Also by Frederic Morton

The Hound
The Darkness Below
Asphalt and Desire
The Witching Ship
The Rothschilds
The Schatten Affair
Snow Gods

AN
UNKNOWN
WOMAN

AN
UNKNOWN
WOMAN

a new novel by

Frederic Morton

An Atlantic Monthly Press Book

Little, Brown and Company • Boston • Toronto

FIRST EDITION

T 05/76

LIBRARY OF CONGRESS CATALOGING IN PUBLICATIONS DATA

MORTON, FREDERIC.
    AN UNKNOWN WOMAN.

    "AN ATLANTIC MONTHLY PRESS BOOK."
    I. TITLE.
PZ3.M84482UN   [PS3525.O825]   813'.5'4   75-45476
ISBN 0-316-58531-9

ATLANTIC–LITTLE, BROWN BOOKS
ARE PUBLISHED BY
LITTLE, BROWN AND COMPANY
IN ASSOCIATION WITH
THE ATLANTIC MONTHLY PRESS

Published simultaneously in Canada
by Little, Brown & Company (Canada) Limited

PRINTED IN THE UNITED STATES OF AMERICA

To Rebecca

"The study of history is useful to the historian by teaching him his ignorance of women. . . . The woman who is known only through a man is known wrong."

Chapter 23, *The Education of Henry Adams*

I

1

The big dog, the St. Bernard whose name she didn't know, walked right behind her, paws thump-thump against the cobbles, and it helped save sanity. The big dog had a wrinkled wise head and black fur on its shoulders like a judicial gown. It walked gravely behind her, snout twitching a little. It strode along, a Supreme Court Justice four-legged with a tic, and what saved Trudy's sanity was that the dog was a remarkableness to fasten on quite apart and aside from Trudy's situation.

"To Captain Doss," she said to a kepi'd cop at the entrance, and he opened the door for her and the big dog.

Probably it wasn't remarkable that in a small Liechtenstein town a police station should be timbered, with a swallows' nest under the eaves. Probably headquarters in the capital had a stork's nest. Probably it wasn't remarkable that the kepi'd cop didn't look twice at Trudy. On the phone Captain Doss had said his staff had been instructed to expect an American woman technician to work on communications. An American woman technician with a dreadful blonde wig and Mr. Justice Dog. Amusing. Probably amusement was good for saving sanity.

The Captain sat behind a huge brown table catty-cornered into another table with an Erector set that must be radio equipment. Behind him was an oil. Probably the Matterhorn. He jumped up. He exclaimed.

"Madame Letarpo!"

Letarpo he pronounced more softly, lingered over the deliciousness of the name. He bent over her hand. "I wish we could meet under better circumstances."

3

This Captain should have been Trudy's comrade. His eyes were red, like hers. Probably he and she were the only ones in town who hadn't slept last night; probably they were the only ones that knew. But his gray hair shone greasy at the temples. His jacket was draped over him like a cape; it kept falling off one shoulder, and she felt that this wasn't the way he usually wore it. Probably he was rising, with maximum dash, to a great top-secret occasion. He wasn't trying to help her. Sweat felt moist under her wig.

"Please. Do take a seat."

"Something very bad?" she said.

"No. No, madame," he said. "Just a change. No — no catastrophe."

"My son is all right?"

"Yes, we shall be in radio contact in a few minutes. I wanted to dispatch a car to your hotel —"

"I like to walk. It's only blocks. What happened?"

"Madame Letarpo, please — be comfortable."

She sat down. But before she even knew what she was doing, she swept the solitaire cards off his desk. Only partly as if by accident. Her Ronnie was holding something mad in his hands, white hands with brand-new brown hair on the knuckles; something all the more insane since she didn't even know what a dynamite stick looked like. And this dashing Captain played cards to while the time away.

"I'm sorry," she said.

"Quite perfectly all right, Madame."

He bent over to retrieve some cards and she caught a whiff of whiskey. Instantly she liked him better. Whiskey was more worthy of the trouble. Probably she ought to try drink herself.

"What happened?" she said.

"Well, you see." The Captain straightened up. "He ordered the plane to take off."

"Where is he now?"

"Somewhere above Milano. He will be calling within ten minutes."

"You don't know my son," she said. "He talks softly. He isn't even seventeen. But he'll blow up the plane."

"Madame Letarpo," the Captain said, "We will do all possible. The Prince himself is most interested —"

4

There was a boop-boop, almost like a burp, from the Erector set.

"Pardon me," the Captain said. "Captain Doss, Liechtenstein Police. . . . Yes! Yes, just a moment." His jacket fell off his shoulder, and that saved sanity when he clamped the earphones icecold against her ears.

"Ronnie! . . . Hello? . . . Ronnie? You know who this is?"

"Yes. Are you in Zurich airport."

It was Ronnie, but it wasn't his voice but something so metallic and toneless there wasn't even a question mark in the question.

"Ronnie! Be human!"

"Are you in Zurich airport."

"No! You didn't want —"

"Are you in Bachberg."

"No, in Liechtenstein, in a small town, just as you instructed —"

"I want to talk to Gospodin."

He was still calling Letarpo "Gospodin."

"Letarpo isn't here yet," she said. "We are trying —"

"I'll only talk about Yussuf and the workers, and I'll only talk to Gospodin."

"But we can't find him right now!"

"Check you again later."

"Wait! Listen —"

Click.

"Ronnie!"

Mummy, if you die, you write my name on a card and put it in your pocket so you remember me when you wake up.

Twelve years ago he'd suddenly said it during their animal lotto, his little eyes suddenly soft brown with tears. Now there was nothing in the earphones. Only static, meteors crackling away through infinity.

"I am sorry," the Captain said. "But we will have contact later."

The Captain removed the earphones from her head, delicately; a gallant helping a princess off with her coat. Then he removed his own phones fast.

"I wish you to know," the Captain said. "When I talked to him, your son, most briefly earlier, he said the young lady is all right. Everybody is unharmed. It will resolve itself."

"Wonderful," Trudy said. "Everything's marvelous."

5

"Perhaps we can be of help to locate Mr. Letarpo? If we can call any of his offices —"

"I've tried!" Trudy said. "Would you have some water?"

"Yes. Of course." The Captain poured from a crystal carafe too beautiful for the simple furniture. "A little cognac? Or coffee, Madame Letarpo?"

She drank, shaking her head.

"The hotel is adequate?"

"I'll go rest there for a while," she said.

"It is empty, but it is the only one with private bathroom. Also best for protecting your identity."

"It's fine."

"The only incommodation is perhaps the dog. But it never harms. It was once caught in an avalanche; it just likes to go with persons at the hotel."

"I don't mind," she said.

"Can we drive you back to the hotel, Madame Letarpo?"

"I like to walk, thank you," she said. "I feel better when I walk."

"You have the air-call? It makes a harsh noise, I am afraid."

"I have it," she said.

"Madame Letarpo, we have great anxiety for your well-being. If there is anything —"

"Everything has been done," she said. "Thank you very much."

The Captain bowed and the jacket fell off his shoulder, and she walked through the inner door and the outer door with the swallows' nest. Probably Mr. Justice Dog stuck close behind her.

She walked into the afternoon of the town. She moved through the rosy-baroque air coming from the glaciers. She passed old men sitting on benches against leafy espaliered walls. She passed old men at the quaiside lighting pipes that hung down silver-buttoned waistcoats. She saw the ferry on its way from the other side of the green river and the horned shadow of the cows on board floating in silhouette across the waves, and there was the smell of wisteria and smoked bacon in the softening of the sunlight. Such a landscape of salvation all around her doom. She felt a sob rising like bitter grit from her throat.

She tried to stop the sob. She told herself that the idea that the world was there to provide comment on yourself was the idea of a

6

neurotic, and a celebrity, and that in an unfortunate way she was both. She walked along the cobbles, the dog thump-thump behind, and she told herself that if she really gave up and cried now she'd be a forty-two-year-old somewhat used beauty crying under a wig. And that was sufficiently ludicrous. It stopped the sob. But it didn't stop everything. A woman came toward her on the cobbles. This woman wore a dirndl and pushed a bike from whose bars hung a shopping bag and next to her walked a tow-haired boy with the woman's features, walking in step with her and pushing a smaller bike.

"How'd you do it?" she said to the woman.

But she whispered and the woman was still too far away.

"I should have known I'd make a bad mother," she said to the woman. "Do-gooders do lousy with their children. Especially half-assed ones like me. Important things like mother love are narrow — you know?"

Both the woman and her boy made a detour with their bikes. Around Trudy and around the big dog whose name Trudy didn't know. Suddenly she asked herself, silently: Am I Ten Best Dressed this year? She couldn't remember. But the question wasn't mad. It had a certain point. She pushed her wig a little askew, her hot horrible dark-blonde wig. She was a harpy talking to herself in the street. It was more seemly, more chic for such a harpy to wear her wig somewhat askew. Matching accessories, dear. Half-assed-do-gooder-Ten-Best-Dressed-Crazy style. She passed a store window full of bottles and stopped. She remembered the alcohol on the Captain's breath. Probably alcohol saved sanity. At least for the night.

"*Guten Abend*," said the woman by the counter. "*Ja bitte?*"

This woman also wore a dirndl. Heavy brown braids were turbaned on her head.

"A bottle of wine," Trudy said.

"Oh, English!" the woman said in quite good English. "Once I worked in Portsmouth. Please."

She handed Trudy a card saying *Amalie Zierl, proprietress, Wines and Liquors, Dennat, Liechtenstein*.

"Nice wine to export with you home?"

"To drink here," Trudy said.

7

"Oh yes. Nice light family wine?"

"Something strong."

"Ah, to celebrate with your friends, a French Burgundy?"

"Just for me."

"I see — the hotel dog. They open the hotel for you? They prepare for you our trout specialty? A white wine with that? Moselle?"

"Please, just give me something hearty," Trudy said.

At first Trudy thought that this Amalie Zierl was staring at her wig, still askew. Not a bit. Amalie Zierl was staring past Trudy at her wall full of bottles. And Trudy felt she was all too well hidden in this town. Nothing could disturb the iron provinciality of pipe-lighters and cows on a ferry and Amalie Zierl surveying vintage labels. If Ronnie crashed tonight the news item wouldn't be nearly so important in this house as the weather forecast. Brutally unfair: All Amalie ever had to do was select wine for minor occasions, in a town that ferried cows through sunshine.

"Bernkastel," Amalie Zierl said. "The English like Bernkastel. One moment. It is in the cellar."

Amalie Zierl dropped into a trapdoor and Trudy knew that to save sanity she had to complicate this woman's life somehow. She knew something from her lawyer Maurice. On a handwritten will she could add codicils at any time without witnesses. She unsnapped her bag to take out a sheet of Hotel Crillon stationery.

"*Codicil to Will,*" she wrote, pressing the sheet against the linoleum counter. "*To Amalie Zierl, Dennat, Liechtenstein, the sum of Three Hundred Thousand Dollars on condition that ten thousand Dollars thereof be spent yearly on a party to be held for the first ten years (after my decease) in Amalie Zierl's house for the world's ten leading female philanthropists.*"

"Bernkastel," Amalie Zierl said, reappearing. "Very springy. Hearty. Excellent. Sixteen francs."

"Fine," Trudy said.

She signed her name to the codicil and folded it into the alligator leather passport wallet Letarpo had given her, and paid while Amalie Zierl wrapped, and walked out in the street again, the bottle heavy in her right hand, the left hand heavy with the aircall inside her bag, and the dog, the big dog whose name she didn't know, thump-thump behind.

8

Many years ago, the Captain had said, when tuberculosis had been a foremost disease, the town had been a foremost Alpine cure and the royal dukes of England were heard coughing here. Now the Grand Hotel was an enormous wooden tomb with rusty chandeliers, cracked Dante chairs and a parquet floor pockmarked by ski boots from the winter. But now it was summer. The Grand Hotel Dennat housed only Trudy and her trouble.

The big lock screeched at the big key. In the dimness of the lobby dozens of antlers floated along the walls like bird-wing skeletons. Bones in flight. Under those swoops, Trudy walked. So did the dog. She smelled cooked meat and felt a twitch of hunger, the first in many hours. She went right on to the dining room. She didn't want to lose her hunger. It was important to be strong, well fed, for the right decisions. She wondered how Ronnie could eat and what. But this thought didn't save sanity and she walked away from it, on to the dining room without washing her hands, the dog after her.

The huge empty dining room was full of small white mountains; white protective cloths thrown over chairs upended on tables. The walls were white and from the white stuccoed ceiling little bits of white plaster drifted down, here and there, white leaves in a white autumn, a very mild pensive snowfall. The St. Bernard whose name she didn't know slumped down, head between paws. But Turk, perched on a little stool at the far end, stood up.

Captain Doss had explained that this Turkish woman was the only one available in the summer off-season; the only one reliably discreet yet able to take care of Trudy in the hotel. Turk wore a blue apron and a black head scarf framing a large firm hairy face. She bowed to Trudy with ceremony. She watched Trudy with the staidness the dog had relinquished when it had lain down. The Supreme Court judgeship had been transferred from Dog to Turk. Trudy had been close enough to the White House bedroom to know how fast such things happen.

"Hello, Judge Turk," she said.

There was only one table not covered by protective cloth. That table was covered by pink linen, set with silver, white linen napkins, and dishes under silver bells. Turk came forward.

9

"*Uegoluepoelo,*" Turk said, lifting the bells. Lamb, gravy, green peas, a mysterious tangy squash-looking thing.

"Thank you. I'm sorry I couldn't eat lunch," Trudy said.

Turk reached into her apron pocket and pulled out a remarkably fresh daisy for a centerpiece. Turk ran to the sideboard, where there were many little flags for winter tourists of all origins. Turk came back with a miniature red-white-green banner.

"Turkish?" Trudy said. "Thank you. Sit down. Join me. I hope my son eats."

"*Puetuaploepu,*" Turk said gravely.

"Come on. Sit down," Trudy said.

For years the world had stood around while she dined, watched her go wrong among the silver dishes.

"Except you're probably better than the world," Trudy said. "This tastes good. You know something? You've got a chin like my aunt's."

She was actually enjoying the lamb, despite the gingery taste.

"Aunt," Turk suddenly said. "I have aunt — Kikago."

"I had aunt — Yew Yorr," Trudy said.

⌒ 2 ⌒

"Yew Yorr" wasn't bad, she realized. It wasn't just mocking Turk's accent. You could say that Trudy had dreamed her youth in a principality called Yew Yorr, just south of George Washington Bridge. Certainly it was as special as Liechtenstein and certainly she'd dreamed it. Damn it. You couldn't *experience* youth; you could only dream it, decades afterward. This was one of her conclusions, eating gingery lambchops, mortified, at the end of a twenty years' maze. At the end of it she sat here, dining all alone in the snow. At the end there was also her son Ronnie, her one child, twenty thousand feet above Milano, with beautiful slim fingers and a stick of dynamite. At the beginning there must have been Yew Yorr of long ago where greenery wandered through Tante's apartment, revising history as it went. Had Tante also wanted to change the time maze? So that the end wouldn't be so damn murderous? Or was Trudy only dreaming her Yew Yorr Tante out of sheer tiredness? The small iron lady with her powerful ex-schoolteacher's stoop, Viennese consonants as imperious as a duchess's? Tante was a refugee from Hitler and wanted to undo Hitler with her gardener gloves. Yes, Tante really wanted to revise history from scratch, starting with primeval flora, trying out in miniature, in her three-and-a-half-room apartment, a new distribution of forests and grasses that would trigger a different evolutionary scenario, hence a different pattern of human origins, which in turn would produce a different history with a different twentieth century containing something other than the Third Reich.

Once a biology instructor in Vienna's Jewish Gymnasium, Tante could make her plants flow, as if by their own power, through a complex traffic pattern in her apartment. Her ivy arrived at the window for the morning light but moved to the vitrine top at noon. Her asparagus fern reached the sill at 2 P.M., after which her African violets spelled them for an hour, followed by her dumb cane, both groups converging on the hutch at dinner time. Such migrations changed by arcane but precise degree with the seasons; but their purpose remained constant: Tante established a new relationship between the needs of chlorophyll and the sun's changing angles. This would set off a more benign, non-Nazi geopolitical sequence, assuming you could find a device to start history all over again.

Once Tante had confided all this to Trudy — when Trudy was still in high school. Later the subject wasn't mentioned again. Trudy's college years were the years in which it got darker and darker in New York. The wrongness of the twentieth century now broke out, not in Germany, but in America. Tante loved Trudy but probably felt she could no longer trust her, that is, trust the savage American force she felt beating in her niece; Trudy's overlong, overripe brunette hair; Trudy's peculiar Ph.D. dissertation on the sociology of age classes; Trudy's toreador pants; Trudy's radicalism, so-called; Trudy's thin bras; Trudy's would-be lover Elihu; Trudy's acceptance of the Max Weber Graduate Scholarship Prize in a dress without stockings; Trudy's eyeliner — to Tante they were all raunchy excesses caused by America. Symp-

11

toms that required decongesting and detumescing. Hence the windows open even in the winter, the drafts shivering plant leaves, the constant cooling chamber music from WNYC-FM (WNYC-FM being just about the only element of the twentieth century Tante would leave unrevised); the everlasting anticarnal flounder filet broiling in the oven, the cleansing, chastening mineral water served with each meal. Yew Yorr. Tante ran her geopolitical apartment as a spa designed to cure Trudy of the U.S.A.

But a curious thing had happened in Yew Yorr. Tante had cured Trudy of nothing. On the contrary, she'd infected Trudy with her own messianic impulse. It was possible to see that now, at a distance, from the vantage point of Liechtenstein. From the hindsight of the ginger lambchops. You could say that the Yew Yorr Trudy had been too damn aggressively messianic. Impatient with herself to fulfill the talents and moral imperatives straining inside her. At twenty-two she'd been absolutely resolved to resist all the clichés of decay.

"Decay is such a goddamn cliché," Trudy had once said to Jennifer. "Let's be original for at least seventy years." They'd been such Yew Yorr buddies, Trudy and Jenn. It wasn't just that they were both sociology majors. But both felt that sociology had to be dragged — screaming, if need be — out of the monographs into the ghettos and garbage of actual life and real politics. Both were outraged by the rumor that the University was going to evict a bunch of oldsters for the sake of better faculty parking. What's more, both Trudy and Jenn had the same oily skin and the same yen for chocolate-covered halvah and the same sense of humor about their Habit. They also joked about being the two Rosa Luxemburgs at Moloch U; so why the hell did all potential Karl Liebknechts in the cafeteria have such jumpy big Adam's apples and mouth such prissy Trotskyite rhetoric while passing bennies? . . . Jenn and Trudy had their laughs together. They borrowed Dorothy Gray cleansing grains from each other, used each other's library cards, swathed each other with so much camaraderie that it didn't much matter that Jennifer was gangly, flat-nosed, plain according to the conventional erotic wisdom. Whereas Trudy's mane, blazing across the campus, couldn't help making male mouths bare their goddamn stud-teeth. Even if it did matter, Jenn and Trudy were still good for each other: Jenn avoided wallflowerdom as long as she bantered with Trudy. And Trudy, with Jennifer at her side, was no stuck-up elitist loner. Jenn even disarmed Tante. In fact, she was Tante's ally against Rabbi Elihu Boneman.

Once, at Trudy's graduation, Acting Chaplain Boneman had given Trudy a gardenia and sort of a hug — and been observed by Tante. Henceforth this rabbi was a piece of American deviltry: someone suspiciously young and even more mendaciously blond for a Jewish clergyman. The rabbi summed up history gone wrong, all the treacheries Tante had to face daily in America, from the smilers who offered to help you carry potting earth in order to snatch your purse, to the A & P specials that were always Just Sold Out. This *goy*, posing as rabbi, personified them all. Whenever Jennifer would come up to the house, Tante would take her aside for a whisper:

"What about this Mister Rabbi?"

Jennifer would roll her eyes to confirm the presence of evil.

"You establish his credentials!" Tante would say. Then she'd hand Jennifer her gradual-watering device, i.e., a basketful of ice cubes, and ask Jennifer to drop four cubes at a time in all the high plant hangers. This was a tribute to Jenn's height as well as a sign of favor. While Jennifer dropped ice cubes, Tante opened the windows. The drafts animated fern fronds and ivy leaves, and set pots swinging like pendulums on their chains. All the ice cubes began clicking, ticking against one another under the foliage as if they were metronomes ticking off Tante's improved geological ages, and Tante would turn up the Händel on WNYC-FM and smile at Jennifer dropping more metronomes into the green. And Trudy, looking back on it in Liechtenstein, loved Tante back in Yew Yorr's magic gardens.

And, funny thing, Tante had been kind of right about Elihu Boneman. In his small-timer style the rabbi was a con man working up his coeds. On the sparse grass of the Moloch U common he had them simmering, simmering, simmering in a semicircle of Bloomingdale's jeans around their far-out chaplain. They sang with him *"Oif dem Pripetshik"* and other Yiddish people's songs, followed by the "Nine Hundred Miles Hobo Blues" and "Molly Branigan." The songs made the simmerers feel Socially Aware. Their shucked-off moccasins, their bare feet, made them Sensuously Free Avant-

13

Gardists. Everybody's soprano sidled up against Elihu's basso. Everybody sneaked looks at his upper lip, his sumptuously curved, lush oriental upper lip of deep, deep pink. This Song of Songs mouth parting in the golden brutality of his mustaches, the open buttons of his shirt . . . it was simply all too exquisite. It was also what Moloch U wanted. Moloch U had appointed an unordained and very unshorn rabbi as Acting Chaplain in order to show that it was some swinging Moloch U. Trudy despised that whole scene. Down she swooped on the songsters simmering around the rabbi, she and Jennifer, to push them all into something real.

"Rabbi Boneman!" she said. "They're going to throw a hundred old people out on the street!"

"*Oif dem Pripetshik*" died away.

"Won't you join us?" Elihu said. (At the Student Council meetings he'd already asked her twice to join his court.)

"It's the Craftworkers Retirement Home," Trudy said. "U will buy it, to raze it for faculty parking. I just had that confirmed!"

"Are you sure?"

"Ask the Dean," Jennifer said.

"We picket tomorrow!" Trudy said. "Everybody invited!"

Everybody looked up at her from the sparse grass. She was upstaging an entire harem. Rabbi Elihu tugged at his mustaches and said, well, in that case, perhaps a Committee of Notables should be mobilized. A telegram campaign —

"Fine," Trudy said. "But meanwhile we picket. Sing your people's songs on the way to helping people!"

"We meet on Broadway and 189th," Jennifer said.

"Oh," Rabbi Elihu said.

"Come establish your credentials," Jennifer said (in private allusion to Tante, so that Trudy had to kill a grin).

"If my hands weren't bound as chaplain . . ."

"Okay," Trudy said. "So stop being a chaplain!"

Next day Rabbi Elihu called to say that he had indeed obtained a leave of absence from his acting chaplaincy to become, for the time being, communications consultant to Slimline Kosher Foods. He could join the picket line.

The trouble was hardly anybody else did. They marched in a

14

very thin line for a couple of hours till poor Jenn, who'd come despite a bad cold, collapsed into a taxi. After this the rabbi suggested that the two of them have a never-give-up strategy session at a groovy new place in the Village, called Le Spot. During its opening weeks Le Spot featured specially reduced Pizza Provençal and Valpolicella, of which Trudy had three glasses to get over the debacle. *"Salud!"* the rabbi said each time, and they went over the anti-eviction telegram campaign to enlist notables. At the end of the bottle, the rabbi played with a few saccharine packets from the bowl on the table and slipped a few into his pocket (for his overweight sister rooming with him) and began to stroke Trudy's fingers. And Trudy, disgusted with it all, knew that if they really ended up in the hotel room of his hope and really became a tangle of tongues and thighs — why then, at the crucial moment that was to deliver her up to voluptuousness — at that very moment she would be so positioned that her eyes would fall on a speckled notice saying GUESTS MUST VACATE ROOMS BEFORE ELEVEN A.M. OR BE CHARGED FOR ADDITIONAL DAY.

The problem with Elihu, blondness, mustaches, upper lip and all, was his ultimate identity. He was a shnook. And the Valpolicella had made her even sorer about all the people that had finked out of the picketing.

"Listen," Trudy said. "I'm sorry. I have a headache. I better go home."

It didn't stop Elihu from calling her up after that. He kept calling her for a whole year. But with his shnook's luck he seldom caught Trudy at home. Tante, of course, was masterful at misunderstanding or misplacing phone messages. And the one message Tante failed to mangle utterly turned out to be from Elihu's successful rival — though nobody knew that yet.

"What's that note on the pad?" Trudy asked her aunt.

Smeared with plant earth, the scribble seemed to say *Spiegerbeck, Waldorf Towels, 40 C, you should be there 5 p.m.*

"That's Waldorf Towers," Jennifer said. She could read Tante better than Trudy.

"You don't mean *Spieger,* Tante? Simon Spieger?"

But Tante was repotting dumb cane too near WNYC-FM's Budapest String Quartet to hear the question.

"Check out Spieger at the Waldorf Towers, would you, Jenn?" Trudy said. "Spieger was on our notables' telegram list."

"Spiegerbeck," Tante said.

"Look, Tante," Trudy tried again. "Could the name have been simply *Spieger*? Simon Spieger — you know whom I mean? The University is building a Library Collection in his name. I sent him my honors paper and he —"

"Spiegerbeck or maybe Pieschgerbeck," Tante said.

"No, *S-p-i-e-g-e-r* — remember, Tante, that nice comment he wrote me? The one you almost threw out? He's one of the big shots we cabled in our anti-eviction fight — could that be the name?"

"He sounds funny on the telephone," Tante said to the dumb cane.

"Well, he's French; we cabled him to France."

"Spieger*beck*," Tante said with finality.

"No soap," Jennifer said from the phone.

"There's no Spieger registered there?"

"They don't give out that kind of information at the Waldorf Towers and nobody answers at 40C."

"I better check it out at five P.M.," Trudy said.

"Maybe your Mister Rabbi plays tricks," Tante said. But she said it bent so deeply into her work, the words seemed to come out of some oracular tentacles of dumb cane. A gust from the open window fluttered ivy branches and tensed the big rubber plant. An ice cube fell out of a hanging planter. It flashed in the sunlight like a bright watch falling and about to break, quite as if it knew that Yew Yorr wouldn't last much longer.

∽ *3* ∽

That had been strange, zooming up to the fortieth floor of the Waldorf Towers when she'd never entered the first before. The desk man adjusted his glasses at her. The elevator man acted like a customs inspector about to ask what underdeveloped country she was from. Stepping out on the fortieth floor, she felt the carpet nap tickle her feet. A succession of hall mirrors produced a succession of Trudys in a sweater-and-skirt very prole under that luxury-resort lighting.

And no matter how familiar it became later, she never forgot her first collision with the Van Gogh in Letarpo's apartment. It was the self-portrait so universally reproduced that when she startled up against the original right in the foyer — the suddenness of that stare, brushstrokes like skin bristling at her entrance — it was like seeing after so many ikons the God himself, naked, in the rawness of his flesh, captive in gold frame. And the Manet and Degas next to it, other divinities, a whole zoo of gods kept here by this lousy small nail-eyed zoo-keeper in a white coat.

A few years later she had Nail Eyes fired. But that day the butler not quite looked at her after she gave her name, and not quite pointed to that heavy carpet she was supposed to cross into the next room. And the next room burst in on her with sunlight, roof-tops, much striped upholstery and mahogany planes and, apparently growing right out of the floor, an olive tree. An honest-to-goodness olive tree; smallish but real; from one of whose branches hung a gray tweed coat.

"Mr. Spieger?" she said.

He didn't look as she'd expected. A tall substantial young man in shirtsleeves, lots of red-blond hair and an Arthur Godfrey face. He was coming in, munching, from a solarium where an art deco lunch was fixed up. Doilied sandwiches, silver spouts, linen napkins on a Lalique glass table. Glamour at which she could afford to smile because it was so Late Late Show.

"Miss Ellner," he said with an accent. "Miss Trudy Ellner? So pleased. My name is Louis Bic."

"Bic?" she said. "I thought the message came from Mr. Spieger."

"Yes, I said on the phone the message is from Monsieur Spieger, but I am Bic."

Spiegerbeck, Trudy said to herself and vowed to bruise Tante's favorite rubber plant.

"Unfortunately Mister Spieger does not feel so hot. He is still in France. But he has discussed the matter with the lady I work for."

17

"This is confusing," Trudy said.

"I work for Michelle Bloit-Letarpo — Madame Letarpo." To give the name some room he had stopped munching. "I handle cultural things for Madame Letarpo."

"I don't understand," Trudy said.

Though actually she was surprised at herself: she understood a lot right away. MICHELLE BLOIT HOOKS OIL BIGGIE . . . MOVIE STAR'S AIRBORNE WEDDING ON CLOUD NINE . . . Why clutter her mind with things like that? MICHELLE LETARPO SNUBS SINATRA . . . True, Tante sometimes brought home the *Daily News* in order to reject the advice of the needlework editor. And Trudy sometimes skimmed the *New York Post*. Yet she had expected herself to be largely ignorant of a Michelle Bloit-Letarpo. She was no garment-district secretary under a dryer, clutching Earl Wilson to her pelvis. Still, she really understood what this Mr. Bic was talking about.

"I don't understand," she said on the Waldorf Towers' fortieth floor. "What is the connection to me?"

"The connection," Louis Bic said. He pulled a linen napkin out of his pocket and wiped his mouth. "I am here for a magazine Madame Letarpo is starting with Mr. Spieger —"

"This has nothing to do with the cable we sent Mr. Spieger."

"Oh sure, Mr. Spieger has an idea. You should do an article on your problem for our first magazine number."

"Thanks a lot," Trudy said.

"In fact, he gave us a tip. You should be editorial consultant."

"This is a little insane," Trudy said. "You're talking about a French magazine you'll be starting or something and I'm talking about people's lives right now, right here in New York, who'll find themselves out on the street if somebody doesn't do something fast!"

"Excuse me, this magazine will be located in America. I am looking for offices here because often it will deal with your culture."

"I spent three dollars coming down in the taxi," she said, turning to the door. "Our culture! I thought this was something real."

"Excuse me, but it is definitely real! I have a budget of two hundred thousand dollars for offices here. Mr. Letarpo is coming across with lots of support. We will be a real —"

"You're kidding!"

18

"A real magazine with influence for good. Otherwise —"

"Two hundred thousand!"

"Why don't you sit, please?" He took out the linen napkin again and placed it, very debonair, on the coffee table. "Will you have a drink?"

"The whole building is just a hundred twenty-five thousand dollars!" she said. "That's what those bastards are selling it out for — that's what the goddamn site is worth. The whole works! The University just wants it for a parking lot. You know something? You ought to buy the building and prevent the eviction."

"My authority is for editorial offices," he said. "How about ordering you an apéritif?"

"How many rooms will you need for your editors?"

"Rooms? Well, circa nine or ten."

"They have three empty doctors' offices — you've got almost enough space right there. Why don't you take a look?"

"Maybe," he said. "We discuss it over a drink?"

"But if you're going to take a look at it, you'd better do it right now because the University's going to gobble it up any minute — if you're really serious, and you should be! Because it's right off the campus, ideal for a magazine of that kind, library and intellectual facilities nearby, graduate students for research help, you get rent from the tenants and you'd save the roof over their heads — you'd do a good deed in the bargain — *if* you're really serious."

"Maybe I should be serious."

He crossed his legs, let his extremely shined black loafers give off light reflections, and pointed at the armchair opposite. He could point all day long.

"If you are really serious, look at it right now, by daylight."

"Boy," he said. "You are a very forceful young lady."

"The emergency is very forceful," she said. "Will you do it? I'm not really a maniac. It's the circumstances."

"You have — élan."

"Will you please look at the building?"

"Very well," Louis Bic said. "Sure thing." He put the linen napkin back into his trouser pocket and reached for the jacket he'd hung on the tree. The jacket wasn't there.

"*Où s'cache?*" Trudy heard him murmur.

19

It hadn't dropped to the floor. It wasn't on the panoramic upholstery. Nor out in the solarium.

"*Je comprends pas*," Trudy heard him murmur. Suddenly his face was the same color as the red on his red-white striped shirt. "Perhaps in the other room. Pardon me," he said. And Trudy felt that the bravado of hanging the jacket on the tree had come to naught. This young man was as new to the fortieth floor, perhaps to his job, as she was to the situation. He walked to the next room rather fast. Trudy was touched. And because she was touched, she wanted to help. She saw a glass doorknob in the shape of a swan's neck. It looked like a closet.

It was a closet, all right. But no male jacket was in it. Trudy had never seen such triple-tiered wealth of silk and satin hung from soft-bolstered hangers. Never, outside Bonwit Teller's. There was a faint powerful exhalation of perfume left over from — from what? What corny high merriments that ate out Sinatra's heart? Maria Callas's fêtes? Monte Carlo soirées? Hell, those were just Madame's *New York* party clothes.

A door clicked. Trudy took her finger off a taffeta sleeve.

"I don't know. Not in the den either," Louis Bic said with a small laugh. At the same time Nail Eyes, the butler, came in with a jacket in one hand, a brush in the other.

"The tree sheds on it, sir," he said.

And that white, ludicrously extravagant little conceit of a car. Its very extravagance must have touched the romantic in her. So did young Bic. His loud yellow gloves. They clashed with the tufted red leather of the upholstery. Yet some part of him must have merged with the car. Otherwise he couldn't have fit in his whole body. It was so massive and muscular and exuberant. The embarrassment of the vanished jacket had never happened. Now he was trying to get out of the rush-hour mess on Broadway onto the West Side Highway and they wouldn't let him get into the right lane, and still his gloves kept waving optimistic signals out the window.

"I'm no help on highway entrances," she said. "I don't drive."

"Don't drive? How do you like that?" Whenever Mr. Bic tried American slang his accent became a little stronger. "A coincident!

Madame Letarpo doesn't drive either! And Mr. Letarpo gave her this car to make her drive, and you must appreciate, there are only two cars like this in the whole smack world, and still she doesn't drive."

"You don't say," she said.

"You better believe it. Specially built for Pilcic, that's Mr. Letarpo's island with no roads. This lane didn't work out either. You are sitting in a Volkswagen chassis with a Rolls-Royce motor in back. You didn't notice no backseat? Look! *Chachacha!*"

Chachacha! was his laugh. He was so deeply rooted in the upholstery the whole car rocked with him. The sun rocked above New Jersey. The dashboard had odd oval dials and the glove compartment muttered. It rustled every time Bic's knee, muscle-bulgy under the tweed, came near it as he shifted gears. He stripped off a glove and she noticed surprisingly delicate white moons on his fingers. Like the car he was peculiarly custom-made.

"I know nothing about cars," she said.

"Of course a young lady so attractive, she doesn't have to drive. She is always invited."

"I've been too busy for invitations," she said.

"Oh yes. You are in the politics game."

"What politics? I'm trying to finish my damn doctoral dissertation," she said. "But I can't let the University get away with it! Kicking out men I did my fieldwork with!"

"This is extremely nice of you," he said, with that extra emphasis which showed he didn't comprehend one bit.

"Look," she said. "My dissertation happens to be on something called 'Sociology of Age Classes.' The people they're about to throw out on the street are the people I interviewed for that. I practically lived with them. I can't just lean back and let them be thrown to the wolves! I —" Something jumped in the glove compartment. "What is *that?*" she said.

"Ah. I didn't show you?"

He pulled back the handle. It wasn't a glove compartment. It was a terrarium — a glass cage built into the dashboard with sand and a black-and-white spotted lizard scurrying, freezing, scurrying again.

"Jesus!" Trudy said.

21

"Supposed to be against the Devil Cricket if it comes into the car —"

"Bugs! In this car?" Instinctively she lifted her legs off the floor.

"*Chachacha*." he laughed. "Not here! On the island. That bug is only on the island, in case Letarpo flies the car to the island! We drive further uptown?"

"Another thirty blocks," she said. "Listen, I'm not very comfortable with lizards. I mean, why keep lizards in New York?"

"Oh. Because Mr. Letarpo says the lizard will not defend the car against the bug if the lizard does not always hang out in the car. Mr. Letarpo is a Croatian."

"Would you close the compartment?"

"Sure."

"Would you lock it, please?"

"Oh sure. Look, I turn the knob. I defend you, *chachacha*. Now spill the beans about your dissertation."

"I haven't even finished it yet."

"That is the nice thing about my crazy job. Meeting attractive clever people. Tell about your dissertation. I would love to read it."

"Like hell you would," she said.

"You don't tell me about it, I don't defend you against the lizard."

"Okay, your funeral," she said. "It's on the retired people in the house where we're going and how they have the kind of culture younger people have lost."

"Boy, fascinating. I'm very interested in culture. This is part of my job with Madame Letarpo."

"I'm talking about culture as a way of life uniting work *and* leisure," she said. He asked for a lecture and he was going to get one. "I mean these old people, mostly woodworkers, they can still repair their own furniture or even make it. And for their grandchild's birthday they'll *carve* a present, not just scribble some damn dry check. And when they hold their old craft-union reunion in the house, they sing a Galician woodworkers' song —"

"Oh, very cute," he said. "We drive more?"

"Yes," she said.

She smelled his shaving lotion along with the expensive leather smell of the upholstery. The tweed-thrust of his knee close to hers disturbed her, a thrust compounded with his lotion scent, the gleam of the dashboard's burled wood, with the lizard, with his ambassadorship from realms rich and exotic. It disturbed her. So she would counterdisturb him with a few highbrowish ideas.

"It's not *cute*," she said. "It's precious and important, what these old people have, and very perishable. That's what my paper is about. Like, in comparison with that, what systems analyst can analyze a little system for his grandchild's birthday present? Or is there a systems analysts' song? Hey, stop! Here we are."

There they were. The timbered old house with the dead beech trees in front looked so mortal. Those tall new campus buildings across the street demeaned it. Above the entrance a sign said UNITED CRAFTSMEN RETIREMENT HOME. But somebody's red paint had turned CRAFTSMEN into CRAP MEN. As if that weren't enough, Mr. Lissberg came down the street with his supermarket cart. Trudy didn't want Bic put off by that kind of encounter.

"Mr. Bic," she said. "Why don't you go right in? Inspect the place."

"Just me?"

"I don't want the owner's agent to see me," Trudy said. "I had my troubles with him. I ought to stay out of the picture. Go in and look at the vacant offices."

"Ah!" Bic said. "Good tactic!" And swung himself out with great swaggering friction between tweed and leather, and was gone long before Mr. Lissberg's arrival.

Of course Mr. Lissberg was one of Yew Yorr's major apparitions, with his two powerful but uncoordinated legs, his four wheels and white beard. He consisted not only of a burly prophet's body but of a supermarket cart he used everywhere, not only as a walker but as freight car. It growled like a bulldog on its rusty wheels, especially when it was full up as it was now. Somehow the wheel-growl made his approach seem massive and fast, but it took him minutes to reach Trudy.

"Our young lady Ellner!" he said. "You missed something at the supermarket. That *momser!*"

Mr. Lissberg could convert his limp into a stomp. His fellow tenants had elected him spokesman not only for his command of English but also for his irascibility, which struck them as forcefulness, probably rightly so.

"The A & P on 191st?" he said. "The *momser* manager? I told him! First of all I belong on the express line. Three-grapefruits-for-thirty-one cents is *one* item. But okay. I wait on the long line. But while I wait I can test my new one. Better than this *dreck* Muzak!"

Mr. Lissberg pulled the flute out of an inner coat pocket. For himself or his friends Mr. Lissberg still carved a new flute every six months and the new flute was his companion and resource on all his outings.

"So this *momser* manager says no! Because they want to dispossess us I'm not a person anymore? A little nice music hurts?"

He lifted the reed to his mouth, dipped his head sideways, a fierce mischievous Pan. Rising above the four-legged cart he really looked half-goat, half–senior citizen. The flute trilled, roiled the twilight and brought Bic out of the house. Yes, Bic came swaggering out with a bigger swagger than he'd swaggered in.

"Fixed up!" he said.

"This is Mr. Lissberg," Trudy said. "He is spokesman for the tenants here."

"Terrific! It is all fixed up!" Bic said.

"Ah, your fine chaplain beau!" Mr. Lissberg said, confusing him with Rabbi Elihu in the half-light.

"No, this is Mr. Bic, but he is also an ally in our cause," said Trudy, while Mr. Lissberg, who embarrassed very easily and vehemently, coiled back so that the cart wheels growled, saying, "Well, he *looks* like the other!" and limped and wheel-growled his way into the building. Probably trying to deny his discomfiture, he blew into his flute a note of such hard jollity it came out like a trumpet blast.

"Look like what other?" Bic said.

"Well, he gets things confused sometimes," Trudy said.

"Anyway, all fixed up!" Bic said. "I looked at the doctors' offices. Not such a hot lot of space. But we kick out the concierge — it's enough."

"I told you," Trudy said.

24

"And I told the boss fellow, the agent, the one with the hat — in America the boss fellow always wears the hat, right? — I told him when he didn't believe I was a Letarpo man, I said, call up the Letarpo Washington D.C. office collect, ask about Louis Bic like in this passport here . . ." (Bic flashed his passport) ". . . B-i-c-. I said, Letarpo is a much bigger name to do business than the University, I give you one hundred twenty thousand dollars, and anytime you come to Paris, give me a ring for classy tickets to the Folies Bergères, *chachacha*."

"Nice work," Trudy said.

"But you realize with a hundred and twenty thousand I am twenty over budget for the site acquisition."

"That's nothing for your Mr. Letarpo," Trudy said.

"It is strategy. Momentum for me. Making it bigger is momentum with Mr. Letarpo. Plus, near the University, that's cultural, also more momentum. Plus saving Jewish people's homes for Mr. Spieger —"

"Jewish isn't the issue. Justice is," Trudy said.

"Oh sure. But it still means more momentum. Plus *fait accompli*. Mr. Letarpo comes back from Java and down payment is already made. Without momentum you can do nothing with Mr. Letarpo. But *you* have momentum, he thinks it's Letarpo momentum, you are in business, you understand? We have dinner?"

Mr. Lissberg's flute sounded again, more muted, three ascending notes answered by deep chords from George Washington Bridge, a few streets away. Some mighty truck must have set the steel girders twanging. A new sudden twilight fell over the fire escapes farther uptown, rust burning like rubies, one of New York's windfall twilights that want to deliver the city's promise at last out of all the soot and litter.

"What kind of cuisine is your preference?" he said.

"I want to thank you," Trudy said. "It's been a very helpful, interesting afternoon —"

"Afternoon?" he said. "*Evening!* We have dinner at the Plaza Hotel?"

"Mr. Bic —"

"Louis. I am Louis. Please."

"All right. Louis —"

"And you? Oh yes, Trudy. You don't like the Plaza, Trudy? May I say 'Trudy'?"

His hand ushered her toward the open door of the car. Inside her elbow she felt the tickle of his red-blond stiff hair on his fingers. He was such a massive boy-child, musclebound with energy, strategy, horniness, braggadocio, enthusiasm, God knows what. He ought to have acne but he didn't and he could conjure power, hundreds of thousands of dollars, out of a dingy super's room that still had a spittoon in the corner.

"Sure, call me Trudy," she said. "But I'll take a rain check on the dinner, thank you."

"You don't like the Plaza? Och, I forgot! Michelle said! The Plaza is not so hot anymore! And the Waldorf is only good for room service. *The St. Regis!* That's what she said. We go to the St. Regis. I am on expense. Then I will show you our Number Zero. It's at the Towers apartment."

"What Number Zero?"

He was a sort of exuberant primitive, a throwback. Maybe that was his charm.

"Number Zero of our magazine. The experimental issue. Number Zero. Everything ready except the cover. I want to photograph something for the cover in America. Photography is my great hobby." He reached with his foot through the open car door and kicked at things under the driver's seat. A small heap of cameras whose clicking made the glove compartment stir. "I must photograph something unconventional. Also the title is a problem because it must be special. The magazine is really different. I will show you a list of possible names for the magazine —"

"Not tonight," she said, smiling.

"Right!" he said. "No more business tonight. Absolutely! You know something? I have Michelle's membership at Nirvana II. How can it slip my mind? That's right, she said either the St. Regis roast beef or scampi at Nirvana II. You choose."

She had to laugh. But she also removed, gently, his fingers from her arm. "Enough for today," she said. "Thank you." She'd already made a supper date with Jenn.

"Enough?"

He stared at her. He just let himself fall sideways into the leather

26

of the car. His shoulder fell against the steering wheel so that the horn gave a little *ploop!* His leather gloves dropped on his tweed lap. Even his disappointment had a certain vivacity. Maybe he deserved to be let down a little easier.

"Why don't you call your magazine 'Anti'?" she said.

" 'Anti'? Yes. 'Anti'! That's great! *'Anti'*!"

"And for your cover photograph," she said. "Well, you might consider shooting the New York skyline, in some crazy variation."

"Yes," he said, sitting up. "That's great too."

"That ought to nail down New York as the magazine location. But not simply the skyline, but something perverse . . . . How about the skyline upside down?"

"*Yes!*" he said. "Upside down is *Anti*. Too beautiful! Oh this we must celebrate!"

"It's just a suggestion."

"No, this is the bull's-eye! Both things!" He was rising out of the car. "To this we drink!"

"Not at Nirvana II," she said. "I haven't got the wardrobe."

"I don't care where! We drink to your ideas!"

"Not at the St. Regis, either," she said. "At a White Tower."

"You are the boss! You know the bistros!"

He'd gotten out to usher her in, and while he went back around the car to get behind the wheel, the lizard was at it again.

The White Tower on 193rd and St. Nicholas had gone out of business, though. And the delicatessen a couple of blocks down was closed on Monday, and it was Monday. But they got hot dogs with mustard and too much sauerkraut from the hot dog stand on the corner. And there was a bench on the Broadway Mall where they sat among dogwood flowering over cigarette butts and cracked bottles. At the curb the Volkswagen-Rolls was parked by a busted parking meter.

This Bic was undampenable, undeflatable. He took the paper napkin the Greek hot dog man had given him and stuffed it continental fashion between the two top buttons of his shirt. Puerto Ricans sat on the next bench, half-drunk, tossing beer cans at each other after they'd emptied them. Bic thought they were marvelous. As a matter of fact with him around New York turned into a kind

27

of Mediterranean port town. There was no fog, but a foghorn sounded from the river through the evening, and the fake baroque of the RKO 190th Street looked in the sunset like the Church of the Madonna by the Sea. Bic ate the hot dog slowly and with surprising *délicatesse* for such a muscle package.

"I love the New York Spanish," he said. "Where do they go dancing?"

"I don't think they dance too much after they get here," Trudy said.

"Oh, but they must, no?" Bic said. "We find out where. They have *joie de vivre*."

"I don't think you'll find out with me," Trudy said.

"But I have a theory," Bic said. "You find out the heart of a city by how they dance there. I bet you. The heart of anybody. I didn't find out about Madame Letarpo until I danced with her at Monodono's. Does New York have a place like Monodono's?"

"Whatever it is, no," Trudy said, smiling.

"A shame. After the Letarpo marriage, Mr. L. gave a magnificent bash at Monodono's — really you never heard of Monodono's?"

"Well, now I have," Trudy said.

"An American journalist buddy took me to that bash. The one who taught me American slang. Is my slang bad?"

"It's just fine," Trudy said.

"Ah, you won't tell. Mum is the word. But maybe you'll improve my slang. Anyway it was at this Monodono bash that I danced with Madame Letarpo. She said, 'Ah. Will you dare do the merengue with me?' Did you do the merengue in New York when it was hot?"

"You've got the wrong girl," Trudy said.

"You could do it beautifully. Madame Letarpo too. She dances like a little sad feather. The day after the Monodono I asked her for the secretary job I have now."

"What is she sad about?" Trudy said. To her surprise she was hungry for another hot dog, but the hot dog man was gone.

"What do you think?" Bic said. "Mr. L. is a very exciting guy, swinging, but if you don't watch out everything becomes Letarpo. Like the Magazine now, or the Hungarian coproduction. You read about the Hungarian coproduction deal?"

"I'm not up on movie deals." Trudy said.

"It would have been just great. In Hungary they dig mature

stars. It would have been great for me, too, to see my father in Budapest, in my native spot."

"I wondered about your name," she said.

"*Biglassy* originally. Somehow it got changed. My father defected as a diplomat in Paris. Five years ago he defected back and they don't let him out again. But you know? *He* is mad for dancing. For my birthday he always sends a bottle of Tokay with a note: 'Drink this in a dancing place!' "

"That's sweet," Trudy said.

"Yeah, but any dance joint I bring the Tokay to, they say, 'Nothing doing. No bottles of your own.' They say that in New York too?"

"I would imagine," Trudy said.

"So I have to order a bottle. But I only drink my father's. It's wonderful Tokay. Next time you drink it with me in a dance joint — we make a pact?"

Trudy had to laugh. Underneath all this raw euphoria of his there was something courtly. He was trying to perform a boy-girl ritual: a couple just met should talk about background, philosophy, family, before moving closer. Probably he'd wanted the ritual to take place in full New York glamour, with nightclub champagne and jazz trombones. Instead she'd forced him to go through with it sitting on a splintery Broadway bench, traffic fuming on both sides and the Puerto Ricans throwing their final beer can at a garbage truck. But he'd gone through with it, the paper napkin stuffed into his shirt; he'd coped with the unfamiliar sauerkraut dangling from the hot dog bun; and throughout it all he'd stubbornly but also very gently kept one finger (with the stiff red-blond hair) on her shoulder.

It didn't occur to her that she might react erotically to someone like that. But she found him touching. She almost never talked about her parents, but when Bic asked about her parents she answered.

"Actually they were from your neck of the woods," she said. "My father was in corporate law in Vienna."

"Ah, beautiful city!" Bic said. "Music. The balls!"

"I guess my father must have been a ball-going type," Trudy said. "But that was before Hitler, before I was born. By the time he got away to this country he'd been through a camp and he did nothing but work full-time for Labor Zionism, if you know what that is."

"Chey! Insult! Beg your pardon!" Bic said, mock-angry. "We are friends of Simon Spieger! Do I know! But your father should once meet my father —"

She shook her head. "He was on his way to some fund-raising in the Bronx." She looked at the street sign on the corner. "Actually it was just a couple of blocks from here. Some trailer crashed into him."

For a moment Bic took his finger away from her shoulder.

"Your mother also?"

"She was with him."

"This was long ago?"

"I've been living with my aunt since I was five," she said.

"Oh. I'm sorry. This is sad," Bic said. "I have lost my mother also. But I tell you what my father always says. 'When you feel sad, go to music.' We go somewhere to music."

"Thank you," she said. "But I really don't dance."

It was true. For someone hopelessly intellectual and intellectually self-conscious, she had the wrong kind of glossy looks. Anytime she walked to the dance floor with a man she had the feeling she became pure window display. "How ya like my hot dish, fellas?" Female paranoia or not, it kept her from catching the beat or enjoying. No, she wasn't going to go dancing with Mr. Bic. But she couldn't just send him packing to the Waldorf Towers either. She didn't have to meet Jennifer before ten P.M.

"You have all those cameras in your car," she said. "Can you take the skyline at night?"

"Sure! The Contax. Night filter and everything. You mean now?"

"There's a spot down the river that would make an unusual shot."

"Chey!" Bic said. "Good! We do that!" He got up and threw his napkin as though it were a Puerto Rican beer can. "And we make music from the car radio!" And his balled-up napkin really hit the wastebasket and they went.

What she had in mind, of course, was the little lighthouse under George Washington Bridge, specifically the circular balcony on top. Once she'd stood there and watched the downtown skyscrapers mass in a peculiarly foreshortened perspective: a cubist panic of giants, frozen in the act of falling. At night the angle might be still more piquant, especially for an upside-down magazine cover.

They happened on a parking space on the Drive, right where the steps went down to the foot of the bridge. Bic hit himself on the forehead. He even turned off Elvis Presley, the music they had been making on the car radio.

"The Waldorf garage!" he said. "I didn't ask for the key! *Merde.* I can't lock."

"I wouldn't leave the door unlocked," Trudy said. "Not this car."

"It is the lizard," Bic said. "The Rolls-Royce part is nothing. But Mr. Letarpo will kill me if they steal the lizard."

The row of dark benches on Riverside Drive was empty except for one Asiatic-looking couple. The man's arm was clenched around the woman's neck. By their bench a heavy golf club leaned, pointing up through the trees at the bleared stars. Nobody else was visible.

"Tomorrow," Trudy said. "Let's not risk it."

"No, no. Not tomorrow."

"In the daytime," she said. "That was a crazy idea of mine. We've got muggers in New York."

"I have a brainstorm. We can't leave the car — we take it with us." He got out. "It goes down there, where we have to photograph?"

He ran clear across the Henry Hudson Parkway, ran back, started the car with a whistle. "It is a sign from heaven," he said. "The railing is kaput." Still whistling, and before she could get out a single word, he drove the car clear across the highway and started down the railingless embankment on the other side.

"You're crazy!" she said.

"I told you. The car was made for a no-road island. *'Oopla!* Four-wheel drive. Hold the strap."

The car trembled, bucked and jumped like a goat, keeled over to the left, righted itself while Bic whistled on and Trudy bit her tongue. The car swerved, bucked, jumped once more, and came to a rest.

"*Chachacha,*" Bic laughed, and put her skirt back where it had fallen above her knee.

In her terror she must have rolled up the window. She rolled it

31

down again to look out. The lizard was, understandably, rattling about like mad, and all the recklessness was for nothing. The shoreline flickered with ditch flares; it was barred and barricaded and dug up all the way to the bridge.

"Damn!" she said. "It must be for a new water main or something."

He'd gotten out too. "What are they doing to us?" he said.

"We can't get up to the lighthouse," she said. "And we can't do it from here. The shot needs a much higher angle."

"Higher up? Wait. We don't give up the ship."

Somehow, by putting his arm around her waist, he'd hoisted himself up to the top of the car. A heavy piece of metal grazed her forehead. It was the camera he'd hung around his neck. It swung wildly and it could have cracked her skull. Bic didn't notice that, of course, nor that her hair was horribly messed.

"Chey, Trudy! Will you make me steady by the legs?"

"I'm looking for my bag."

"I need you. You will support my legs?"

The car was still on an incline. His legs were straddled on the roof. She held them by the powerful calves. Through the trouser-cloth she felt his European-style sock garters. She'd never felt anything like that before, and she also seemed to feel calf-hair, probably also red-blond, just above the garters.

"No, not quite high enough for the skyline," he said. He jumped down. "I have a brainstorm. *You* go up."

"The roof! You're kidding."

"This is easy."

He simply lifted her up, as if she were a barbell. But it felt as though the whole night were sprouting hands, the bridge lights, the ditch lights, the shadows all coming round her and pressing her in unlikely places, and she had to keep herself from screeching like an ingenue taken advantage of in a grotto.

She found footing on the car roof, dizzy. Her palm suddenly felt metal. A camera.

"You have it?" Bic's voice said. "Hold it. Now you move just a little." He was standing next to her without his jacket. His striped shirt was like the bridge, a dim, massive established fact in the night. "Now. *'Oopla.*"

32

Again she was lifted. This time, incredibly, she landed on his shoulders.

"You are stark raving crazy mad," she said.

She was sitting piggyback on the shoulders of a man who was standing on the roof of a Rolls-Royce Volkswagen, under George Washington Bridge at night. Only her panties were between his neck and herself. His nape hair tickled the inside of her thighs.

"Okay, now you find the skyline with the camera finder," he said.

"I want down!"

"You don't wear stockings," he said. "Nice. You found the sky-line? The camera is all fixed, shutter and exposure, everything. You are not light, but I love this. The release, the little button, is on the side."

"*Get me down!*"

"You found the skyline? Press the little button."

She found it. She pressed. "Good!" he said. He gave his shoulders a sudden tilt. She clutched her thighs around his neck and grabbed his hair for balance and heard herself laugh an absurd girlie laugh foreign to herself and they both fell.

But they sure fell cleverly. It was more of a sliding-slipping, topsy-turvying down each other and down the car window, her head just missing the rearview mirror, the bridge's light-arc cart-wheeling, transmuted into his shirtsleeved arms around her.

She was lying on the ground, in deep crazy Yew Yorr, she felt grass blades through the back of her blouse and his face through the front. Just before his mouth caught hers she knew she had to get this at least under joint control. If Trudy Ellner suddenly went all the way amidst the scents of upturned earth, brine, river pollution, maleness, it wouldn't be because she was seduced but because she provoked. She thrust her hand deep into his shirt. No hair, to her surprise. Just warm firm flesh and a hard nipple that made her own nipples bristle. And no squirmy breathy preliminaries either, no Elihu theatrics. Somehow he'd folded up her skirt with the same motion that caressed her hair out of her face. Bic-teeth gently pulled her bra away, and Bic-fingers, many of them, whole devout pilgrimages of Bic-fingers, went all over, inventing a sacred body she never had till now, spread on dark crabgrass under the bridge. For a moment she opened her eyes and saw her panties flicker to

33

the flicker of the ditch lights, panties lying by the car like an artifact from a primeval eon in her life. Yew Yorr, Yew Yorr . . . She
closed her eyes because he was already there.

"Oh Trudy," he said.

They were already joined down there, the air cool and free
between her legs together with his heat, heat which he fed her,
with strength but also with a touching solicitude (somehow she was
proud to have the detachment to find him touching), with the delicacy of a mother feeding a child. And just as his delicacy changed
to depth and speed, just as she learned to be hungry, the Negro
rose out of the ground.

Not even the car sheltered them. Nothing stood between them and
the sudden footsteps and the sounds. Bic must have gotten hold of
his jacket. She felt tweed rough over her arms and knees, but her
face remained uncovered and in her terror she opened her eyes.

It wasn't a man but a tall gaunt black woman in a torn black
coat too long even for her tallness and dragging behind. The
woman played a mouth organ, a low monotonous tune, and with
her other hand scattered paper scraps into the Hudson, and the
amazing thing was that some gulls followed her, swam alongside
her like a fleet of gray beaked little gondolas, stabbing at the paper
scraps for food, the woman trailing her coat along, moving slowly
over the torn-up earth, the mouth organ fading toward downtown,
the gulls rippling into the night.

And then, the procession gone, Trudy and this boy so amazingly
above her — they both started to laugh. Because it was no mugger
and because the crabgrass on which they lay smelled of spring and
because the stars were still there, and he had begun to grow again
inside her like a sweet baby of her flesh.

Thank God she'd never told Jennifer about the Bic thing. At
least she could keep the aftermath to herself: the cornball humilia-

tion of having been rolled around on the grass only to be abruptly and neatly abandoned. So what in hell, then, was the meaning of the invitation? The Pleasure of her Company requested at the opening of the Simon Spieger Judaica Collection at the new university library. It was printed on cardboard so thick you probably couldn't tear it up with the proper contemptuous ease. On the margin a hand-written phrase said *At the invitation of Mr. Louis Bic.* She didn't even know whether the writing was his.

Her impulse had been to visit the Chem Building on the campus, soak the invite in sulfuric acid and mail it back marked *Attention: Mr. Louis Bic.* But that was ludicrous emotionalism. She simply decided not to go. She also ignored the R.S.V.P. On the day of the opening she happened to have a dissertation conference, and when she came back found Tante's note: *Mr. Bickle called EL-5-8100.* She checked the phone book. Sure enough, that was the Waldorf Towers number, allowing for Tante's usual two misrecorded digits. Trudy did not return the call. She threw away the note.

On a last-minute whim she did go. But she kept on her old gray raincoat with the loose buttons. Nor did she change the scuffed sneakers she'd worn all day (mostly in order to irritate stuffy Dr. Zopf of the dissertation committee). Furthermore she took her time, strolling those ten blocks uptown. She walked in not at five P.M., as the invitation had said, but at nearly five-thirty. And the moment the guard took that invitation and admitted her among the illuminati she knew she could never sufficiently despise the occasion, and not just the occasion but the interior of the whole new university library, if the Simon Spieger collection was at all representative.

Surrounded by pompous black marble and *chutzpatik* white composition bookshelves sat forty pharaohs, sweating slightly. The air conditioning seemed to be on the blink in the high-and-mighty windowlessness of it all. The scene was so charged with exclusivity and celebrity (and therefore with Trudy's nobodyness), it was so airlessly self-conscious, Trudy wondered if it was real. It could have been an arty movie set — the all-highest burial chamber inside an MGM pyramid. And the only empty chair was next to a bull-shouldered blazer.

Bic. She didn't want to sit down next to him. But up at the

lectern Dean Goldeck paused among his sonorities. He stared at Trudy, the stand-up disturbance. She had to sit down.

And the moment she did, the coffin lids jumped into her view, right behind the rich buffet table, hung on the wall. They were of course the Simon Spieger coffin-lid paintings and actually a good thing to focus on, away from Mr. Bic on her left. All four coffin lids showed faces half-disintegrated except for the anger, cheeks askew but inflamed, yellow stars burning bitterly in eye sockets, shoulders and arms blurred into gray beards. Trudy was trying to decide whether this was clever expressionism or really haunting art, when Bic's whisper started.

"So glad you could come!"

Trudy didn't answer. Up on the lectern the Dean was talking about the monumental sociology work Simon Spieger had written before the war on the Old Testament's structuring influence on Western society. Spieger and Schweitzer, the Alsatian twin stars, one Jewish, one Christian —

"I phoned you! . . . I also wrote! . . . You never got it?"

Trudy ignored this lying whisper. Up at the lectern, the Dean was occupied by Simon Spieger's versatility — a versatility not only of gifts but even of fate: Simon Spieger arrested by the Nazi minions and put in the same cell with Alexander Letarpo. The very man whose generosity (scattered applause) joining that of others made possible this Collection today.

"You see, I had to fly to Paris the next day! I had to leave quick! Madame Letarpo got very unwell suddenly!"

But Trudy listened only to the Dean, who was now discussing genius as the force that could transmute unpredictability into necessity. Didn't it seem almost necessary in retrospect that the shock of the holocaust Simon Spieger had escaped so narrowly would make him abandon erudition to create — out of left field, as one said in America — those immortal coffin paintings of which the University had been fortunate to borrow a few?

"I had no chance to explain to you!"

The Dean's account of Simon Spieger's decision to return to scholarly pursuits was interrupted by applause in which Trudy said, very evenly, "Explain what?"

"Explain I must return to Paris. The magazine is postponed because of Madame Letarpo's health —"

36

Trudy joined the tail end of applause. At the lectern, Dean Goldeck rejoiced in the University's good fortune: that here Simon Spieger would write the long awaited second volume of his treatise, and here he would lecture. . . .

"But we have a rain check for the magazine. Also, while Madame Letarpo is under care, I work for Mr. Letarpo —"

. . . and here it was the Dean's happy duty to thank so distinguished an assembly for having come to celebrate this event and this Collection. . . . Tremendous applause bounced off the marble.

"Trudy!"

The Dean was finished. Everybody was getting up, so Trudy finally could too. But if she had moved away from Bic as fast as she'd have liked, she would have bumped smack into the Honorable John V. Lindsay.

"Look, Trudy, please!" Bic didn't have to whisper anymore. "I will be in town till Wednesday, and tomorrow there is a *vernissage* where I have two tickets from Mr. Letarpo. It would be wonderful if you —"

"Yes, wonderful," Trudy said. "Meanwhile the University has gone right ahead and bought the house. They are going to evict."

"If you will give me a moment —"

She saw no reason to give him a split second. It was much more interesting to watch the pharaohs simpering at each other: a panorama of self-congratulation and moral altitude among the cocktailing elect.

"Oh there he is!" Bic said. "Mr. Letarpo! I would love you to meet him!"

"We're suing the University to prevent evictions," Trudy said. "If your boss is involved with the University we're suing him too!"

"Mr. Letarpo," Bic said. "Mr. Letarpo and Mr. Spieger, may I introduce a special young lady, Miss Trudy Ellner. Trudy, you know these gentlemen."

She knew them all right. Tall Simon Spieger with dark, wide, sadly astonished eyes in a pearl-pale face, thinner and taller than his photographs suggested. Whereas Letarpo was just like his picture in the papers; a roguishly nostriled overage little Puerto Rican busboy Lothario. Obviously both were off to a soirée. Both tall man and short wore the same boiled-white-shirt-and-tux costume. Trudy decided they looked like a famous comedy team.

"Bravo, Bic," Letarpo said. With an arm quite long for a short mogul, he reached clear across the buffet table, almost knocked over a goblet, grunted something at it that made it regain its balance, broke off a carnation from the centerpiece, and pushed it into Trudy's buttonhole. An action most wonderfully absent-minded because with his free hand he poked the governor of the Empire State, who had stepped up to the pâté de foie gras.

Mr. Simon Spieger, however, went his friend one better. After all, Spieger was the one V.I.P. here who was supposed to know Trudy. This was the man who'd supposedly taken a few hours out of his important life to read the essay she'd sent him, who'd written her about it, who was really responsible for all this, including Bic. Now he gave her just one mumbled word. *Enchanté*. Plus four limp versatile-genius fingers.

Silence.

"Mr. Letarpo," Trudy said. "Do something for some deserving old people and buy back from the University a house —"

She was drowned out. A fanfare of superb laughter from another group swept away her whole sentence. *Her* group kept staring at her with mild curiosity, at this juicy little nothing in the funny coat with the unpublished face that had actually never been printed in the papers.

"Mr. Letarpo," Trudy started again. "If you want to do something to help —"

"Chey, you're the girl for when we do the magazine," Letarpo said. He lifted up Trudy's arm, turned up the sleeve of her raincoat, probably to hide the sleeve button that was hanging by a thread, turned it up all the way to her elbow with a surprising modish flair, reached for her other arm to turn up *that* sleeve too when somebody stopped his hand by shaking it.

"Tarp!"

"Chey. Commissioner," Letarpo said.

"Trudy, you must meet Senator Javits!" Bic said. He pulled Trudy, who pulled back. She wanted to give Letarpo a chance to turn up her other sleeve. But the Commissioner, who had a picaresque wart on the cheek and the ribbon of God knows what decoration on his lapel, was whispering in Letarpo's ear. At that point it became too much. She was too ridiculous. Who was she to expect a Letarpo to do her grooming? She was this nobody of a fucked floozy amidst the flowers of creation. She was this cunt jived, balled and discarded without ado; only now she was being warmed up again because Mr. Bic was spending a week in New York again, and after all he had to have something to stick himself into at night.

It was too much. Bic pulled her toward Senator Javits. Trudy wouldn't let him. She dug the spoon into the caviar bowl that stood on the buffet right under one of the coffin paintings. She smeared black fish eggs on the stiff red-blond hair of Bic's fingers and for good measure also smeared some on the white cuffs. It only took one second. It was enough to make Bic stop. The next second he looked at her with wide blue eyes. In that second Trudy knew that she was about to cry.

She ran out, past the guard. She wanted to run out into the street, but the outer entrance was blocked by a group that alarmingly resembled the Rockefeller brothers. She backed into a small room with magazines stacked helter-skelter on tables. She beat her fist on a pillar of *Commentary* magazines and still couldn't stop the tears. Apart from everything else she was appalled by her lack of control. But she knew that getting mad at herself would only make her sob aloud and she didn't want to alarm a guard or a Rockefeller or both. She found a Kleenex in her bag and tried to be rational, see things in perspective. It wasn't her fault she had looks that attracted animals her brain despised. It wasn't her fault that she had no loving overprotective parents who carried on against staying out late at night and whom she'd have rebelled against by developing a healthy sex life, the kind of sex life for which a Mr. Bic was a minor entertainment. She ought to say to herself, To hell with my orphan-girl's puritanism! She had better uses for her energy, she was as special as any of the swollen pharaohs in the Burial Chamber and she vowed not to let them stop her from making her special social and intellectual contribution. The idea was to get on with life and she'd have gone out into the street if a man hadn't blocked the doorway of the room.

"Miss Ellers?"

It was Spieger. She had just time to sneak the Kleenex back into her bag. At least she hadn't used mascara for the occasion, so nothing could run.

"It was so stuffy in the other room," she said.

"I wanted to apologize," Spieger said. "I am so glad to find you here!"

"I have to go home," she said.

"I am an admirer of you, Miss Ellers—"

"Ellner," Trudy said.

"Of course, Ellner. You must excuse me. I am two hours off the plane. I am still giddy. I didn't hear the name properly on our introduction. You are the author of this most interesting essay I had hoped to meet—" He stopped. "There is something wrong?"

"The air was stuffy," she said. "I told you. And not just the air." The best way to hang onto control was anger. "Our Dean here," she said. "You've listened to his flatteries, his humanisms! This man is going to evict a lot of old people. For a parking lot. A parking lot!"

"Oh yes," Simon Spieger said. "You have sent me a cable. When will this happen?"

"As soon as they pull down the house right opposite there. Sixty old people. Out into the street!"

"I did not realize it was so soon," Simon Spieger said. He touched the pillar of *Commentary* on which she supported herself. "You are admirable."

"We've formed an ad hoc committee suing this great institution," Trudy said. "People in your position—you can help if you really mean it!"

"We must speak to some authorities," Simon Spieger said.

"Oh I've spoken to the Dean," Trudy said. She said it loudly because she saw Deansy coming with Letarpo. She'd love to take on Deansy right now. She was just in the mood.

"Good grief, they're in the periodical room!" said Dean Goldeck to Letarpo. "Just what I wanted to hide because we haven't fixed it up yet."

"We must make amends to this young lady, for a lapse," Simon Spieger said.

"Miss Ellner!" the Dean said. "I was going to write you a letter!"

"I hope you enjoyed getting our court notice," Trudy said.

"I sure did; that's what the letter is about," the Dean said. "That notice came at a perfect time. It'll strengthen my hand against our Real Estate Vice President. We have two of those," he said to Simon Spieger, smiling, "as if one wouldn't be enough. You gentlemen know our brilliant Miss Ellner?"

"She does not feel too well," Simon Spieger said.

"She's much too pretty to be our social conscience," the Dean said. "But that's what she is and maybe she overworks herself."

"Yes, I did not realize she would look like this after her learned fine essay," Simon Spieger said. "I didn't catch the name."

"I'd better go," Trudy said.

"To make up for my lapse, may I take you home?" Simon Spieger said.

"I was about to offer her a University car," the Dean said.

"Thank you, but we will use the one at my disposal," Simon Spieger said.

They moved to the door and a deep Balkan voice said, *"Halt."* It was Letarpo, and except for Trudy they all stopped.

"It has fallen," Letarpo said. He seemed to say it with great mock solemnity. He picked up the carnation he'd given her and which had really fallen to the floor just now and pushed it back into her buttonhole again. With almost the same motion he turned back her other sleeve. It was part of the same sophisticated little joke. Everybody smiled. And then they all walked out of the Periodical Room, a small pantheon of dinner jackets around Trudy in her old carnationed raincoat and her sneakers. She saw Bic agape from the buffet table, still rubbing away at the caviar stain on his cuff. And Trudy in Liechtenstein, past the age of forty and nobody for company except a dog whose name she didn't know and a bottle she didn't know how to drink up — Trudy wished the world had stopped there. It was a world in which the only triumphs were the small ironic ones, like a girl entering a burial chamber in a pumpkin and coming out retinued by the gods, a regular Washington Heights Cinderella. Only if they'd all dropped dead right then and there, right there on the black marble floor, only then would they all have lived happily ever after.

41

But nobody died for quite a while.

Five minutes later Trudy sat with Simon Spieger in a black limousine, her legs tucked back to make the sneakers invisible.

"You tell him, please," said Simon Spieger.

"Eighty-five Haven Avenue."

On the front seat the driver's august black face turned around. "Eighty-five Haven Avenue," Trudy said again. Apparently it was hard to comprehend an address tucked away so deeply into the lower middle class.

"It's just ten blocks south of this great university and a couple of blocks west," Trudy said, and the car rolled.

"Now I must make two apologies," Simon Spieger said.

"No reason in the world why you should recognize my name," Trudy said.

"Much reason, but that is the minor apology. The major one is — you helped me by crying."

He had a French voice of huskily muted elegance and his long black trouserlegs, crossed at the knees, matched the gray cape someone had hung around him before he'd stepped into the car. His head had fallen back. She wasn't ready for so much classy melancholy. She'd just discovered that her left sneaker was unlaced.

"I was *not* crying," she said.

"I did not express myself well," he said. "I mean, I saw you, you see, someone so young and strong and attractive but with such bitter eyes — I am so exhausted by the plane and by what I must do in America — but when I saw you in a similar state in the little room, I took heart. Could you open the window, please?"

There was a whole mess of buttons inside the limousine door. Finally she pushed the right one, and the traffic blew in.

"Thank you," Simon Spieger said. "When I saw you so disturbed I felt better. This is what needs apology. Because of you I didn't feel so alone in my weakness, I didn't feel so unworthy of — of things said about me. But — but one shouldn't feel better on seeing someone else suffering — and you were suffering to protect some old people. Would you open just a little more, please?"

She opened just a little more.

"Thank you for letting myself unburden."

She had a sudden great need for irreverence. "This idiot," she

42

heard herself saying to Jennifer. "He doesn't know I was suffering because I had to sit next to a pig that once conned me into fucking." But Jenn wasn't there. And Trudy wasn't being fair to herself. And the man sitting next to her was no idiot. He was very important.

"You shouldn't have left your reception so soon," she said.

"There will be many receptions. But perhaps not another person like you."

"You must have a busy schedule."

"They will show my paintings in twenty-one cities in the U.S.A. I must make little talks everywhere. And I have the lectures at the University here in the fall." He drew a pained breath.

"Why do it if it bothers you?"

"Because this is the country — the important country to make an impact for the right things. Only . . ." His head, still dropped against the seat back, shook slowly. "It is too official, all my arrangements. I feel the need for a real connection — real feeling, which you showed —"

"All right!" she said. "Then do a teach-in! A teach-in at Craftsmen Home in the fall!"

He lifted his head off the upholstery.

"Teach at the house they want to raze! Where my old people are supposed to be evicted! You can start your lecture series there! That's how you could save the roof over their heads!"

The car had stopped. He looked at her. His face was ravaged, yet graceful, and his eyebrows arched, dark-silky and astonished like a child's.

"We have stopped before your home?"

"Yes."

"By any chance, may I use your telephone?"

"Yes. Why not?"

"You see, Letarpo is expecting me at a function tonight. I would like to call and say I cannot come."

"All right. Feel free."

"Otherwise they will delay everything, waiting for me. But I am too fatigued."

"By all means use the phone," she said. "I am sorry I sprung this other thing on you."

"Sorry? I am glad. I am thinking."

43

The limousine door had been opened and as he helped her out she brushed against his cape, which was smooth like his hand on her elbow, smooth soft cashmere.

The light on the brownstone stairs was damnably dim. Probably it made her house look slummier to Simon Spieger than it actually was. But the dimness had the advantage of obscuring Trudy's un-laced sneaker. Tante, alas, stood very brightly illuminated when she opened the door.

Tante wore a green feathered hat and carried a pepper mill. On opera days that was her way of cooking. The day of her Met subscription she wore her hat constantly by way of warming to the occasion. She'd wear the hat even while repotting cactus; she got ready all day for Leonard Bernstein, whose tempi she always despised afterward. And behind Tante stood Jennifer, with whom Trudy had made a movie date. Trudy had forgotten all about that.

Introductions. Spieger bent down into almost hand-kissing posi-tion. His tallness arced into a classic curve. Tante's hat looked overdone. Jennifer's shawl seemed pretentious, though it was slung so tightly round her neck only to obscure chinlessness. Both women stared at Simon Spieger as if Trudy had brought home a giraffe.

"The last showing of the Fellini is at nine-twenty," Jennifer said; somewhat gratuitously for it was not even eight.

"Mr. Spieger just wants to use the telephone," Trudy said.

"*Das Telefon ist under den Pflanzen,*" Tante said.

Talking in German was a sign that she did not much care for this gentleman caller. But Simon Spieger needed no translation, for he was already getting his dinner jacket sleeves wet, groping for the phone under the ice-cubed plants. He happened to face the door left open into Trudy's room. He had a splendid view of the unmade bed, the book litter on the floor, and on the desk the manuscripts, with two combs for a letter weight. Not to speak of the lidless jars messing up the night table. Jennifer must have been through her toilet kit again, in search of a new lotion against oily skin.

"I am so sorry, I cannot find the phone," Simon Spieger said.

Tante took a big Teutonic step forward.

"Simon Spieger! *That* is your name?"

44

"Yes, Madame."

With her pepper mill she pushed out something from under wetted-down fronds of fern. Not the telephone but a book. *The Illustrated History of Israel.* There was Simon Spieger's name on the cover.

"A book of you?"

"That one, not really," Simon Spieger said. "I have only done a little introduction."

"You will sign this book for me!"

"Oh, with pleasure," Simon Spieger said. "But I cannot find the phone. My faculties are very poor today."

"Trudy can always find the telephone," Tante said with an irony Trudy hadn't thought she could muster in English.

"Would you telephone on my behalf?" Simon Spieger said to Trudy. "Please." He had pulled out a small blue address book. "Would you leave a message for Letarpo? I am too fatigued, I have already retired, would they excuse? You would help so much."

"Okay," Trudy said. Dialing, she kicked the door to her room shut.

" '*Letarpo!*' " Jennifer said, very softly. "Hotcha."

". . . Club, good evening," said a West Indian voice.

Trudy couldn't make out what club because that moment something clanged to the floor. Simon Spieger had followed Tante and her *Illustrated History of Israel* to the kitchen table and had with his cape brushed a copper pot off the wall.

"Is Mr. Letarpo there, please?"

"Who is calling?"

"I'm calling on behalf of Mr. Simon Spieger."

"Yes. Please hold on."

"No, no need to get him, just tell him Mr. Spieger is too tired to come tonight and would like to be excused. Good night."

"*Letarpo!*" Jennifer said again, with soft-whistling thin lips.

"I think I've got something in the works on the eviction," Trudy said, putting down the phone.

"With Letarpo? *The* Letarpo Letarpo?"

"Not exactly with him. But it might work."

"Tell!"

There was no time. Tante came out of the kitchen with Simon Spieger, who held a huge bottle of mineral water.

"I am so grateful," Simon Spieger said. "But my capacity for liquids —"

"You take it home," Tante said. "Specially Swiss-imported. Against all travel upset. Three times a day."

"Most kind of you," Simon Spieger said. "Would your niece have a little flashlight to walk me downstairs?"

Down on the street the house looked wizened next to the big limousine. Simon Spieger pointed to the car door held open by the chauffeur.

"Would you sit with me a minute?"

She got in. The chauffeur closed the door behind them both as if they would drive off together.

"You know, the teach-in would be political," Simon Spieger said. "It would violate my visa."

"Hell," Trudy said.

"It is the reason I had to turn down speaking at a dinner for Governor Stevenson. But you I cannot turn down."

"Oh, that's beautiful," she said.

"I will make the teach-in on one condition."

He hugged the mineral-water bottle against his cape.

"You will help me on my American tour this summer."

"Help you?" she said.

"You have already made a job arrangement for this summer?"

"My God," she said. "I have an interview coming up, for a summer-session tutorship at N.Y.U. —"

"You come with me. You will be my bridge to real people."

"Jesus," she said.

"I will tell you something," he said. "In 1946 I was in a funeral chapel in Strasbourg for my cousin from Buchenwald. But there were hundreds of cousins from Buchenwald there, so many they had a heap of coffin lids in the yard. Afterwards — you mind if I tell you this?"

"No," she said.

"It is related to this moment. I could not work on my sociology after the coffin lids. I came back to the chapel that night with my paints. I started to paint on the coffin lids. Suddenly. Maybe it was crazy. Painting was just a hobby before."

"You've produced haunting stuff," she said.

46

"I don't know," he said. "I do know with me suddenness is genuine. It is strength. It is a good strong thing, my asking you to help me. It is good because it is sudden. Only now the issue is life, not death. You will be my bridge to life in America. My connection to real people."

"You know whom you should paint," Trudy said. "A man named Lissberg, the spokesman for the evictees. A Simon Spieger painting of the spokesman at the teach-in!"

"Yes. But you help me on the tour."

"What do you mean help you?" she said.

"I wish to go beyond the official things. I want to do the teach-in and paint the friend you mention. With you I don't care about visa restrictions. Will you help me?"

"I am not so good at suddenness," she said.

"You are not to decide now!" Suddenly he turned to her and the mineral-water bottle clinked to the carpet and she was stirred that she had moved this man to a gaucherie.

"We both should think a little," she said.

"I have thought!" he said. The folds of her raincoat were now between his hands, as though he were praying with the help of her coat. "I have seen your telephone number," he said. "I glimpsed it on the telephone when you used it. Audubon six-two-nine-four-four! I shall never forget it! I will call you tomorrow. You will help me in America!"

She stood on the sidewalk as the long black chassis pulled away. Out of a dim storefront came a woman's voice singing *La Paloma* . . . and the wind rolled an empty Coke bottle along the sidewalk and banged it against a trashcan.

She put the flashlight in her raincoat pocket. Inside the torn lining of the pocket her fingers came on something silken. Simon Spieger's address book. She climbed the stairs slowly. Plenty of time to make the movie with Jennifer.

47

II

1

It had been one of Fellini's weaker films. But it was the last movie she and Jennifer enjoyed together, wisecracking at the clumsier subtitles and munching Goobers, which were such murder on the complexion. A couple of months later, when she saw Jennifer on the ship off Miami, it was already different.

And yet it shouldn't have been. Nothing had really changed between them. They kept regularly in touch by phone. Jenn held the fort on the anti-eviction front. In fact, Jenn was supposed to have been Mr. Lissberg's airborne escort. Since the Simon Spieger schedule was so hectic, Mr. Lissberg was supposed to have caught up with Spieger in Miami and to have sat for a Spieger portrait there.

"Those airline bastards," Jenn had told her over the phone. "They say they'll bump Lissberg because of the supermarket cart. If you can't shove it under the seat, they won't allow it in the cabin."

"Bastards is right!" Trudy said.

"I told them," Jenn said. "That shopping cart is like a blind man's cane. To him it's a necessity. It's like talking to a wall. They won't let him fly with the cart and he won't fly without it."

"We'll find another way," Trudy said. "Meanwhile you come down anyway. It's on Spieger."

"Just myself?"

"For a strategy session. We are doing an interesting thing on a ship down here."

"I understand you are doing lots of interesting things."

"Come down. You'll make me feel less homesick."

So she came down, and Trudy and her old pal stood on the deck, Letarpo's ship, which Trudy herself had seen the very first time that day. The shore lights held in their glitter not only Miami but Baltimore, Washington, Kansas City, St. Louis, all the places where Trudy and Simon Spieger had done readings together over the past two months, the many eyes staring, many hands clapping. Those two months were a phosphorescent space in her brain. Through Jennifer she wanted to make the phosphorescence more homey. But Jennifer had given her an oddly correct handshake when they'd met. Trudy suddenly felt a loss. A nostalgia for the Yew Yorr Jennifer.

Of course the big deck on which they stood was in itself unhomey. Half-naked men pushed kliegs, cables, cameras, Simon Spieger's coffin paintings. Spotlights flared off and on, moths swirled in twitchy little shadows. The scent of jasmine ripened in the heat. Jennifer appeared to reject it all. Her New York overcoat was buttoned up to the neck against it.

"Take your coat off, Jenn," Trudy said.

Jenn didn't. "I still don't get this ship," she said.

"Chey, don't get it?" Letarpo said. He had a habit of coming suddenly out of the dark with a paintbrush and a crushed bosun's cap. He'd been with a detail of sailors whitewashing a remote corner of the deck, remote and humble in contrast to the silver flashes of the film crew.

"Jennifer, you've met Mr. Letarpo," Trudy said.

"Had the pleasure when I was piped on board," Jennifer said.

"This ship is *Michelle II*," Letarpo said. "Number Two Michelle named for my Number One, my wife, you get it now?"

"You always film on board?" Jennifer said in her overcoat.

"Dirty Croat pictures. *Chachacha*. But this film, Michelle's crazy to see Simon reading, so we film it on Number Two Michelle and show it to Number One, her birthday surprise next month, chokay?"

Another brief, powerful hoarse laugh. *Chachacha*. Suddenly the smell of turpentine spiked the air. Two men followed Letarpo wherever he went, one with a can of turpentine, the other with what must be a bowl full of water; on the water man's shoulder, towels gleamed white in the dark. Moving very fast, Letarpo had

52

turpentined, rinsed, dried his hands, touched Jennifer lightly under the chin, which made Jennifer's overcoated shoulders rise and freeze in risen position.

"Isn't — the yacht moving?" Jennifer said.

"Not a yacht," Letarpo said. "A tanker, little bit converted."

Chachacha. He'd vanished in the dark.

"Sporty friends you have," Jennifer said.

"I'm not exactly a Letarpo friend," Trudy said. "I never even met his wife. But he was in the same Nazi jail as Spieger."

"Sporty remote acquaintances you have," Jennifer said.

"Oh, cut it out," Trudy said.

"Anyway, it would have been great if the Lissberg thing had worked," Jennifer said. "The media would have loved it."

"If Simon can't do a Lissberg portrait here, he'll do one in New York," Trudy said.

"We'd get twice the coverage at the teach-in," Jennifer said.

"Look," Trudy said. "Simon's going to make an interim trip to New York anyway, to talk to the immigration goons. I told you, they sent him such a nasty letter on the teach-in."

"An eminence like your friend Spieger," Jennifer said. "Imagine."

"Oh, he expected it," Trudy said. "They say a teach-in would be political activity in the U.S.A., it'd violate his visa in this free country."

"No kidding, the yacht *is* moving," Jennifer said.

"Of course Simon won't back down," Trudy said.

"Bravo," Jennifer said. "Bravo to you both on the press you've been getting."

"Simon's a terrific presence," Trudy said.

"Don't be modest," Jennifer said.

"It's also the mix in the audience, the bright oldsters with students," Trudy said. "For that I'll take credit, that's my idea. It's a whole new kind of electricity, it just takes a little advance work."

"Oh yeah, somebody sent me a clipping from out of town someplace," Jennifer said. "Comparing you two to — what was the actor pair? Lunt and Fontanne?"

"Oi," Trudy said. That particular write-up had been about how attractively Simon and Trudy complemented one another in age,

53

accent and good looks, the great pale continental scholar-artist and the young dark-maned West Side Joan of Arc.

"It's crap, but the more of a buildup we get, the better for the teach-in," Trudy said.

"Sure." Jennifer said. "Great." They both stared at the shore lights that were really dwindling. Letarpo had disappeared altogether, so she couldn't find out why.

"You are going to marry Mr. Simon Spieger?"

The question came so flat and sudden, it somehow caught her off base.

"Yes, and we'll adopt Tante with the plants," she said.

But Jennifer didn't smile. Not as far as Trudy could make out in the dark. Amidst the jasmine and the moths Jennifer had become humorless, unlike the Yew Yorr Jenn.

"How is it, traveling with Spieger?" Jennifer said, again flatly.

How was it. How talk about it? About the thing Trudy had found under her hotel room door in Baltimore one morning: a sheet of hotel stationery on which there was painted a long-petaled fine pink flower with the unmistakable line of Simon's coffin paintings and underneath something like an inked signature which wasn't a signature and which took her a minute to decipher. It had been scrawled so very tinily and fiercely. *Be my wife.*

How talk about that? She'd told him she couldn't reply before the teach-in, and he'd covered her hand quickly with his, for one second, then turned with a deep breath to his cousin Thérèse — his factotum on the journey — who had come to massage his neck. Next morning Trudy found another flower painted on another sheet. It was signed *Please.* He never mentioned the proposal to her face; just translated it into childlike chaste gallantries like putting a pillow on her seat in the plane, or jumping up, outrunning a waiter so that *he* could bring her the mustard jar. The haste in his tall elegant frame was powerful. So was the way his dark eyes burned at her in that white, abstaining face. He surrounded her with oblique fond pressure. How convey it to a Jennifer?

And that night it was as though Simon had sensed how hard it would be to make himself conveyable to her friend Jenn. (Often he was intuitive like that.) He didn't come out on deck until

54

Letarpo called out, "Ready! Please!" The lecterns had been pushed into place and the kliegs catapulted into brightness the coffin paintings grouped in the background. Finally Simon came out of a stairwell onto the deck.

"Good luck," said Jennifer.

"I don't know if it's going to work here," Trudy said. She walked into the glare.

Instead of an audience, there was the artificiality of the camera. Also the ship, heading out still further, had begun to roll just a little. Yet when she began as usual, reading from Simon's text, the words rang right. She'd learned from Simon not to declaim but to try and chat personally with a particular face in the audience. The lectern light gave Simon eyestrain, but he could blink his eyes as if he'd just heard a most interesting reply. "You talk as if you had just listened," Simon once told her. The advice helped her enormously. And the book Simon had written and from which she read helped too. He'd finished it before the war but seemed to have meant it, idea-freighted as it was, for a romantic night, for a backdrop of wave-lapping and warm stars. So now she talked to the camera as if she'd just listened to it. She talked out loud a passage from Simon's book: about redemption as the evergreen obsession that kept the West young; how the redemption dynamic continued under secular masks like "progress"; how it animated laboratory and lecture room; how it produced the great rejuvenators of the occident from Gutenberg to Luther, from Marx to Edison. . . .

The camera swung away, closed in on Simon. Redemption, he said, was an heirloom passed through the generations. He'd like to read something from his dear friend Trudy Ellner, her Sociology of Age essay, the passage on the old ironworker who had made a beautiful patron saint for statisticians, as gift to his grandson who was an actuary at Omaha Mutual. . . . She saw that Simon didn't turn pages as he read. He'd learned her words by heart; his whole body was turned past the camera toward her; and the prophets on the coffin lids rose and fell very gently to the ship's roll, the moths settled on their wasted faces as butterflies do on flowers, and even the end was not an anticlimax.

Here Trudy thought the audience with its applause would be needed. And that the sky provided.

Clapping came out of the air. Applause droned and swelled down from the sickle moon. A helicopter sank onto the deck with red lights flicking and blurring windy blades. The gusts made one of the light screens topple over. Letarpo shouted. His shout made the kliegs swivel their shine onto the landing scene.

Out of the helicopter jumped Bic, who lifted down Mr. Lissberg. Mr. Lissberg complete with beard! Then came his supermarket cart, whose rusty wheels squeaked the moment they touched the deck.

"Mr. Lissberg," she heard Jennifer yell.

She wanted to start forward with Simon — but Simon was gone. Letarpo was there, taking her arm.

"Did you do that?" Trudy asked him. "Did you have Mr. Lissberg brought in?"

Letarpo pulled her sideways, grinning.

"Your plane and helicopter?"

"Here," Letarpo said. "Go down. Be nice to Simon." In front of them was an iron door; behind, the noise of the Lissberg arrival. "Tell Simon yes," Letarpo said. "And it's okay, they can't kill his visa."

"I don't follow," Trudy said.

"This film we just did," Letarpo said. "Anytime they want to demolish that eviction house, you take the film to the house, you with Simon, you show it, you sit down with a lot of friends, you do nothing but watch it, have a nice brainy time. Not a teach-in, a film-in. Somebody says it's political activity in the U.S.A., my lawyer says Ha ha, what U.S.A.? This film was made outside the U.S.A.!"

"I thought this film was for your wife —"

"Sure, filmed for her outside the three-mile limit, captain's affidavit!"

A hoarse, tremendous, moth-scattering Letarpo laugh, a tap-caress on the back of her neck, an expert touch, turpentiney, conspiratorial, humorous. "Go tell Simon."

"He doesn't know about the three miles?"

"He just knows he got into a lot of trouble for you. So you be nice. Say yes. Don't make trouble with each other."

She got a little push through the open door. Down in a dank stairwell sat Simon, head between hands. She was enormously touched.

"Simon?" she said.

The door closed behind her.

"Simon? You know we just did this outside the three-mile limit? Outside American waters? We can have a film-in and you'll still be all right — Simon?"

He was lifting his head slowly. Against the rough steps the fineness and thinness of his cheekbones were shining. He looked wounded and beautiful. Letarpo was right. Why make trouble for each other?

"Simon," she said, walking down the steps, her hands held out to make him get up. That moment the flute sounded. Mr. Lissberg's flute which he played when kept waiting too long at the A & P checkout counter or at any other emotional moment. *"Havah Nagila"* came fluting through the steel plates into the dreary stairwell. Simon was suddenly up, grasping her, wheeling her about in dancing desperation on that very narrow platform between stair flights.

"You don't answer!"

"Answer what?" she said. "Your proposal? Watch out!"

They both nearly fell down the steps. His eyes were sepia-luminous through the dimness, moist crazy stained-glass windows in his pale face. She felt her own eyes filling as she had to smile. They were staggering around, boxed into that tiny stairwell.

"All right, I'll answer," she said.

Outside, the Caribbean waited with jasmine and moths and a millionaire's ship pushing shore lights beyond limits, and Mr. Lissberg's flute. She nodded to Simon. He had crazy-lovely eyes, and her nod continued all those things out there and made them swell into the great exciting arc she'd always expected of her life. There was a lot they could get done together.

"My Trudy!"

He tried to dance with her again, joyously now.

"Let's go out on deck," she said.

Arm in arm they went up the stairs.

∽ 2 ∾

Trudy had always sworn never to marry out of compulsion, however subtle — especially if the prospective marriage was a "good" one. In a "good" marriage she had to be doubly careful not to do the compulsively ingenue thing and invest her good looks in some proper blue chip. She'd observed the vow. Her marriage to Simon was "good" all right. But it was no shivery-panicky dash into some sort of mink-lined safety. Not a bit: it was gearing up for further risk. By marrying an activist American citizen, Simon took a shortcut to his own U.S. citizenship and hence to being unrestrictedly active.

So it was a noncompulsive yet still romantic occasion up on the high meadow above the Bürgenstock Palace Hotel, which in turn balanced on a flower-studded cliff above Lake Lucerne. The wedding was held here to make attendance easier for Michelle Letarpo, who stayed in a sanatorium by the lake. At the last moment it turned out that Madame Letarpo wasn't well enough to come. Letarpo remained with her. Jennifer had returned with regrets the round-trip air ticket sent her. But Tante arrived, of course, and on Simon's side there was his cousin Thérèse.

"Also," Simon said. "I've asked the two Antones, father and son. You know them?"

"I don't know anybody fancy, Simon," she said. He always seemed touchingly surprised that she didn't share his entire network of renowned chums.

"Old Antone used to be in business with Letarpo," he said. "A fine man, most kind to me always. He was the first to collect my pictures. But his son leads a union, the Building Workers."

"That one," she said. "I think we once thought of reaching him for our anti-eviction fight. He's quite a glamour-puss."

"The old Antone calls him a traitor to his class." Simon smiled. "A man so good-looking doesn't deserve to be so *simpático* too. You will see."

"I've seen him on the Six O'Clock News," Trudy said.

In a way she was uneasy about meeting people she didn't know, such a select motley crew, at her own wedding. Yet here on the meadow their sweat proved them all real friends. It had been Simon's idea to get married under a home-made *chuppah* and by God, here they were, not *Chasids* but classy *goys* most of them, working away, making a wedding canopy. They had all put on hotel porters' aprons. Young Antone had pulled the rough green apron over the shining white linen of his shirt; it looked as peculiar on his lankness as it did over his seignorial bald father, who had pulled it on over his blazer. Tante had tied the apron over her formal black skirt; Simon's cousin Thérèse (face of a perennially insulted bird) over her flounces. Simon had put the apron over his white kaftan, specially made for the ceremony, and Trudy over her chemise. The men hoed four holes into the ground. The women were busy with kitchen knives (in an affectingly clumsy way) trying to sharpen the points of the four poles. A couple of hotel porters, de-aproned, watched astonished. Simon had forbidden them to help. There was also a wire-service photographer who'd somehow gotten wind of the thing; and of course the rabbi from Lucerne, who kept stroking his mustache, dazed. He'd been summoned so suddenly by Simon Spieger.

The men speared the four poles into the ground. Then Simon permitted one of the porters to bring a stepladder forward. Simon climbed it. Trudy held on to his legs, his slim tense calves, steadying him. He tied the four corners of a huge prayer shawl to the four pole tops. It was the roof of their wedding canopy. The wind pulled at it, at this holy white sail, high in the Alps. Nick Antone, with the handsome boy-face under the gray lock, threw some stones up to Simon. Simon caught them and weighed down the canopy with them against the wind. He climbed down; everybody took off their aprons — and Bic came running up from the hotel with a bottle. A porter uncorked it when Bic suddenly whispered to Trudy — the first words spoken on the meadow for minutes.

"Special Dom Perignon from Mr. Letarpo. Will you sign the label?"

Trudy kept on combing her hair for the ceremony. Bic kept whispering.

"For my autographed label collection? I already have labels of bottles Letarpo drank with Willy Brandt and Jean-Paul Belmondo. I already took the label off this one. Here."

He held out the label.

"Would you mind?" he said. "I had something to do with this occasion."

He still held out the label at her. She took it, tucked it under her sleeve, turned away in dismissal. That moment the rabbi began the ancient chant, first in Hebrew, then, like a good Swiss rabbi, in German and in English.

He who is strong above all else . . .

And the September breeze stopped. Leaves stopped rustling. The sunshine swelled into a young brilliance which swept all Bics away. The pine woods on the highest slopes sent down scents of sweetness and greenness, the sun umbrellas on the hotel terrace below opened like marigolds and the lake fired up an April dazzle wonderfully naive and quite out of season. They all swam in a spring morning of their very own.

He who is strong above all else,
He who is blessed above all else,
He who is great above all else,
May He bless the bridegroom and the bride. . . .

Though it wasn't easy to do on grass, Simon stamped so passionately on the goblet, it shattered right away. He kissed her with champagne-spiced lips. Bic, thank God, had gone down to see to the wedding dinner, and she didn't mind kissing the others. Antone the younger only blew her a kiss because he was on the run: he had to catch a plane back in order to substitute on Spieger lecture dates during the honeymoon — the first one being tomorrow. But he yelled as he ran down; would the bridal couple make an appearance at his Union convention next month as an exchange-*mitzvah?* And they both yelled back smiling (he pronounced *"mitzvah"* well) maybe they would, and everybody laughed, even Tante. Tante then began to cough imperiously to defend herself against sogginess; Trudy, kissing her, felt something moist between their cheeks. She kissed the others, and then all the others left, the porters too. Simon had requested this in advance.

He wanted to take down the *chuppah* all alone with his bride. Only the photographer, discreet behind a tree, remained.

Again Simon went to the stepladder; again she steadied his legs as he untied the prayer shawl from the poles. Together with him she pulled the poles out of the ground and together they carried them into the luggage cart. They each kept one of the stones which had weighed down the wedding canopy against the wind. Suddenly he took her hand and kissed it and pointed to the new ring on her finger. Instead of a gem, it had an ancient Davidic hexagonal coin. But that wasn't what he pointed at.

"My Trudy, did you see? There is something missing."

He pointed at the two small prongs on each side of the coin. Only one prong had a tiny blue stone in it.

"Hey, no blue stone on this side," she said. Simon had the gentlest touch.

"It's not a stone. A piece of old mortar. From the synagogue of Berdichev, where we came from before Alsatia."

"My God," she said.

"It was called the Blue Shul, and the ring is from my oldest granduncle."

There were bird calls and they stood alone on the meadow.

"Don't be surprised if I cry," Trudy said.

Simon kissed her.

"I wish I had something like that to give you," Trudy said. "I don't even know where we came from before Vienna, what kind of Polack or Russian Jew."

"Trudy," he said, "I always wanted to go back to Berdichev. The Blue Shul is still supposed to be there."

"Take me along!"

"May I?"

"I'll kill you if you don't!"

"We could squeeze it in before the anti-eviction act," Simon said. "This could be our honeymoon. You could look for a little blue mortar piece. You could put it in the empty part of your ring."

"Simon!" she said. She had to kiss him.

"All my old-age sociologizing!" she said. "My thing about old folks! It's just a substitute for roots!"

"You are my root," he said.

61

Together they pulled the *chuppah*-cart to the hotel, and the breeze came back and grasshoppers leaped like crocus buds gone mad, and they heard nothing but bird calls and their footsteps and those of the photographer following discreetly behind.

So fresh was the film out of the lab that the sound track hadn't yet been mixed. Therefore Simon and Trudy did the narration live. What they saw now, Simon said, was the surrounding of the synagogue. Those were the birches and lawns of the People's Culture Park of Berdichev. And the little house in the middle was the Blue Shul, whose congregation was long gone and where Simon's grand-uncle had been the last cantor. And this was the inside of the Shul, Trudy said; it had been a granary for a while, then a tractor barn, but it was a library now, with the librarian's desk where the tabernacle used to be. And *this,* Simon said, was the miracle's start: After being dead for two thirds of a century, the synagogue would come to life again for two hours. The Soviet authorities had given permission. Here he, Simon, was doing a *brucha,* pronouncing a blessing over wine poured at the librarian's desk, the first time such words had been heard under that roof in many decades. Here the walls were being sprinkled with wine thus blessed, to resanctify the house. And this now, Trudy said, this was something never *ever* seen before in Berdichev: Simon and his wife Trudy each carrying into the Shul a Torah scroll, a *woman* carrying the burden of the Law. (Trudy, watching that shot, wished her long black dress didn't look so much like an evening gown.) And this, Simon said, was Trudy pronouncing the *Shema Israel;* and this, his Trudy and himself each reading one symbolic sentence from that week's portion of Pentateuch and Haftorah, reading the Hebrew to impassive emptiness, to library chairs and tables and, over there, to faces swift in the window, village boys jumping for glimpses outside. And this, Trudy said, was Simon chanting the eighteen benedictions and the concluding *kaddish shalom*. And now, Simon said, one would have to look close. See the small bit of paper he was dropping on his way out with the Torah? This was a corner of a page from his granduncle's prayer book; he had wanted to leave behind at least one syllable of God's. And finally this was a bit of mortar taken from the wall of the synagogue. The building had been repainted and so the bit was a little brighter than the blue mortar bit set into his granduncle's ring.

The screen went dark.

At Trudy's request mention of the ring as her wedding ring had been left out. And there was no credit of Letarpo Energy Ltd. as sponsor of this CBS documentary, inappropriate here in a preview-lecture format.

For the commercial, Trudy substituted her own voice, live. This documentary, she said, also applied to America: where often the souls of buildings die because of the constant rent-minded turnover in tenants; because of the constant tax- or mortgage-minded turnover in owners. Where often only the maintenance staff, that is the building workers, provided the continuity which gave a roof its warmth and pulse. To these providers, their audience tonight, she and her husband wanted to dedicate this film.

The lights went up in the ballroom of Chicago's Regency Hotel. Three hundred hands, belonging to the Cultural Committee of the International Brotherhood of Building Workers, clapped.

Arm round her waist, Simon bowed together with her, led her into the backstage room. And here stood, of all people, Louis Bic in a black suit.

"Look who's here," Trudy said. Applause kept drumming through the door. She was high enough to be airy even about Bic.

"My Trudy, now I can tell you," Simon said. "Our friend here already telephoned me about the matter this morning."

"What matter?"

"I didn't want to mention it just before going on. I knew you were going to be marvelous. I didn't want you disturbed."

"What happened?" Trudy said.

Usually Simon went to bed, pale and spent, after an appearance. But now he stood very erect. His cousin Thérèse had already given

63

him the fresh handkerchief to dry his forehead with and he had already wiped himself with it, but didn't give it back to her. He held it with both hands and looked at Bic.

"You see, Michelle Letarpo died," Bic said.

"Oh, I'm sorry," Trudy said.

"Michelle was an extraordinary woman," Simon said. "I owe her very much."

"I never met her," Trudy said. Still she felt a little sheepish she couldn't scrounge up a sense of grief. The applause kept drumming.

"Let this reporter in, sir?" the Pinkerton guard said. There was a local interview waiting. Simon shook his head. He kept looking at Bic.

"Mr. Letarpo wants to do something in his wife's memory," Bic said. "He wants to establish a School of Religion at the University, named after her, but only if Simon becomes head of the Yeshiva unit."

"There are so many better qualified," Simon said.

"You know Letarpo," Bic said.

"But so fast," Simon said. "This winter I planned —"

"This winter?" Trudy said.

"You see, we could use the Pharmacy College," Bic said. "I've already looked into it. The facility for the Pharmacy College where the financing didn't work. That building would be just right for our school. So the plant is already there."

"But — this winter!" Trudy said.

"We're talking about a six-figure donation," Bic said. "And this year is the only feasible year for Letarpo. We ought to start now on organization and staff. It'd be some wonderful memorial to Michelle. The biggest Yeshiva in America."

His slang didn't go with the black suit.

"This winter," Trudy said. "We were going to act against the evictions. But now, if Simon's going to be part of the administration —"

"Yes, one should explore that," Simon said.

"Let me tell you," Bic said. He could speak very gently. "We have already discussed it very quick confidential with the University. They don't want to have any more trouble with a Mr.

Simon Spieger. For sure not with Letarpo, not with this donation. They're going to back down. They'll give some helluva fine housing to your protégés."

"Trudy," Simon said. "I wish Michelle could have heard you tonight!"

"Wish I could have," Bic said. "But the University will relocate your old people very well. Give them a whole new floor in their brand-new graduate dorm on Washington Terrace. And as Yeshiva head, Simon would have more influence against future evictions. He'd be on the Board of Trustees."

"I am not meant to be a trustee," Simon said.

"A trustee, or not a penny from Tarp," Bic said smiling.

"It is hard for me to think," Simon said.

"We just want a provisional Yes," Bic said.

Simon took a deep breath. He linked arms with Trudy. "Very provisionally," he said.

"Good enough," Bic said. "Now I must catch the young Antone."

"My Trudy," Simon said when they were alone. He was sweating again and very pale. Suddenly he had his postreading exhaustion. "It happens too fast," he said. "Can you do the interview by yourself?"

But she couldn't do the interview by herself. At first she thought she could, after Simon was helped through the side door by his French cousin. She asked the Pinkerton to give her a tiny bit longer. She thought she'd be ready in a minute. But she wasn't. She felt out of breath. She couldn't get her hair right in case there was a photographer and she felt ludicrous and pointless, struggling with her comb before a Pinkerton. She ran.

She ran. Through the side door to the back elevator that shot her three floors up to the Spieger suite.

"Simon!" she said.

He had already changed to his paisley robe. At her entrance his cousin Thérèse turned, but didn't stop rubbing his forehead with alcohol.

"We should have a talk," Trudy said.

"I hoped you wouldn't be long!" He touched his cousin to make

65

her stop rubbing. She not only stopped but went off with a very erect, pained neck; Trudy couldn't care less.

"Listen," Trudy said. "I couldn't discuss it with Bic around —"

"Yes! We must go back to Berdichev! Just by ourselves!" With his little finger he dabbed away a drop of alcohol from his brow. "We go back to Berdichev! — But on a real honeymoon — no network cameras, no crew, just ourselves, no pressure! Would you do that?"

"All right," she said. "But —"

"It wasn't really *us*. But the film will be on one hundred and forty stations, best prime time, I was told this morning. I just didn't want to bring it up on the news about Michelle."

"*Wait a minute!*"

Maybe she was screaming a little. He rose up from the bed, astonished.

"I'm not talking about starring on TV," she said. "I'm talking about the evictions. With this Yeshiva thing we make it easy for the damn University to go right on evicting —"

"Evicting? My Trudy, it is only relocating. I understand the dormitory is only two blocks away —"

"*Evicting*. I know those college dorms. That's the reason I lived with Tante! Four jammed together into a plastic box! At least students go out a lot, and they have the parent house. But with old people, their world is the apartment! I know from my fieldwork. A dorm will kill them!"

Simon sat down on his bed again, very gently.

"Maybe it seems like a small consideration, next to running the biggest Yeshiva in America," Trudy said.

Cousin Thérèse had come back into the room again. He must have given her some signal.

"I just don't want those poor old things to get lost in the shuffle!" Trudy said.

"We must think about it calmly for a while," Simon said.

"Let's tell Bic to hold everything," Trudy said. "I better catch him before he leaves."

The cousin was rubbing alcohol on Simon's forehead again. And Simon, as if his hearing were blotted out by that, said nothing.

"I'll tell Bic to wait!" Trudy said, and ran to the phone in her room.

66

But when she was connected to the desk she was told that no Mr. Bic had checked in; there wasn't even a room number for him. She ran again. Down the stairs, to avoid the sluggard elevator, to catch him in the lobby, have him paged if necessary, cornered somehow, and by God there he was by a house phone next to the bell captain's desk.

"Simon hasn't decided; he can't accept yet," she said.

Bic put down the receiver. He put his foot, a buckled slipper-shoe, on his overnight bag.

"It is a little late," he said. "I should have been told before I went to the long-distance booth."

"But we talked to you less than half an hour ago!"

"I have phoned Letarpo since then. It's settled. He's given the University the green light."

"So please phone him again!"

"He is in the speedboat, off to his mother."

"But you could reach him before!"

"Yes, just in time at the marina in Trieste. He cabled the green light to the University and went back to the island."

"You're bound to catch him if you try him again!"

"His wife died," Bic said quietly; a very clever wistful untouchable quietness. "When he has a loss he is in isolation with his mother. The only thing that helps. He will be like that for another week."

"Yes, I understand," Trudy said. "I sympathize with him. But we're not giving the University the green light."

"I am sorry." Bic picked up his overnight bag. It was pigskin with the initials L.E.B. imprinted in gothic gilt. "Not every day is another victory." He spoke to the lobby babble rather than to Trudy. "Not every day is a champagne wedding. Pardon me, I got to give a message to Nick Antone."

She had to step back to let him pass.

"If you'd sign that little old champagne label sometime," he said.

She could barely keep her hand from slapping that massive cheek inside which there was a fucking smile. She wheeled into the elevator whose door was opening just then, hammered at the No. 4 button.

67

"Simon!" she shouted from the suite door.

No answer, except sign language from Simon's French cousin. Cousin Thérèse rose from the sitting-room sofa to shake her head wildly at Trudy and point at the bedroom.

"But he couldn't be asleep yet!" Trudy said.

Cousin Thérèse of the incredibly long stringy spinster neck made her neck longer still and opened her blue ostrich eyes wide at Trudy's noising.

"I just want him to make a quick phone call to Letarpo!"

The blue eyes became wider still. It was no use. Trudy didn't know Letarpo's island number, though Simon probably had it somewhere in his three tiny-scripted and curiously coded red address books. And Simon, even if he dropped off for only one minute, needed to revive himself at length with coffee and the *Jerusalem Post* before he managed to become audible.

Trudy ran again, this time to her bedroom. She nearly overturned her tortoiseshell toilette kit, managed to pry loose the false bottom and pulled out, from under the stone that once had weighed down her *chuppah,* the champagne label of her wedding day.

She *had* to catch Bic with Nick Antone. The information desk said Mr. Antone's Executive Board meeting was at the Palladium Room, and at the Palladium Room she simply pushed past the Pinkerton. Or not quite so simply. The Pinkerton had gotten an "admit" sign from Mr. Antone.

Inside, under the spidery chandeliers, there were some fifty men shirtsleeved, chair-sprawling, smoking around Antone Junior, all so intensively focused they barely moved. She'd butted in and maybe she would have butted right out again if she hadn't seen Bic over in the corner.

So she stayed put, got her breath back in a chair and planned exactly what to do at the right time. She would NOT go over to Bic, would NOT say, *You poor harried messenger boy, too bad you hate me just because I overtook you when I married Simon Spieger — here, take this if it makes you any happier!*

No, to save the roof over the heads of a few hundred people, she'd tiptoe over and give him the champagne label of her wedding day and say, *Look, I've signed it, it's what you wanted, now please ask your boss to do the right thing and wait with the Yeshiva until the evictions are canceled.* She would do that. And from that moment on she'd hate Louis Bic for unimpeachable reasons for the rest of her life.

But she never needed to say any of that, she never had to give him the champagne label, thanks to Nick.

Nick changed everything: Nick strolling-talking in the Palladium Room, Nick of the gray temples and the boy cheeks, Nick whose open white shirt collar looked singed, Nick with his eyes flashing darker than any Venetian fisherman's, Nick with his sleeves turned up beyond his tanned elbows, Nick kicking a cigarette butt out of his way, easy.

"So we'll put a few ideals first on the agenda," Nick was saying, hands in pocket, walking among his seated Executive Board. "We're a pretty high-minded bunch. What do you think?"

"Sure are," somebody said, and their grins followed him.

"We don't spit at dollars and cents," Nick said, "but I mean, principles are also the business of this convention. So we'll be busy with principles, huh?"

"Yessiree, we dig principles," somebody said.

"So we ought to draft a rap against Pentagon spending, shall we?"

"That'll take at least two days," somebody said, and they all laughed.

"Minimum," Nick said. "Then we ought to take a stand on tax reform. Hell knows when my father did an honest day's work."

They really laughed at that.

"Also, let's not forget, we've got to come up with a solidarity message to the Cubans."

"*Venceremos!*" a little blackhaired fellow yelled, smiling.

"Then there's a minimum wage."

"Like last time, only stronger, Nick!"

"And longer. Plus a position on welfare."

"Now you're talking, Nick!"

"And after that," Nick said, "maybe we'll buckle down to their lousy wage offer."

"Remind us," somebody said to general amusement.

"After all," Nick said. Suddenly his hand was light on Trudy's shoulder. His ambling in her direction hadn't been random. "After

69

all, Moses had forty days up on the mountain. We can take a little time too."

That really broke them up. But it also made them stare at her.

"This is Trudy Spieger," Nick said. "She just previewed her film for our Cultural Committee. Let's show some appreciation."

They applauded.

"Maybe Moses didn't take a beer-break up on the mountain," Nick said. "But we ought to. Then we'll do the agenda formal, with resolutions. Half an hour?"

"Half an hour! Seconded!"

"*Aye!*"

"So moved."

"Come on," Nick said to Trudy.

"I just wanted to catch Bic!" she whispered. That instant Bic turned around over in the corner and it was a beefy redhead with hornrims.

"Bic must be at the airport by now," Nick Antone said.

"Christ!" Trudy said. "I bust in on you for nothing!"

"Come on," Nick Antone said. He had already drawn her into the next room, a pantry whose coffee urn and wet dishes Trudy could still smell, so many years later, in Liechtenstein.

"Now tell me," Nick had said to her in the pantry.

In the pantry of the Palladium Room of Chicago's Regency Hotel it had occurred to her for the first time that Nick looked like a gondolier. The gray hair over the young face was a roguery, a golden earring. She'd never seen a real gondolier. But then she'd also never known an Exeter boy, yet she felt that the vowels in his "Now tell me" must be Exeter. He was snatching a couple of cups off pantry hooks. He could have been a busboy working here for years. A *conde* playing gracefully at drudgery, that was gondolier-like too. It was attractive to watch but it didn't help her.

"Tell," he said. "You are disturbed. Is it Michelle Letarpo's death?"

"Not just that," she said.

"Sorry I couldn't do that little introductory talk before your film. Too much came up."

"I should apologize," she said. "I busted in on your meeting."

70

"Don't worry, they were ripe for a break." He was drawing coffee from the pantry urn. "Bic called me this morning on Michelle. Rough. I try not to show it here."

"I'm sorry for Mr. Letarpo," Trudy said. "Though I never knew his wife."

"You don't know any of us," Nick Antone said. "Simon locked you away."

"We've got this enormous lecture schedule," Trudy said. "You see, Simon and I were supposed to fight the University administration on a building they want to raze for parking. The bastards want to kick a hundred old people out."

"Is that the problem?" Nick Antone said. A few drops came out of the coffee-urn spigot even after he'd turned it off. He caught them in the cup in the most adept manner.

"So now Letarpo is going to give the damn University a whole big School of Religion or something, with Simon to run the Yeshiva —"

"Which is not going to solve the eviction problem," he said.

"Well, they're going to phoney a solution, but I don't want us to be snowed into accepting it! I wanted to tell Bic to hold everything! Damn it, I thought I'd catch him here!"

"Well," Nick Antone said. He jumped to see what was on the upper shelf of the cupboard. He jumped well. "No cream there either," he said. "I guess Tarp's naming the school after Michelle?"

"I don't care if he's naming it after his lizard! I'm not letting these people get thrown out on the street. You shouldn't either!"

"No cream anywhere," he said. "We'll have to drink it black."

"The hell with cream. You're a pal of Letarpo's. Exert pressure!"

He gave her a cup and pulled two stools together.

"So Bic brought you all that bright news today?" he said.

"I mean it!" she said.

Her hands managed to be as steady with the coffee as his.

"Now I'll tell you what Bic brought *me*." He sat down next to her. "Word from Letarpo there'll be a little price war among the tanker boys. By January we'll have the first tiny price drop in home fuel since the end of the war."

"That's all terribly exciting," she said.

"Usually we vote on the contract offer at the convention," Nick

Antone said. "But not with that bit of news now. We'll do numbers on charter revision, ideology, nice points like that. We won't get to vote on wages."

He was sitting next to her, sipping in the same rhythm as her.

"We're not going to force the money thing till January," he said. "Not till fuel drops and we can prove that owner costs are down. Then the public's going to be with us when we open up heavy on wages."

"That's brilliant," she said.

"You wonder why the hell I'm blathering on like that."

"No, I just wish I were in the mood to appreciate the confidence —"

"It's not a confidence, it's temporizing," he said. "I'm just trying to impress you because I can't find a way to help you with this goddam thing."

He could flash a rather fetching bitter smile. At the same time he held her by the elbow, so she couldn't get up.

"You've got a building workers' union," she said. "Use it to save a building! Enlist your members! Mobilize —"

"*A resolution*," he said suddenly, quietly. "A strike resolution against any unfairly evicting landlord."

"Hey! . . . ," she said.

"I always thought we ought to pass a concrete public-service resolution. Not just gimme-gimme wage yells or leftie abstractions. Anti-eviction. Good girl."

"That would be fantastically helpful," she said.

"Okay. Tonight it goes on the agenda."

"Boy, I'm glad I stumbled in here," she said.

"Me too," he said. "Shake!"

How the heat and strength of the coffee suddenly worked inside her now! They stood up. They shook. They gripped arms. That wasn't enough, but since she shied away from anything further, they shook hands again. Their fingers interlaced, and then they stopped touching each other.

"Let's see," he said. "Over at your campus, I think we've got about two hundred men organized. The University evicts — they'll hit."

"Boy!" she said.

72

By the coffee urn a buzzer suddenly went off and a voice came out of the intercom.

"Hey, Clarence! How about the Danish for the Gold Suite?"

"This is a CIA listening post," Nick said into the intercom. "I'll rustle up Clarence, if you'll tell me where you keep the cream."

Laughter in the intercom. She had a sense of not only relief but of wires and gears meshing and interacting in this gargantuan hotel-hive, the musky coffee-ish smell of a giant's nerve center, and it warmed the undersides of her knees and moistened her nostrils into the need, of all things, for a Kleenex.

She opened her bag. The first thing that she saw was the signed label of her wedding day champagne.

"Here," she said.

" 'Dom Perignon,' " he said. "What's that for?"

"Just to say thank you." And thrust it at him. And ran out and away and waited till she was out of earshot before snatching a Kleenex and blowing her nose.

～ 4 ～

Yet for a long time she'd lived in more interesting unison with Simon than she had thought possible with a man. Before Simon she'd always been struck by the anomaly, the goddamn bedeviling contradiction in the urge. Once you'd really bedded down with somebody, sex was a crass heat that had nothing to do with the face or quality of the man that had entered you. It was the race-lust beating hips together. Okay. But after that was over, then you became captive of an opposite unreasonableness; you became rather pointlessly sensitive toward your partner; and this again had little to do with the man's face or quality (*vide* Bic) but simply with the fact that his genitals had been inside yours and now were out. Absurd.

Here Simon's specialness came in. His face and quality governed their bed life. Somewhere below his gray wistful eyes was the possibility of ardor. Together they nurtured it into an erection, shaped it as two celebrants co-shape a Sabbath candle, her smile kissing his frown in the dark, and when they'd finished molding their candle, and lit it, and put it out quickly inside her to his sigh that always came like the wind in a winter woods . . . it was like an important chore only the two of them and no one else could have performed; it was unique, masterful, almost public-minded in its tenderness, almost like their journey to Berdichev, their only journey there because they never went back.

And she was also indebted to Simon for the showmanship he'd taught her and which he encouarged even after it produced results not quite congruous with his new status. As head of the yeshiva-to-be, he now appeared with her in distinguished forums paneled with walnut, before barbered button-down collars. But Trudy always insisted on recruiting part of the audience from both the local campus and some local old-age home. She herself picked up both contingents in the same bus and led them both in personally, canes thumping behind her, sneakers scuffing; she referred to both in her introduction — that both the studying young and the retired old were out of the system and therefore free to help in reforming it; and the sneaker-shod and the cane-bearers applauded and infected with applause the button-down collars, and that's how she warmed up the place not only for herself but for Simon and his coffin-paintings. And when it was all over, Simon bowed out with his hand round her waist, a gesture sovereign and grateful, public-minded and tender all at once.

Right up to the big *Save Uptown!* demonstration their marriage still functioned in its own disabused way. Trudy's student rapport rubbed off so well on Simon that the Interfaith University crown was offered to him just then. Simon in turn strengthened Trudy's causes like her anti-eviction fight. He gave her celebrity and dignity. Of course she often wished there were more chance for direct activism. For example, she'd have preferred to spend the days before the demonstration preparing for it, instead of flitting off to the Caribbean first, to give a lecture on a Letarpo cruise. But when she did get into action now, the action had clout. It made a big

74

difference that the Spiegers were among the demonstration sponsors: their name roped in some of the scaredy-cat liberals.

Yes, Simon risked the demonstration even while his career was accelerating into still higher altitudes. Even while he and Trudy were being hoisted in a rope cage to the cruise deck a phone call was waiting for him. High up on the prow of the *Michelle II* stood old Antone, Nick's father, holding a white telephone, pointing it down at them. Naturally a telephone. By then an epidemic of telephones had broken out in Trudy's life, and no Tante's plants in which to smother them.

"Maybe this means a call from the Charter Commission," Simon said. "They have changed their mind. The Cardinal should be president."

"No, I think you're stuck with it," Trudy said.

"Head of a yeshiva is one thing. But a whole new university — they didn't give me time to think. Do you think it's a good name, Interfaith University?"

"As good as any," she said.

"You wish we wouldn't come here," he said.

"No, it's beautiful."

It was an idyllic moment. The rope cage swung very gently as it rose toward the deck. They floated above little whitecaps and blue glitter and gulls curving white through sunshine and silence.

"I just wish we wouldn't have the demonstration Monday," she said.

"We will be back in time," Simon said. "We must talk about it. And the Interfaith, I long to talk more with you about that."

Actually Interfaith had happened only that very day: the expansion of the idea of a Letarpo-financed Religion School into a full-fledged University with a separate campus, with Ford Foundation backing, federal cofunding, and Simon Spieger as president. That morning, the first organizational meeting had taken place on the wording of the public announcement and the Cardinal himself had accompanied the Spiegers to Dulles Airport, describing how he'd played soccer with the Pope when they'd both been seminarians in Rome. Of course the project was very exciting. But Trudy and Simon hadn't had much chance to discuss it on the flight. Their plane was very accomplished, leaving the Washington runway on wheels and landing by the ship here on pontoons. It was also an extremely noisy plane. Because of his cough Simon couldn't strain his voice. Now their rope cage rose up along the hull in this lovely quiet.

"Always like this in America," Simon said. "Everything is too big, too complicated. Too fast. Too many things at once."

"It's you, Simon," Trudy said. "Personalities trigger energies."

"You are angry." He smiled. "Because you can't bus old people to the ship."

"Not a bit," she said. "So the Pope is really a goalie."

"I shall tell them I refuse."

"You'd be an idiot," she said.

"I will never get back to my sociology if I must run a big institution."

"Face it," she said. "Things wouldn't let you get back to it even before this came up."

"You will keep helping me if I go through with this?"

"Yes, and I have an idea," she said.

"Wonderful! At least we can talk a little here."

He put his arm round her in the rope cage. The motion made them swing again, very gently, like a bell, through ocean serenity, from one horizon to another.

"I've been thinking while we couldn't talk," she said. "There's one advantage to starting an institution from scratch like that. You can really write the ground rules."

"Exactly my thought! This is the excitement!"

"And the most unused potential in our universities is the student."

"*You* made me sensitive to that," Simon said, with a squeeze.

"So I think the dean of students should carry out Student Council decisions, for students to share power with the administration, and that should be in the charter."

"Yes!"

"And you might even consider the idea of giving someone like me a crack at being the first dean of students."

"Trudy!"

He stared at her, with a delighted mouth.

"Nepotism wouldn't apply, because I wouldn't be responsible to you but to the students."

76

"Yes! You could lead a demonstration against me!" He laughed.
"Or I could stop one. And through my rapport with old people
I could be a bridge to the outer world."
"All right," he said. "Seriously, it is my condition for accepting."
"It's just something to think about."
"Dean Trudy!" he said. She got a quick kiss before the rope cage
was pulled on deck.

The Rough Diamonds did their cruising on the converted
Letarpo tanker, and old Antone stood on deck in a safari shirt,
light gray, long-sleeved, belted, a sort of tropical raincoat. "Wel-
come," he said. He gave the phone not to Simon but to Trudy.
The voice in the earpiece was Jennifer's, of all people — Jennifer
had taken Trudy's place on the Graduate Student Council.
"Trudy? Where are you?" Jennifer said.
"We arrived this second from Washington," Trudy said. "What's
up?"
"The Shoreham gave me this number. What are the Rough
Diamonds?"
"Hey, you better be calling me collect," she said. "This is the
Caribbean."
"Oh how nice. Where?"
Jennifer liked to sniff out Trudy's whereabouts, by way of
reproach on the glossiness of it all.
"Around Bermuda someplace," she said. "It's a lecture we owe.
And it's going to be a rat race, flying back to the demonstration —"
"It's tonight."
"The demonstration — *tonight?*"
"Goddamn cops changed the permits on us. But that's not even
the main reason I'm calling —"
"*Tonight!*" she said. Yes, always like this in America.
"A bigger problem is, another group's muscling in tonight —".
BOOM!
Actual gunfire. Simon staggered back, and Trudy instinctively
held the phone over her head.
"It's just the Rough Diamond trapshoot," Antone said, smiling.
"Right into our ears?"
"This is near the trapshoot part of the deck."
"Can't they stop for a moment?"

77

"Unfortunately it is a tournament."

"Jennifer!" she yelled into the phone. "Hold on while I get to a saner part of the ship."

Simon already sat in the Rolls-Royce Volkswagen that would take them to the other end of the endless ship, with the fancy tents and the pool. But old Antone shook his head.

"Right now this is the only phone on board that speaks."

"What?" Trudy said.

"An Anaconda gentleman shot up the extensions line. I am staying close because I expect a call myself."

"Burn Eisenhow. . . ," she heard Jennifer's voice squawk between volleys.

Antone reached for the receiver. "Will you allow me? My right ear is deaf. Which is an advantage now."

So there was Jennifer, connected to a Venetian condottiere who reclined his profile into the shotgun-boom-boom and said as though translating from demotic Egyptian:

"Something about burning Eisenhower in effigy . . ."

"What?" Trudy said.

"Burning Eisenhower —"

"But they were going to stick to anti-eviction and urban issues!"

"Something about the American Legion coming . . ."

"There's going to be a massacre," Trudy said.

She grabbed the phone.

"Jennifer, I'm coming tonight!"

She couldn't understand what she answered because of the racket.

"I'm coming! You'll hear from me again! Stay at headquarters!"

She hung up and stared at Simon Spieger, who had gotten out of the car.

"The demonstration is tonight," she said.

"I heard. I heard everything," he said, frowning against the noise. But just then the trapshoot stopped. She smelled a barbaric brew of brine, oil, gunpowder.

"I am sorry," Simon said. "I will go to New York."

"*You?*"

"These other people will have to be stopped."

"I'm not sure that's good for your cough," she said.

"My responsibility. I go to the demonstration."

She saw he really meant it.

"All right. We both go."

"You give our talk here," Simon said. "First I go back to Washington to take the Cardinal with me to New York. For extra strength at the demonstration."

"The Cardinal," she said. "That's a good move, but —"

"We have to save the demonstration."

"All that flying, Simon —"

"Is there a plane here bound for Washington?" Simon already asked old Antone.

"You are overdoing it," she said. "That's two more trips for you today."

"They are very short flights," Simon said. His cape and his thin face rose with the ship against the swell and against a wave-slapping interval between shots.

"A plane is going to Washington to fetch my son here," said the old man.

Simon clasped Trudy's hand. "With your permission I will take the plane," he said. "My Trudy will give our talk here." And they started to shoot again.

The guest suites in that ex-tanker must have been officers' quarters. Letarpo or his decorator had made them bristle with big-time informality. The cabin where Trudy was trying to block out the lecture was styled à la Portuguese harbor tavern, fishnet draped over the telex machine. On the antique wood of the little bar lay the mimeo'd "curriculum," which explained that the Rough Diamonds were a bunch of underprivileged chief executives running corporations (assets five million dollars up) without benefit of college education; a lack they tried to correct by going to their school ship once a year under Dean Alexander Letarpo; this year's faculty being John K. Galbraith on "The Fallacy of Plenty"; Margaret Mead on "American Male Myths"; and Trudy and Simon Spieger on "Inventing Tradition."

"Inventing Tradition" was one of the chapter heads in the outline of Simon's still unwritten new sociology book. They would have had time this afternoon to sketch out a talk based on the

79

concept — if Simon hadn't flown back to the mainland for the demonstration's sake. Trudy sat alone with the fishnetted telex and not a sliver of inspiration.

Far off the trapshoot had started once more. Much nearer, yelling came through the porthole. Trudy walked over and looked down. Last time she'd been on this ship it had been night and she hadn't even noticed the pool on the upper deck. Last time Mr. Lissberg had dropped out of the sky with a shopping cart, and Simon had proposed to her. Now it was daylight; she'd come a long way from uptown. But somehow everything had become more mysterious yet on the huge boat. A lot of Rough Diamonds stood around the pool, all tanned, some trim in their pastel trunks. They shouted at a floating ball. A pirate in bare feet and a red sash wrote the shouts down on a pad. He was a steward. Another pirate bartended behind a huge black barrel that had CHIVAS REGAL chalked across the hoops. Apparently the shouts were bets on which direction the pool ball would float in response to the movements of the ship.

"Five hundred South-South East!"

"What do you know, Proxy-Joe?"

"Three hundred straight South, Big-Mouth!"

Trudy couldn't understand the rules of that game. The shine of sun against the metal of the derricks and on the glitter of the pool, the yell of the Rough Diamonds and the sequence of far-off trapshots all seemed to be part of a complex code. The solution would tell her why she was on this ship. But she couldn't break the code. "Listen," she heard herself say down the porthole. "You bastards. I'll be a University Dean long before I'm thirty."

The sound of that sentence oriented her. She'd have her own power base. Fine to be featured in Simon's noble show; but time to step up from actress to activist — with leverage all her own.

"Diamonds, hold on to your hats," she said. Suddenly she knew she could solve the code and think up something good on "Inventing Tradition" within an hour. Only she never had to. There was a knock on the door.

It was still another pirate. Would Madame Spieger pardon but the only telephone working was still on the other end of the ship, and there was a call for her?

A fifth pirate drove her back across the deck in the VW Rolls.

Again old General Antone was holding out the phone for her. By then the shooting had stopped. And this time it wasn't Jennifer but Nick Antone.

"I'm sorry, it's my son," Antone said.

"Trudy," Nick's voice said. "Don't panic. Simon arrived on the plane in a faint. But he's already better."

"What?"

"He's okay. The doctor said it's fatigue. No hospital — just rest — absolute rest for a day, that's all."

"I *told* him!" she said.

"I got him back into the Shoreham. His French cousin's taking care of him. She won't even let him phone."

"Right, she shouldn't," Trudy said. "But, my God, I'll have to go back —"

"He's really all right. He had a cheese sandwich —"

"No, I have to go to New York because that's where Simon was going —"

Cack. Disconnected.

"Hello? . . . Nick!"

The ship swerved into rollers of sun. It jostled a clump of Rough Diamonds sideways and Trudy glimpsed Letarpo, the first time she'd seen him since that filmed reading on this ship. He looked like a chunky little bo'sun in black pants and a black polo shirt and a black squashed cap and he held a rubber limpness, a balloon which a barefoot pirate was blowing up.

"Nick? . . . Hello? Hello!" she cried.

No answer, but she saw that the balloon inflated into a dead plucked wrinkled chicken, which unwrinkled slowly into a fat dead plucked chicken as the pirate blew into it, to great laughter.

The ship dipped. Trudy floated down into heat and glare. Her hair messed in the breeze for lack of a scarf and she felt, crazily, that some centrifugal flash had flung her head and her heart apart, and Nick came back on the line and she screamed, *"I'm coming to New York! They changed the demonstration to tonight!"*

"I know," Nick said. "My New York local just phoned. I'd better —"

"It's going to be terrible there tonight! Simon was supposed to defuse it —"

"We'll defuse it," Nick said.

81

"It's not just my friends' eviction, there're a million like them in the city and if we mess this up —"

"We won't," Nick said.

"I've got to make it to New York!"

"But I'm going too," Nick's voice said.

"No, no! Just help me get to the city!"

"We'll meet in New York. Give me my father."

"Are you serious?"

"Is my father still there?"

"Yes."

"Give me my father. He'll get us planes," Nick said, just as the plucked and dead naked rubber chicken sailed high on laughter across the railing and fell into the sea.

She always loved coming back to New York. Like touching earth again after a long stay elsewhere. This return trip had been head-over-heels; two hours in the plane that lifted Trudy away from the Rough Diamonds, and twenty minutes in the copter from La Guardia to the top of the Pan Am Building and then the taxi bumping her along the West Side Highway — and now reunion with reality.

After all the glossy faraway of being Mrs. Simon Spieger, after levitating on podiums, balancing on tops of microphones, high smiles at receptions, room service on many a thirtieth floor, telexes under fishnets — after long months of all that, back to good old uptown.

Homecoming. She got off at 165th and Broadway in the smog of the evening. She touched the dear dirty pavement of Washington Heights, the real grimy McCoy of her youth.

And as if to make up for long-time-no-see the city had herded together for her benefit its force and numbers, its voltage and weight and pressure, all its electric muck. She stepped out into a thousand shadows, cluster after cluster, under the bleared street-lights. The thrilling thing was that she had helped in this mobilization, even if her part had to be done by phone. Immediately she picked out "her" old people, resting on brownstone steps, canes and crutches poised like emblems in the dark, so many she couldn't find Mr. Lissberg with his cart. She saw a sizable contingent from

Moloch U., a solemn black mass of academic gowns. There was a big battalion of Nick's building workers, brooms and mops raised as pennants. Fantastic. A bakery local came trooping with oven peels for halberds. Guitars strummed all over, a beard hawked *The Catholic Worker,* meat-sizzle from frankfurter stands spiked the musk of many breaths, feedback whistled out of loudspeakers, white-blue lights of a police car rotated confetti gleams over the crowd. Somehow it was more exciting than the big student demonstrations Trudy saw later on. Man, this was New York with not a thing missing. Not even Elihu.

Elihu came running, the former University Chaplain and uptown Pancho Villa, her old Old Flame. He was just in time to pay her taxi. In the rush she'd forgotten to take cash.

"Trudy! . . . Your husband didn't come?"

"He suddenly got sick," she said. "Didn't Nick Antone tell Jennifer? Nothing serious."

"Nobody tells me. Liaison here has been unbelievable."

A beam from the patrol car brushed her. Elihu stared: her pastel jumpsuit with beltcoat to match, rather jazzy for the occasion.

"I didn't have time to change," she said.

"If you're cold, I'll get you a wrap," Elihu said. "Now. Put you in the picture. They'll only let us march to Hundred Sixty-ninth Street. Hundred-seventieth and the Square itself they sealed off. Fucking cops! Only ones allowed in the Square are the oldsters and the Legionnaires counterdemonstrating, those assholes. Theory being the Legion wouldn't touch the oldsters. Bullshit! When those types start burning Eisenhower —"

"What types?" Trudy said. "How do you know they're in there?"

"Ten wild men in an empty store! All-out radicals! With an Eisenhower doll! We *know!* The cops let 'em in, those cocksuckers want a little blood!"

Trudy had never known an Elihu so brisk, so hard, so leonine with obscenities. Of course she was alarmed about the cops. But a part of her was still in an inexcusably good mood and Elihu enriched it.

"Now," he said. "Strategy. We'll sneak you past the cops into the

Square. You and Nick. When you get there, tear the heads off the wild men! No dice! Not tonight! Let them burn Ike next week. Otherwise no support from us for any of *their* things. No old-people support! No student support! Nick Antone will ditto for the unions. He better lay on his charisma! No Legionnaire trouble tonight! No digression from Inner City crisis! Okay?"

"Yes, sir."

"I'm sorry. I'm barking. It's all this disorganization. I'm sorry, Trudy. Also, I'm sorry your husband is sick."

"That's all right," she said. "Where's Nick?"

"That's the shitty thing. They said, Meet him at Rugow's Bakery. They didn't say at Rugow's Bakery *where*. I'm not even sure it's on this side of the street. The liaison on this is unbelievable. Hold it. I'm going to ask that union fellow. Hold it. Be right back."

He vanished into a storefront. She held it. Before her some Puerto Rican union people in overalls began to link arms.

BUST BANKS NOT BLOCKS . . . BUST BANKS NOT BLOCKS. . . .

The Spanish accent made it sound ardent, not angry. People stepped on Trudy's soft pastel moccasins which matched her jumpsuit meant for the Caribbean. She didn't mind. Hope pulsed in her wrists, hope for crazy America. She felt connected again to the craziness and the hope. And she felt that Elihu's buoyancy had been abetted by her arriving alone. He regarded her husband's sickness as a personal compliment.

"Hey, Trudy Spieger? Didn't I hear you speak at Rutgers?"

She smiled, nodding at the redhead saying that. Suddenly she knew she'd make a damn good dean of students. The months with Simon hadn't been a detour after all. She and the Street hadn't lost touch with each other.

"Let's go," Elihu said, rematerializing.

He steered her through the crowds. "Rugow's Bakery, that's all they know. They think it's somewhere on the north side of the street. Unbelievably shitty liaison. . . . You see any Rugow's Bakery?"

"There!" Trudy said.

There was RUGOW's, the store sign, and, underneath it, the dark window with empty doilies on the cakestands and, in the door, also dark but open, three men, one of whom was actually Nick Antone, Jr.

"Good luck! Take care!" Elihu whispered. She got a sudden hug round her shoulders. Then they closed the Rugow Bakery glass door behind her and Nick Antone.

"They asked me not to turn on lights," Nick said. "We don't want to attract cops. Hold on to my coattails."

She did. He was groping his way to the back of the store. "Where are you, trapdoor? . . ." he said. "Here we are. . . . Where are you, ladder? . . . Good boy, ladder. Down we go. You okay, Trudy? . . . Now they said, close the trapdoor behind you."

Never in her life had she closed a trapdoor from below or even above. The door was heavy, but she closed it well. Closing trapdoors with Nick Antone. Sometimes her life amazed her.

"They said twelve rungs down and the light switch to the right. . . . You falling off, Trudy?"

"I never fall," she said.

"Bravo. Twelve rungs down and a switch to right. . . . Nine, ten, two more to go."

Down they went into limbo and he found the switch to the right.

In the sudden harsh naked-bulb light of the bakery cellar, in a flour-dusted yeast-smelling cave, they discovered each other; she in her jump suit, he in a striped turtleneck and windbreaker, grinning.

"Beats getting into the Square under police escort," he said. "That's the precinct captain's bright idea."

"He offered that?" she said.

"Sirens, motorcycle escort, anything that'll kill credibility with the Ike-burners. Let's see. They said, go past the oven, the mixer, there's supposed to be a door. Right. Now watch yourself." Past the door there were two deep steps into the basement of what seemed to be the next building. It was pitch black.

"Down into the sewage?" she said. He was lifting her down by the waist.

"We're supposed to find a door with a staircase behind it." He switched on a flashlight. "And up that staircase and we'll be right in the Square to kill that Burn Ike stupidity, if we don't break our necks. Hold on to my jacket."

Under the flashlight, laundry machines loomed up, glass-mouthed squat mummies in a catacomb. For the possibility of rats alone it was nice to have his jacket to clutch.

"You'd probably make a very decent burglar," she said.

"I got directions from janitors in the Brotherhood." Surprisingly he'd begun to kick at something.

"Is that door supposed to be open?" she said.

"It's the staircase door and I'm supposed to have the key," he said. She realized he was searching himself. He was searching himself so thoroughly she had to let go of his jacket.

"I musta losta da key," he said in the voice of a mournful old Italian organ-grinder. It was very quiet in that basement, no hint that a street-ugliness might be brewing just a few yards up. Trudy had always been too poor and too brainy to be a frivolous school belle but suddenly she guessed what it must be like to be a seventeen-year-old minxy minky piece of mischief, in on some classy high jinks with an Exeter boy.

"Gotta go back looka for da key," Nick said.

They retraced their path through the laundry machines, searching the floor. She had to grin when the flashlight lit on his yachting shoes.

"Your shoes are still off to the Caribbean," she said.

"Big deal, Rough Diamonds," he said, and went back to the Italian organ grinder: "Musta losta da key on da strit."

By then they'd found greaseballs on the filthy floor, matches, dried dough bits, cigarette butts, everything except a key. They went back up the ladder to the trapdoor, but the trapdoor wouldn't open.

"One of those self-locking jobs," Nick said. "Okay. Stand back. Go down a couple of rungs."

He took off one of his yachting shoes and began to bang against the trapdoor with it. With a deep ancient organ-grinder's anger.

"Ragazzi! Hear!"

Nobody heard. Nothing happened.

"You're competing with a lot of noise outside," she said. Even through the trapdoor, far back in the bakery, they heard the Puerto Rican BUST BANKS NOT BLOCKS . . . BUST BANKS NOT BLOCKS. . . .

86

"All right," Nick Antone said. They climbed down the ladder again. "Steady. Let's make sure."

He went slowly through all his pockets and their contents: dollar bills; a jacknife with a beautifully carved wood handle; a badge which, he explained, was the Honorary Police Commissioner's of Gary, Indiana; a clean handkerchief and a rather worn little leather-covered notebook, a thin, beautiful little alligator-leather wallet with a big tear in it, a key ring with irrelevant keys.

"Will you look at that?" he said.

He'd pulled out his pants pocket. There was a little hole in it just big enough to let a single key slip through. Like his father with his luggage tag dangling from the raincoat, years later in Liechtenstein. The waifdom of the great glamorous Antones.

"That's too much," she said, smiling, putting her finger through the hole. Somehow the hole produced a brainstorm. "Phone somebody!" she said. "In the basement! Wasn't that a pay phone?"

"Yeah!" he said.

They rushed back to the basement, he lifting her down the steps again. But he set her down with a groan.

"If I know me, I haven't got change."

He knew himself. Of course he had no change. The hole in the pocket had drained it. He played the flashlight on her bag. She didn't even bother to look. She remembered from the taxi: no money at all.

"*Niente*," said the organ-grinder's voice.

"Listen," she said in the dark. "Somebody's bound to come looking for us."

"Sure. Tomorrow. The bakers," he said. "Outside the cordon they think we're inside. Inside they're not even sure we're coming. Lovely."

"Let's get out of the dark," she said.

"My father would love this," he said. "All for nothing. The calls and planes and copters and strategies. For nothing."

"There might be rats here," she said. "Let's go where it's bright."

He lifted her; half-tossed her up the steps, back into the lit bakery cellar. She closed the door and looked around what was no longer just a passage for them: a small raw cluttered workshop, oven chrome and steel kettle of the dough mixer encrusted with flour, the girlie calendar with a mildewed maraschino cherry pressed between the legs of Miss November. But the bench was scraped clean, two wedding cakes brightened a rack and next to a grease pot on a shelf stood a water glass with a freshly budded daisy.

Jovial men working here at their jovial craft. Snug in the very coziness of their limitation. She envied them. Her euphoria was gone. These bakers understood their lives. Why the hell didn't she, sometimes? From a stack of flour bags Nick Antone was heaving a sack from the top down to the floor.

"How's my husband?" she said. "I didn't even get a chance to ask."

"Fine." Nick heaved down a second bag. "Doctor says a day in bed will do it."

"He wanted to bring a cardinal to the demonstration," she said.

"The cardinal could have helped me with the flour bags."

"What are you doing?" she said.

"Floor's filthy. Might as well be comfortable." He leaped up to bring down still another flour bag. Thud.

"How's the eviction situation at my old people's building?" she asked. She wanted to distract him from the bags.

"My office was supposed to send you a note," he said.

He was pushing off more bags. Actually, she'd just received the note: pressure from his union still prevented eviction, but the University kept harassing by nonservice, no hot water, etc.

"I haven't gotten it yet," she said, not quite sure why she lied. Maybe because only bland noncontroversial conversation would slow him down. He was tossing flour bags on the floor like a fiend.

"I'm not much in touch with my office. I'm going to quit the Brotherhood," he said.

"You are?"

"I'm going to run me for Congress. I'm going to lose bigger things than janitors' keys. I want to foul up the whole country."

He'd taken off his jacket to drag about the bags. In his slim turtleneck, short-sleeved and zebra-striped, he looked more like a gondolier than ever, moving with force and smoothness at once.

"And I'm going to ask a bright girl like you for help," he said. "Us foul-ups need help."

88

"Don't be so mad at yourself because of a key," she said.

"Long live the key," he said. He stretched out on the mattress of flour bags he'd made, and reached for a wedding cake on the bottom pan of the rack and broke off the bridegroom's head and popped it into his mouth.

"No!" she said.

It was so unexpected, she kneeled down and tried to stop him.

"Oh, we pay cash," he said. He reached up and plunked a twenty-dollar bill on the work bench. "Taste some," he said.

"But that's lousy! You could eat cookies!"

"Cookies is for aunts."

He was munching and smiling the Nick Antone smile. But not really. It was a spoiled rich Nick Junior face.

"I'm not hungry," she said.

"You don't have to be," he said. "My father would love this because he loves things to add up to nothing. But we got news for him. We'll add up to a lot tonight. Taste it. Please! Go on."

He held out a piece of wedding cake icing; half a pink rose made of spun sugar.

"Please?" he said.

Kneeling beside him, she took a small bite. It did taste pepperminty; refreshing. Welcome, because the day's strain had caught up with her all of a sudden. She felt wickedly tired.

"Here. More." A bit of icing was still on his finger. "Finish up," he said in his presumable Exeter accent, the zebra turtleneck slenderly muscled against the drab of the flour bags. She sniffed male thrust. Not so much sweat as the scent of physical momentum in a cave too small to contain it.

"Come on. Finish," he said.

"Did you know," she said, "that the Religion Faculty Letarpo wanted to establish, it's going to be a whole university now?"

"No kidding? Finish up."

"With federal subsidies. And I might be dean of students."

"Beautiful. Finish up."

She had to lick the piece from his finger. Her tongue felt the hard of his nail. She jumped up.

But the zipper in her back was undone.

"Please zip that again!"

"Come down again."

She came down and he reached round her and zipped it up and then zipped it down, and with swift, startling gentleness kissed her down into the flour bags.

"Oh come on," she was trying to say. "We know you're a ladies' man —"

But he didn't answer maybe because she couldn't quite get it out. He'd broken off a sugar garland and placed it under her bra and a bridegroom's shoulder into her navel (somehow he'd freed her midriff), he managed to kiss her outraged laughter and began to pick up these same icing bits tenderly with tongue and teeth, leaving warm, barely wet spots on her skin till she stopped him, hard. She took him by the ears.

"You — are — absurd," she said.

"All right," he said. He stopped everything. He looked at her, straight, unsmiling.

"Till now we were not absurd," he said. "Just apart. And unhappy. *I was very unhappy.*"

The harshness of that, the unsmooth, un-Nick-like drivenness, flabbergasted her, undercut defense or argument. They stared at each other. He started again with the sugar bits on her body, but now with a desperate mulishness, with a tongue tip that turned her skin upside down. Her hands came down on his ears again but she couldn't pull at them anymore. She had to accept a bridal arm thrust between her lips. Her thighs felt shocked and nude, sliding against the coarse weave of a flour bag. My God, she thought, and right under a demonstration with my naked gondolier. Her fingers found a handful of icing and smeared it against his forehead. The trapshoot started again, they laughed sugar onto one another's tongues and sailed into the Caribbean together after all.

III

❧ *1* ❧

And now, many years later, a car cracked into the evening's gravel, the gravel of the driveway of the Grand Hotel Dennat, Liechtenstein. Such a nice jovial crackle through Trudy's stress and solitude, it must be a mistake.

By the time she opened the door, the taxi had already crunched to a halt. A man was getting out, tall in a raincoat, bald, narrow-cheeked, very old, yet not old in the way he uncoiled from the back seat on slow strong springs, not at all like an ancient retired oil man, or a long-retired general of the U.N. Relief Task Force. Yet it was him all right. Old man Antone. His suppleness vitalized her for some reason. She ran toward him.

"My dear," he said.

How many years had it been? He still had the peculiar combination of New England drawl and light Venetian accent.

"My God," she said. "How'd you find me here? How do you know?"

"I have spies."

He had turned slightly. His elbow presented itself to her, slightly raised. A second passed before she realized she must take his arm. He needed to be led. This was a blind man. Old General Antone had gone blind.

"Oh, I'm sorry!" she said.

"It's all right." He said. "One adjusts. That's not the point now."

On stunned squeaks of gravel Trudy led him to the hotel. His step was still crisp and long, and he walked hatless with his head held high. The blue veins on his temple looked like a treasure map of a river delta that had defied the deciphering of generations. And the eyes which she still couldn't believe were void — the eyes were still black enough to remind her of his son Nick.

Behind them walked the taxi driver, carrying the suitcase; the dog, the big dog whose name she didn't know, trotted on the General's other side with the kind of sexist contentment some dogs show only in the presence of tall human males. They entered the lobby to echoes of indoor emptiness, antlers perching alertly along the walls. The dog sat down by the Dante chair; as if that had always been the General's traditional place. The General stopped too.

"*Hier,*" he said.

The driver put down the suitcase, bowed. He walked out and the General tapped the chair, to guide himself in sitting down.

"Let me take off your coat," Trudy said.

"Thank you. I'm a little cold."

Reclining now, with his knees crossed, wrapped in that high-collared raincoat, he was the same. The same superior immobility which put an onus on whomever he was with. An aristocrat's gift, and blindness had enhanced it.

"The woman who cooks here has already left," Trudy said. "But I could try to rustle up something."

"I'm not hungry, thank you."

"Or if you want to wash up . . ."

"I'd just like to sit and smoke a while, if I may."

"Of course." She pressed a Dubonnet ashtray into his hand and looked for a match. But he was already lighting up the pipe, ashtray well balanced on his lap.

"Now, my dear."

"There's probably no point in dragging you into this mess."

"That's my forte," he said. "Pointlessness. That's what Nick always told me."

He puffed an immobile pipe-puff and he smiled a seeing smile, and it did no good. She couldn't talk.

"Jennifer said something about Ronald with a girl and explosives up in a plane."

"My son's gone crazy," she said. "I don't — I can't talk about it now without blubbering —"

94

"Letarpo's plane?"

"Yes," she said. "They've set up a radio contact through the police station here. They'll call me if — if —"

The main reason she couldn't talk now was the luggage tag. It was hanging from the belt-loop of his trenchcoat, saying FIRST CLASS BOAC MUNICH-ZURICH GEN. N. ANTONE SR.

They had tagged his coat to make it easier for the stewardess to find the garment of a blind man. And nobody had thought to remove it afterwards. No wife or companion had noticed it. With all his presence and poise the General seemed pitifully womanless and that too, of course, was Nick-like, it was the womanlessness of the Antones that attracted women, disarmed them. Trudy knew it all too well, yet her heart went out to him.

"Why the hell burden you?" she said.

"Ronald is my grandchild," the old man said. "Now, what can we do?"

"I don't know!" she said. "Ronnie will only talk to Letarpo and we can't find him!"

"You have a telephone here?"

"It's right above you," she said. "It looks like a stethoscope."

"Would you dial Letarpo's Paris office for me?"

"I've tried that," she said.

But she was dialing it. The old man's immobility compelled her finger. He held out his hand and she pressed the receiver into it.

"Thank you. Please pay the driver."

In exchange for the receiver he gave her a wallet. She went out into the evening and paid the taxi driver 120 francs, the meter fare from the Zurich airport, plus tip. The fine leather wallet was worn at the corners. Was that aristocratic self-assurance or the Antones' waiflike-ness? Or both?

By the time she came back he had already hung up.

"Did you reach anybody?"

"His night man at the office. I said I'll be in radio contact here with Ronald. It will make Letarpo come."

She stared at the pipe the old man was relighting.

"Letarpo will be jealous that I'll succeed here, not him. He will come."

The match, flaming yellow-blue, was like a little campfire against the hollow jungle of the lobby.

"Don't worry; Letarpo is a fixer," the old man said. "When my fisheries were going to hell, he gave my men Christs lit from the inside. He fixed things up with Christs made in Hong Kong. Don't worry, my dear."

"You can't fix up Ronnie like this!" she wanted to cry. But she disciplined herself. She forced her mind away from the hysteria of any direct Ronnie thought. It was better to focus on Christs made in Hong Kong. They made Letarpo a cozy rogue.

"Let's talk about that," she said. "At least now I can talk with somebody. Would you like some wine?"

The old man shook his head.

"Tell me more," she said. "The fisheries and the Christs. Letarpo never said much about those days."

That was a lie. But she had a sudden child's need for nice story-telling. It'd make the waiting for the phone more bearable. "Tell me more about the crazy Christs," she said.

A grin came from the old man. But since his face didn't move, it must have been the pipe that grinned.

"His Christs made me keep the fisheries too long," he said. "I was already in oil. But he made fishing pay off with the Christs. They hung on the cross and they had a little flashlight under the navel." The old man leaned forward out of his immobility as if he'd decided to assume management of the crisis, and she did feel better. "It went by the month," the old man said. "A man caught more than three hundred kilos of fish a month, Letarpo gave him three bottles of Frascati stamped with the man's own name. They caught more than four hundred, he had their boats painted blue for free. They caught more than five hundred, they got a Christ made in Hong Kong. He had them fish like mad. He started early."

"Sonofabitch, he couldn't have been much older than Ronnie is now," she said.

"He was the only fishery foreman in Dalmatia whose voice was still changing."

"Tell me more," Trudy said, for the old man was leaning back again.

"Please tell me more," Trudy said. "It makes me feel better about him. I'll need it when I see him."

"My dear," the old man said.

Did it embarrass the old man to hear her beg for fairy-tale therapy? Or did it amuse him? She didn't care. She was making a deal with fate. If she became humble, really humble, if she humbled herself to old Antone, things would come out all right. Her son would come down safe.

"Tell me more," she said. "Please. Something about honey and donkeys? It was in some article on Letarpo. He made fun of it."

"Bridles," the old man said. "He put honey on the bridles, to soften up the donkeys. Later he softened up prime ministers, but he started with my donkeys. The honey made them move at night; we had the only night-moving donkeys. By morning he got the fish directly to the restaurants. He had a way. A donkey didn't move, he hopped on one leg and made a rude noise and the donkey moved. I never saw it, but all the drivers talked about it."

"Bet he always knew, someday he'd paint donkey ears on a Rolls-Royce Volkswagen, the bastard," she said.

"On my birthday the domaine put on a show for me," the old man said. "He made ten donkeys raise their tails at the same time."

"Yeah, he would," Trudy said.

"And then there were the Early Lesion Louse Ants," the old man said.

"Louse ants?"

"We talked English even back then," the old man said. "I don't speak Croat. He pretended he didn't know any Italian, so he could practice his English on me."

"My God, yes, he still has his barber business-card in English," Trudy said. "He showed it to me. He was picking up English from tourists, cutting their hair. When'd he sleep? I hope Ronnie can get along without sleep like that. Oh yes, and once he showed Ronnie the sheep shears he used."

"He bought them from my shepherd," the old man said.

"And the tourists really believed they were ancient Croat barber instruments? That's what he told Ronnie."

"Even if they didn't believe him, they gave him an extra tip," the old man said.

"He was always a great joker," she said. "Maybe he could get Ronnie down safe on some playful basis. What do you think?"

"Maybe," the old man said.

"And he's so good at acting fast," she said. "He can be so goddamn fast. He's loused me up often enough with his suddenness." Again she thought of the way Letarpo had hooked Simon into the Yeshiva business. "Even in my first marriage," she said. "He sprang a couple of nifties on Simon."

"Simon wasn't slow either," the old man said.

"About the Louse Ants," she said. "Tell me."

"Just before the war," the old man said. "Just before I married Abigail, I explained to Letarpo why I was selling my island to him."

"But 'Louse Ants'?"

The old man really smiled now. "I explained it to him. It wasn't enough, becoming an American citizen through marriage. I had to give up my European residence before I could get my Early Lesion Louse Ants."

"What?"

"Oil Depletion Allowance."

When was the last time Trudy had laughed like that?

"You know something?" she said. "He doesn't pronounce it much better now!"

"But he understood what it was," the old man said. "He understood that the island thing was a formality. After a year my Swiss corporation was supposed to buy it back. He understood that all right."

"You wanted Pilcic back?" It was the first time Trudy had heard of it.

"It was always understood," Antone said. "I brought Abigail to Europe just to see Pilcic. She was pregnant with Nick but I wanted her to see my island. Friend Letarpo was just waiting for that day."

"With some donkeys?" Trudy said smiling.

"Oh, many," Antone said. "The week before, he'd moved right into our villa with his mother and three pigs and fifty black Croat chickens with diarrhea. The vases were full of olive pits. We even found a donkey in the dining room."

"Always with his donkeys," she said.

"There were lizards in our beds," the old man said.

"He is something," Trudy said.

"And he smiled in a waistcoat. He'd bought himself a waistcoat

98

in Zagreb just to watch us with this. Abigail almost threw up. He knew we would never move in there after that. He wanted to keep the island. He kept it."

"He never told me you had wanted it back," Trudy said.

"Now, Mama Letarpo," the old man said. "I should have taken her by the bosoms. I should have pulled her out of the bedroom by the Croat tits. Right in front of Abigail and our friend in the waistcoat. But I didn't. I let him have the island."

"I never knew that about Pilcic," Trudy said. "But you kept on being friendly!"

"I loaned our friend the rigs," the old man said. "With my rigs he found his first oil in Macedonia. When Nick made union president, I let Letarpo fly in twelve fiddles from Bucharest. I let him give my son a party." The old man smiled. "Twelve fiddles in Union Hall. A thousand dollars apiece."

"Why'd you keep on being friendly?"

"It's all right," the old man said. "He watched me lose Pilcic. So I watch him. It's best from up close."

The old eyes had shut. For a moment she thought he had fallen asleep. But the pipe still puffed, and a moment after each puff his eyes opened as if he could see puffs only after they had already dissolved among the antlers, saw them transformed into something astounding in the dimness.

"You wanted to watch him lose too?" Trudy said. "You wanted to watch him fail? But he's going strong as ever! Has he failed?"

It was no longer nice storytelling, but it compelled her. "Tell me!" she said. "I should be prepared when Letarpo comes here; I need help to save Ronnie! Why stay friends if you're no longer friendly?"

"My dear," he said from far away under his closed eyes. "You stayed married to Simon Spieger."

"But that was different!"

His head had dropped back. His hands with the pipe lay on the crossed knees.

"It was different!" she said.

Silence.

"You can't compare it, it was different!"

Silence. He had really fallen asleep.

She'd fallen asleep herself, but the dog woke her. It had begun to growl.

"Shut up!" Trudy whispered to the big dog whose name she didn't know. It thumped its python of a tail against the parquet. In the Dante chair, old Antone slept a deep luggage-tagged sleep in his raincoat. With each exhalation the hand on his knee, which held pipe and ashtray, moved slightly. Each exhalation made the pipe strike the tray softly. *Ping!* . . . That very soft *Ping!* . . . shivered through the hotel lobby, amplified by magnetic dusk and the alertness of the antlers along the walls. *Ping!* . . .

The dog didn't like the sound. "Brrr! . . . ," it growled at the *Ping!* . . .

"Don't wake the old man!" Trudy whispered. "I need him fresh when the phone rings! I need him for Ronnie! Shut up!"

The dog's eyes stared up, in bloodshot astonishment at her nerve.

"*You* got nerve!" Trudy whispered. "This old man you're growling at, he's a much more successful parent than me. His Nick never acted up with him. Not like my Ronnie. No crazy stuff in planes!"

Ping! . . . went the pipe. But now the dog didn't growl. While Trudy whispered, it didn't growl, just stared at Trudy. She was very tired, vexed to the bone by guilt and lack of sleep, but she had to keep whispering so the dog wouldn't growl. "That old man should be a lesson to me!" she whispered. "He did much better with his son. He made Nick come out of Yale to help him with refugee relief! You don't growl at a man like that!" The dog didn't growl. "Right, shut up!" she whispered. "The old man here, he had Nick do liaison between Polish DP's and the Building Workers Brotherhood which was lousy with Polacks. And even when Nick broke with him — God, my son should only break with me like that! Shut up!"

The dog had growled again, slightly, at a *Ping!* . . .

"Shut up!" she whispered. "Even when Nick broke with his old man it was political, not personal. Even after he went to the Brotherhood he still showed up at the old man's parties. You follow? He was a mother with the ladies and who should know better, and he was a mother with the electorate, but he didn't go hog-wild with dynamite like my Ronnie. He was a real mother when it came to snowing ethnics. The old Brotherhood brass was Polack, but the new guys were spick and nigger —"

She stopped. The old man no longer *pinged* in his sleep. And the St. Bernard lay quiet now. It was a conspiracy to make her stop the foul-mouthed whispering, just when it gave her such nice relief. "Spick and nigger!" she went right on. "Fucking pejoratives make me feel better. Spick and nigger versus Polack. So Nick made himself president, a classy compromise. What'd my son Ronnie ever make himself? Nick opened a black local in Memphis! That's tougher than going crazy in a plane. I ought to tell my dear son. I ought to shame him."

She grabbed into her bag for the Crillon stationery pad. She was going to write more codicils.

"To my son Ronald Spieger I leave nothing," she wrote. The dog slept too now. Writing, pressing the ballpoint hard against paper, was a better release than whispering to a couple of snorers. *Assuming a happy end to this mess,* she wrote, *assuming that my son Ronald should come out alive and that I will predecease him, I leave him nothing.* If she wrote in large letters she could write even in this dim light, and though the Crillon stationery sheets were small she still had some left and she used both sides. *My son Ronald needs no money,* she wrote. *I understand he is already a beneficiary in the present will of my husband Alexander Letarpo. I owe Ronald nothing, except perhaps a little candor. Probably he owes me more. He has led me a pretty tough life.*

Tough from the very start; literally *ab ovo*. She had ample right to be angry at Ronnie. Perhaps if she let the anger rise, the worry would become less. Ronnie had made it very tough for her *ab ovo*. From the moment he'd been an egg just fertilized. Even when he'd been nothing but a twinge of nausea and a positive lab report he had crossed her up; he'd prevented her from flying to New Mexico where Nick Antone was settling some damn strike. She couldn't come rushing after Nick like some shopgirl knocked up in a panic in Rugow's Bakery uptown. In a sense Ronnie was a perverse accident on flour bags. *To my son Ronald,* she wrote, *I leave nothing in dollars and cents for the above reason. But I do bequeath him a memento. A striped doll. A little king. If that's being perverse to him, he's been perverse to me.*

It seemed to work: as she nursed her anger at Ronnie, she became less nervous about his fate up there in the plane. And damn little Ronnie *had* been perverse, from the very start, right in her belly.

The embryo had positioned itself laterally, Dr. Greenberg had said: which meant that it stuck out as a lump when she was only three months pregnant, just at the time Simon had come down with the ulcer. It was at Doctors' Hospital that he'd made the discovery. He'd fondled her, amazingly conscious after such surgery, and come upon the bump. She remembered Simon's cry. Simon pulled out her blouse to lay his finger on it and to kiss it; he recognized it as his own child by an act of faith and by murmuring Jacob's blessing over her belly, whispering at it, proclaiming that little lump a boy, even naming "him" Ronald after Rehoboam, Solomon's son (all this while he had plasma tubes running into his veins), whispering-explaining to Trudy that he meant Solomon the sinner, not Solomon the king, smiling, quite possibly getting through the night because of it.

Yes, Ronnie's lateral position had elated, perhaps saved, Simon. So Trudy couldn't respond to the roses sent anonymously to the hospital. Nor to the heart-shaped cake delivered to her c/o Tante's apartment in the carton of Rugow's Bakery; nor to a message, again c/o Tante's, asking her to please call Nick at the House Office Building in Washington.

To my son Ronald, she wrote, *I leave another souvenir, namely my toilette kit, all 97 bottles and flasks. As a tribute to his looks and how much more interestingly he deployed them than I did mine.* As a newborn he'd already had a cleft tiny chin and the nurses giggled over the furlike hair rimming those perfect little ears that would soon exchange the fur for freckles. And there was that photograph, inimitable, done by the gay Parisian photographer Simon's French cousin had sent. It showed baby Ronnie shaking both his big toe and his forefinger at the same point in pink space. This picture she'd taken along with her on her first stay away from the baby. Her trip to San Francisco to make arrangements for Simon's come-back lectures after the ulcer, his tour to start on the West Coast. She'd come down into the lobby of the St. Francis Hotel after unpacking and the desk clerk gave her a While You Were Out message that said, unsigned: *"Would Mrs. Spieger ask Miss Rugow to come into the bar here at five p.m.?"*

She had no idea, of course, that Nick Antone was right here in town with her. On the plane she'd seen his picture in the *Los*

Angeles Times, dancing with some Mexicali rose at the Grape Pickers' Benefit in Sacramento. Now she had just enough steadiness in her voice to find out from the room clerk that, yes, Mr. Antone Junior was also staying at the St. Francis. She was shaken with fury at this juxtaposition of newspaper picture and coded note. It made him such a splendid rogue and her such a sodden rehash of the Scarlet Woman, and she just kept standing in the hotel lobby, sweating into her dress. Then she remembered Ronnie's toe-pointing photo in her wallet. She took it out and wrote on the back of it:

Ronald Amos Spieger is pleased to announce the death of Miss Rugow.

She put the photo in a hotel envelope, had the clerk place it in Mr. Antone Junior's box, elevatored up to her room to get her things together, elevatored down, paid her bill, taxied to the airport. She managed to make most of the lecture arrangements from a phone booth before the night plane took off for New York. For some years this was the last time that Nick Antone and she unpacked bags under the same roof. And Baby Ronnie was involved with that too.

To my son Ronald, she wrote, *I would like to explain —*

She stopped writing. Something had begun to happen in the empty hotel lobby in Liechtenstein. The dog had begun to dream. The huge brown-white heap of hair began to tremble in the dusk. The forepaws came together as it lay on its side, big blunt claws praying; its head lolled from side to side and from the snout came a nearly human sound: "Ah . . . ah. . . ." A sound so heartfelt and noble it made you think this was a prince trying to struggle free, out of the St. Bernard's fur.

"Ping! . . ." went the old man's pipe. He still leaned back with closed eyes, sleeping. But now his lips bent into exactly the same curve as the mouth of the antlered skull above him, two grins aligned at a dog trying to dream himself into a prince in an empty hotel.

No, she hadn't seen much of Nick when Ronnie was small. But somehow old man Antone and his smile were always there, especially at the Big Moments. That time at the High Club — some ten years ago and fifty floors above pollution. Fifty floors below there must have been thousands finagling sex or business in their cocktail crevices at five P.M. But up at the High Club the light was royal. It came like butler-poured white wine through the windows. It flattered Trudy's still somewhat oily skin (she could see that from the mirror opposite); it firmed Bic's already puffing face. It made classic the smile of old Antone; he looked like a faintly, lethally amused bust of a Roman emperor. Did old Antone know that in the fineness of that light, things might start which would deform her marriage altogether? Which would drive Trudy and his son back to each other, toward a very special disaster? Or did the old man smile simply because he liked the light? Maybe he felt anything beautiful was worth an elegantly suppressed little laugh. And that light *was* beautiful. That light shone on the forelock of the Honorable Sherr Winnis, Democrat from Indiana. It shone on this damn red-blond tub of a rube who wielded rubedom like a foil.

The Congressman wanted his good friends to know that the Speaker of the House had taught him how to pronounce "locks." He'd practiced that word a lot because he'd been warned about it: they'd never serve him smoked salmon in New York City unless he knew how to pronounce "locks," and he was very partial to smoked salmon and he knew the best Scotch stuff was sent to New York City and he really did resent being told by the High Club here they didn't have any just because he'd probably said "locks" a little wrong in his excitement when he'd tried to order it just now, and it wasn't a fair shake either they wouldn't bring him the Sazerac he'd asked for, just because of that little "locks" booboo.

And while they were all smiling he said, still deadpan, that he was throwing all these tantrums for a reason. He had to work up enough gall to ask Mrs. Spieger something: Her husband's wonderful speech about his future Interfaith University, was there any objection to putting it in the *Congressional Record?*

"Simon would only be pleased," Trudy said. "And it wouldn't hurt his university either. It might help get the funds passed finally."

"Now dad bang it," the Congressman said. "If there's one thing I hate, it's giving credit where credit is due. But I better come

104

clean: Young Nick Antone pointed my nose at your husband's speech. Was Nick's idea to have it printed in the *Record*. But I had to tell him a dirty fact of life. Marvelous speech like that, it'll get much more attention printed under the name of an old fogey like me, just because I happen to be Vice Chairman of the Rules Committee and all that junk. And Nick handed me permission on a silver platter. I just wanted to own up on that."

"Well," Trudy said. "My husband is recuperating from a virus, but I'm sure he'll be so pleased."

"Well, if he's pleased, I'm flattered," the Honorable Sherr Winnis said. "But to make up for it to Nick Antone, I'll tell you what we've got to do with him. I don't care if it's embarrassing his distinguished father setting here. We can't treat Nick like just another freshman in the House. A union boy landsliding the Silk Stocking district! That's pitching a big bale! I say, stuff seniority, and slip him into the Finance Committee! The House could use a brain there. Not just brains either. Hell, Nick's got more labor clout than Moses! Why, if he snapped his fingers now, they'd be rushing out of the kitchen with 'locks' for me! They might even bring me my Sazerac!"

Everyone was properly entertained by that, especially Bic, who could laugh with great emphasis. He apologized for the service.

"Never mind my Sazerac," Sherr Winnis said. "But there's dumbbells think Nick Antone's a commie because the blue collars believe in him. Like there's dumbbells think my state will go to hell if Sherr Winnis gets into the Senate next year. They think Montana'll just drop through the trap door straight into hell! Just because I voted against that extra ten million on the Parochial School bill! They think I've got a cloven foot! Well, I got no cloven foot and I haven't got it in my mouth, either! I'm going to print Mr. Spieger's inspiration in the *Record,* and I'll be tickled purple to co-sponsor that religious Paul Newman premiere down at Key Bahama for Sclerosis, if the General really means his invitation?"

"I do mean it," old Antone smiled. "It's a film about King David, who could have used a good congressman."

"Oh, no, no!" Sherr Winnis said. "That's not a good congressman spouting at you now! No sir! That's a swell-headed uppity pol! Maybe Mrs. Spieger ought to walk out on me right now! I'm goin' to say something really nervy in a minute. No excuse for it. I'm not even drunk 'cause I'll never get my Sazerac —"

"Seems to take a long time," Trudy said to the congressman, "almost as long as it takes Congress to fund our University."

"I'll give that waiter hell," Bic said, getting up.

"Touché," Sherr Winnis said to Trudy. "I hope I pronounced that right. Now this nervy thing I want to ask — to give the premiere real class, would you and your husband introduce it with one of your remarkable readings — that is, if my co-sponsor, the General, don't mind?"

"I don't, not at all," old Antone said. And Bic, who had returned with the waiter in tow; Bic, who by that time had already lost his French accent and spoke a fake BBC English, Bic said, "Congressman, you may kill me for this, but I've got to tell our friends my suggestion."

"Don't you *dare,* Louis Bic!" the congressman said.

"It's just a suggestion," Bic said.

"Bic, you'll get your martini right in your eyes!"

"The suggestion —"

"Martini's gonna blind your eyes, Bic!"

"You see," Bic said to Trudy. "A movie premiere plus the General's charity plus the Simon Spiegers in person, altogether that would be very newsy —"

"I'm warning you!"

"The suggestion is simply that the Spiegers dedicate their reading to the congressman that evening. . . . Help!"

Bic covered his face against the attack. Nothing happened. The congressman put Bic's glass down on the table.

"Lucky for him he done drunk his martini," the congressman said. "I told him, it's the most nervy idea I ever heard of. I don't even know if your remarkable husband can fit it into his schedule. It's in April."

"I can try to recommend it to him," Trudy said.

"It's a very popular benefit," old Antone said. "The Keys' Free Clinic. My friends are always very generous about it. So I wouldn't dream of letting the Spiegers appear except for their full fee."

"Which I'm going to take care of," the congressman said.

"Never mind," old Antone said. "It is my benefit."

"I will so take care of half, 'cause that's what co-sponsor means. Otherwise I'll use filthy language on you, General!"

"I'm sure you'll do it wittily," old Antone said.

"Just a moment," Bic said. "You're fighting in Letarpo's club. He will be the umpire on the fee."

"I feel bad," the congressman said. "I started all this messin'. Right in front of a lovely lady like Mrs. Spieger."

"Oh, I'm enjoying it," Trudy said.

And she was, on the assumption that everybody would get his at the High Club. Or hers.

"Now, Congressman," Trudy said. "I was going to ask you for some advice. I mentioned appropriations for Interfaith University. You know why all the delay in getting them passed?"

"I'm just one of the dumbbells on the Rules Committee," Sherr Winnis said. "It's the brains on the Education Committee carrying that ball."

"They're scared of our University charter," Trudy said. "Because we've got ten percent of our operating budget going direct to the Student Council."

"Oh well, that's a tough one today," Sherr Winnis said. "Riots and all."

"To get around it we might make a change. Ten percent direct to the dean of students disposing of the money *in consultation* with the Student Council. Think it might help?"

"I'll be glad to pass that along to them Education dudes," Sherr Winnis said.

"Will you go to bat for it? It's my husband's idea I should be the dean of students."

"Hey!" Sherr Winnis said. "Bravo! With your popularity with young and old."

"Thank you for exaggerating," Trudy said.

"Even so, it's a pretty hot potato."

"Hot for somebody like you? You're still exaggerating," Trudy said.

"On the other hand, you're a very able, attractive young lady."

"Congressman, you do keep exaggerating," she said.

"And you'll put in a good word for me with your husband's readings?"

"Now you're not exaggerating," she said.

That moment the waiter finally brought the Honorable Sherr his drink.

"Well, here goes what they call the moment of truth," Sherr Winnis said.

"Sorry it took so long," Bic said while Sherr Winnis drank.

"By God," Congressman Winnis said and put down his glass. "The Speaker of the House is going to get kicked. We bet a kick. He bet me I couldn't drink a Sazerac in New York City that didn't taste of a rat's tail. Well, this here ain't no rat's tail. That's a fine potable. Let's all drink to kicking the Speaker!"

And they all drank to that, even old Antone with his antler-skull smile.

2

To my son Ronald, she wrote. *Instructions on the little king I'm leaving him. This is a very old doll now. Once the king's eyes were anchored in the fabric, but the hooks are exposed now, and rusty. Ronald should take care not to cut himself. Except maybe a little. When the dybbuk rises up inside him, he should give himself a small scratch on the back of his hand and drain out the dybbuk with one drop of blood. That is my legacy to him.*

The St. Bernard was still dreaming in Liechtenstein, still trying to be a tender and desirous prince inside matted fur. Old Antone was still sleeping, smiling together with his pal, the antler-skull. Now she was sure they were smiling at her as well. Hadn't she been like the dog? Desirous, through all the beastliness in her life, for some damn princely fulfillment? Maybe that was *her* dybbuk: fulfillment. Fulfillment, the old American demon. Fulfillment, fulfillment! Fulfillment in America! What a cry, what sacred anguish sounding through the open-ended paradise! A whole continent stuffed coast-to-coast with great lovers, great poets, great revolutionaries, great jackpot geniuses, all *manqués.* Fulfillment sent two hundred million suckers hustling day and night, panting after some lousy chamber pot of a Holy Grail. She of all people should have found out fulfillment much earlier. She should have known from her sociology and her experience. Did it matter there had been fulfilled fucking on flour sacks instead of wise words at the demonstration? Nope. Did it matter that the demonstration had gone all right, sort of fulfilled itself anyway? Nope. In the end nothing was done to stop evictions or slums or the grinding up of Mr. Lissberg, supermarket cart and all. Fulfillment, shmulfillment. Bad enough, nothing had taught her to exorcise the fulfillment dybbuk. Worse yet, she'd probably passed on the dybbuk to Ronnie. In even more dangerous, mysterious form.

To my son Ronald, she wrote. *This is to disinherit him from the dybbuk I may have left him unbeknownst while still alive. I'm sorry I never understood that or him.* She hadn't understood Ronnie as far back as Key Bahama. That far back, when Ronnie had been barely seven, a charming, impulsive child, quick, peculiar, impenetrable. He didn't look like Nick yet. The freckles covered, of all things, only his ears and his long slim little fingers. His little trousers flared when he whirled about in his sailor suit. Every weekend Nanny sent him off to wherever Simon and she appeared, and every time Nanny dressed him up in a sailor suit.

He couldn't have played more sweetly with his "Daddy," twirling the *dreidel* and whirling along with it when it whirled. It was that beautiful *dreidel* Simon had gotten in the mail from an admirer, a striped dicelike spinning top latticed in white gold and red gold, and the Hebrew letters on the four sides of it were wrought of onyx.

Simon was resting up for the reading. He lay on the couch of their suite at the Key Bahama Inn, explaining how to play the *dreidel.* He had explained something pretty abstract for a kid, the number values of the Hebrew letters, yet the faint chant of his voice had been enough to press Ronnie's little face into his little fists with fascination. The player who came closest to the number 114 won, Simon said; for that was the numerical value of Shaddai, the name of a shoemaker raised up to be the Angel of the Presence, the very highest of the Angelic Hosts, with eyes of lightning and lashes of cloud, for it was this shoemaker who had already wanted to talk to God when barely out of the cradle, when he was too small to pray a prayer and therefore wanted at least to *play* a prayer — and made the first *dreidel*.

Ronnie listened; then spun himself around fantastically fast to the spin of the *dreidel*. Ronnie won, or at least so Simon said. He gave Ronnie the paper-thin chocolate mint that was the prize. He stroked the child's face. He put his finger on his lips and fell asleep. Ronnie tiptoed away, munching the chocolate. Ronnie slowed down; turned around. He looked at Simon sleeping. He tiptoed back and suddenly, simply, reached into Simon's trouser pocket and pulled out the *dreidel* and was about to pad away into his bedroom to take his nap as he'd promised, if Trudy hadn't grabbed him. She'd watched the whole spectacle through the half-open door of the salon, and she had Ronnie by the scruff of his neck.

"Put that back!"

"It's striped," Ronnie said, also whispering so Simon wouldn't wake.

"What's that got to do with it? Don't you *ever* steal again!"

"I'm going to magic it into striped candy."

"You heard me! Put it back!"

"Maybe the shoemaker will make him another one."

"Back! This minute!"

His little body had pressed itself flush against her. For that reason she found it difficult to spank him. She pulled Ronnie away from herself and saw that he had put the *dreidel* in his mouth, an angelic, freckle-eared child sucking on a striped thumb and looking at her in a way that was either trusting-sweet or a diabolic simulation, and she hesitated another moment before spanking him. Then it was too late. General Antone walked in with the young Macedonian prince who was his houseguest.

"I'm sorry — I knocked," the General said.

"That's all right," Trudy said, staring at her son.

"Since you wanted to look at the house, I thought it might be convenient now."

"The house!" Ronnie said. "Oh, Mummy, we've been there. It's beautiful! Please! Please, Mummy!"

"Put that *dreidel* back! On the coffee table in Simon's room," she said. "This instant."

"We could make it another time," the General said.

"Right now is fine," Trudy said. She watched Ronnie creep off, place the *dreidel* on the coffee table, perform a curious sardonic bow toward Simon sleeping, creep back.

"Now say thank you to General Antone for saving you from a spank," Trudy said.

"Thank you, sir," Ronnie said, and walked out ahead with the young prince.

From the start Ronnie had had a peculiar effect on this prince. This Yussuf, heir to Macedonia, would someday inherit millions gushing from oil sites first leased by old Antone and now by Letarpo. Trudy had met Yussuf the day before and it was as if the weight of his inheritance had pulled everything tight in the young man's face, his olive cheeks downward and inward, and his thick black eyebrows into an over-alert frown; he looked much older than fifteen. But now, with Ronnie, he was all of a sudden just a happy swarthy kid. Ronnie, who was eight years younger, had made such fast friends with him this morning, the two were running ahead, holding hands with wild innocence.

Trudy watched them as she followed with old Antone. Maybe it was the momentum of Ronnie's changeability which produced change in others. You wouldn't have thought that this exuberant, skipping little heller had been a very quiet, very expert thief a little while ago. She was wondering how to cope with that as a mother and within a minute had more to wonder about. They'd come to a canal, edged with flowering cactus, which separated the Antone domaine from the rest of the island. Old Antone guided her across a little bridge into a garden of palms and jasmine. The house itself looked like a lovely Portuguese mission, secluded among umbrella pines. But a few feet from the portal the air changed — as if Ronnie's unpredictability had infected it. The sweet floral scents became acrid. The smell was nastily out of key with the jasmine and the cherry espalier patterned against white-washed arcades.

Trudy looked at Ronnie, who smiled at his new friend Yussuf. The General patted both, at ease in the stink.

"A few years ago," he said, "we had a record hurricane."

A Negro in a white tunic held the door open for them. On the

111

carpet of the anteroom stood a madonna, baroque, beautiful and grieving in rich folds of time-darkened wood. Her cheeks were fondled by claws. Something had reached for her through a grating.

The smell was rank and Trudy's hand, which had gone up to protect her nose, was caught in her mouth: the grating closed off the next room, a huge Spanish salon whose furniture crawled with beasts. A gray monkey jumped from a credenza, another hung from the crucifix and bit into an apple, a third reared his purple behind in an armchair. Droppings mottled the parquet, an orange parrot pecked at the portrait of a conquistador, and on the dining table stood a white long-legged bird on one leg.

Ronnie had already pressed a lever that squeaked open a gate in the grating. He and the prince ran inside. "No!" she wanted to yell, but the old man touched her.

"Over there is the damage," the General said.

At the other end of the salon there wasn't a wall, not even a picture window, as she'd thought at first, but simply jungle. A chaos of shrubbery and leaves. Right under the dining chairs grass was growing and ferns twined round a highboy.

"How can you live here?" Trudy said.

"Oh I don't; I'm in the cottage," the General said. "I thought you knew. But the wind also smashed my zoo house. So I combined."

"Why?" Trudy said.

"Economics," the General said. He'd taken out a pipe and knocked it playfully against Ronnie's head. "Until Nick comes back here, those are my heirs."

From the chandelier that once must have been gold something black hung upside down. The smell was getting worse. She turned her head away and saw stairs.

"The upper floor is undisturbed," the General said. "We have my friends sealed off. I suppose Nick could restore the whole place in a couple of months."

Trudy wanted to cut out of there. But she didn't want to panic before Ronnie.

"I'd like to look around upstairs," she said to get away.

"Please," said the General.

The marble steps and the scrollworked balustrade seemed absurd in the stench. But the air was better on the upper floor, though she thought she detected droppings on the flagstones of the corridor. She opened the door to the first room and sniffed; hardly any smell here. Just dust and musty light from a shuttered window. But she knew instantly whose room this was. Midget ghosts stared at her. Sheets gravely suspended over low objects, objects that took on shape as her eyes adjusted to the dim. Veiled small chairs, a veiled little bed, even a veiled little piano. Once upon a time the child Nick had run around these things. Little Nick's room. But even this dusty floor had a dropping. This enraged her, she kicked it. It bounced. It wasn't a dropping but something rubbery, shrunken, a hollow big raisin made of wrinkles. She bent down. It was a mummy of a balloon. The relic of a children's party decades ago. Nearby, in a corner, lay a little king. He was very dusty but she only had to shake him to see that he was a remarkably unfaded bright cloth doll, rather flattened because the stuffing had compacted, but with a gay yellow clown's face and pert blue eyes and a huge crown and a cloak of purple-white stripes. She scooped this king into her shoulder bag and beat it out of the room and down the stairs.

Shock jolted back her head.

Not the smell for which she was braced but the sight of Ronnie and his friend. Those two had put on white houseboy tunics and they'd gone mad inside the grating. They must have set the dining table. Beige Wedgwood china plates on silver silk place mats, cut-glass goblets, but of course the glass was caked with mud, the silk mats splotched, and excrement smeared over the Wedgwood. Yet Ronnie — as if all were candlelit daintiness — Ronnie poured water into the goblets from a cracked decanter, the prince heaped fruit into the plates, and from everywhere the dinner party came hopping, jumping, screeching, slavering; ape necks and tailfeathers bobbed round the table, and it was all doubly weird because of Ronnie's face. Such a sweetly tousled boy-face, as cheerful as his friend, the prince. The two bustled about in their domestics' uniforms, buttling and serving amidst smacks, snorts, claws, snouts. She had never seen her son so content as now, mimicking elegance and reason in the inferno.

"*Ronnie! . . . Ronnie!* Ronnie! . . . *Ronnie!*"

Finally he stopped.

"Take that off and come out!"

She rattled the grating.

"Allow me," old Antone said. He opened the gate. Ronnie came out with his friend and she pulled her son away so fast out of the house that the strap of her shoulder bag got caught in the door-knob. Not until she'd disentangled herself and was far enough to smell sweet jasmine again did it strike her that Nick's king doll, which she'd stashed inside her bag, had a cloak which was striped.

As a rule she had a cast-iron stomach, but shortly afterwards that day she became nauseous. It could have been the experience she'd been through. That plus the fact that it was near her time of month, though she couldn't recall being so affected by her cycle before. At any rate she had to skip dinner. When she dressed for the evening she still felt awful.

"Simon," she said. "I can't go on with you today. It's my lousy stomach."

As introduction to the movie premiere, they had intended to do the most abridged and popularized version of their reading-from-each-other's-work act. But she couldn't trust herself on stage even for five minutes.

"My Trudy." Simon went to her and kissed her hand, and, very lightly, her stomach. "I will try to do something alone," he said. "It is a King David film. I will try to do some psalms."

And he did, with an aplomb she had to admire. She watched him from the wings in that wedding cake of a little opera house. The spotlight flashed on Simon, all alone on a bare stool before an audience darkly gorgeous with brooches and velvet lapels, old Antone with his U.N. medal, Congressman Winnis with a carnation in the buttonhole, and Ferdinand and Isabella wreaking florid greatness in frescoes all over the walls and ceiling. Very alone Simon sat, legs close together under the cape, elbows propped on his knees, face down and covered by his knuckles so that only the sparse gray welter of his hair stared at the audience like a mask of desolation. With hopelessness that was melodious and unremitting he began to speak the Twenty-second Psalm through his fingers.

I am poured out like water, all my bones are out of joint. . . .

Not a cough or a sneeze in the opera house. Not a rustle of clothes. But little Ronnie, standing with Trudy in the wings, said, low, "Where's the movie?" Trudy put her hand over the small mouth.

Behold, thou hast made my days as a handbreadth. . . .

"Mummy, I want to see the movie," Ronnie whispered against Trudy's waist.

Thou turnest man to destruction,
A thousand years are but a watch in the night. . . .

"Mummy, please!"

"Look," she said into Ronnie's ear. "The movie starts much too late for your bedtime —"

In distress I called upon the Lord,
And the Lord answered me and set me in a large place. . . .

"Mummy, just a little bit of the movie?" Ronnie's whisper chewed his little teeth against her waist. It was too much for a little boy, the excitement and the festiveness here, the screen already unrolled for the film — and off to bed. Ronnie shouldn't have been brought here in the first place. But Simon had wanted him to hear the psalms.

"*While I live!*" Simon called out. With a swirl of his cape he stood up into tallness.

While I live I will praise the Lord,
I will sing while I have any being. . . .

She was about to say, "Okay, the first ten minutes of the movie," but she realized how cruel the eleventh minute would be, especially for this volatile little boy. "To make up for it, you'll get a surprise tomorrow," she whispered. She knew exactly what to give Ronnie,

115

who was mad for striped things; she'd give him the striped little king tomorrow, Nick's little king that weighed down her evening bag, even now.

Praise ye the Lord! ...

Simon had shrugged off the cape with a single shrug that flung it on the stool. Now he bestrode the stage erect, in the elegance of his brown blazer and the long black Gary Cooper trousers.

Praise ye the Lord,
ye dragons and all deeps;
fire and hail, snow and vapor;
storm winds fulfilling his word,
creeping things and flying fowl,
Princes and beetles....
Praise ye the Lord....

The last word was the cue that made the spotlight die. In the darkness Simon said, "Dedicated to our friend and co-host Congressman Sherr Winnis," and Ronnie bit very quietly into his mother's waist.

Their plane to New York next morning ran into bumpy weather. It didn't bother Ronnie. He dropped off, and Trudy got up, straightened his little legs across her seat for comfort, and then found three empty seats on which to stretch out herself. It was the best thing to do in view of her still somewhat funny stomach. An hour later she woke up, very much better. She went back to her seat — and found Ronnie huddled in a blanket, knuckles pressed against his face. Did he have a fever? Trudy was about to run forward when she realized that he was reading out loud. He was reading a children's book the stewardess must have given him: *Pierre Panda's Flying International Phrase Book.* He had the book propped up on the seat table and he was reading it through his fingers covering his face. He was performing it the way Simon had performed the psalms, hunched in his blanket-cape of misery, and with a child's desolate voice he said:

116

"Hello — helloh . . . Guten Tag — good day . . . wie heissen Sie — what is your name . . ."

He had Simon's slow powerful mournfulness, even his French accent, exactly right.

"Leider regnet es — Unfortunately it is raining. . . . Sprechen Sie Englisch? — Do you speak English?"

Ronnie stood up from his seat, dropped his hands from his face. With sudden thrilling huge hope he announced:

"Es gibt Coca Cola! — We have Coke! . . ."
"Sie können bestellen — You can order now. . . .

"Stop it!" Trudy said.

"Ice cream, please!"

Ronnie was shouting in spiritual triumph.

"Milcheis . . . Hot dogs — Wiener Würste! . . .
Ham sandwich — Schinkenbrötchen . . .
Waffeln — wafers . . . Pretzels! . . . Crackers! . . .
Peanut butter! Chocolate doughnuts!
Cookies! STRAWBERRY ICE CREAM SODA! . . . "

All around him passengers stared and smiled. She had time for one discreet sharp spank, and then they had to fasten seat belts for La Guardia.

∽ *3* ∾

Every Monday she went with Ronnie to a certain rendezvous at Letarpo's Waldorf Towers apartment. Thank **God** her stomach was back to normal by the time they reached the Waldorf. And Ronnie was sweet again. That was the uncanny part, that generally he was a sweet child, and the Monday after Key Bahama he excelled in sweetness.

Now he was no *dreidel*-thief, no mocker of psalms. He was quiet, a little pale despite the exposure to Caribbean sun, and in the ride up to the fortieth floor pressed his cheek against Trudy's rib cage. She felt she'd have to give him the striped king-doll for a present after all.

Letarpo himself greeted them at the door, and took off his jacket immediately to cut Ronnie's hair. Ronnie always submitted tamely. Bic hung a kind of bib round Letarpo's shirt and pushed the stool next to the Renoir (it hung where the Duchamp used to hang so that the olive tree in the middle of the room had the look of a permanent enduring classic). Bic handed Letarpo the scissors and draped a Snoopy tablecloth round Ronnie's neck. The butler spread sheets of the *Wall Street Journal* under the stool, then stiffed away.

"Hokay," Letarpo said, clicking the scissors. "Sit down the stool, Spieger Junior." Letarpo always exaggerated his accent when talking to Ronnie. He walked around Ronnie, clicking the scissors and giving him little pushes as he appraised the hair. The huge paneled room began to look like a little barbershop in Dubrovnik. Letarpo started to snip.

"Your hair grows too fast again," he said. "Grows too fast in jet planes. No good."

"Aw, you're making a joke!" Ronnie said, sweetly, if a little loud.

"Hay, quiet," Letarpo said. "We got Mister Nick in there in the dining room. He's eating ice cream with some of the United States Senate. Much too much hair in the back."

"What kind of ice cream?" Ronnie asked.

"What kind?" Letarpo said. "Bic, find out what kind of Senator ice cream. Hold still, Junior, I tell you a story."

"All right," Bic said and went into the gallery.

"A nice story?" Ronnie said.

"Ho sure," Letarpo said, snipping delicately. "You know Spieger Senior, your head of family? He needs a nice school. So we been finishing one for him. But to finish a real nice one, a new law got to help us. You like school, Junior?"

"Sometimes," Ronnie said.

"Chey," Letarpo said, giving him a growl-laugh and a little push. "This school you'll like right now, son-of-a-gun Junior, hold still, huh?"

"You're giving me pushes," Ronnie said.

"It's banana-blueberry ice cream," Bic said, coming back.

"You want to eat the ice cream the Senate is eating?" Letarpo said.

"The banana part," Ronnie said.

"Hokay," Letarpo said with another little push. "First you hold still. Then the bananas. It's a deal? We call the lawyers?"

"Yes, sir," Ronnie said. "But why do you want to make him a school?"

"Why? Dumb Junior!" Letarpo said. "Because it's going to be in New York, so Senior won't have to go lecture all over the country, so your hair won't grow too fast in jet planes, hokay?"

"Yes, sir," Ronnie said.

"They make a nice law, we finish making a nice school. So Nick is having banana-blueberry with them to fix it up. You with me?"

"I'm with you," Ronnie said. "But I itch."

"Where you itch? I scratch you."

"Here, sir," Ronnie said.

Letarpo scratched him beside the armpit. And Trudy loved the whole thing. As Mrs. Simon Spieger she'd become a connoisseur in showmanship. This she really appreciated — not just that Letarpo made such an ebullient, handsomely weathered little Balkan barber; but also that a very private compliment was being paid to the very private fact of Ronnie's paternity. She was sure that Letarpo knew; he had to, if he was as close to Nick as everybody said. Letarpo knew, and Letarpo cooperated. The Letarpo apartment and the Letarpo personality, two extravaganzas, were produced for her each Monday, so that on the fringe, in the shadow, Ronnie could see his father Nick and she and Nick glimpse each other briefly. Once a week the absence in her life received deft, prestigious treatment and could continue to be borne.

"You going to leave this lousy Junior here a little while?"

119

Letarpo said. He made believe he'd caught an insect in Ronnie's hair, smelled it, threw it down and stepped on it.

"Nannie won't be back till four," Trudy said, smiling. She said it every Monday.

"Sshshsh! Senate shoving off!" Letarpo said.

"They leave some ice cream?" Ronnie said, sweetly.

"Shshshsh!" Letarpo said. His scissors clicked very soft, slow, conspiratorial clicks. Judging from the sounds out in the gallery, there were about four senators with wives saying their goodbys. But the only voice Trudy heard distinctly was Petite Paulette's.

Paulette was a fly in the Monday ointment, a minor bug, though equipped with a piercing chirp.

"Thank you!" Petite Paulette was saying. "No — no, it doesn't hurt, it just looks so awful — thank you and Mrs. Lantzen! . . . And thank you, Senator Mill," Petite Paulette was saying, "No, don't you try to be polite about it! It's an eyesore and I deserve it! But thank you for coming! . . . Not at all, the pleasure was ours," Petite Paulette was saying. "Oh no, how were *you* responsible? . . . I leaned too close to it! My own silly fault! . . . Anyway, such a pleasure, even more than in Washington," Petite Paulette was saying. "Oh, it'll be a lesson to me! . . . Huh? My, that's too *funny*, Senator!"

Followed by little rapt peals of little-Southern-girl laughter. The first time Trudy had heard this sound was the first time she'd met Petite Paulette, whom Nick was escorting at some Interfaith luncheon. Petite Paulette had lost the heel of her left pump and did her chirp act looking for it barestockinged and trilled a high C as she stepped on an ice cube. Trudy had also heard the sound on Fifth Avenue, where the Simon Spiegers had run into the same odd twosome just as the wind had blown Petite Paulette's hat under a taxi. The men, Simon and Nick, had vied after it, despite Petite Paulette's chirps to let it go. And now the laughter-cries tinkled away in the gallery until Petite Paulette herself tripped into the room. On she twittered about a small singed rent above her bosom.

"From the steak *flambé!*" she cried. "Would you believe it?"

Petite Paulette was everything Trudy despised in women: the helplessness coutured exactly to male requirements; the pretty pathos, the lipsticked flutter, the professional girlsieness with which she'd do everything and anything: pour tea, spread legs, stroke beards.

"Ronnie's hair!" cried Petite Paulette. "Can I keep a lock?" And bent to pick one up.

"Costs a nickel," Letarpo said, snipping. "A deal? Want to call the lawyers?"

"Oh, you!" Petite Paulette said.

Trudy had to admit that this time P. P. didn't look like a kewpie blonde just taken out of cold storage. She was very tanned, enough to make a good contrast with the overrinsed hair and the ever-so-feminine pink print.

"Trudy!" Petite Paulette said. "How are you?"

"Hi," Trudy said. "Are you limping a little?"

"Skiing!" P. P. said. "I'll never learn the parallel turn! After three years! . . . Don't you dare look at my *flambé* hole!"

"Hey, everybody," Nick said, coming in. Actually, P. P.'s presence was another factor that helped Trudy face Nick coolly. Next to P. P. she felt like a very controlled cool customer.

"How's the Congressman?"

She raised her hand in a man-to-man long-distance salute that precluded a hello kiss. Next she gathered up her handbag with an emphasis not lost on the butler. He went to get her coat.

"I'm off on my errands," she said.

"We got to finish the hair," said Letarpo, the barber from Dubrovnik.

"Can I baby-sit the baby?" Nick asked the ritual question. He asked it every Monday.

"All right," Trudy said. She said it every Monday. "Nanny's due back at four, to pick him up for skating." She went to kiss Ronnie. " 'By, darling. See you at dinner."

"I sure would like to have my banana Senator ice cream," Ronnie said with model sweetness.

"Your Mama's kissing you!" Letarpo said. "You hold still! My Mama's kissing *me* — I am still! In a minute I go skiing myself."

"You going to be as tanned as Nick?" she heard Ronnie say, just as she was waving goodby all around. Which meant that she left about two seconds too late.

The question and the too-lateness didn't really strike her until the day was further gone. Her taxi jumped red lights all the way up Park Avenue, radio jiving. It went fast enough for Trudy to squeeze in a visit to her oldsters, overdue anyway. And when she got out at United Craftsmen Retirement Home, the house seemed like a continuation of the cab, with bass fiddles and drums thumping from gray windows.

But Mr. Lissberg of 4A didn't appreciate that at all. He remembered of course that Trudy had married Simon Spieger yet seemed too distracted at first to recall Trudy's name. He was still getting about fairly well with his supermarket cart, but there was no flute sticking out of his jacket pocket. All the lamps were turned on in the apartment and the dowdiness of their shades and the yellow of the electric light made the living room seem barer, drearier than it probably was. From the antenna of the TV set hung a black cloth.

He'd put up the black flag as a protest, Mr. Lissberg said. To show the manager if he ever came. Because the TV was dead and the repairman said it couldn't be fixed due to the hepcats that had moved into the building. Their electric mandolins were blowing the fuses. They were playing drumsticks on the radiators. It banged right into Mr. Lissberg's ears at night. They played so loud they scared the dawn away. And the manager didn't come because the hepcats paid him off.

"Mr. Lissberg," Trudy said. "I wouldn't be surprised if the University — that's your landlord, as you know — I wouldn't be surprised if they put music students in vacancies as a kind of pressure. But we are starting our own institution, and we'll take over this whole north part of the campus next year —"

His bathroom ceiling was all moldy and wet, Mr. Lissberg said; sometimes it got so bad he had to obey nature's call under an umbrella.

"We will take title by next year, Mr. Lissberg —"

Yes, Mr. Lissberg said. The lights went out when they were turned on, and sometimes they came on in the middle of the night.

"Come with me, Mr. Lissberg," Trudy said. Playing the part of the supermarket cart, Trudy supported him to the window looking out north. "Do you see that building site over there? All the cranes? Where the Ear and Nose Hospital used to be on Hundred

Ninetieth Street? Remember that? Well, they're building Interfaith University there now, and we're running that and we'll take over your building too, except we're going to maintain it better — now do you feel better?"

Oh yes, Mr. Lissberg said. Except right now the water was coming out funny from the tap. Mr. Elinsky had seen a hepcat put drugs in the water tower on the roof. There was a chemical in the water made the roaches act crazy. They were running around in circles. Mr. Lissberg was scared to kill them now.

"Well, we'll do something about it soon enough," Trudy said.

Yes, Mr. Lissberg said. There was a hepcat walking through the lobby all the time with a balloon tied to his big toe.

"Will you write me a note?" Trudy said. "Not about the balloon but about noise conditions and the lack of maintenance? You can write it in big printed letters, if that's easier, as long as you sign it in your regular signature."

"Oh, Mrs. Spieger," Mr. Lissberg said as they got up. "The worst is the TV. I missed your husband speaking on Moses because the TV is broken. It's broken all over the house. I told everybody it's got to be fixed in time for Mr. Spieger because his wife has done so much. This new colored handyman we got, I think they paid him off to wreck the TV."

"Well, we'll have to see about the TV too," Trudy said.

At the door there was a difficulty. Mr. Lissberg's police-lock rod had dug itself too deeply into the floor and couldn't be disengaged at first.

"I'll try the Building Workers Union," Trudy said. "Maybe they'll go to bat for you again."

"Thank you!" Mr. Lissberg said, supporting himself on the police lock rod. "God bless you!"

"I'll see you soon," Trudy said. Where was his flute? "Cheer up."

But suddenly there was no cheer in Trudy herself. Mr. Lissberg depressed her, but in the university library elevator she suffered devastation. The elevator had a mirror under a harsh futuristic light. It trapped her. She looked lousy. Pale, puffy, and the huge mane only magnified the paleness. Some contrast to Nick.

And then, as she stepped from the elevator, Ronnie's question

123

came down on her — Ronnie's question to Letarpo when Letarpo had said he'd go skiing. *You going to be as tanned as Nick?* She hadn't looked closely at Nick. It was her policy not to. But no doubt Nick was tanned. No doubt beautifully tanned like Petite Paulette; no doubt in the same place. Letarpo's Alpine paradise where she'd heard you could even summer-ski on glaciers, no doubt those two had bronzed and cuddled together in some such idyll. A wonderful thing to contemplate; especially for a pale-face struggling with police locks.

It was one of those grin-and-bear-it days: The first person she ran into at the university library was Jennifer.

"Jenn!"

It was the same old Jennifer with hair stringing down her thin cheeks, just her face a little harder under the green eyeshade.

"Hello, Trudy."

"My God, are you working in the library now?"

"It's temporary. They don't like to give radicals anything that leads to tenure."

"Those bastards! Just because you were in on a couple of demonstrations? Are you sure?"

"I don't care. I'm splitting for Israel."

"I'll be damned," Trudy said. "You know I wrote you a couple of times."

"I moved. I guess they didn't forward."

"Listen, we've got to see each other. How are you?"

"Not as well as you."

"You should only know," Trudy said. "Right now I'm chasing after the head librarian here."

"Oh yes, of course," Jennifer said.

"It's about the transfer of the Simon Spieger Collection to Interfaith University, messy details," Trudy said.

"The head librarian isn't in," Jennifer said.

It was one of those days. "Damn!" Trudy said. "He said I didn't need an appointment."

"I'm sure *you* wouldn't, but we're closing," Jennifer said. "New hours. We close at four and the head office is always gone earlier. But it's nice to run into you."

"We've got to see each other," Trudy said.

"Remember Elihu?" Jennifer said. "Rabbi Elihu Boneman?"

"Are you kidding? Has he still got the Pancho Villa mustaches?"

"He and I, we're in the same organization. It's called 'The Three Generation Aliyah' and it's pretty exciting. The idea is setting up emigration groups to Israel, but multi-age level, grandparents, parents, children, starting in a camp here, ending in a kibbutz in Israel."

"Good," Trudy said.

"We've got it all together, except the money," Jennifer said. "If your husband would give a reading, or just give us a tape of a reading, it wouldn't have to be in person, we could raise enough to start things going."

"If you want that from Simon, take it up with Simon."

The moment she said it, she knew she shouldn't have, not that way. But did her old friend Jenn have to be so snide? The Spiegers as a team were now as well known as Simon alone.

"Of course anything from you both would be great," Jennifer said. "I just didn't want to involve both of you, since both of you must be so busy."

"Oh, the hell with busy!" Trudy said, still feeling bad. "Can you grab a bite with me for a few minutes?"

"I have cataloguing duty after we close," Jennifer said. "That's another couple of hours."

"Damn," Trudy said. "I've got to see about a present for my son. Will you write me? Interfaith already has an office at One West Fifty-seventh, easy to remember. Will you write me and we'll set something up?"

"Yes." Jennifer looked very green under the eyeshade and her skin was still broken out, and Trudy, who wasn't much less pale-green nor entirely without little bumps on the complexion, wondered what kind of a contrast they both made to tanned, smooth, Nick-cuddling Petite Paulette of the bronzing ski slopes.

"I'm sorry the head librarian isn't in," Jennifer said.

"Who cares?" Trudy said. "Write me your phone number! We'll get together!"

She gave Jennifer a very quick kiss and ran out to catch a taxi to F. A. O. Schwartz.

Some days are like that. F. A. O. Schwartz was outrageous. They had only one gift box that matched the striped king-doll in size and design, and for that plus some measly wrapping paper they charged three dollars. After Trudy was through there, her watch said 4:35. She was so early because of the library closing; but if she knew Nanny McCoover, Nanny had picked up Ronnie very late at the Waldorf to take him skating. There was no point going to the Rockefeller Skating Rink because those two wouldn't even be there yet.

Trudy stood among the swirling crowds on the corner of 58th and Fifth, and she hated every swirler. It isn't pleasant to flounder alone amidst so many happy purposes. All the lover-couples had ski tans. Across the street was the Fleur de Lys Beauty Spa. Something inside Trudy said, What the hell. She jaywalked across Fifth Avenue, brakes screaming left and right. She walked into the Fleur de Lys Beauty Spa.

"Do you have sunlamp treatments?"

"Oh yes, ma'am," said Mr. Overmelodious. "But if I might suggest, only after a cream bath. In justice to your skin — and hair."

"All right, all right," she said. She knew the wind had messed up her already messy hair. He didn't have to rub it in.

"How long would it take?"

"Oh, no waiting, ma'am. Monday is our light day."

She walked out with a comb-out and a sunlamp facial and her cheeks glowed. It was nearly six by then. At Rockefeller Center the ice was being cleaned for the evening session. In the skate house a few people were left, unlacing their boots. No Ronnie. No Nanny. But an attendant pointed a finger at her.

"Are you looking for your little boy?"

"Yes!"

"Mrs. Spieger?"

"Yes!"

"Here. You should call this number."

It was her own Central Park West number and they let her use the skate house phone.

"I have taken the boy to your apartment in the bus," Tante said without so much as a hello.

"From skating?" Trudy said. "Where's Nanny?"

"She telephoned. She had an automobile problem in Connecti-

cut. They wanted to send the boy home with a chauffeur. But he
has to learn the bus."

"That bitch!" Trudy said. "Automobile problem! *Who* wanted
to send him home with a chauffeur?"

"This Mr. Anatole."

"You mean Nick Antone?"

"The politician. But it is not good for a boy."

There was a cough at the other end. Tante still believed in open
windows, despite her bronchitis lately.

"You shouldn't have come out specially for Ronnie," Trudy
said. "Can I talk to him?"

"He is asleep. The nurse is here now."

"Damn!" she said. "I wanted to give him a present."

"He was very tired. He was on the plane with you today. Are you
flying off tonight?"

"Simon needs me in Chicago," Trudy said.

"Well, good flight. I am sure you know what it is you are doing."

"I'll be back the day after tomorrow for the rest of the week. I'll
see you and Ronnie then."

"Yes. Good flight, Trude."

"Tante —"

She had hung up.

Some days are like that. Trudy hung up too. She thanked the
skating people for letting her borrow the phone. She was usually
talking on borrowed phones. Everybody else was either at home at
this hour or rushing home. Everybody else had *something*. Tante
had righteousness and many plants, Simon had spirituality and a
whole big university being assembled just for him. Old Antone had
manners, monkeys, whatnot. Nick had the conquest of Washington
before him, not to speak of ipsi-pipsi Paulette. Even Nanny
McCoover had her little roadhouse fucks she called automobile
problems.

And Trudy? Trudy had a gift-wrapped package with no child
accessible to give it to. She also had cheeks darkened by a fag
sunlamp with no sexy ski-holiday preceding. She also had a lot of
cunning, dynamic, heart-pounding loneliness. . . . What was it all
for? Dean of students at thirty-two?

Some days are like that.

But then, suddenly, she knew how to get the better of that damn day. She was only a few blocks from the Waldorf. But she took a cab because she couldn't stand those happy crowds. The Towers elevator man widened his eyes at her, either because he'd never seen Trudy bust in like that or because he wasn't used to seeing her hair so nicely done. The butler, cupping a cigarette in his palm, said, "Uh. Mr. Letarpo has been driven to the airport."

"Yes, naturally," Trudy said and brushed past him.

She swept into the living room, jostled the olive tree, spat at the Degas, poked into the empty dining room, burst into the den, where she'd never been before. And here, shirtsleeved and piquantly disheveled as she knew he would be, Nick Antone, Jr., rose from a leather couch.

"Trudy!"

She didn't put Ronnie's gift on the cocktail table, but at the end of the couch, where she had a view of the open door into the next room.

"It's a gift for my son," she said. "Could someone give it to him tomorrow?"

"Sure. I'll be here."

"No need for you to bother. Letarpo could arrange it."

"Tarp's gone off to ski."

"Oh yes, same place where you and Paulette had fun?"

"Paulette," he said. "With her ankle?"

"You shouldn't lead such a frail thing down rough slopes," she said.

"Oh, for God's sake," Nick said. "Tell that to her father. It happened with him."

"Oh come on," she said.

But the fact was that the next room, indeed the bedroom, only showed a bed cover covered with books and papers, and that Nick held a foolscap pad in his hand.

"I've got the cops' communion breakfast tomorrow," he said. "And they wrote me such a lousy speech."

He was really all alone, working. No Paulette.

"I didn't know you'd still be here," she said.

"I can't use my New York office till next week," he said. "The painters never finish. You do look nice."

She felt her skin contracting as though her whole body had been under the sunlamp. He looked so rumpled-innocent-attractive-good and he was so goddamn bloody tactful. She was making such a fool of herself, she was so obviously lying in her teeth. And he did nothing to capitalize on her vulnerability. No easy wit at her expense. No Nick Antone cleverness. He just waited and inclined his handsome head, almost in humbleness.

"Oh Nick," Trudy said. "She is such a silly girl."

"But — that goes without saying," he said.

There was no breath in her now. Trudy was choking hot in her coat.

"What do you and Ronnie do together?" she said. "Do you play games?"

She hoped for recovery through some safe subject. But of course Ronnie wasn't safe. Nothing was safe.

"I'm proud of Ronnie," he said, toneless. "I never see you alone. I don't get a chance to tell you."

"Listen," she said because he was coming toward her. "I just checked on that building where they want to evict those old people, the University should be required to have their — their maintenance personnel live in the building, not crazy music students, you should put that in your bill. . . ."

"Yes," he said, close.

"Or use your old influence with the union till we take over the building."

"Yes," he said. "You don't need a sunlamp."

"I'm an idiot," she said. "I shouldn't have come here."

"Me too," he said, toneless. "I should have come to you. I should have come begging a long time ago."

She was thunderstruck. If this happened, it should happen under more meaningful, purposeful circumstances.

"I have to fly to Chicago," she said.

Without unbuttoning her coat he parted it so that some buttons broke and put his hands inside and pressed her harshly against him and pulled apart from her again. Their faces stared at each other, both with tears in their eyes. And from the time he shut the door with his foot, still staring at her wet-eyed, from the moment the door clicked shut, to the end of his life, they were together.

IV

❧ 1 ❧

Had Simon ever guessed? He must have, after a while. And he fought back in Simon fashion. He became sweetly resourceful in clouding all her attempts to do something about a marriage turned obsolescent.

Obsolescence, in fact, was a mild word for it, the year before the opening of Interfaith University. Taxiing to a session of the University Organizing Board, she managed to corner him, sort of. Actually a taxi was the place to broach the subject. Elsewhere Simon kept too busy either with setting up his President's Office at Interfaith, or with his painting which he'd started again, or — most cunning — with work on his inaugural address. He'd asked her to write it jointly with him and agreed to let her express many of her ideas on inner-city problems regardless of how they'd sit with tory archbishops or chief rabbis. Whenever she said, "Simon, let's talk about us," he'd veer into a fond nonsequitur. "My darling," he'd say, "this point in your speech draft, it is the most insightful heresy. We must give it more room. Will you flesh it out a little?" After which she'd feel uncomfortable about pressing the end of their marriage.

But in the taxi he had no such subterfuge.

"About us," she said. "Shall we try the separation this summer?"

"My Trudy," he said. "We work so well together."

"We'll keep working together. Maybe even better once we face it that the other thing — the other relationship is over."

"My Trudy, some things really start when one thinks they are over."

"All right," she said. "Let's find out about that through a trial separation this summer."

"Maybe," he said. "If you'll visit me now and then."

"Simon, then it wouldn't be a separation —"

But the taxi stopped. They had arrived. She firmly intended to bring it up again after the meeting and this time really see the issue through. But it turned out that they weren't alone in any taxi afterward. The big Letarpo limousine waited for them and for Letarpo (who'd come in at the end of the meeting), and Ronnie sat up front next to Yussuf, the Macedonian prince. Ronnie had used the limo to go to the airport and meet his old friend, in for a quick visit from his studies in London. The two were conducting quite a boisterous reunion.

Not that Trudy minded that. No, what irritated was that merriment bubbled in back too, where she sat between her husband and Letarpo. Joshing volleyed back and forth across her. Simon was being perversely humorous. As if everything were *tout va bien* tra-la-la, and no hard decisions had to be made about his married life.

"No, no. No deal with you," Simon said to Letarpo. "You are a dangerous person."

"What dangerous?" Letarpo said. "You give me the oil paper. I rent you cheap my whole Paris house, whole summer. Chokay?"

"No, I take a nice room at the Hotel Pont Royal," Simon said. "I hide my oil paper there."

"Nice big house," Letarpo said. "Eight broom closets, five bidets. Chokay, you rent it free."

"No," Simon said.

"No?" Letarpo threw up his arms in exuberant helplessness; the car veered him against Trudy. "Excuse me. He says no. You know your husband here? This is a blackmailer."

"Because I reject eight broom closets, I blackmail?" Simon said.

"I'm talking to your wife," Letarpo said. "This great sociology painter, he's got a paper saying he's fifty-fifty with me, the first little oil field I ever had, southern Macedonia. Someday he's going to hit me with it.

"Maybe I'll make a painting of it," Simon said.

"Blackmailer," Letarpo said. "He's going to exhibit his fifty-

fifty at the Louvre! He never told you about this fifty-fifty we made in jail?"

"I guess he didn't," Trudy said.

"Nothing about the fifty-fifty when the Nazis put us in the same hole? Chey, Prince Yussuf, your father never told you about that, when the Nazis occupied him?"

"My father tells me very little, sir," the prince said, and there was laughter up front.

"You will hear it told now, with much distortion," Simon said, smiling at Trudy.

"First I cut his hair in jail. Excuse me." Letarpo's arm reached across Trudy to Simon's hair. "Like this. I pull his hair down like this. Barber him tough. Then I say to the Nazis, 'You see this tough Jew here? Very tough. Smart! You know those oil fields you occupy, southern Macedonia? The one I own? That tough Jew here, he owns fifty percent. You let him out with me, and this smart Jew will make Morgenthau —' You remember Morgenthau?"

"Oh yes," Trudy said.

" 'You let this tough Jew out with me and he'll make Morgenthau protect his oil. He'll make the Americans stop bombing the oil you occupy, believe me!' And the Nazis look at him with his hair cut tough. And they say, 'Oh boy. Yeah. Chokay.' I sign a paper saying he owns fifty percent, for the record —"

"I got the carbon," Simon said.

"Chokay, I give you my Paris house for the summer and you give back the fifty percent paper."

"I will make a still-life of the fifty-fifty," Simon said.

"Get out of here," Letarpo said. "This guy is worse than the Shah."

He gave Simon a vicious kick, which somehow never landed, and at the same time managed to kiss Trudy's hand. By the time they got out, Ronnie and the prince had run ahead into their building on Central Park West, each boy holding onto a strap of the prince's overnight bag. They vanished into the staircase entrance in the lobby. Simon and Trudy stood waiting for the elevator, alone.

"I'm not going to use his house in Paris," Simon said, still smiling. "It is too formal, in case you want to visit me."

She didn't want to visit him.

"Did Morgenthau really stop the bombing?" she said.

"I don't know if because of me. But somebody had sent Mr. Morgenthau my book."

"But the Allies really stopped the bombing?"

"It was a miracle. Everything in those days was a miracle, Trudy."

"Listen, about this summer," she said.

"There has never been a smuggler like my friend Tarp," Simon said. "Somehow they really stopped the bombing for a while. But the unbombed oil got to the partisans after Tarp was let out."

"That's pretty good," she said.

"He is also a very good hair cutter. Maybe if he cuts my hair in a way you like, you will visit me in Paris?"

"No," she said. "I haven't changed my mind about this summer. That's what I wanted to tell you."

"After the summer, then."

"Let's not rush things," she said.

By that time they were in their apartment; that is, in his studio, where he'd led her. His cousin Thérèse followed him with the cup of herb tea. No doubt Simon had led Trudy here because this was his place of strength. The huge window hardened and thinned the light as it fell on his new series of paintings on the wall. They were on conventional canvas now, showing spider nets, nearly all of them. Huge eyes were caught in those cobwebs, blue round eyes complete with lids and lashes, and the peculiar thing was that in the morning light each eye looked fierce and skulking like a spider; but toward evening, as it was getting now, the eyes would hollow out, hang helpless in the web, sucked dry like the husk of an insect long eaten. It was a marvelous trick. Which is exactly what Simon was himself.

"I thought the summer would give you enough respite from me," he said. He could stir a cup of tea with a very fine, wistful bitterness.

"Respite isn't the word," she said.

"No? . . . Then what would be the word?"

"I mean this summer would be a chance to sort of ease into the separation. With least harm to Ronnie. And we also ought to look at it from the viewpoint of the University."

"I don't understand, Trudy?"

"In terms of the credibility I'd lose as dean of students married to the University president."

"I am amazed," he said gently. "What can I say? You yourself wanted to be dean."

"Yes. Years ago. Life has gotten a lot more suspicious since then. It's a much tougher thing to get away with now. Didn't you sense the resistance to it at the meeting just now?"

"*You* could get away with it. Someone like you could." He was speaking softly, sadly, to his tea-stirring spoon. "But if you rise higher, yes, I agree with you. When you become provost, marriage to me would become an issue."

"*Provost?*" she said. "I am aiming for provost?"

"It may be one reason why you are bringing this up."

"You really figured that out!"

"I may be wrong. I am very clumsy with power politics."

"No, Simon. You could give a seminar in it!"

"I am wrong, then. Forgive me."

He had risen from the chair. Very slowly he walked to the couch and lay down with his cup. Not a drop of camomile was spilled, though he moved with eloquent haltingness. He had made her sound strident. He had also put her at a moral disadvantage. And practically speaking, she realized, he had her by the short hairs. The surest way to destroy a political future was for a woman to come to a politician after abandoning an entrenched saint. Especially the saint on this couch, who could project the loftiest victimization by just lying down with a cup of tea. Holding it with both hands yet.

"I admire your gesture," she said.

"I am sorry," he said softly.

They stared at each other. Ronnie burst into the room, arms full of white balls, followed by the prince.

"Excuse us! Please watch? I'm rehearsing for the end-of-term show!"

"Go ahead," Trudy said.

The prince sat down crosslegged on the floor and began to wail an Arabic tune. He was so lanky, he wasn't much less tall seated than Ronnie standing. Ronnie began to juggle five white balls to

137

his friend's melody. The five balls thinned into four without being dropped or palmed in any visible way. They kept rising and falling to the wail, became three, two, then one, and — all through the wailing and the devilish skill of the thing — Ronnie kept the innocence of his face, his freckle-eared, long-cheeked happy trance.

"Very good," she said, as the last ball vanished.

"Watch! Now I get the balls back!"

Ronnie ran over to the couch, to Simon Spieger, and pulled something out of Simon's breast pocket.

"Oh!" Simon said. "Marzipan!"

As a matter of fact, marzipan balls were Trudy's favorite. Ronnie ran over to her and pulled another such ball out of Trudy's pocketbook and put it in her mouth.

"Trying to make me fat, huh?"

"Aw, please! I practiced so much!"

Her teeth took the marzipan from his pale little fingers. She hugged him close, her slim quick sweet-blurring boychild, he moved so fast.

"Tomorrow you fly?" he said.

"Well, I better check on our place for our summer in Europe," she said. "Or can you do that with magic too?"

"You're not going to crash?"

"Silly," she said.

"If something terrible happens, you put my name in your pocket so you remember me when you wake up."

He had said that sort of thing before. This time he actually took something from his pocket and stuffed it into her handbag.

"For God's sakes," she said. She pulled it out of her bag. It was a picture postcard of the New York skyline on whose message side was written *My chiled is Ronnie* in a small but rather exquisitely looped hand in red ink.

"On the plane you put it in your dress," he said.

"Hey!" she said. "Come here! You don't know how to spell!"

Her mouth needed to give him a kiss. But he had suddenly blushed a vehement red, maybe because he'd acted like a mama's boy before his older friend. He grabbed Yussuf violently by the hand and ran with him away from the spider eyes, through the door.

Simon Spieger and Trudy were alone again in the excessive brightness of the room. She put the postcard in the passport wallet of her pocketbook.

"You see," Simon said from the couch. "Ronnie too — Ronnie would also be a very hard thing to give up."

"You wouldn't exactly give him up. You would see us on some regular basis. That would be part of the arrangement."

"Will you two come with me on my tour this summer?" Simon Spieger said.

"This summer?" she said. "I've already rented a place in Switzerland."

"I realize it would be a change of plans."

"But this summer you won't even be speaking in America," she said. "You don't need me in France."

"When don't I need you?" He sat up and put down his cup. "But you and Ronnie, you two go with me this summer, and we'll make the arrangement in fall. I let you go in the fall."

"You mean that?" she said.

He nodded. Very slowly he sank down on the couch again.

Of course Trudy had already planned her Swiss summer, had staked out a little flat for rent above an inn just outside St. Gallen. Four rooms with Wilhelm Tell wallpaper and a cast-iron sink and very high soft beds, and it was all slightly too good to come true; the idea of hiking with Ronnie and seeing Nick. Nick had promised to fly over for at least a couple of weekends while Congress was in session; after the recess he'd join them for more.

All that was out the window now. She'd have to be with Simon July and August in exchange for final freedom. Still she could save a fraction of the summer: two June weeks, the last two weeks before Ronnie's semester ended, when she'd just distract him from exams. They were also two very important weeks in which to be free for Nick. Those weeks Nick would be near Switzerland at the World Parliamentary Union at Luxembourg; and the little flat with the Wilhelm Tell wallpaper was available, and instead of hiking with Ronnie in July she'd be able to ski with Nick in June. Nick had arranged for them to ski the glacier on Letarpo's shoot at Bachberg, just across the border in Austria.

Apparently that was also a little too good to be true. Trudy got to St. Gallen all right. The little inn smelled of good strong tomato soup, and upstairs the flat glowed with lemon-oil cleanliness. But Nick got delayed in Washington. There was trouble with both his bills, the Minimum Wage and the Urban Housing Maintenance. On top of that, the good governor in Albany tried to gerrymander him out of the presidential picture, the convention being only a year away.

"*Bueno, bueno,*" Nick said to her over the phone. "So I'll run for secretary in my old Brotherhood Local. So I'll be presidential from Spanish Harlem."

But when he finally got to Luxembourg, to the World Parliamentary Union, he was six days late there, and too busy for jokes. Being an Antone and therefore something of an international name, he could barely avoid being named chairman; being a leftie, he had to push the resolutions on behalf of deputies jailed in Spain and Greece. Day after day he was in too deep over his ears, and couldn't come.

He couldn't come. She had to be alone. There was a sense of deprivation which somehow licensed her to accept all the sybaritic stuff Nick had arranged through Letarpo's people: the car picking her up every morning; Tony, the former downhill champ with the embarrassed pipe, waiting for her at lower Bachberg; Tony making the local ski-shop owner open the shop for her in June; Tony fitting her with the right buckle-on boots, the right fiberglass skis; the chair lift creaking into gear just for her and Tony; tons of machinery and hundreds of thousands of volts to lift just the two of them past the pines and the scrub pines towards the ice.

Nine thousand feet high, and still she didn't get altitude-sick as Tony had feared. On the contrary, she latched on to the parallel turn pretty fast. She did much better here than in Sugarbush last winter. Tony was so happy, his cheeks gave a leathery blush. He made her a red wine fondue at the lodge, which had a sauna and an indoor pool into which Tony had pumped water just for her. Probably it was the unconscionableness of the luxury which gave her a fillip. She was cheating back at the world that was cheating her. She missed Nick. Lately she'd missed Nick too much and too often. She resented him for that — but at least he wouldn't laugh next time he saw her on skis. She also missed her little Ronnie. She telephoned New York, and the governess told her that Ronnie was working and practicing so hard for the end-of-term show, the school nurse had prescribed a mild sedative. When Ronnie came on the line he sounded fine, maybe a little guarded, as he often did on the phone with her. After he hung up, she wanted to fly home. Sometimes, at such moments for instance, total disorientation ambushed her. She mistrusted Simon's promise of a separation in the fall, mistrusted herself, her future with the University, her ability to do some real good — she even mistrusted Nick. Yet when she stood high up in the mountain glory again the next day, air like cut glass, all uncertainty blew away. She tilted down into the steep; she carved spraying curves out of the snow and let the glacier freshness sting her face. Who the hell ever said the world was hopeless? . . . Whooom!

On the third day she had charley horses in both thighs — a sign she used the right skiing muscles, according to Tony. On the fourth day she forgot to cream her ears after creaming the rest of her face against the high Alpine sun. She came home with the skin of her earlobes hanging down in red shreds. Tony drove all the way to Innsbruck for an ointment. By the sixth day her muscles adjusted and the innkeeper no longer crossed himself at the sight of her fried ears. Towards the end of the second week, she stopped using makeup. She hardly needed cold cream. She wasn't just tanned. She was burnished by the altitude, the sun, the pine-tart air, the privileged loneliness. She couldn't wait for Nick's expression when he saw her.

She couldn't wait for that, though their two weeks in Europe had shrunk to taking the Swissair flight together to New York. Their departure day he had to spend in Zurich, for reasons so sudden and mysterious he couldn't say on the telephone. And what was his expression when they met as arranged at the Zurich airport bar? The expression had nothing to do with Trudy's looks: a fast roll of dark Nick eyes meaning, "*Oh boy, watch out.*" He was talking to another man.

"Governor," Nick said, "this is Trudy Spieger. The Spiegers are old friends."

"Of course," the governor said. "So nice to see you. That's my luck. I don't run into any lovely ladies till the moment I shove off."

He bowed to Trudy and poked Nick in the chest and looked

smaller and fatter than in the photographs. "We work together, huh, *paisan?*" he said to Nick and walked out with a wave; at the other end of the bar a whole retinue walked out after him.

Nick did something reckless. They were all still in eyeshot of each other, but he put his arm round Trudy's shoulder and steered her to a row of public phone booths.

"We make a call," he said. "Your ears are a little red." He asked the operator for a New York number she didn't recognize, collect.

"Some hello," she said, standing with him in the booth, their nearness solid in the crowded unreality of the airport. He wore his Norfolk jacket and a scarf, very handsome-*léger*. His jawbones twitched inside the skin.

"Governor making trouble?" she said.

"Oh, this is a marvelous man," he said, leaning into the phone.

"Is it the gerrymander?"

"Gerrymander? Baby stuff!" Nick said. "This is a major personality. Presidential timber. . . . Hello? . . . I'm still with you, operator. . . . This is a big insightful brain that looks ahead. He knows they'll nominate somebody Goldwaterish, you know? Some damn Western piece of reaction, and for balance they'll need an Eastern liberal on the old team, like this marvelous governor with the common touch. Hear how beautifully he pronounced *paisan?*"

"He got you all tensed up," she said.

"It's an experience, listening to this great liberal pronounce *paisan*. He must have a voice coach."

"I wish him boils on his balls," she said. "I wish I knew Yiddish curses. Maybe we could have had one day on the glacier together, except for that liberal."

"Oh, after he fills the Senate vacancy with Nick Antone he'll be a certified liberal."

"What?"

"Yes, sir. That's what he thinks."

"*No!*" she said. "Is that what this is all about?"

"Our marvelous governor was in Paris," Nick said. "And he flew here specially, just to lay this thing on me, that's how liberal he is."

"That bastard!" she said. "He tried to gerrymander you!"

"So once I'm kicked upstairs out of the district it'll gerrymander easier. And he's getting me out of the House just when my bills are getting through. And he thinks upstate will kill me in the primaries when I'm up for Senate reelection. Just before convention time. Great man!"

"Say *No!* to the bastard!" she said. "A big no with all the reasons at a big news conference!"

"Ah," Nick said. "He's too marvelous for that. He wants to announce it Monday. And he's got it all checked out. I have no forum between now and Monday."

"Create a forum! Call a press conference!"

"Create a forum, and this marvelous governor will say, 'This was my boy! I fly to Zurich special to make my boy Senator! Make my boy a liberal voice in the upper chamber! My *paisan! Mio caro bambino!* And my boy turns around on me! The boy is jealous, he wants the White House, he drums up a news conference against Papa! *Malo, malo.* Now I've got to gerrymander my boy double!! ... Marvelous man."

"He'll get his," she said. "Don't let him tense you up —"

"Nobody gets a marvelous man like that. He even made sure to spring this on me in Europe on a weekend. So I can't reach my people in New York. . . . Hello? Hello, Janey!" Nick was talking to his secretary Janey. "Well, where else would you be? First thing you do is charge this collect to the office. Second, hang on, I must explain to you that the world is a friendly and loving place with especially lovable governors, and the only trouble is that the Speaker has a cold. . . . Hello? I said that the Speaker, the Speaker of the House, he was at the World Parliamentary Union with me, he has mucus in the sinus, Janey, one hundred two degrees fever. In Luxembourg. He'll cancel *Face the Nation* Sunday, he can't make the plane. . . . You follow? . . . Even at your mother's you got the notepad with you? Janey, not even the lovable governor deserves you. Now we have this nice pal at *Face the Nation,* remember? Pal Freddie? . . . That's right. And since this is such a warm loving world, we ought to help out a pal and be nice to a needy TV show. Right? So you tell Pal Freddie I'll pinch-hit as guest though it's not at all sure about my accepting the Senate appointment. . . . Hello? . . . Oh, yes, that's exactly what I said, *the governor's offer to appoint me,* but I'm not at all sure whether I can accept that kindness — you heard right, appoint me to the

143

Senate, I want you to hear me right with your notepad there. But if they'd ask me on that on *Face the Nation*, I'd first of all say how much the state legislature loves the marvelous governor. And I'd have to say I'm not so sure about accepting the appointment. Know why? Because I'd have to presume on their great love for the governor. I could only accept the appointment if for the sake of that love they'd promise not to gerrymander my district. . . . You got that? . . . And that's not the only unfair presumption I'd have to make. Because there's also a group of about thirty congressmen, upstate and New England, they also love the governor so dearly. Now if I left the House at the governor's request I'd have to invoke their love for him too, to support my bills I'd leave behind, the Minimum Wage and the Urban Maintenance, even if those bills go against their grain or the dear governor's. And that wouldn't be a fair presumption, now would it? No more fair than the idea that the governor is playing it presidentially, sidetrack me as a nowhere junior senator. . . . Tell Freddie that. Tell him the weather was lousy in Luxembourg, but the smoked trout is great, and that's really my message till tomorrow. . . . 'By, sweet. Have a good dinner with Mom."

He yanked down the phone hook. The receiver he kept in his hand. He did a couple of small dance steps out of the phone booth and back into it again, holding the receiver like a gun; his face had suddenly taken on a brute chewing-gum dash. He could have been a Sicilian Mafioso. She hated that. Of course she knew it was Nick's way of unwinding. On his shapely pale-freckled hands with the slim fingers the veins stood out thick and blue as though something old had been painted on something young. The muscles of his jaw worked, making the white scar come and go.

"Get out of politics," she said. "It's not worth it."

He still aimed the receiver, mowing down the airport crowd while doing a faint dance to the Muzak tango.

"Come on, let's catch our plane," she said.

"Lovable governor reserved me a room at the Hilton here," he said. "To crown me senator in. I got my luggage there."

The elevator Muzaked the same tango and so did his room, which was really a big suite, wall-to-wall beige cubism cluttered with typical male sloppiness à la Antone, shirts on an undone bed, valises spilled out into bathrooms, and the only thing that wasn't characteristically Nick was Nick. He was still moving in absorbed dance steps.

"Let's pack," she said. "We want to make the plane."

He packed, but like a tango-zombie, in a very slow, abstracted rhythm. She didn't know how to snap him out of it.

"Nick!" she said. "I know it sounds trivial right now but I want to get to New York in the morning. I'd like to get in a day's rest — I want to be fresh for Ronnie's end-of-term party!"

"Our lovable governor thinks you're nifty," he said tonelessly, still half-tangoing.

"Oh, fart the governor." She was folding an incredibly crumpled Nick sweater. "Just get your bills passed," she said, "and then the hell with it. The hell with the White House."

"Yup. The hell with it," he said. "All the noble losers say that. That's something I ought to practice: 'The hell with it.' "

"Who's a loser?" she said. "Get back to the union. They're still dying for you! And I'll be free in the fall, we'll have time for each other! It could be so terrific!"

He was taking off her blouse.

"Hey!" she said. "It's an hour to boarding time!"

Her skin felt the young hands with the old veins.

"You've got your TV on Sunday!" she said. "You too, you ought to get to New York in time!"

"Yeah," he said. All of a sudden he was alive, the zombie gone. "Look," he said. "She's not tanned there. She didn't take any sun-baths like that. She's been a good girl."

"We'll miss the night plane, Nick."

"But she's got red ears. . . ."

And it was already flowing through her, between her fingers, lips and thighs, the sweet and powerful Nick disorder.

The Swissair dayflight to New York took off at one P.M., so she should have known when he tickled her awake before eight in the morning. Before *eight,* when they'd spent very little of the night sleeping. Nick, who never needed rest, was already a jovial blur in a Norfolk jacket, aromatic with fresh-shavedness. Trudy was simply too groggy to understand what was up. Her watch seemed to be wrong and she was too numb to question just why they had to rush off instantly, no time even for breakfast.

All she could do in the taxi was to get that bobbing face in the mirror into some sort of human semblance. Her tan masked her fatigue and at least she was in the good part of the monthly cycle. The only thing she could really focus on was that she seemed to have lost both her hairbands.

But the rush of wind on the open airfield jarred her awake.

"This is a helicopter!" she said.

"Fastest way to Tarp's glacier," Nick said.

"*Oh no!*"

"So I want to do some skiing too, you mind?"

He led her to the open bubble.

"But I have my stuff checked through with Swissair!"

He pointed. Her luggage was stacked in the back of the copter together with his, thank God. He must have arranged that while she slept.

"But I must be in New York tomorrow! Ronnie's end-of-term party! And you've got a TV —"

"So we're booked on the nightflight tonight. Say hello to your old friend Tony."

Yes there was Letarpo's ski guide Tony again, and there they were in a glass bubble vibrating above Lake Zurich toward the unreality of white peaks, drinking the coffee that Tony had had the foresight to bring in a thermos. In her daze the coffee was Trudy's salvation, but Nick smelled it with much alarm.

"*Madrrrracula mia!*" Nick said. "Tony-coffee! Watch out! Remember, Tony? Long time ago, my Papa the General, he leased the whole mountain from Tarp? For a shoot — boom boom? I was *this* big? A *bambino?* Remember the coffee you made us then?"

"Och," Tony said, blushing his leathery blush above an alp. "Long time ago, sir."

"Goat's milk! That's what Tony used for cream in that coffee! Tony had a special coffee-goat. *Café au lait de chèvre!*"

"Oh, but no more," Tony said. "Cow now."

"Well, let's see," Nick said, tasting from the thermos. "Uhu. Mostly cow now. Little bit goat still. Tiny bit pig."

They laughed and whirred together in the sun. Nick gave the bottle mouth a tiny kiss before handing the thermos back to

146

Trudy. His thumb and forefinger were lightly around her neck, the collar of his Norfolk jacket turned up. He'd never been a zombie; never an assassin in a phone booth. He was all European playboy, with a peasant's vivacity and a princeling's fun.

Of course she knew why. She knew her Nick. He liked to fight any stressful complication imposed by others with a stressful gambol of his own, almost like fighting fire with fire. In the teeth of all good sense he'd produced this day partly as therapy for himself; and partly by way of making amends for their missed two skiing weeks together. But there didn't seem to be any calculation in it at all, just happy outbursts.

"Hey!" he said. "It's June! Hey, Tony, when I was a youngster, that chamois mummy, remember? That was in June! . . . You *patzer*, you forgot? The chamois-mummy leading up her kids to the best water up on top? You told us they always do that in June?"

"Yes, right, June," Tony said.

"But you don't remember how we followed the chamois-mummy? That's how we got to that fantastic spring. Hey, Trudy, you drank *nothing* if you didn't drink that — you wait, *ragazza!* Hey, I think I see some chamois now! See those dots? One of 'em is a mummy-dot. Make him go down lower, Tony, so we can see!"

"He is going down," Tony said. "We are here."

Bachberg Lodge was tangy as ever with the smells of firewood, ski wax, and bacon; but now, in this dizzy way, the dream had come true. Nick was with her. The best Nick she ever knew.

She stopped in the ski room downstairs to pick some bootlaces as replacement for her lost hairbands when she heard his yell.

"*Madrrracula mia!*"

Down the stairs he came shooting in his shorts. He waved a pair of ski pants through whose split seams he'd shoved his fist.

"I forgot! Three years since I've been to this crazy place! Goddamn Tarp played a joke!"

She smiled, though three years ago must have been the Petite Paulette era.

"Don't look at me with those torn pants," she said. "I never heard of needle and thread. I'm not a nice girlsie."

"*Hey, Tony! I need pants!*"

He got pants, even if they were so baggy on his slimness they

147

were slightly Chaplinesque. Laughing, they ran across the meadow to the copter. They had only one day; for one day they couldn't bother with the slowness of the ski lift. They flew up.

They jumped out on top, snapped on their skis, breathed deeply, slowly, to accommodate the altitude — and it was almost too much. It wasn't only that he stood beside her in the brown taper of his sweater and his baggy blue pants. It was everything. The luck with the weather, the air, the glacier. The glacier had changed incredibly in the forty-eight hours since she'd seen it last. No more smudged snow at the edges. All melted. Instead, the ice was framed by long cascades of flowers that must have shot up and bloomed overnight, silver-green leaves, topped by little golden blossoms, thousands of them, making the boulders more rugged and the ice creamier and filling the swirl of peaks and valleys all around with an amazing scent.

She pushed off after him, as fast as he, not skiing as smooth-legged, of course, not leaning so boldly into the turns, but keeping close, careering round the same moguls, catching the rhythm of his curves, aligning her hips and knees into the speed, listening to the hiss of ski against harsh glacier snow, listening to the sough of wind in the woods below, the scented sough, and to something else, something like balalaika music, feeling the charley horse in her thighs again, but not badly, when they finally came to a stop.

"Look at her, she's good," Nick said.

She knotted the bootlaces more tightly round her hair.

"Another two minutes of this and I'd be dead," she said after catching her breath.

"Does the music bother you?"

"My God, I thought I was imagining it."

He jabbed his ski pole at the loudspeakers on the lift stanchions.

"I had that switched on in case Janey cables on my college talk."

"What college talk?"

"Warren College. In case there's a hitch about it."

He grinned at her and she knew that she was meant to be surprised.

"You mean in addition to the TV?"

"I got bumped by LBJ from *Face the Nation*," he said, and pushed off so fast the only way she could catch up was by a shortcut through his long easy swings. She sideswiped him with a snow-plow.

"Wait a minute!" she yelled at him and at the breeze.

"It's the marvelous governor," he said. "He's got fast phones. Good for him."

Nick smiled, apparently not at all confused that what he was saying was galaxies away from the landscape here.

"But — what now?" she said.

"LBJ bumped me, so I bumped the chancellor of Warren for the commencement address, that's all. Janey phones fast too."

Again he pushed off, but she caught his baggy pants with the point of her pole.

"Just like that?" she said.

"Sure, I can't give the governor all the loving credit on TV, so I'll give it to him at Warren College — listen, you tear *these* pants and I'll really be sunk."

"You bet I'll tear them," she said. "Tell me everything!"

"That's all. We'll have AP and UPI dropping by. Those boys have a genius for news, with a little help from friends."

"You bastard!" she said. "When did all this happen?"

"While my love was asleep."

He grinned again. This time he did get away from her and they glided on down together, she after him. But not for long. A few slalom turns later, a silence suddenly came out of the lift stanchions. No more music in the loudspeakers.

"Sir." It was Tony's voice from the base lodge. "*It is a cable from Paris.*"

"Paris?" Nick said. "False alarm. That's for Tarp. He's due tomorrow."

"And you didn't tell me all this governor stuff till now!" she said.

"You weren't alive till now," he said. "You were still unconscious in the chopper."

"You are pretty goddamn treacherous," she said.

"I learned from marvelous people. At Warren I'll say the governor is so marvelous, he can drag a sick ex-President out of bed to pull strings. Hey, you know what that scent is? All those flowers?"

"No," she said.

"*Wermut.* That's wormwood. Usually they don't come out till July. They came out for us. Now you go first. Go on. Ski. Let's see how you turn."

"No," she said. "I'll be self-conscious."

"Please."

"No."

He stroked her belly with the ski pole; he was a master at belly-stroking under any circumstances.

"Okay," she said. She stamped to shake away the charley-horse in her thighs. Then she did go ahead. They spiraled down, the glacier snow loosening in the warmth of the day, spraying up in many little white fountains around her ski tips, and it was crisp and glorious and wind-whistling, and she was glad to see the copter by the base lodge so that they could soar right up again.

Only the pilot wasn't in it. He stood beside Tony outside, and Tony held out a folded slip of gray paper. It was the cable. But it wasn't for Letarpo and it wasn't even for Nick. It had Trudy's name on it and it was two days old because it had been forwarded from St. Gallen to the Swissair desk in Zurich to the lodge here. It was a cable from Simon Spieger's cousin, the one who had stayed in Paris. It said, in garbled English, that Simon Spieger was deceased of a heart attack at a radio station in Paris.

Trudy handed the gray slip to Nick. He read it and handed it back to her. They looked at each other, still standing on their skis, in the middle of Simon Spieger's death. Gusts of sun-blue sky brushed their faces and the scent of many small gold blossoms blew down from the glacier. It was only eleven in the morning. But they didn't go up again.

~ 2 ~

It was an awful, wrong kind of loneliness. During Simon's burial in Strasbourg she walked all alone between the coffin and the Spieger clan following behind. A large phalanx of a *mishpoche,* dentists and rabbis to the community, and strangers to her. They had thin white faces swathed in black and spoke a mysterious Alsatian Yiddish with each other and a superb elegiac French to the press. Trudy herself said nothing; at that nothing the Spiegers nodded. About Ronnie they asked only once. She was dismissed at the airport with dry kisses on the cheek. They had reclaimed from her their Simon and their Simon's fame. Goodby, *ma chère,* and good luck.

The wrong kind of loneliness: when she walked into the apartment in New York she was struck by that again. Simon's clothes had already been sent to Strasbourg as the Spiegers requested. She was amazed by her absence of feeling at the sight of those two empty closets. Not entirely empty, because in one closet lay some poles and a white cloth. Remnants of the *chuppah* on their wedding meadow in Switzerland. The poles and the cloth hadn't been sent because nobody had remembered what they were. Chilling. And what chilled her was the apartment where she'd lived for so many years; this big bright Central Park West suite with the menorah Chagall had made for Simon; the big studio with the eye paintings; grim relics in a cold shrine. Suddenly she longed for Tante's plant-smothered little apartment in Washington Heights. It was gone. Tante had moved to Miami. She had an impulse to call Tante, and at that moment Ronnie's governess seized both her hands to vent sympathy. This governess, Mrs. Moore, with her permanent wave and badly self-manicured hands, was more joined to the apartment than Trudy. Mrs. Moore lived here with Ronnie more consistently than Ronnie's mother. Trudy had chosen the Kaethe Kollwitz woodcuts, but it was Mrs. Moore who had had the time to nail them on the walls.

"Where's Ronnie?" she asked.

The governess raised her shoulders and tiptoed toward Ronnie's bedroom. They passed the potted orchid, an end-of-term present from Tante in Miami. Mouth-organ music came from the bedroom and Mrs. Moore stepped aside to let Trudy peek through the partly open door.

It was quite a spectacle. Behind Ronnie's bed was the black-draped magic stand. Behind the stand worked a little clown with a harness round his neck that held up a mouth organ before his face: he could play it without using a hand. The clown played Prince Yussuf's wailing tune on the mouth organ while pouring golden water into a beaker that never became full.

Two men in dark elegant clothes sat on the floor. Legs folded, they watched the miracle. Nick and his father. Old Antone must have come from Key Bahama for this; Nick had taken time off from his political emergency. And warmth blessed Trudy's blood. *This* was her new family. They'd rushed here to be with Ronnie and with her.

"You see," the governess whispered; she beckoned Trudy away, out of earshot of the performance. "Ronald practiced day and night for this —"

"I know," Trudy said.

"It was for the end-of-term party, but because of Mr. Spieger he couldn't — but he practiced so hard, we thought it would be all right to let him do it here in private. . . ."

"It's all right," Trudy said. "It's a good compromise."

"And it was Ronald's own idea to use sadder music. He practiced for that too after the terrible — after the passing."

"Isn't that something?" Trudy said. She wanted to rush to her little son to give him her present, a six-color Swiss pen. But the governess held her by the elbow.

"Dr. Sessfor is in your bedroom," the governess said.

"Dr. Sessfor?"

The last thing she needed was a Dr. Sessfor, a busybody principal of the New York Studio School.

"Dr. Sessfor asked me to ask you," the governess said. "Could you see her before you talk to Ronald?"

Probably Trudy would have simply ignored that. But Nick came out of Ronnie's room. They hadn't seen each other since the glacier. He didn't say a word. She couldn't. He just put his arm around Trudy's shoulder. She needed the arm, desperately, but if she'd walked in on Ronnie like that, she would not only have interrupted the show, she would have started to howl.

"Nick," she said. "Nick, I'm supposed to see Dr. Sessfor."

At least Dr. Sessfor offered the convenience of being the one person in Trudy's life least likely to move her to the quick: squat Dr. Sessfor wore large, creatively shapeless dark hats that implied that she was really tall and sensitive. She had an echoing, well-modulated voice with which to richly suggest and forgive parental lapses. And of course Trudy found her staring at the bedspread.

Ever since Ronnie had learned to sew (at the Studio School both sexes did), Ronnie had fallen into the habit of ripping off luggage tickets from his mother's bags and sewing them into her quilted yellow bedspread. But Ronnie had also used tags of his own trips to Trudy, and when you looked at the bedcover studded with tags — Cleveland, Dallas, Los Angeles, St. Louis, Des Moines — you could really think along with Dr. Sessfor that Trudy resided exclusively in DC-10 Sky Lounges, five miles in the air above her only son.

"Mrs. Spieger," echoed Dr. Sessfor. "My condolences. Such a loss."

"Thank you," Trudy said. "This is Congressman Antone, an old friend of the family."

"Oh yes," Dr. Sessfor said. "One reads such good things about you. I hope we meet again at a less sad time."

That meant, of course, "Go away." Trudy held on to Nick's sleeve. Nick made no motion to leave.

"It was kind of you to come, but it really wasn't necessary," Trudy said to Dr. Sessfor.

Dr. Sessfor lowered her eyes slowly toward the airline tags. "Apart from the sad occasion," she said, "we should have a confidential word." She raised her gaze again, straight and hard at Nick.

"I've been very close to the family," Nick said. "With Trudy's permission I'd like to stay."

"Stay," Trudy said.

"Well, then," Dr. Sessfor said. She walked to the door and closed it. "Ronald," she said (she slightly re-shaped her hat brim). "Ronald is a special child, with special gifts — and inclinations."

"Yes, we discussed it once," Trudy said.

"Well, that was quite a while ago. Now there've been — developments which involve new planning for Ronald, and that's the only reason I am detaining you on this heavy day."

"New planning?" Trudy said.

"It's just that we at Studio feel that another school would be more suitable. Say, with emphasis on outdoors and on music, where Ronald has such gifts."

"Did he flunk spelling?" Trudy said.

153

"No, actually he got by quite nicely on that, an improvement over last semester. And, as you know, he can do brilliantly in other subjects."

Dr. Sessfor stared at the airline tags.

"You're suddenly dropping him," Trudy said.

"Mrs. Spieger, if you'd like us to, we'll help place him in another school."

"You're not taking him into the next grade?"

"I realize this is no day to burden you —"

"It's no day to beat about the bush," Trudy said.

"It would be helpful to be frank," Nick said.

Dr. Sessfor took a deep, subtle breath.

"Well, she said. "Ronald relates very well to teachers. Sometimes better than to his peers."

"Please, let's get to the point," Trudy said. She sat down on the bed, on the sewn-in airline tags, and Nick sat down with her.

"He has been especially close with Miss Fasser, his homeroom teacher."

"I'm in pretty good touch with my son," Trudy said. "I know in my sleep that Miss Fasser is his homeroom teacher."

"I appreciate that," Dr. Sessfor said. "When you were in Europe these past two weeks —"

"My one vacation in the year," Trudy said.

"Of course. I am sure. In that period Ronald practiced his musical magic show day and night."

"I am aware of that," Trudy said.

"Especially at night, and he complained of headaches, as your nice governess —"

"I know," Trudy said. "I was on the phone with her and Ronnie while I was overseas. I understand the school nurse gave him some light sedative, and frankly I was wondering about that."

"It was very light and it was also a misjudgment," Dr. Sessfor said. "But what's done is done and you asked me to come to the point. The point is Ronald took the sedative bottle to school with him."

"I wasn't told!" Trudy said.

"You see, your governess, what is her name?"

"Mrs. Moore," Trudy said. "She never mentioned with one word —"

154

"She doesn't know what I have to tell you now," Dr. Sessfor said. "It's not even her fault. She kept the bottle out of reach. Ronald used a stepladder. He was quite open about it. Afterwards."

"Then why didn't *you* tell me! I left word how I could be reached in Switzerland!"

"It's not a thing I could talk about fast on long distance," Dr. Sessfor said. "You see, the homeroom teacher had her lunch with Ronald that day. She had him to lunch in her office, to talk to him, make him less intense. Ronald poured the sedative bottle into her tea."

"My God," Trudy said. "But then Miss Fasser should have called me. Instantly!"

"Miss Fasser didn't know. Ronald poured it so she didn't notice."

Silence. The mouth organ trembled faintly from Ronnie's room.

"When was that?" Trudy said.

"Five days ago." Dr. Sessfor took off her hat. She had a hairdo like an old black poodle. "I told you," Dr. Sessfor said, "it's a very hard thing to talk about. I haven't mentioned it to anyone except you. I'm just sorry it has to be on this day."

"What happened?" Trudy said.

"Miss Fasser became unconscious and Ronald cut off her private hair."

Trudy stared at her, then at Nick.

"Pubic?" she said.

"Miss Fasser had a scissors on her desk," Dr. Sessfor said softly. "He removed some of her clothes and cut off some of her hair there."

"I don't believe it," Trudy said.

"He didn't molest her otherwise," Dr. Sessfor said. "He even put her clothes in order afterwards. She didn't even know at first anything had happened. She thought she had fainted. Ronald went to the cafeteria to bring her coffee —"

"He can be a strange child," Trudy said. "But — not *this!*"

"None of it has gone further, beyond Miss Fasser and myself," Dr. Sessfor said. "We've changed his spelling mark from C to Failure as reason for not continuing him at Studio —"

"Excuse me!" Trudy said.

She was up from the bed and out the door. On her last day in St. Gallen she'd gotten a letter from Ronnie — a sweet bland note plus a small envelope that said *To Mummy* and which had nothing inside except some short brown fibers. It had not so much puzzled as touched her because he often sent her things like that, a feather that had come out of his pillow during a dream or threads unraveled from his shirt, she'd thought it was something of that kind and now, rushing to Ronnie's room, she was carrying in her handbag a small envelope of his teacher's pubic hair.

"Ronnie!"

The little clown-arm, magic wand and all, dropped. The mouthorgan music stopped. Old Man Antone got up from the floor. But she didn't care about him.

"Ronnie — *why?*"

The clown tore off his head. Above the black-buttoned pink smock was Ronnie's face now, looking doubly pale and elongatedhandsome, doubly freckled at the ears, doubly like Nick despite the mouth-organ harness he didn't bother to take off.

"Mummy."

He ran to her. His head almost reached to her breasts. She caught him, held him away slightly. The skin inside her arms ached for his small face, but she didn't give a damn for her skin.

"Look at this," she said. She tore open her handbag and took out the little envelope so violently that her handbag fell to the floor and her end-of-term gift spilled out.

"Ronnie, *why?*" she said again. She thrust the envelope at him.

Old Man Antone picked up the handbag and the gift, and Ronnie snatched the handbag from him and closed it and gave it to Trudy, and then held on to the gift with both hands. His face was wet-eyed now, and without the mouth-organ harness; what made him even more pathetic was the way he fought crying by pursing his lips in a half-whistle.

"Answer me!" she said. She lifted the harness off him; old Antone took it as though he were a stagehand to the scene.

"The nurse was lying," Ronnie said, almost soundless. "She said the drops don't do anything to you."

"*One* or *two* drops don't," Trudy said. "And it's not just what you did with the drops! It's this!"

She whipped the envelope into the wracked half-whistling little face. "Why send this to me? What's the matter with you?"

He stood before her, holding on to her gift. "You didn't tell me he was going to die," he said.

"I didn't know!" she said. "It's terrible he did, but that's no answer! Answer what I asked you!"

"You went away," Ronnie said.

"Ronnie," she said. "I didn't know he was going to die. But he probably felt it somehow, so he wanted us to be with him this summer and that's the only reason I took off a couple of weeks just now, to — to do some work before our summer together — *now answer my question!*"

He stood before her, small and comely, with his unwhistling trembling lip.

"Ronnie, how could you do this with your teacher?"

"Because — " he lowered his face; he rubbed her graduation gift against his chest so that the wrapping paper rasped against the clown smock. "Because . . . I wanted to . . . to send you something I did when I was very scared."

She didn't know what to say.

"I'm sorry," he said.

She sat down on his rocking chair. His head buried itself fast and hard in her lap, a tousled bullet, and they both rocked together with the impact. He still held on to her gift.

"Oh, Ronnie," she said.

She had to let her hand stroke the silky hair. At the same time she saw Dr. Sessfor and the governess watching from the door as though the magic show were continuing, and old Antone walking toward the watchers with a stern arm, sweeping them away.

"Ronnie," Nick said. Nick was on his knees, at their side. "Ronnie?"

He nudged up Ronnie's wet, heaving face.

"You listening?" Nick said. "From now on we'll be straight with each other! It's very sad Simon's no longer here, but I'm your Daddy, your real one, from now on. You understand?"

Crying had released Ronnie's face into tinyness, cheeks baby-splotched. He looked from Nick to Trudy. Trudy nodded. Old Antone was gone too, it was just the three of them, and she knew

157

it was okay for her to cry too, but she didn't even have to. Nick had his arms round both of them.

"I'll show you how straight we'll be with each other, we three," Nick said. "I'll tell you something nobody knows in the whole world. I'm going to run for President of this country."

"President?" Ronnie said.

"I'm not going to wait to be senator first. I wanted to run all along, and I think I can help this country, and I want to be straight with the people about what I want — but first I'm going to be straight with my own, and that's you two characters, you and your mother, you hear?"

He kissed them, kneeling. His lips brushed her cheeks and Ronnie's, he was his warm European peasant-prince self. She loved the way Ronnie looked at him.

"No one — no one else knows?" Ronnie said. A small sob had interrupted him.

"Not a soul," Nick said. "I just decided today. Next week I'll announce it at a college speech but nobody knows now, Ronnie. Not the marvelous governor of this state, not the biggest bigshots. Except you. With you I'm straight. And from now on you'll be like that with us?"

Ronnie had begun to unwrap her gift, crying. He nodded.

"Anything that's on your mind, you'll tell us first before doing anything about it?"

"Ronnie," Trudy said. "He's really your Daddy from now on. He is right. Will you do that from now on?"

Ronnie nodded again. He got up, still heaving slightly. With a child's trudge he trudged to the corner of his room where his toy office was set up, and he drew out the toy file which contained nothing but pieces of wrapping, a motley-colored crush consisting of papers in which his mother's gifts had been wrapped over the past years, gifts lost or used up or discarded by now, yet the wrappings in which they had come were still preserved here, the essence of all her past gift-giving to him compressed into this little green file. Now he wedged into the drawer the shiny silver sheet into which her end-of-term gift had been wrapped, and he closed the drawer with a crispness which for a moment restored his pathetic too-composed half-whistling upper lip. But then he opened the gift

158

box and saw the six-color Swiss fountain pen. A sob shook him into a child again. He ran to her and kissed her waist and drove his head into her lap again, and Nick's arm, the presidential arm, came round both of them and they were together.

<h2 style="text-align:center">3</h2>

It was ten P.M. in the great lobby cave of the hotel in Liechtenstein where she kept vigil by the two sleepers. She still watched the luggage tag on old Antone's raincoat. She'd watched it for hours. It moved like a falling leaf that didn't fall, it trembled to the merged dreams of an ancient Venetian tycoon and a shaggy St. Bernard. Watching it, she heard, shortly after ten P.M., a groan outside the house. A sudden, somehow familiar noise. The dog was up instantly. So was she. She found herself limping. Her left leg had fallen asleep, her joints were gritty with insomnia and fatigue. By the time she unlocked the door, the groan came again. The muted sound of a car horn she knew. Outside in the driveway, in the gnat-flickering lamplight stood Jennifer by the Rolls-Royce Volkswagen.

"Jennifer!"

"Hello, Trudy."

"Is my husband here?"

"He'll be coming in a few hours," Jennifer said.

Just as well. She wasn't ready for him.

"You know about that awful business?" Trudy said. "My son's up in the plane. He'll only talk to Letarpo."

Jennifer nodded. She held the black folder with prints of the Simon Spieger paintings, of which she was curator. She carried the folder as if this were life as usual. Yet she kept standing next to the car, locked into that bug-ridden lamplight.

"Don't mind the dog," Trudy said. "It comes with this crazy hotel. But it doesn't bite."

"It's — your hairpiece," Jennifer said.

159

"Don't look at me," Trudy said. "I haven't slept for days. Come in. Did you come by plane?"

"Letarpo wanted me to check out Zurich airport," Jennifer said. "To make sure there're no reporters."

"No. Nobody knows," Trudy said.

"That's what I phoned back. Oh."

They were in the lobby. Old Antone slept with the luggage tag, with the smiling antler skull above him. At his feet the big dog had stretched out again, in the same strange position of praying paws, begging to catch up with the old man's dreams.

"Old Antone, he's blind now," Trudy whispered. "He called the Letarpo office in Paris —"

Jennifer had turned to stare at her again.

"I know I look a fright," Trudy said. "Would you do me a favor? Watch the old man for me? Take care of him when he wakes up? I've got to take a shower. I'm such a mess. I've got to get in shape for Ronnie and Tarp."

"Sure," Jennifer said.

"Thank you!"

She went to the stairs. But on the first step something occurred to her.

"You have no luggage!"

"There was no time," Jennifer whispered back. She had sat down in Trudy's chair, had taken over sentry duty.

"How come you're here?" Trudy said. "I mean, did Tarp send you?"

"I — I just camped in his office when the trouble started," Jennifer said. "I told them, if there's a message to be sent to you, I should be the one." A whispered laugh, very thin and jittery in that enormous wooden cavern. "You know me. I meddle."

"Thank God," Trudy said. "Thank you!"

She went up the staircase, down the corridor, sconces floating past. In her room she took off her clothes, spreading them out across the dusty plush to make it look less forsaken. Naked, she was suddenly struck by the inadequacy of her "Thank you." She sat down on the floor where her shoulder bag was and opened it and dug out her Crillon stationery for another codicil.

To my friend Jennifer Berg, she wrote, *the sum of four hundred*

thousand dollars in partial, very partial, recompense for her ser-
vices. When I asked her to be Literary Executor of Simon Spieger's
papers, I didn't have in mind all the secretarial chores, the personal
services she did render me. Like, for example, coming here today.
If Bic had come instead, it would have sent me over the brink.

But she felt over the brink anyhow, almost. She couldn't go on.
To do something routine, daily, sustaining, she took the astringent
bottle out of her toilette kit. She unscrewed the lid so that it would
be ready for application right after the shower when the pores
were wide open. The herbal smell of the astringent buoyed her.

She stepped into the shower stall, tiled in yellow arabesques like
the chapel of a Byzantine saint. The plumbing didn't just wheeze
when you turned on the faucet, it was a whole drowned choir of
voices and seabottom screams. They poured down on her tiredness
as she soaped herself. She heard a wet graveyard of Trudys shouting
up at the waves, one Trudy yelling at the anti-eviction picket lines,
another arguing with Tante, another chairing a Nick campaign
meeting, another reading with Simon on a dais . . . they all croaked,
sputtered, flushed through the hotel's old pipes and tumbled out
of the showerhead, and she was so beat and hallucinated that she
realized too late she was using the soap in the shower stall's soap
dish, not her expensive Laszlo shampoo.

But it wasn't bad, that plain soap. Furthermore, her hot-air gun
really started blowing when she plugged it into the baroque outlet,
and her hair dried fast and rather silky after that soap and then,
suddenly, shaking it out before the mirror, she noticed strands of
gray she'd never seen before.

Mummy, when you die, put my name in your pocket so you'll
remember me when you wake up.

In the service of what beautiful great thing, in the course of
what true enjoyment, had these strands turned from brown to
gray? Was that any way to consume a life?

She dabbed on more astringent. It did make her feel a little
better. Seeing the Crillon stationery on the floor, she decided to
go on with her bequest — candidly, as one should in a Last Will
and Testament.

To my friend Jennifer Berg, she wrote, *the sum of four hundred*
thousand dollars in full knowledge that she might have had ego

161

reasons for accepting the job I offered. She became Simon Spieger's Literary Executor and in effect my assistant, so that she could watch me closely. So that she didn't have to read at a great jealous distance about my Mrs.-Letarpo-life. So that she could see her fill of the warts on my glamour.

Time to stop, to do the fifty strokes on her just-dried hair. This wasn't vanity now. Combing her hair was a device to keep half-sane by observing the little rituals by which one declares oneself normal and functioning. Only after the fiftieth stroke did she go back to the codicil.

To my friend Jennifer Berg, she wrote, *the sum of four hundred thousand dollars in full recognition that we kept using each other, as one must in an enduring friendship. I used her as a root, a hired root to my earlier and unstained ambitions. I guess I thought that with her around, my hair would never turn gray.*

"Decay is a cliché," she'd said to Jenn, decades ago, at Moloch U. "Decay is a cliché. Let's be original for at least seventy years." Yes, ma'am. Oh sure, ma'am. But there'd been a period when such sophomoric bluster really seemed to come true. During Nick's presidential campaign it seemed quite possible that she'd become great and happy, and remain good and noble and young and original forever. Nothing would turn gray. Everything worked. Interfaith University even agreed to give her a leave of absence from Dean-designate though it was the very year the University was to open. Nothing could stop her. She herself became one of the main agents of Nick's unstoppability.

"Hey, Miss, Studio C's closed!" the NBC guard had said. "You can't go in there!"

But she went in there. The guard said "Oh, I didn't see you, Joe," for the man with her was Security Chief and personally unlocked the door for her. Nothing could stop her. The world was child's play in those days. Literally. Studio C was cluttered with the set of Dr. Hasenpfeffer's kiddie show. In Studio B, Senator Sherr Winnis had just taped the governor's endorsement of the Winnis-for-Prez try, an utter sour-grapes futility because of Studio A. Studio A, the big one, was crawling with stars and lights and unstoppability. There the telethon boiled and glittered and sucked in the loot to sweep Nick past the primaries already won, past California, Pennsylvania and New York to the crescendo of the convention, no matter how industriously the governor slapped Sherr Winnis on the shoulder in Studio B for Channel Four.

And Sherr Winnis knew it too when he walked in. He did come in briskly in his tweeds and his tan made of pancake. But he wasn't quite the chubby-hearty rube genius she once knew. Only Sherr Winnis's very white teeth existed in the dusk. The rest of him hung on like grim death to his smile.

"Hi, Trudy!"

He looked around at Dr. Hasenpfeffer's props dying in the gloom. "Shoot," he said. "You couldn't find a better place in which to seduce an old man?"

"It fitted best into your busy schedule," she said.

"Oh, Trudy," he said. "I wish you were running my schedule instead of Nick's. I'd be so much busier still."

They laughed and did the embrace bit.

"My God," Sherr Winnis said. "Remember when? You came to me on that University bill?"

"Going to be the best new university, thanks to you," she said.

"Dean of students or whatever? Must be awfully small potatoes to you now."

"Listen, they're doing so well, they gave me a leave of absence pretty fast. They don't need me."

"Holy Moe, you're even tops in modesty," Sherr said, and they laughed again.

Child's play. That night she'd felt infallible, grotesquely infallible. She knew her hair was just right, and her clothes too. A black-and-white pants suit with little shoulderstraps on the blouse to play on her status as plenipotentiary from a major power; but also a semidecolletage to pull erotic rank if necessary; and her bronze shoe buckles with the *Nick Now!* logo on her patent leather pumps.

"Oh, that's a beauty," Sherr said, looking down at her buckles. "I've got to tell Mae about that when I see her, if ever. Hey, you know what Mae said the other day? She said, 'I can't wait till all this nonsense is over so we can see Nick again, just friendly, and Trudy too and that whole crowd.'"

"Amen," Trudy said, smiling, though they'd never been Just Friendly. What "whole crowd"?

"How *is* Nick?" Sherr Winnis said. "Goddamn it, all we do these days, we pass each other in them Studio corridors. How is that handsome scoundrel?"

"Tired, I guess."

"Well, for God's sakes tell him to take a long vacation!" Sherr said laughing.

A counter-roar from the telethon. Every time the pledges went up by another thousand, Dick Gregory hit a gong and applause seeped through the door into the Dr. Hasenpfeffer half-light. Sherr Winnis's laughter rode smoothly across it. There was a lot of cool left in the man after all. To Trudy the situation became more interesting just because it wouldn't be quite so easy.

"As a matter of fact Nick's going to take off for a few days," she said.

"Bless him. How's your boy? Ronald, is it?"

"What a memory," she said. "Ronnie's fine. He's in Switzerland, in school."

"Cutest thing on legs. I remembered him from Key Bahama. How's your friend Letarpo?"

"Letarpo," she said. "All right, I guess. He's more a friend of Nick's father."

"Well, now I'm going to level with you." Sherr sat down on a big empty bird cage. "I came in here to sidle up to a lovely young lady I haven't talked to in much too long a time. But I'd also like to shoot my mouth off on something. You mind?"

"Shoot," Trudy said.

"Do me a favor. Tell Nick he shouldn't rely on Letarpo too much."

"Well, that's interesting," Trudy said.

"I don't mean money from the guy. Son-of-a-gun Nick, I wish I had half his hundred-bucks-a-plate dinners. I mean, he can lean all he wants on buddying around with Letarpo, it still won't save him from the bolshie label."

"Oh, is he a bolshie?"

"Honey, we know better. I'm talking about the label."

"My impression is, Nick hasn't really buddied with Letarpo for years," she said. "He's been too busy."

164

"He's still trading on it, sweetheart."

"That's awfully complex of him," she said, smiling.

"To the left he plays slum-champ. But to the right he's trading on growing up with Daddy Antone and Number One Funny Oil Boy. It won't wash, Trudy. Not in November."

She rather liked Sherr's little offensive, enough to play it out some more.

"It should've been a less funny oil boy?" she said. "A Rockefeller?"

"Be a helluva lot better — real solid clean-assed banker. You know, those fifty million slobs out there, stepping on dog turd on their way to the salt mines, you ask 'em, 'What's a Letarpo?' Bet they answer 'Uh, that's some funny fancy-shmancy society gorilla, pinko leftist pals, all that stuff, sort of a wop pinko too.' Not the type to get Nick off the bolshie hook."

"Well," Trudy said. "Nick will be fascinated with the information. I mean, that he's on a hook."

"Aaaah, Trudy," Sherr said. He kicked his foot against the bird cage. "Nick's important to me. As a friend and as a candidate. As the most important candidate, between you and me, and I wouldn't repeat that in front of my own staff. See, there's another trouble. Nick's movie star thing. That's what's really going to kill him in the end."

"I won't let him make blue movies," Trudy said.

Sherr didn't smile.

"Listen, good looks is great. Glamour is great. Bein' a bachelor ain't presidential usually, but he's making it work for him — great. Even carrying on red is great. That's excitement for the kids, dandy for doorbell ringing, marchin', yellin', hollering — hell, they might even stampede the convention in July. More power to 'em. Only one trouble with Christmas in July — and that's death in November."

Gong! went Dick Gregory's gong. Another thousand dollars worth of applause fluttered over the Dr. Hasenpfeffer set.

"Yes, that's how a lot of people are trying to console themselves over Nick," she said.

"I hate to frighten a pretty lady," Sherr said. "But here's what's going to happen in November. Fifty million guys with holes in their soles, they're gonna wake up on the bar stools and start

165

walking to the polls. And they'll be scared to death of the stuff Nick's been selling to the Platform Committee, the Urban Maintenance, the Minimum Wage for the blackies, stuff he couldn't get passed in Congress —"

"Are *you* scared to death of it?"

"Trudy, I know we got to move socially, but without good politics ain't gonna be *no* movement nohow at all! Tell Nick."

"He's been told," Trudy said, smiling.

"Trouble is too many guys are telling each other now. Might get to be a stalemate at Chicago and give a critter like me a chance."

The time had come.

"Sherr," she said. "Don't you miss your chance tonight."

"Hey, finally you're flirting," he said.

"I'm too worried to flirt. I'm worried about you."

"Ah. About time somebody pretty was."

"You'd pass up a lot if you didn't support Nick's planks for the platform."

"I'd love to, honey, but you just give me one good reason."

"We don't just want your support." She was talking slowly. "We want your support as a winner. We'd make sure you won big in Montana, if we could count on you."

"My, my," the senator said.

He rocked back and forth on the bird cage, and Trudy was again surprised by her own zest in such fencing — the crispness, confidence of her tongue.

"Think about it," she said to Senator Sherr Winnis.

"I'm thinkin'," Sherr said. "I'm thinkin'. You want old Sherr to go to bat for Nick at the third ballot if Nick can't swing the first two —"

"Nope, no need to trouble you on that," she said. "Just support Nick's planks and he won't even contest you in Montana —"

"Honey, that's one state I'm not contestable. No way."

"Those college kids of Nick's can do a lot of screaming. And I've got my contacts with the senior citizens. We want you to look good."

"I'll never look as good as you, honey."

"You know what I mean."

"But Jesus. I must look even dumber than I am! All you're giving me, you'll help me where I can't lose."

He was strong and smart. She decided it had to be done.

"Sherr," she said. "I'm not just talking about giving *you* something. I'm talking about giving the party a strong running mate."

Sherr stopped rocking.

"I tell you what I think Nick needs," she said. "A running mate that's okay with the guys on the bar stools but still gets past the kids without a hassle. And who's proved it in a presidential primary."

"Oh, now, you wait a minute," Sherr said.

"You're no fascist pig," Trudy said. "You didn't vote against Nick on those things. Just support them for the platform and talk them up in Montana. You'd win Montana anyway, but this way you'll come out looking like a Vice President."

BANG. Everything worked just then. Someone shot off a starter's pistol in Studio A. It meant another Ten Thousand Dollar milestone had been turned in telethon pledges. The applause was huge and the studio walls muffled it into an enthusiasm distant, pure and sweet.

"Trudy," Sherr Winnis said. "You made all that up all by yourself? You laying a yarn on your old buddy?"

She took cool satisfaction in her nerve.

"If I'd made it up, it'd be a bad mistake to tell it to someone like you."

"Sche-he-re-za-de," Sherr Winnis said. "Watch yuh neck."

"And just because it's me," Trudy said, "I can't afford to say it lightly."

She slung her handbag over her shoulder to emphasize the very personal Nick-implication she'd just dropped, and also to get a move on. Nick was waiting.

"Got to hand it to you." Sherr got off the bird cage. "Politics was a lot duller before you two came down the pike."

"Thank you."

"Let's all do a little brooding, huh?"

"We'll be back Monday," she said. "You know Nick's lawyer. Have somebody give him a ring Monday."

They were walking out of Dr. Hasenpfeffer's melted fairyland.

167

The white smile had drained from Sherr's mouth into his body, filling it and hardening it somehow.

"Trudy, I'll use any excuse to see you again."

He held open the door, blew her a kiss. Some quiet staff shadows joined him as he walked off to the right. She walked to the left, toward Studio A's hurricane, past the monitors reverberating with Streisand on stage, through a glitter and mutter of campaign peons and great legends it would have been fun to meet. She walked among staff faces she didn't even know, now that the campaign had grown so big. She was walking in a backstage crowd studded with sudden reappearances. Nick's success had pulled them out of nowhere. Elihu Boneman (Pancho Villa mustaches intact) back from Israel to coordinate the Jewish Student Section — Trudy ducked around him because it was so late. Dean Goldeck, balder and more sausage-lipped than ever, whose approach she stopped with a Hello! — Goodby! wave. Nick's old flame Paulette smiled, arm in arm with a gray-mustached gent. Tanned jocks of the Rough Diamonds Cruise type stared at her (right past Faye Dunaway) which was all the more reason to hurry toward the campaign secretary, who had her coat ready at the exit.

"Taxi's waiting," the secretary said.

Trudy ran through the light rain. In the cab the ride was just long enough to get her hair into order. And sure enough, at the Loew's Motor Inn stood the little green Secret Service Volkswagen she recognized and the off-white Chevvy, beside which she told the driver to stop.

She hopped from one car to another. She was moist with rain, with eau de cologne just dabbed on, with the fine sweat of power, and with love.

"Figures," Nick said. "You'd be the one. You're the last person left in this lousy country with the nerve to keep me waiting."

They laughed. Off they were together, to the airport.

Nick wore his raincoat directly over the blue sport shirt. The first shirt button was closed, the second open, the third closed again, and through the openness of the middle button an unembarrassed curl of hair licked, very black against the young gray locks of the gondolier's head.

It was typically, proverbially, tangily Nick, that unkempt shirt. It also went with the big yellow foolscap pad sticking out of his briefcase. In the car he'd jotted down some of Trudy's thoughts on his Democratic Governors' Conference speech coming up next week. He hadn't bothered to push the foolscap all the way back in. It kept sticking out, and by that time in his career even such negligences became master strokes.

As they walked up the gangway she felt again the quick silence all around that meant the upturned smiles of ground personnel, the excitement that remained surprised and bashful till the first *"Hey, Nick!"* broke out together with the first handclasp. They loved their godling sloppy; foolscap, buttons and all. It confirmed the idea that his rise had been improvised with casual elan. *Hey, Nick! Nick Now!*

Everything worked right, including the mechanics of their get-away. Not a single flashbulb. All the Economy Class passengers were in and seated by the time Trudy walked in with him. The Z.K.'s (Zoo Keepers, as Nick called the Secret Service men) lounged in the last row on both sides of the Economy Class door; faces of boiled ham and legs faintly jiggling. Tom, the new speech man, and Dorothy, their research chief, already sat in the special section, four seats facing across a table. Tom and Dorothy were waiting for their "spouses," in whose names the reservations had been made officially.

To Trudy the whole thing was the start of something like a dream: three days away-from-it-all. The slovenliness of Nick's shirt was too much, of course. But she didn't have a chance to tell him at first. Stewardess Cleft Chin kept bending over Nick to set the table while the plane still taxied on the runway. Right after the take-off Stewardess Dimple Cheek began twittering for their side orders to the coq au vin. Stewardess Pert Cap did a sort of Sally Rand for Nick, using oxygen mask and life preserver for fans, when out came Mr. Striped Sleeves from the cockpit. Pilot Captain Jeff Towitt, sir, an honor, sir, he was a Republican, to be quite frank about it, but this was a privilege, and would it be all right to ask him to autograph the flight menu for his son Jesse — Jess*e, e* at the end — Jesse being such a hotshot in the Nick Antone movement at Virginia State, the boy would be so thrilled?

"Pleasure," Nick said and wrote on the menu, *Jesse, set Dad straight — Nick Antone Jr.*

With resplendent laughter the captain returned to the cockpit, while Cleft Chin titsied up, bosoms and Instamatic cocked at Nick. Would Mr. Antone mind, one little candid?

For a couple of seconds it was dicey. Nick managed to gain time by faking a full mouth. Well trained in such matters, Dorothy used the interval to crawl under the table and emerge next to Nick. By the time the click came, Trudy was out of the picture.

Trudy still didn't have a chance to ask him to button his shirt. The very next thing that happened was a man in a wheelchair. He came barreling through the Economy Class door together with an Economy Class stewardess, who actually got him past the Secret Service men. He rolled to a stop by Nick.

"Oh, Mr. Antone. The rumor is true! You're on the flight. I'm Edgar Bellis. The Economy restroom has a step up, so Pan-Am allows me to use First Class."

"Good for them," Nick said.

"I am glad to use this opportunity. You've said nothing about a Federal Real Estate Tax Limitation Law."

"Yes," Nick said, faking a polite full mouth again.

"Because it's eating up the nation's basic wealth, otherwise I won't be able to cast my ballot for you."

"Write me . . ." Nick had begun to cough convincingly with food-freighted cheeks, ". . . your opinion . . . would you?"

"I'm sorry. I didn't realize you were dining. In Economy they haven't even started serving us yet."

The man rolled on sullen to the john, half colliding with Striped Sleeves No. 2, who came out of the cockpit just then.

"Mr. Antone, it's Tony Silva, your co-pilot. I don't have any kids like the captain, but, boy have I got a bet riding on you election day! I also have a menu — would you mind?"

"Pleasure," Nick said. On the menu he wrote, *"To Captain Silva — make money in November! — Nick Antone Jr."*

Captain Silva loved that. The stewardesses to whom he showed it loved it too, with many titters. Nick's head fell back with closed eyes, so swiftly that Trudy didn't understand the idea until she saw the wheelchair coming out of the john. He passed the napping probable next President, glared at the open shirt button, breathed gloom through his nose, and nobody smiled until the Secret Service men had closed the door behind him, and Nick sat up and said, "Jesus Christ. Any clues from the telethon, Dorothy?"

For Dorothy pulling her notebook out of the bag and flapping it open was one single motion. "The total's holding up all right," she said. "That's as of eight P.M. Only it's the old story. The five, ten, fifteen bucks people — fine. Better than ever. Also the three-hundred-and-up. I know how you feel about the over-one-thousand ones —"

"Many of them are hypes anyway," Nick said.

"I really don't know how that ten-thousand pledge got on camera," Dorothy said.

"I'm glad somebody feels guilty," Nick said. "Apart from the psychology of showing big ones, we got burned too often. Like that ancient nudist — where was it, in San Diego someplace?"

"Right, the coffee heiress," Trudy said. "Who sent you her picture along with the check. Thirty grand to be paid to the order of Henry Wallace. You should have been flattered."

"Not by that navel," Nick said. "But I thought I'd made it clear. Four- or five-figure pledges don't go on the air. They might all be phoney or nutty."

"It won't happen again," Dorothy said.

"Nudists and betting pilots," Trudy said. "You do have certain areas of voter support."

"My cheerleader," Nick said. "My drum majorette."

"Anyway," Dorothy said at her notebook. "The rich and the poor are all right. It's the in-betweens. Like, not enough fifties from the luncheonette-owner types. That's the problem category. And the Midwest is still the thinnest. It's still the W.W. problem."

"Excuse me — 'W.W.'?" Tom said.

Tom, of course, was the new speech writer.

"W.W. — Wanton Wop," Trudy said. She jerked her thumb at Nick. "It's to explain his charisma to us." The stewardesses happened to be clearing, and their giggle made the coffee cups shake. After this flight they'd be able to dine out on a lot of delicious Nick Antone stuff. As soon as they left Nick pressed the recline button on his chair. He pressed it on Trudy's too. And that was sufficient signal to the others.

Dorothy vanished behind the front page of the *Washington Post*. Tom pulled out a paperback novel. The stewardesses also seemed to understand. The cabin lights dimmed away, leaving only baby spots to read by, in the smooth mystic whir. But Nick and Trudy didn't read. It was really a trip from a national election to a tryst, even if they still had to get rid of some business first.

"The Sherr thing," she said, softly.

"Bet he was chewing on a straw," Nick said in the same tone.

"He knows he has Montana with or without us."

"I wish we'd go away to a valley and grow cucumbers, you and me," Nick said. "You know why?"

"I know why," Trudy said.

"No point getting the damn nomination if I don't also get the support of pricks like Sherr, that's why. I hate politics."

"So you'll make politics better."

"He's a real bad animal and I hate to use him for a good program. He'll put the straw in his mouth in Montana and he'll make Minimum Wage sound like a cattle subsidy. Let's find a valley."

"Nick," she said. "I sprang Vice President on him tonight."

Nick's whole lean body with the funny-buttoned shirt turned toward her.

"It seemed like the moment for best leverage," she said.

She felt Nick's eyes on her.

"Of course, it's not a hundred percent commitment," she said. "Just a hundred percent bait. He'll be less jealous. He's so jealous of you."

Nick was still staring at her. She loved to make those tough gondolier eyes go feminine-wide with astonishment.

Nick laughed, suddenly.

"Beautiful," he said.

"I think it worked. He'll be in touch Monday."

"*Eminence rose,*" Nick said, dipping one forefinger quickly through her hair.

"Button your shirt," she said.

He took a deep breath and arched his body in the chair.

"You said jealous before," he said. "What makes Sherr jealous is what keeps the middling dough out of the telethon. It's a problem."

"You're too bloody glamorous," Trudy said.

"But that's gotten out of hand," Nick said. "It's gotten so it has nothing to do with anything anymore, with the right program or with people suffering — that's why my old man sends me all the Wanton Wop clippings in Earl Wilson."

172

"Still does?" she said.

"The hard political reform stuff, what we're trying to do, Papa doesn't see. But Wanton Wop, all the froufrou, that's what he picks up on. He loves that because of the emptiness."

"You sure carry on about your father," she said.

"So what we ought to do, we ought to get rid of Wanton Wop," he said.

"Good luck," she said.

"The two of us could do it." He said it very softly.

"The two of us?"

"If we both agree."

"What do you mean?"

"Maybe we ought to play up Paulette a little more. I mean, play her up in the campaign and with me personally. Her and nice little WASP cows like that."

The only impulse she had right then was to adjust her chair in the extreme recline position. He adjusted his too.

"I mean, so far the media have held back about us," he said. "But it's getting around a little bit. You're making me too bloody exciting and colorful."

"Me? Trudy from Washington Heights?"

She was proud of her light laugh.

"Yeah, you, the slinky Jewish liberal siren. Look in the mirror, for Christ sakes. For the goddamn campaign, the Paulette types are a great cover. Like at the Governors' Conference Dinner."

"Petite Paulette," she said.

"Boy, I'd love to commit political suicide and marry you tonight."

"No, you wouldn't love that," she said.

"Yes, I would. I told you, I hate politics. And I kinda like you."

"I saw Paulette at the telethon," she said.

"Yes, old Paulette's been behind a lot of our fund-raising down South."

"Was she?" Trudy said.

"She's great with the glassware at those money dinners. With the right goblets they give more. It takes one to know one."

"I think she was with some sugar daddy tonight," Trudy said.

"White mustache? That's her father. Old man Bunton is Chief

Judge of the Louisiana Court of Appeals, with five pillars to his portico. Actually that's the point about Paulette. You see?"

"Oh, you've been to their house?"

"Once. Had to get myself photographed with them and their pillars. That's very important in Louisiana. Those pillars. Paulette'd be a great red herring for us until the election, her and her likes, if you agree."

"I have no veto," she said.

"Sure you do. We ought to plan this together. And if I really make it and get in, boy, we'll plan the coming-clean together. Like what kind of bagels at our White House wedding."

"I don't like bagels," she said.

"And I don't like this whole discussion, no more than you," he said. "If you want to know the truth, I've been sitting up nights over the thing. All through the Southern swing. Because our program is the gut part of the campaign, the truest, best thing about it — for God's sake, you drafted it, Trudy, and I'm not going to have it sunk by the Wanton Wop myth, and believe me, they'll try to sink me with it, I could feel it down South, they'll really clobber me on it in the fall."

He sneezed suddenly and hard. In a peculiar, neutral way she was pleased by the comeliness of the convulsion. With him even snot came out comely.

"The problem is, make the Wop less Wanton," he said. "Make him nicer and dowdier. You know? Like, dull him down with some dull Miss Rights at some dull white-tie dinners."

"Like Petite Paulette at the Governors' Conference," she said.

"You see, then I'll have an easier time selling Minimum Wage to the goddamn middlings. You follow? Like, doctor the image, so we won't have to doctor the program. But correct me any time."

He waited. She could think of no correction, nothing to say. He sneezed again. And again.

"A little allergy?" Pert Cap came tripping. "A little Dristan?"

Trudy shouldn't have let him nod Yes. Nick was sloppy about his remedies. Dristan knocked him out, with the sneezing usually worse after he woke up. Trudy should have said "No" to Pert Cap. She should have done the only thing that helped — pinch Nick's nostrils together. She didn't.

174

"Paulette knows she'd be a cover?" she said.

"She'll come out fine," Nick said. "She'll end up with a DuPont or something, especially after this. I'll end up with you, so I'll be all right too. The only one to get screwed is you." He smiled and sneezed. "Because you're going to be one First Lady much too fucking bright for the job."

Pert Cap came tripping with two white pills on a golden napkin and a cut-glass tumbler on a silver salver. Nick swallowed and drank. It was like a reprieve. Then the reprieve was over and they were alone again.

"I mean it," Nick said. "Worst comes to worst and I really win, what's a brain like yours going to do for four years? Smile in the receiving line in the East Room?"

"Button your shirt," she said.

And here any further real talk became impossible. The stewardesses from Economy Class, who must have finished serving, came in. They sat down to eat in the last two rows of First. And the Secret Service men had gotten up to give them room and now sat in the seats empty till now, the row immediately behind Trudy and Nick. Privacy was finished at this nice juncture.

"The Dristan is killing me," Nick said.

"You shouldn't have taken it just because she brought it," Trudy said.

"Hey, I just remembered, you should have squeezed my nose!" Nick said.

"Button your shirt," she said.

Finally he did, his head lolling against the seat back, looking at her.

"Does it make sense?" he said.

"It's — a pleasant enough fantasy."

"We'll talk about it at Bachberg."

"There are small details. Like the effect on Ronnie. Or whether I can really keep up with such — such a lofty level of manipulation."

"We'll straighten it out at Bachberg."

"Yes," she said, closing her eyes. She heard Secret Service breathing behind them: conversation was really impossible. When she opened her eyes she found him still looking at her and so she turned away and counted the green petals on the cutesie-flowered wallpaper of the plane, and when she'd reached fifty she looked back to find Nick asleep, duly knocked out by the Dristan, immobile, stretched out slim in the chair, and he had the longest black lashes ever likely to look out of the Oval Room.

Pert Cap pushed a button near the cockpit. The section dimmed out entirely. After all, the Prince slumbered. Pert Cap also pulled down all the window shades. Trudy was suspended in a tight dark drone over the Atlantic. Tom, the new speech writer, stared into his paperback under his little night tent; there was the whisper-clink of Economy stewardesses eating; the Secret Service breathed. It was enforced torpor and it condensed like steam on Trudy's skin. She pulled up her window shade to let the moon cool her temples. But the moon was a disgusting pale green maggot on the night's cadaver. In the East, where they were going, sunrise festered, sore and blood-soaked. She pulled down the shade. She couldn't get up and pace up and down because of the stewardesses and the breathing, zoo-keeping Secret Service. She turned off her reading light. She screwed up her air vent for more ventilation and all through that she managed not to look at Nick. The air jet was cooling. She closed her eyes. Yet somehow her mind stayed lit and clammy with a sore sunrise somewhere inside, melting down her lids into a fatigue that closed in so fast she couldn't tie her scarf to protect her hair against sleep.

In Munich, where their party disembarked from the plane into the two cars, his sneezing fit didn't come back. It should have. She knew him too well not to find the return of that fit essential. For Nick a little fit of some kind was a rite of passage — the passage back from the flashbulbs and the microphones, back to being just himself. The fit was terribly important because it released him from fake. Nick was an incomparable faker of ease. The more serious the world became over him, the more seductively casual did he act vis-à-vis such seriousness, thereby attracting more of it. His flair had killed off the governor and all the Sherr Winnises. And now her.

The only difference being that Trudy knew the final paradox: Nick's ease was no cinch for him. There was a clenchedness somewhere inside it. When the performance was over he had to unclench himself. That he usually managed only in Trudy's presence. Sometimes, when they got back to their suite, his shoes would get unbearably tight. In Santa Fe, after the National Chicano Caucus, he'd ripped off his loafers and thrown them out the window into the hotel pool, and only after *that* could he laugh and they put on their wig disguises and drove off together, and he was his off-hours European *roi-fainéant* self and everything was fine. Or after the endless handshaking in Minneapolis he came in with his thumb in a spasm so that Trudy had to sign room service for him; but then they Indian-wrestled — a sudden idea he had — real dirty Indian wrestling with foot cheating and nail scratching, and then everything was fine too.

But the most usual release was through his sneezing, fits that he often exaggerated with wild wheezings. Dristan always made it worse, and therefore it was bound to come back doubly after he woke up in Munich after the plane trip. And it didn't. The allergy simply didn't come back. He was Nick — full of beans in the car, joking about the Bavarian weather to Tom and Dorothy and waving to the Secret Service men, who could relax abroad and rode in the car behind. Trudy was stunned by that. Somehow his failure to sneeze reminded her of Ronnie falling, skinning his little knee badly and then just sitting in silence, doubled over his leg. Ronnie had often failed to cry; Nick now failed to sneeze even more weirdly. The failure made all his previous sneezings seem like forgeries.

No, she couldn't believe it; Nick unsneezing in the car, his arms round Trudy, fresh as a daisy after the night flight, after a fairly taxing conversation, his foolscap pad on his crossed knee, talking to Dorothy and Tom, who sat on the jump seats.

"Everybody game for a little work?" Nick said. "Get a fix on the Governors' Conference speech now? Then all you two guys have to do is polish it in Innsbruck and then goof off? Okay?"

"Sure," Dorothy said.

So that's what they did, right off a transatlantic crossing, at an ungodly eight A.M., in a hairpin-curve limbo, cutting through rain and moist pines, and Nick was still clear-eyed, not a single sneeze.

His crispness dazed her. Trudy felt as if *she'd* been lamed by too many Dristans. She couldn't quite follow his criticism of the first draft of the speech. Something about the wit in it being too postgraduate. They passed the salute of caped guards at the German-Austrian border. "Governors, my distinguished friends, six of you will be up for re-election on the day I hope to be elected and, gentlemen, I've never seen a finer set of coattails." Yes, Nick said, the idea was to be less ashamed of *Reader's Digest* yuks. Reform was for the sake of folks, it had to be voted in by folks, it was worth trying to package it a little more folksily. The car veered. Sudden tree branches stuck out of the mist and struck at the window.

"Trudy — so quiet?" Nick said.

"I'm trying to collect my thoughts," she said.

There was wet black cotton behind her eyes. Dorothy's computer mind contributed facts to the folksy packaging. Tom, who used to write for the Johnny Carson Show, turned out to be a good phrasemonger. Trudy's usual job was idea-thrust and overall structure. Now all she could think of was the ludicrousness of wearing last night's dress this morning.

"I have a headache," she said when they kept looking at her.

Innsbruck turned out to be as rainy as Munich or New York. They reached the hotel where the others were to be dropped off, but Nick felt the speech still didn't have quite the right flow, though it had to be delivered right after the weekend.

"We're close," he said. "Might as well finish it off right here at the hotel."

While Dorothy's and Tom's luggage was carried to their rooms, they all settled down in a small beer-smelling banquet hall where a vacuum cleaner ground away, relentlessly, next door. The others didn't seem to mind. It was like a drill into Trudy's forehead. The others worked on, verbalizing folksily the suburban stake in Urban Maintenance. Trudy combed her hair. Combing sometimes had the effect of a refreshing massage. This time she couldn't even get the tangles out.

"I better go ahead up to Bachberg," she said to Nick.

"Are you all right?"

"Just the headache," she said. "I'm not in working order."

"Poor thing. Sure. Catch up with you in a couple of hours."

He looked concerned, always a rather startling production in a slightly scarred gondolier face.

So she went back to the car alone. It drove her out of Innsbruck, curved steeply into the Alpine woods. She rolled down the window, not caring how wet the rain might make her. She needed to be refreshed. Refreshment refused to come. In the afternoon the car reached Bachberg's high meadows and the rain stopped. But that didn't help her. Even here, at nine thousand feet, mist sludged heavily along the slopes. Below the lodge she noticed a mist-veiled derrick working at a wall around the chalet complex. It shrieked and whirred away like a giraffe gone deafeningly mad among the peaks.

At the lodge she didn't bother to have her bag unpacked. She went upstairs and dropped face down on the double bed. Instead of relief or sleep came noise. Growls, gratings, the cries of the steel giraffe. She called Tony on the phone.

"Oh, this is the fence they are building because Mr. Antone's union project is kaput," Tony said.

She understood nothing. She did know that vacation bungalows had been put up for Nick's building workers. Letarpo had leased them the land at some nobly low figure. The nobility didn't make the noise any less or explain why the project was kaput. Nor did the noise stop at seven. It stopped at seven-twenty. At that point Trudy was too frazzled for sleep. But she didn't want to take a pill. Too much like the abandoned maiden escaping into oblivion.

"Is the sauna working?" she asked Tony on the phone.

"Sauna?" Tony said. "Ah! We had pipe trouble because of the construction. But I get going the pump and you have enough water for sure in the morning."

Trudy knew she had to do something, ventilate herself tonight. "How about the glacier lift?" she said.

"Oh yes, okay. But now it is getting night —"

"The lights still work Mr. Letarpo put up?"

"Oh yes. The lift is okay too. But now at night? You want me to come?"

"No thanks," she said. "I'll just try a couple of runs."

Downstairs in the ski room, changing to her snow gear, the window dark outside, she recognized the weirdness of the impulse; she welcomed it. After the weirdness that was happening to her, it was therapeutic to try a little weirdness of her own. Just clanking out the door with her skis stamped away some of her funk.

Tony had thrown all the switches. The vast fog-hung mountain night hummed for her. Lift chairs moved empty and solemn through the brightness between the floodlights and the seamed white glass slope of the glacier. Trudy jumped a chair. Weird — yes, she felt rather piquantly weird: flying up the light beam of the universe, and the only trouble was that despite the altitude and the chill it was still the same old sodden mist clogging her lungs.

But even that changed halfway up. The air cleared. A thousand stars sprang at her. From the Silvretta range, peak lights glittered. She jumped off at the top of the lift. Deeply she inhaled, deeply and happily for the first time in many hours. The next moment had her staggering with dizziness. She bent down to rub some harsh glacier snow into her face. It restored her completely. She put on her goggles against the floodlight glare.

"Fuck you, Paulette!"

The shout echoed down the verticals, and she pushed off.

"Fuck you, Sherr Winnis!"

She wanted to make it easy for herself, so she turned in wide slow arcs, pleasant despite the stiffness of the snow. The filter of her goggles fused into the same green spectrum, stars, floodlights, snow and scrub pine. Through panoramic greenness she swayed, in total solitude and freedom. The muscles in her thighs felt the pull of the slope, but the rest of her luxuriated in release: she was tied to nothing! To no man, no career, no swollen political imperatives. Only to her Ronnie and to herself. She skied well and stopped for a rest at the slight bend in the glacier where the dwarf firs clustered. Free.

"Trudy!"

A silhouette shouting up there in the glare. Nick was coming down after her.

"Trudy! . . . Hold it, will you?"

Instinctively she pushed off. She didn't want him near. He was bad for the freedom she'd just begun to relearn. But of course he was so much faster and better.

"Trudy!"

Rather than being caught, helplessly, she decided to allow him to catch up.

"Trudy! ... Hey! ..."

She heard him sneeze before she heard the hiss of his skis. He held both his ski poles in his left hand. His right pressed the handkerchief against his face.

"You angry? ... Paulette? ... That's why I wanted this weekend with no business ... just you and me to —"

The sneeze shook him. His goggles were pushed up his forehead. The rawness of the floodlights battered his cheeks. Suddenly his gray hair was no longer boyish-premature. She'd never noticed such seamed erosion under his eyes before, his skin jowling and wrinkling after each sneeze.

"Trudy! Pinch my nose."

She pushed off again. Nothing could be trusted anymore. Not even his allergy, his mesmerizing, infatuating funny little frailties. He snowed her with those the way he snowed the world, with wit and looks. She skied faster. She didn't dare schuss, but she traversed at a pretty good clip, and the increase in speed increased her anger because he caught up so easily. She stopped short to let him have it.

"Listen!"

She didn't get beyond that one word. He flew right by, giving his head a light shake, goggles still pushed up, two ski poles in one hand, handkerchief in the other, whizzing past sovereignly, going into a fine taut slalom round the pines to show that nothing could daunt or refute him.

One of the two poles dropped from his hand. His wedel sprayed into a snowplow. She was astonished. What she saw next was something she had never seen before in her whole life, Nick totally out of control. For a moment his hand with the handkerchief seemed to reach for the lost ski pole. The left ski went up, out of balance. His parka, which wasn't quite zipped, ballooned like a green football inflated in the glare. He got his left ski down just in time for him to shave past the dwarf firs. He vanished doubled over, sneezing. A small clatter, a tap, pervasive through the night. Then nothing. No call or sneeze or noise of skiing. Just the lift

181

chairs floating empty with the tiniest clicks against the cable, and cowbells far off in the black scenic silence.

"Nick," she said to herself.

She pushed off hard as she could. In her panic she fell just before the jutting of the scrub pines. Snow punished her belly. She scrabbled up, stabbed with her poles at her bindings to unsnap the skis, crawled past the pines, saw.

She looked away instantly, whispering to herself: *Don't touch — phone! Don't touch — phone!*

Her forehead burned and her stiff high boots were murder on this steepness. She fell again in her haste toward the telephone box with the red cross painted on it.

"A helicopter! Tony! Wake up! . . . Something happened! We're in the middle of the run — where all the pines are! . . . A hospital helicopter! . . . Right now!"

And then she just let herself sag onto the snow, ripped off her goggles, let herself look.

Just outside the dark's edge, the floodlights produced him so brutally out of the night. He lay there, thrown slim and askew across the boulder, arms wide open, one ski broken, the other pointed up at the little moon, his head downslope, long neck bent almost lovingly round the sharp cropping of rock, the hair so young-gray, silken again, so fine a contrast against the dark green of the goggles and the lighter green of the moss, against the white of his half-open eye and the blood that came out of his ear, wetting and darkening the parka, darkening a path into the snow and into the silence, and a breath came down the mountain and shadows of lift chairs flew past, solemn and slow and empty, and small pine twigs trembled and cowbells sounded in the dark far away.

V

1

It was after midnight in Liechtenstein when she heard the car. The first thing she did was not put on the wig. No one would be awake in town to see her; her hair was too freshly washed; she was too tired to endure the sweaty thing. She put on her big hat.

"Letarpo is at the police station."

Jennifer spoke in the doorway, breathless from having run up the stairs. The dog, the big dog whose name she didn't know, stood next to Jenn, a monumental four-legged piece of dream-porcelain that would shatter and set up a chain reaction of shatterings through the night, at the first wrong move. Fatigue had alerted Trudy to split-lines, cracks, mortalities everywhere; you had to thread your way through urgency and fragility in the dark. She went fast down the stairs, but one step at a time, past the antlers and old Antone sleeping, and waved goodby to Jennifer.

The ride took her through a black town of drawn curtains and empty streets, the moon staring rheumy out of the river. The eye of a drowned zombie.

The car stopped. Getting out, Trudy understood less than ever how a police station could look like a timbered villa. Irrational low twitter came from the nest in the eaves. Swallows were dreaming the same dream that shivered Antone's luggage tag and made the big dog pray.

But inside, in the office, there was Letarpo (with the police captain, who cried "Madame!"). Tarp was there at last. The earphones on him were as black as his polo shirt. Off they came. He gave her a big vibrant wave with them.

185

"Trood!"

"You've already talked to Ronnie?"

"No. In about five minutes. You had a tough time, Trood?"

"What do you think?" she said. "Where've you been?"

"Come on. We get a sieve."

He didn't try to kiss her. Arm lightly around her shoulder, he ushered her out and the three assistants that moved with him as always, moved along too.

"Where are you going?"

"*Kapitän*," he said. "You got a kitchen sieve?"

"Sir?" the police captain said. "A sieve?"

"Kitchen sieve. Like, strain soup through. You got a kitchen around here?"

"Yes, Mr. Letarpo. In my house next door. If you are hungry —"

"Just get a big sieve. Come on, Trood."

Even now Tarp had an energizing effect on her. She needed energy so badly.

"Where the hell are you going?" she said.

"Come on, couple of steps. Here. That's too many baby swallows."

They stood under the soft twitter of the nest in the eaves.

"Hear that? *Peet!peet!* at night? That means too many baby guys. We had a *peet!peet!* problem on my island, I tell you?"

"We ought to go back for Ronnie," she said.

"Ronnie calls, we're inside in a second. You got a sieve, *Kapitän?*"

"I have already sent a man, Mr. Letarpo."

"Waiting, doing nothing is nervous," Letarpo said. "We do something. We take out the extra *peet!peet!* Otherwise *peet!peet!* is going to be pushed out."

"You are right, sir." The Captain seemed resolved to be thrilled at everything that might happen. "Indeed, a little swallow was pushed out last year!"

"Chey, somebody get a little grass," Letarpo said, and one of his assistants moved out into the night to pluck grass blades from the lawn.

"Will we hear it if my son is making contact?" Trudy said.

"Of course, I have a man standing by," the Captain said. "Ah, excellent. The sieve."

A kepi'd cop had brought a big wire-meshed sieve, which the grass-gatherer took and quickly filled with grass. Sudden loud chirping. Trudy turned and saw Letarpo lifted high by an assistant, reaching into the nest under the eaves.

"Chey," Letarpo said. "Easy in there. I just want one little *peet!peet!* Make it easier for you. No, there! . . . Nice little *peet!peet!* Little white-necked one. We don't let them kick you out. Take good care of you."

He jumped down, put the tiny whimpering twitch into the grass of the sieve. A buzzer sounded.

"Ah — radio contact!" the Captain said.

"Ronnie!" Trudy said. They all rushed inside.

"I'm taking little *peet!peet!* to the island," Tarp said. "We haven't got any little white-necked ones. . . . Ronaldo, my boy?"

They'd clamped on the earphones, Letarpo with one hand because he cupped the grassy sieve with the other.

"Gospodin," said the voice in the earphone.

It was Ronnie's voice, more metallic than ever.

"*Ronnie, it's me!*" she said.

"I have business with Gospodin."

"Now, Ronaldo," Tarp said. "Number one, we got the refuel plane right behind you. You let them air-fuel through the hose and you got another nine hours' flying time, nine more hours to be tough with me, deal?"

Silence. Crackling in the earphones.

"Answer him, Ronnie! Please!" she said.

"All right," the voice said. "But I want Yussuf safe. And I want proof. No tricks."

At the word "tricks" the voice broke slightly into something more human and teenage, and made Trudy gasp. Letarpo threw the sieve with the little bird into her lap. Just in time. The touch of her hand against soft grass and soft feather kept her from a scream.

"Tricks," Letarpo said. "Guy like you, with dynamite up in my plane, no sir, no tricks with you."

"I want proof," the voice said.

"Listen," Letarpo said. "In seven hours I have Yussuf talking to you here, alive, safe. You know his voice. No tricks. Seven hours or less. That tough enough on me?"

Silence. She stroked the softness, grass or feather.

"Maybe," the voice said.

"Ronnie!" she said. "I'm not trying to sway you or anything. But do you get enough rest so you can think?"

"Yes," the voice said. "Gospodin."

"I'm here," Letarpo said.

"I've got Yussuf's sister with me," the voice said.

"Don't remind me," Letarpo said.

"Say what she reminds you of, Gospodin. How many barrels of oil. She's a princess of Macedonia."

"You mean how much oil we got in Macedonia? Oh you are a real tough one, Ronaldo."

"How many barrels, Gospodin?"

"Seven million barrels a day. And in seven hours I get you Yussuf. Now you got my nose bloody enough?"

"When the princess and I land, Gospodin, you'll bless our affair with a kiss."

"A kiss?"

"A kiss before photographers. Yussuf in seven hours and a kiss before photographers. Yes or no, Gospodin?"

"Yes," Letarpo said. "*Proklinjati!*"

"Mother, you're a witness," the voice said.

"Ronnie!"

"Goodby, Gospodin. Mother, goodby."

Silence. The hum of electromagnetic nothingness.

"Foooh, I don't want *him* in a proxy fight," Letarpo said.

"He better come down all right," Trudy said, stroking the soft feather.

"Sure he will," Letarpo said. "Now you go to sleep, I go to work."

"I can't sleep. I tried at the hotel," Trudy said. "I want to stay right here, just in case."

"Okay, stay here and sleep here."

"Sleep here?" she said.

"Sure. You got a jail here, *Kapitän?*"

"Beg your pardon, Mr. Letarpo?" the police captain said.

"You sleep great in Swiss jails; I know," Letarpo said. "Got anything like that around here?"

"Well, next door," the Captain said. "We have a little detention facility."

"This door?" Letarpo said, and opened one and then another, and behind the double door was a small bare room with nothing in it but a cot and a crucifix.

"Something breaks, you're right next door," Letarpo said. "Sleep!"

She wanted to ask him a lot of questions. But suddenly all the compressed fatigue sagged loose and pulled at her limbs. All her veins became sandbags.

"You'll get Yussuf?" she said.

"One hundred percent. I come through before morning. Sleep!"

The doors closed behind her. She put her hat over the crucifix, to muffle that agony into rest. A few grass-blades stuck to her thumb from the swallow sieve she had given him. She closed her hand over the thin green. Then she fell on the cot.

❧ *2* ❧

Letarpo had always come through. Even at the worst moment at Bachberg with the two doctors and the chief of police for all of Tyrol standing around Nick's body, writing out certificates and depositions, and the incredible number of reporters materialized out of nowhere, flies converging on a huge fresh death, reporters she could see from the windows of the lodge, reporters shouldering their cameras behind the roadblocks, reporters by the flicker of the trashcan fires they'd made, reporters rubbing their hands against the frost of dawn, reporters tilting flasks against their mouths, reporters who waited for her too, for they all knew she was there, the police chief had told her the Austrian radio had already mentioned the beautiful young lady surviving and co-starring in the great ski death — even at *that* moment Letarpo had come through, from God knows where. He had come himself, amazing, even if he was the lessor of that glacier. He'd suddenly showed up in a Snow-

189

cat tractor, dressed in overalls and a cap too big for him, and he'd taken Trudy down the same way, unrecognized, bypassing the helicopter pad and the roadblocks past the flask-drinkers and hand-rubbers, cutting through the underbrush while Trudy lay on the ribbed floor of the tractor, by way of extra precaution.

And then he'd more or less vanished for a little while, to come through again, in an entirely different way, about a month after the funeral. He called her up, out of the blue, during still another backbreaking session over the disposition of campaign funds.

"Hey, my lady Trudy."

The rough jovial voice was like a massage. It was also a relief. Usually the phone ringing meant still another Nick-obituarist who had cracked her unlisted number or still another yap from the *National Enquirer*. At least this was neither.

"Chey, why you want to make Swissair rich?"

"What?" she said, smiling.

"I got a spy, says you go to Zurich Wednesday, Swissair."

"Yes, I'm picking up Ronnie at his school."

"So you got a lift, my jalopy. I'm going Wednesday myself."

"Well, thank you!" she said.

"Where you sneak off with Ronaldo?"

"We've got to get away from it all," she said. "Old Antone invited us to Bahama Key for the summer."

"Old Antone! *Zaista ne!* Key Bahama! Where the grave is? Sit with the father on the grave all summer? Always be reminded? There's no other place? You kidding! My driver picks you up, noon Wednesday."

His driver picked her up, noon Wednesday, and he was right. Nick had been dead for weeks, but every day she was still reminded, and sometime it had to stop. In Letarpo's plane she realized how it still hadn't stopped. Some part of her couldn't believe that this plane wasn't still part of the *Nick Now!* campaign, wasn't just another whirring piston that would thrust Nick into the White House, dead or alive. It had all the smooth acceleration of the *Nick Now!* apparatus with bits of gnomishness here and there for an extra twist. Behind the cockpit, the same cove with consoles, lights flashing, soft communications clatter. And if the installations here were a little bigger, that only made Nick's victory seem all the more imminent. The bedroom had sepia mahogany dressers and the lizard poised a scaly bright green on the yellow bedspread. He raised his head as if to judge the hum of the starboard engine. And the abrupt folksiness in the next section, coarse wooden chairs with cotton bolsters, the olive tree in the brass pot, leaves moving faintly to the vibrations, the bark-covered Chianti bottles and the salami rods hanging next to the oxygen masks. A harbor tavern cruising thirty-five thousand feet above the Atlantic. And the three men in gray suits and black turtlenecks who smiled up from their work on notepads. They, too, struck her as part of a startling new posthumous Nick playfulness.

Letarpo stopped her before the next partition. Beyond it she saw the Louis XIV table, burled and burnished, with three people. Ronnie's friend Prince Yussuf, now a goateed young man under a turban, and his kid sister in a dainty yellow summer frock; and, black-bearded, blue-eyed, their father in a Cardin blazer. That this blazer enclosed the Moslem king of Macedonia seemed much less bizarre to Trudy than the fact that Nick wasn't on board nor would never be seen again in mortal time.

"Don't think Nick all the time," Letarpo said. He gave her a little push. He had a special husky whisper. "Think this king here. Europe or America, every street corner got a car with his oil in the tank. Man like that doesn't know what to do with his son. Interesting? Think that."

"All right, I'll think that," Trudy said.

"Come on, let's be hungry," Letarpo said. And they went to have dinner with the Macedonians.

But at this, her first meal with a king, they talked about Nick again. She'd met the king just before takeoff, yet he got up as if they were to be introduced all over again and smiled inside his probably dyed black beard.

"Please, enjoy an apéritif," he said. "You will ignore that I am forbidden by my faith."

Except for the phrasing he sounded American-Irish. This wasn't surprising, the king said, as he had been brought up in Macedonia by a lace-curtain nanny. "My father pirated her — is that the expression? — from the Kennedys."

"Good stuff, pirate the pirates," Letarpo said.

"But I have no Boston manners; I was remiss," the king said to Trudy. "I neglected to extend to you in the name of my family and my country our sorrow at the loss of Mr. Antone."

"Kind of you," Trudy said. The dining cabin of the plane was half-lit by electric sconces: a mercy in view of the probable color of her cheeks. She still reacted like that to congratulations for being the bereaved mistress, the most intimate survivor of a great charisma. Congratulations to a great love Nick might well have dumped, had he lived to see the White House. Anyway, she'd be damned if she'd call anybody "Your Majesty."

Letarpo pushed her down into a chair between the king and the prince. "Drinks?" Letarpo said. "No? Everybody a good boy? Okay." He threw his fingers in strange patterns at the steward. The steward looked Chinese, an apparent deaf-mute. He was bald, worried-looking, smaller than Letarpo even, and he moved in fast spurts in his white uniform, like a ballboy at a tennis tournament. Nobody touched the lamb stew, not even Letarpo, until the king reached for his fork.

"Now, Madame Spieger," the king said. "Are you going to be prominent in this great new university in New York?"

"Well — I'm sitting that out for now," Trudy said.

"None of my business, but they'd just use her for fund-raising," Letarpo said. "Use the publicity."

"I'm trying to get back to my own work," Trudy said. "I haven't even finished my Ph.D. dissertation."

"This young lady," Letarpo said. "She's written social science stuff way above my head."

"Indeed?" the king said.

"We got her back on her own track," Letarpo said.

"My daughter Dara here," the king said. "In a much more modest way she has a track of her own also." He stroked her on the arm and the pale princess began to cut her lamb pieces fast into tinier bits. "Indeed she has. She is only eleven. But already she sings our Sufi songs with much feeling. I am told your son's school is attentive to creativity?"

"Well, it's closing now," Trudy said. "That's why I'll be scouting for a new one."

"Perhaps my daughter could also attend whatever institution you select for your son? Could you also scout for her?"

"Well, I couldn't afford anything fancy," Trudy said.

"I don't desire fancy," the king said. "Modern is desirable. My daughter has not much gotten about. With your approval, my son Yussuf could escort my daughter on your scouting? Also some attendants? I would be pleased."

"Why not?" Trudy said.

"Know what kind of an unfancy king?" Letarpo nodded his chin at his neighbor. "He's got a much better plane than me. Sauna, pinball machine, everything. But *his* plane, we land and the roofs fall in. Protocol, boom! Ambassador, boom! Flag, fuss, boom, boom! This way with me, he just sneaks up. Guest of a business-man. That's all."

"Not just a businessman," the king said. "A good friend."

"I hope so," Letarpo said. "Ten years from now my lease with you — *finito*. Letarpo's no friend then, he's nothing."

"*Perhaps we should make provision for ten years from now.*"

The suddenness with which the prince spoke up made it seem like a shout.

"I have sufficient, thank you," the king said to the steward who came around with seconds.

"Such planning should be done a long time ahead," the prince said.

"Madame Spieger doesn't wish to be bored," the king said, dabbing his mouth.

"It is not a boring subject," the prince said.

The king raised his hand. A man with a fez stepped forward from a door Trudy hadn't noticed. On the man's wrist stood a brown curve-beaked bird.

"He won't eat while he's drugged," the prince said, very erect. His sister cut the lamb into tiny pieces.

"I'm not feeding him," the king said. He took the bird on his own wrist and began to stroke the feathers with a tenderness peculiar in such a very bony hand. Abruptly he handed the bird to his son. So fast, as if the bird had leaped at the prince.

"You will hood the falcon in my bedroom," the king said. "Perhaps my daughter will enjoy the film with me?"

The prince got up, went off, fast, silent, pale.

"Film coming up," Letarpo said.

No, this was definitely not the *Nick Now!* jet. Sconces dimmed. A white kite unfolded from the ceiling into a screen. The fez began to strangle the king from behind.

"I am sorry," the king said. "I have only this one set of earphones."

The fez had adjusted the phones around the royal neck and ears.

"We go drink Turkish?" Letarpo said. He gave Trudy a little push.

"Interesting?" Letarpo said. "Little bit of king family-trouble? Takes your mind off Nick?"

"In a way," Trudy said.

The Chinese served them coffee in a tiny bar in a tiny cabin with a window looking out on a jet wing that had a red light at the tip.

"Just a small sip from the top. Let it settle lower down," Letarpo said.

"It's good," Trudy said, sipping the coffee from the top.

"Always brings his own films," Letarpo said. "King's got every one Ava Gardner ever made. His own earphones too. Not with the regular — what do you call it? — the regular dialogue. He knows that backwards. But dirty stuff on Ava. What she does with matadors. Interesting?"

"With matadors?" Trudy said.

"I don't know," Letarpo said. "He won't let me listen. But he's a nice chap. The prince too. Hello, Yussuf."

The prince had come in, very pale.

"I must apologize, but it was too much," he said.

"It was interesting," Letarpo said. "Gets the young lady away from things a little bit. Drink Turkish, Yussuf."

"Thank you," the prince said. "But first I must tell you." He had turned to Trudy. "I've been wanting my sister to go to your son Ronald's school. My father has consented now only because of you."

"I don't even know what Ronnie's new school will be," Trudy said.

"My father doesn't care because you are very famous now."

Trudy always hated her own pleasure at such statements. She had no illusions about herself as the vehicle of Nick's posthumous image. Senator Sherr Winnis had succeeded to the mechanics of the *Nick Now!* machine. She had inherited the Nick Antone glamour, elegantly spayed. She was the woman of the Great Romantic Ski Disaster. The heart of the Nick movement, the true tough core, had gone up in pot smoke in college cafeterias. Maybe there were some people around still uncynical enough to be heartbroken. At any rate the messianism Nick had triggered didn't live on in her. But Nick's perfume did, piquant, headily notorious, safe. Even an oriental autocrat could now become a Nick Antone fan by kissing Trudy's hand. All that she knew damn well. So why be pleased about her fame?

"If I'm famous it's for the wrong reasons," she said.

"No, no," the prince said. "And furthermore — or rather first and foremost: I, too, am grieved by Mr. Antone's death! Much more than my father! I have a right to be! I met Mr. Antone in London last year. I am reading economics in London, probably he didn't mention it to you — trivial for him — for me extraordinary! I was so flattered! We agreed on so many items!"

"Yussuf, drink Turkish," Letarpo said, and poked him toward the cup.

"The Senator agreed," Yussuf said, "the last thing that should happen after Mr. Letarpo gives up the oil sites — the very last thing is nationalization."

"The first thing happens," Letarpo said, "we drink Turkish and we find a school."

"But nationalization means my three uncles get three hundred thousand acres! I'm sorry, Mrs. Spieger! I shouldn't impose this on you. This is very bad manners. But I even tried to explain it to your son."

"Did you?" Trudy said. "To Ronnie?"

"Oh, he is most intelligent. I told him how thrilled I was about Mr. Antone. Mr. Antone was so sympathetic when I opened my heart to him. He also agreed, there's no point my reading at the

London School of Economics. I know all the economics I need about my country! Not five giant estates, the rest slum! No! Individual community ownership of resources! A Nick Antone program applied to our conditions. I've sent the Antone program to thirty of our mayors — I am truly sorry! Such a tirade! The worst manners."

"No," Trudy said. "Not a bit."

Her eyes had begun to run down her cheeks. Why had she become so goddamn weepy? This turbaned prince with his naïve theatrical face and the idealistic shoulder straps on his white shirt — had he really discussed things with Ronnie which Ronnie had never even mentioned to her? What kind of tie did she have with her only child? She had so few real solid things as she was being flung across the Atlantic again. Nick was dead. The zeal that trembled in this Yussuf and which she'd once felt burning in her rib cage . . . where was it now? She was even scared that a return to her doctoral work might be beyond her present powers of concentration; and, as the plane bumped, she felt she'd lose Ronnie too, there'd be no one waiting for her at a disintegrating school in Switzerland. She needed someone. What the hell had happened to the strong Trudy, the Pink Eminence of Nick's sweep?

"I'm just tired," she said. "Please excuse me."

"Oh, I'm most dreadfully sorry," said the prince.

"We let her go," Letarpo said, patting the prince on the neck.

Then he escorted Trudy along the bumping plane. In the dark dining cabin the king watched Ava Gardner cross her legs, his head leaned into the dirty whispers of the earphones, his hand stroking the arm of his daughter. In the tavern part of the plane, the triplet-looking turtlenecked men jumped up and then sat down again after Letarpo shook his head at them. By her own cabin Letarpo opened the door, released her with a slight squeeze on the elbow.

"Sleep," he said.

She stood alone behind the closed door. The plane bumped. A hoarse cawing cry came from somewhere, perhaps from the falcon. She fell on her bed.

"Ronnie!" she said. The percale sheets had been meticulously turned. "Ronnie, be there!"

~ *3* ~

Actually she'd always felt a little guilty about Ronnie being at the École Mannritt at all. She'd chosen the school because it was in Switzerland, far from Ronnie's pubic-hair misadventure in New York. Yet it was close to Zurich airport. It had a good music department and last, not least, there was Madame Mannritt's willingness to go along with Trudy's requirements.

"I want to see my son whenever there is a chance," she'd said to Madame Mannritt at the initial interview. "I might snatch him away for a few days in the middle of the term. I'd just like that understood."

"Oh yes," Madame Mannritt had said. "You are in politics?"

"Yes, at the moment."

"Oh, Mrs. Spieger," Madame Mannritt said. "Politics. My late American husband was in New York politics. He made enemies — people trying to attach the income of the school to this day! They want to ruin us! I could not pay the mortgage. *Vicious* people, using politics with the judge!" The pack of file cards Madame Mannritt had held in her hand were now all in a heap on her desk. Her blonde pompadour seemed to have an erection, her culotte dress bosomed out, her cheeks gleamed with passion. "It is dirty politics! *Kress* versus *Mannritt*, Southern District Court of New York. I am sure you are in good politics; if you could help in any way. . . ."

"You overestimate my influence," Trudy said, ambushed by all this. The École Mannritt might not be the place for Ronnie after all.

"Of course," Madame Mannritt said. Smoothing back her hair, she was smoothing away the outbreak. The file cards were a neat stack once more. "I only mentioned it because you mentioned politics. Please, do not be put off. I welcome your son."

But of course Trudy was put off. Why, then, did she keep Ronnie at Mannritt just the same? By any chance, because deep down she knew she was a pretty unentrenched mother due to her hectic Nick-life — because, leaving Ronnie at Mannritt, she felt

197

she could reclaim him easier from an unentrenched, contested, unstable school?

Was that possible?

It was possible. Trudy tried to know herself. And to fight that part of her psyche she'd been several times on the point of pulling Ronnie out of the Mannritt establishment. If she didn't at the end, it was because she discovered that the school was peculiarly right for a peculiar child like Ronnie. In five modernistic silos on the outskirts of Zurich, the school flailed away at every athletic and aesthetic skill. Apart from subjects academic, Mannritt also taught opera, mountain climbing, yoga, ballet, judo, painting, skating, sculpture, skiing, drama, squash and three-dimensional chess. At night everybody was lifeless with self-improvement. Even then there was little letup. The faculty (mostly Swiss university students who always had coughs, perhaps from all the overwork) kept their charges busy with trilingual Scrabble.

And La Mannritt herself glided about the Student Lounge's sparse Finnish furniture among her faculty's sniffles. Perhaps living at the edge of professional extinction gave her extra vitality. You wouldn't guess a lawsuit was killing her. She looked much younger than forty-five (the age given in the catalogue). She had full flushed cheeks, a vibrant pile of blondeness, and a long green gown to hide the waistline. "*Ah, Freddie!*" she said. "*Qu'est-ce que tu as? Un petit mal de tête! Och!*"

The author of all that draconian activity in the daytime, she was at night all Junoesque solicitude and bosom warmth. She floated among the exhaustion of her children like a huge mothering cherub to rub black-and-blue spots, to stroke foreheads and detect fevers. She passed out aspirins (personally placed the tablet on the tip of a child-tongue and then patted the neck to help with the swallowing). She massaged the scalps of kids headachy from too much broad jumping, glued Band-Aids on knees scraped during stage-prop moving and gave Ex-Lax to the pole-vault champion slumped before the Scrabble board.

Most of the Mannritt parents were high-speed international executives who could give little time to their families. They wanted to have their children thoroughly taken care of, if possible to the fatigue point that would leave no energy for drug-fun or sex.

Trudy, who saw through the psychology, found that she herself was not above it either. She had her own manic schedule around Nick and wanted to minimize a corresponding void in Ronnie. But there was one big difference — and no copout either: Ronnie actually did need the Mannritt regime. His energy not even that school could drain. Evenings Trudy would find her son whipping around the student lounge, always bizarrely hatted, a costume item swiped from whatever plays were being put on at the school. Not that Ronnie wore these hats with a sense of fun exactly. He hadn't inherited Nick's playfulness or her own inclination to irony. No, these funny hats were part of an adeptness that was inventive, graceful, smileless, a little weird. Others might laugh, but not Ronnie. If he put a cardinal's biretta on top of his blue jeans he'd needle his fellow students into an oratorio whose lyrics he improvised out of the ingredients list on a mineral-water bottle. If he wore a shaving-brush Alpine hat he got the other kids out of their sags into a Schuhplattler kicking dance. No matter how comatose, those kids obeyed. And La Mannritt indulged him, though she'd told Trudy of the house rule against "contretemps," especially evenings which were meant for soothing and curing. In view of the threat against it, the school had to be careful about mishaps and cuttings-up. Yet Ronnie, in his earnest way, continued to cut up. *"Mais c'est extraordinaire, votre petit,"* La Mannritt had once said to Trudy. "I have charge of Ronaud myself. We are working on a Hugo Wolf song. He is making a dance of it. The only person I know truly understand Hugo Wolf! At such age! *Si jeune! Extraordinaire!"*

Ronnie awaited them. Because of possible reporters they'd avoided the main entrance. With old Antone, who must have arrived just before, Ronnie stood inside the back door of the Dining Building. He stood there so tall! Not that he'd grown so much since the last time she'd seen him, but it was a shock to see him reach the shoulders of old Antone. Ronnie was one tall kid. He wore a fringed leather jacket and a red skullcap this time. But he whisked it off, came at her with an almost expertly affectionate kiss for which she no longer had to stoop down so much and whose expertise she didn't mind because she knew it had to varnish the embarrassment of real feeling. His lush hair, dark brown, had the same wavy spring against her cheek as Nick's gray locks once did.

"Hello, Mummy."

His voice wasn't quite the little-boy one any more. Pale freckles had surfaced on his cheeks, made them leaner somehow, pointed up the long-jawedness, again an echo of his father. He got poked in the stomach by Letarpo and covered up grinning. His old friend Prince Yussuf introduced him to the princess, his sister. Ronnie shook hands gravely. This was almost like a youth, a dear stranger. "Come back, little Ronnie!" she wanted to cry, probably after the manner of all mothers.

"My darling," she said. "We'll be looking for a school together with the princess."

He stood suspended. "It's a good school," he said. "We want to save this school! We'll put on a show to raise money —"

"No, no!" Madame Mannritt said. "Ronaud, no!"

"I want to show you," Ronnie said. He pointed both his forefingers at Trudy with an intensity that reached round her heart. At the same time she was ashamed of a smile hidden in her mouth, a not very nice pleasure: her boy was at the end of his school, she at the end of Nick. Both their lives were disrupted, therefore she wasn't alone in starting over again. And meanwhile two fat little fellows were pushing chairs and tables back to create a stage in the dining room. Ronnie always had his helpers.

"Please — no!" Mannritt said in a high C quiver. "Not before such guests!"

"It's all right," Trudy said.

She had no idea how a Letarpo or a little Macedonian princess would take this, but she was glad that Ronnie (taller or not) did what he so often did at the start of her visits. He rushed a performance at her. Usually for some practical reason, but underneath it was an outburst, an emotion, a rush to impress and win her all over again. He was still her little Ronnie.

"I hope this goes all right," the prince said.

Ronnie had thrown him a mouth organ and after three quick tuning riffs he went into the "Merry Widow Waltz," but oddly, with a muezzin's wail in the beat, and the next moment Ronnie danced. Ronnie danced along the Finnish sleek of the dining furniture. Hands in jeans pockets, shoulders lifted, he danced the "Merry Widow" as it might be danced around a minaret, slow and tranced. Blood burst from his lips and cut off the music in mid-phrase.

"*Sto se Desava?*" Letarpo said with a grin.

The princess gasped. Trudy knew her son. It was a theatrical fluid, some capsule he must have bitten open.

"Ronaud," La Mannritt whispered. "He is dancing the Ten Plagues from the Pharaoh ballet. . . ." Her whisper was a choked hysterical screech, and Trudy wished she'd shut up for Ronnie danced on with his cheek gory, waltzing on wounded yet still slowly, orientally majestic until another break in the waltz froze him. A frog, wet and rubbery, jumped from between his teeth. The waltz came on again and Pharaoh Ronnie danced once more, more damaged yet still with an iron grace, arms and brow imperial despite the feebler turns.

"Ten plagues. . . ." La Mannritt said. "Blood, frogs. . . . I am sorry!"

Thump.

No waltz. Mannritt lay in a faint on the floor, on a long massive green spill of a gown that rimmed Letarpo, his three assistants, old Antone, the princess. Yussuf had run to the corner sink.

"Madame!" the prince said and threw a moistened towel to Ronnie and, again in instant teamwork, Ronnie caught it, knelt down (bloody face and all), dabbed wetness on Madame Mannritt's forehead, dabbed her into sitting up. She began to pant out a faint coloratura.

"Forgive. . . . But to save my school! . . . One photograph! Mr. Letarpo and Madame Spieger and their Royal Highnesses! . . . To show what personalities in my school . . . It would attract backing! One picture to save the buildings!"

"*Never mind the buildings.*"

Letarpo's voice — not exactly loud but with such casual rough thrust it could pierce walls. Ronnie dropped the towel.

"*Don't worry about buildings.*"

Quite convivially that voice made other voices and actions superfluous. Letarpo had begun to move furniture. All the tables and chairs that had been moved back for the performance Letarpo now began to move forward again, to restore each piece to its exact place. His turtlenecked assistants made no move to help him. His whole retinue watched him quietly with the intentness of connoisseurs. Trudy watched him, old Antone watched, Mannritt, from the floor, watched. It was weird; it was as though Ronnie's plague-waltz and Mannritt's swoon, the whole confusion, had been meant to climax into the solo of one swarthy little man pushing chairs around.

"Never mind buildings," Letarpo said. He pushed a table. "You lose buildings, we get you buildings. Okay. Those Bachberg chalets. I build them for Nick's union. So without Nick they say No. So we put your school into the Bachberg buildings. Okay."

He said "Okay," every time he finished the restoration of one table with its complement of four chairs.

"*Dieu . . . ,*" Mannritt breathed from the floor.

"*Dieu* reminds me," Letarpo said. "Our little friend the princess. She's going to be a student. King's very Moslem. You have no religion department? Hello, *Madame la patronne* on the floor? You hear me? No religion teachers?"

"Religion?" Madame Mannritt said from the floor. "Religion? . . . We have yoga. Religion is difficult to recruit. But it would be wonderful!"

"Lady Trudy here, Mrs. Spieger," Letarpo said, carrying a chair. "She can swing religion. She knows more than professors."

"Wait a minute," Trudy said.

"Come on, terrific brain-lady like you," Letarpo said.

"First of all I'm in sociology, not religion," Trudy said.

"All right, consultant sociology and religion," Letarpo said. "Live in the school with Ronald. We got plenty chalets, stupid union. You can make your dissertation there too. Nice and quiet. Back to basics. Okay."

"Wait a minute," Trudy said again. But Letarpo had an irrefutable way of carrying three chairs at once.

"*I'll give you a shot!*" Letarpo said to Ronnie who tried to help him with the chairs. Letarpo threatened him with a mock-kick. "Okay," he said. "What else? Prince Yussuf. Yussuf, you manage the relocation, huh? I send you helpers. You move the school, re-model chalets, like that. Administrative experience. Just what you need."

"I'm due in Macedonia," the prince said.

"Macedonia," Letarpo said. "You kidding? Make your father mad? Every minute you're there, he gets madder. When my lease is up, he gives it all to Exxon, he's so mad. Okay."

"To *Exxon?*" the prince said.

"Or Texaco. Not nice chaps like me. To spite you, follow? Stay away. Let him cool down. Forget London School of Economics. I'll straighten it with him about no London School of Economics. Do this school. Executive experience and protect your baby sister. Ho-*hup!*"

With the pull of both his hands on both her wrists, small Letarpo had put big Mannritt on her feet. He needed her out of the way to restore the last chairs and tables.

"Now Ronald and his mother," he said. "We look over the Bachberg chalets this summer."

"This summer," Antone said.

It was the first time the old man had raised his voice.

"This summer Ronald and his mother will be at Key Bahama with me," Antone said.

"Ah."

Letarpo stopped in his tracks. Chair in hand he went directly, slowly, at Antone.

"You had Nick's funeral on Bahama," he said.

"You were there," the old man said.

"You got Nick's grave on Bahama," Letarpo said. The chair legs were pointed at the old man. "You got the grave. You don't need Ronald too, and the mother."

"My Croat friend," Antone said. "Don't sweat. Leave it to the mother."

Letarpo turned about on his heels. "How many buildings you got here?" he said to Mannritt. "Five? Six? Hm?"

"Eight," Mannritt said. "And the gardener's cottage. Also the garage. Oh, but this would be wonderful good fortune!"

"We got at least thirteen at Bachberg," Letarpo said. "Thirteen buildings, water, electricity, everything. That stupid union. You just need remodeling, installment of stuff, bookshelves, school equipment, cinch. Financing! I'll be Mr. Partner. Hey, big executive? Budget for relocation, remodeling, so on. We move this summer, Madame Partner?"

"Yes!" La Mannritt said. And Trudy realized someone had gone. No more old Antone.

"Where's the General?" she said.

"I'll get him," Ronnie said. With Mannritt he ran out the door. Trudy felt she ought to run too, talk to old Antone about postponing Bahama for just a little while to give this crazy idea a try. But the old man had just gone away.

Trudy ran out of the room. She passed the dark pantry and the bright student lounge, where droopy kids blinked up at the neoabstract chandeliers. She was just in time to see a teacher unlock the main entrance for old Antone — barely in time to coil back from the rush of photographers outside. For a moment she was dizzied-dazed. She couldn't understand anything. Why Nick was dead or why the world was so starved for a death like his or a survivor like herself. She stood alone among the stares of the students.

Passing the pantry on the way back, she saw silhouettes in the murk of a corner; for a moment so brief she wasn't even sure that had been an embrace. Mannritt and Ronnie. She didn't understand that either.

"We are so happy, I can't express!" Madame Mannritt said a moment later. At Mannritt's side, Ronnie came running to his mother, and together they walked back into the dining room toward Letarpo.

It wasn't the nearness to the place of Nick's catastrophe. The Bachberg valley lay only a mile below the glacier, but a huge brow of fir trees hid it from the ice. In fact it seemed hidden from just about everything. The road leading there was screened off by larches and by a stone wall stippled with moss. When they drove into the valley itself it was like opening the door on a sequestered chamber. Gray rock, dark woods, green slopes closed in a perfect ring around the meadows. It was quite something after the wild irregular canyons of the Alps all around. This sudden natural symmetry struck Trudy like a vitalizing shock. My God, a hint of purpose tucked away in chaos, of order possible even in her life.

No, there was nothing disturbing in the way it looked. The chalets built for the Union were scattered pleasantly through the hollow. Ronnie seemed to get along well with the princess, sister of his old friend Yussuf. Yussuf and Madame Mannritt walked far ahead, the two younger kids in tow, with the turtlenecked Letarpo assistants following. Against the scenery they looked like figurines in a romantic oil.

There was nothing objectionable about the chalets either. None of them were cursed by the project look. Some of the roofs still needed shingling, but they were all distinct from one another, idiosyncratic with off-angled corners, waywardly jutting eaves, some with oriels, some with fretted balconies, all within the Tyrolean style. Hearts, eagles and crosses were carved in bas-relief on gables and balustrades. A miniworld, grace notes and all, in which one could live. Cords with paper twisted around them marked off huge seeded lawns. Tips of grass needled out from the earth. She smelled a cleansing, a growing in the pine-tart blue air. She watched Ronnie run around the biggest chalet.

"What's the big house?" she asked.

"Community center. It was supposed to be," Letarpo said.

The place didn't exhilarate him. He wore horn-rimmed glasses on a steel chain round his neck. Occasionally he picked up the glasses, but not to put them on; he dropped them again into a dangle and marched close and compact next to Trudy, picking up wood shavings and mortar bits, tossing them aside, treating them as if they were great obstacles in Trudy's way. His hair fell sideways with the bending over, rather thick and glossy-black for a man his age.

"That's the house for you," he said.

They went in and it was a joke. It had a big hall and about eight rooms on each of the three floors, all blindingly whitewashed.

"It's only about twenty times too big for me," she said, though she was taken by the lovely balconies. A couple were even connected playfully by staircases.

"We use it as school library," Letarpo said. "You take the rooms on top. You got books near, good for research. Quiet too. *Cul-de-sac*. Here's the marsh." He picked up a nail from the balcony floor and threw it, morose, down into the bushes. Down there it glinted wet between the ferns. The valley, she saw, wasn't a quite flawless hollow round after all. Behind a fir copse it developed a long wet bushy spur that tilted down into the lower Inn valley. She liked that. This nook was a shelter against the world, but a shelter juicy and alive. One could really live here. Here she could finish her long-unfinished Ph.D. dissertation and learn enough German to teach at some Swiss university nearby. Live a nice small solid real life.

"The wet comes down from the glacier," Letarpo said. "We drain it."

"Why didn't this work out for the union?" Trudy said.

"Mummy!"

It was Ronnie running up.

"It's so big, Mummy! We can have a music room!"

"Hold on," she said. "A couple of rooms will do for us."

"Why?"

"We can't afford a palace. But it's nice here."

"Oh. No money?"

A leather-fringed ten-year-old, full of headlong innocence. Had he really kissed Madame Mannritt? In any case she wished he hadn't brought up money before Letarpo.

"Not enough to furnish a whole house, dumbo," she said.

"Chey, the school pays," Letarpo said. "School furniture for you. You'll be a school consultant."

"I don't want school furniture," she said. "I want to build my own life here."

"We arrange for an advance in salary."

"No," she said, walking out of the building. "Come on, Ronnie. Look at the marsh!"

He ran out to join Mannritt, just as she'd hoped. She didn't want him to hear the discussion. In fact, she didn't want to discuss finances with a billionaire. "Why didn't the union want this project?" she said.

"Why? Long as they had Nick, they had a brain. Now it's a bunch of headless chickens."

He picked up a pebble, hauled off for a big throw. The pebble flew low and far, dove into a pool between ferns and like a frog sprang out of the water into the green. It came to her what might have been the trouble all along. His tricks. She had a sense this exquisite valley was not nature but a production of his. Trudy suspected herself of not being sufficiently wary of the man. From

206

her *Nick Now!* experience she knew that the people who wanted to change the system (like herself) were patsies vis-à-vis the people who operated the system. The changers took the system rules so seriously they wanted new ones. But the operators employed and broke the rules with equal virtuosity. Compared to such ambidextrousness the greatest revolutionaries were simpletons. She was no longer a revolutionary (if she'd ever really been one). But she sure didn't want to be Mr. Letarpo's simpleton. His moroseness today was probably a trick within a trick.

"I wish you'd leave the marsh the way it is," she said.

"We just drain it." He bounced another pebble. "Nine-hole golf for the school. You play golf? We teach you. An excellent attraction for the school, golf. Terrific for Madame Partner."

For a moment he straightened up, swelled out in front, became Madame Mannritt teeing off like a huge-bosomed Prussian general. But he didn't smile. He stayed morose.

"No," she said. "I don't want to learn golf."

"I don't play much either," he said.

"Don't make a golf course," she said. "I'd hate it if I lived here. I want to concentrate on my son and my dissertation, start all over again in a real way, and if there's going to be a lot of building here, and tampering and manipulation and embellishment — my God, I had too much of that in my life!"

He seemed to smile now and she didn't know what had come over her. Maybe a desire to assert herself, impose a move of her own since he made so many. So many maybe tricky ones.

"What I mean," she said. "The marsh is lovely. The whole setting here is just right. Why not leave it as it is?"

"The golf would be good for the school," he said. "With the golf we can charge top tuition. I have become a tremendous expert in tuition."

"Sorry. I forgot there are other aspects," she said. It was embarrassing. Here she was talking money with a billionaire again.

"But you are right. No golf," he said.

"I have no right to be right," she said. "I'm not paying for this project."

"There should be no top tuition either," he said. "I fire myself as a tremendous expert."

"No, please, forget it," she said.

"I am fired," he said. "Now we get your rooms furnished." With a touch he turned her around and they began to walk back to the cars.

"I have some old furniture," she said. "It's all right."

"Not all right. Nothing old. You said you wanted to start all over."

"Don't take me too literally these days," she said.

"I got an idea!" he said. "I'm closing my place in Paris anyway, one day. You take some furniture from there."

"Oh, come on," she said.

"You save me storage! See how you like it. You don't like it, you make beds from marsh wood." He picked up another pebble, as though it were an obstacle in her way, and he didn't smile. "Meanwhile you save me storage."

"I don't know your furniture in Paris," she said.

"Come look with your son."

She watched Ronnie point high at a roof, Mannritt and the Macedonians following his finger.

"Our Nick was a big friend," Letarpo said. "You let me do something."

She was really dying to live in a small alpine library — perfect for starting all over again.

"Kind of you," she said.

"You look at my stuff, I have to be in Paris anyway," he said. He threw the pebble fiercely, like a boy.

Next morning they were in Paris, looking at his house on the Avenue Foch. It had a lovely baroque façade but inside was an overdone mausoleum. Trudy hadn't expected the late Madame Letarpo — movie star and all — to be so conventionally grand. Or that Letarpo would simply let the grandeur gather dust like this, for so many years after her death.

An old woman with a gray braided bun and authoritatively thick glasses led Trudy and Ronnie around. She didn't so much show as reveal. Behold, the third floor, Madame's study. Everything was dustcloth-covered, unshrouded and shrouded again by the old lady in the ritual light of half-drawn curtains. Behold, the chaise longue, all ivory and silk bolsters; behold, the inlaid escritoire; behold chairs of buffalo horns all glued together — Madame's one attempt at avant-garde whim.

On the floor below, behold, a pomposity of a boudoir; behold a presumable Manet hovering in the dusk above a mincing Louis XV table. Behold, highboys, armchairs, all unshrouded and shrouded once more. (In front of a small rather simple very dark room — the one in which Letarpo must be sleeping when in Paris — stood a pair of men's slippers, marooned in the vasts of the tomb, and she found herself touched.) Even the rugs of the drawing room downstairs had a dust cover. The old lady insisted on drawing it back to expose the Persian design. Behold. Ronnie pulled hard at the fringes of his leather jacket. Trudy made a polite noise. The old lady became defiant. She straightened up and said in hard bad English: *"Sometimes — often — wonderful parties here."*

On the ground floor they were ushered into a bird-cage elevator. It was slow and, thank God, so small that only the two of them could squeeze in.

"Yech," Ronnie said.

"Let's be polite," she said.

They walked out of the elevator into a fluorescent hive. Above and below ground were reverse worlds, *chez* Letarpo. The basement seemed to be his Paris office. IBM machines blinking, muttering, in something like a big, secret and automated post office. A turtleneck triplet led them from the big cavern into a smaller one that could have been the waiting room of a Bombay physician, full of dark men, well dressed, with jiggling trouser legs, long-patient in their armchairs. The turtleneck opened another door.

Letarpo all alone. In a gray business suit he perched on a board table. He had a blueprint across his lap and he was eating a salami sandwich.

"Ah. Sorry. I wanted to have lunch with you."

"I know you're busy," Trudy said.

"Aaah." He was still morose. "Iraquis, Iranians, Turkish. I must make them creep in the same pipeline. I wouldn't be lunch fun."

"Look!" Ronnie said.

An olive tree grew from a sunken pot next to the big desk, the way the flag stands next to the President's desk.

"From my island," Letarpo said. "I have lunch ready for you at a little place, next street."

"Don't worry," Trudy said.

"I worry. The furniture is no good. Right?"

"Well, the house is gorgeous," Trudy said.

"It's no good. All wrong for you."

"Not my personal taste, that's all."

He frowned down on the blueprint. This morose Letarpo was somehow younger than the ebullient one she'd known first. In that classic animal face of weathered olive there was a kid that lost his jackknife.

"I want to change this place," he said. "I tell you. We try New York. I have a conference flight there tonight on my ship, but I book you Pan-Am."

"New York?" she said.

"We dig up something at the Waldorf."

"Are you kidding? Your Towers apartment?"

"I have two rooms full of storage there. All kinds furniture cluttering me up. You too tired to fly on?"

"That's not the point," she said. "We had a good night's rest at Zurich. But —"

"Big boy, ready to fly?" Letarpo gave Ronnie a tap on the neck, but such a broodingly subdued tap it was almost a caress.

Perhaps she had agreed because New York meant more time with her son. Originally he was supposed to have returned to École Mannritt. Yet there Ronnie was seated at her side. She was traveling with him, as more regular mothers do with more regular sons. He had developed a stuffed-up nose, obviously a cold coming on fast. But he was being awfully adult and gallant. Insisted on carrying her light cosmetics bag onto the plane for her. Rose on his toes to help her off with the cape, protected her: as they found their seats a tall ruddy-faced joker smirked and ogled down Trudy's dark glasses as if into the décolletage of her incognito. *Ain't you that Nick Antone chick?* Her son Ronnie bluntly stepped between that stare and herself.

And after takeoff they did just what she longed to do. They talked about their Bachberg plans together.

"Couldn't I help plan my own room at Bachberg?" he said. "Can I be in on that, Mother?"

Mother. It was the first time he'd called her that. She was both touched and nostalgic about her decease as *Mummy.* But also hopeful: better to be a steady Mother than the fitful Mummy of the past. Going through that Bourbon grotto of the house in Paris together; traveling together; weren't those new bonds?

"I can even build furniture a little," he said. "I took woodwork at Mannritt."

"Good," she said. "And you can choose the furniture in New York."

"Mother, see, I don't want to use his stuff."

"Maybe we'll use nothing. Maybe just a couple of things. I just want us to start on a home together! It'll be that much faster if we find something right."

He arched his back, exactly as Nick used to when impatient.

"I want to tell you again," she said. "That dance of yours, the Ten Plagues, that was really terrific."

"Well, I didn't know you'd come in with Letarpo and everybody."

"Letarpo loved it," she said.

"I don't want to use his furniture," he said slowly, rheum in his voice, quite changed.

"Don't worry," she said. "Perhaps I can track down some of our old Central Park West stuff."

"You sent that away last year," he said, rheumy and low. He coughed.

"We'll get you aspirin in New York," she said.

"If we'd gone to Bahama this summer, I could have started making my furniture there. Mr. Antone's got a carpenter."

"Is that what's bothering you?" she said, surprised. "We can do that for a while, visit Mr. Antone. We're free agents, Ronnie."

"I don't think there'll be time."

"Yes, there will be — "

"There never is."

"From now on there will," she said. "That's the point."

"I feel sleepy," he said.

211

"Yes, darling, sleep," she said. "But I can't wait for us to have our own place!"

He fell asleep almost immediately with the instant-sleep knack of the Antones, before Trudy could ask the stewardess to bring him some tea with lemon. His head didn't quite touch her shoulder, but leaned toward her closely enough so that her neck could feel his breath.

He slept on and off till New York and even in the limousine waiting at JFK. He didn't really wake up at the Waldorf. The room Letarpo had reserved for them wasn't a room but an enormous suite, much too much draped velvet and much too big a gesture. The kind of gesture that alarmed her, though she didn't know why. Ronnie had dropped on the gigantic sofa to go on sleeping. She picked up the phone in the bedroom, whispered at room service: thermos of tea, lemon and aspirin for when he woke up. She didn't open any suitcases partly because she didn't want to disturb him; partly because she felt she was warding off these oversize accommodations by staying shut tight against them. She tried to lie down but it didn't work. She didn't want to go up to the Waldorf Towers to look at Letarpo's furniture without Ronnie by her side. She felt terribly restive. The traffic noise from the window sounded like lunar music, not like New York at all. Was she really back in her native city?

Suddenly she found herself thumbing through her address book to see if she still had Jennifer's number. She not only still had it, but Jennifer was still living there, despite her Israel plans.

"Jennifer. I dunno. Out shopping someplace," said the hoarse fed-up voice. "I'm her cousin. Who's calling?"

"It's Trudy," Trudy said. "She'll know. Tell her to come visit me at the Waldorf soon as she can, please. I'll be here only very briefly, thank you very much."

She had to smile at herself for not giving the telephone number. Somewhere deep down she must still be convinced that cousins and aunts would, like Tante, mess up the digits. Her New York past! On the spur of the moment she decided to inspect the furniture left from her marriage to Simon, the Central Park West stuff. If she found something, she could use that to fend off Letarpo with;

212

she could give Ronnie something nice and familiar from his little-kid days. Off she rushed to the elevator.

The Attal Brothers warehouse was below Dyckman Street, and she had her cabbie get off the West Side Highway at the 168th Street exit. Her old uptown neighborhood passed through the car window like the stage set of a dead play, vandalized and littered with Spanish store signs and dented cars parked hubcap-deep in dog turds.

On 190th Street rose the verticals of Interfaith University next to those of her own Alma Mater, all so brutally tall amidst the rubble all around them, the rubble from which her old friends had long been evicted. She was glad not to be involved in the contrast, especially not on the dean level. But the mere sight was depressing. With Nick's help her old friends had been relocated to a nice home — where? The Rockaways? She couldn't remember. Where was Mr. Lissberg now?

The Attal Brothers warehouse didn't exactly give her a lift. She had to deal with a black who made up for his skinniness with a raspy voice. She produced her receipt, the one she always carried around in her passport wallet.

"Storage ain't been paid the last six months, honey."

"I know," she said. Why the hell hadn't she paid it — to repress her whole Simon Spieger marriage?

"Must be over there, your stuff," the voice rasped. "Look around."

She looked at the enormous dust-lit dimness. Hundreds of sofas, tables, lamps, loveseats; countless family organisms dismembered and interred here, the amputated limbs of different dead living rooms stacked on top of one another on a floor mottled with cold cigar butts. After a minute she found the old apartment all right, heaped together in a corner. But it was like finding a cadaver: recognizable, yet unfamiliar and eerie. A cold tingle traveled up her ankles. Only two chairs made her feel better. Two bland blond pieces that used to be Ronnie's. One had a mysterious red stain on the seat. The other was unflawed.

"Those," she said. "I'd like to have them sent to Europe."

"Two hundred and ninety dollars," the voice rasped, instantly.

213

"Two hundred and ninety?"

"Honey, that's storage charges, plus arrears penalty plus interest. Then you got your overseas shipment — what's the place?"

"Bachberg, Austria," she said. *"But two hundred and ninety dollars!"*

It seemed not only exorbitant but arbitrary. She tried to recall her checking-account balance without actually taking out the book. Could matters be arranged, if say, ten dollars cash changed hands? She reached for the wallet-purse inside her big travel handbag, the wallet-purse she'd long wanted to throw out because it was so frayed and the clasp didn't work. Her fingers tried to push open the clasp with all her might till she not only opened but upended it. She heard its contents pour tinkling all over her handbag. It became impossible to keep standing there, grubbing around for a bill to bribe that rasp with.

"How much would it be to ship just one chair?"

The black lips performed a computation soundless, enigmatic, swift, in the mangy light.

"One hundred ninety-five dollars and twenty cents, honey."

"All right," she said. "Send the chair without the stain."

On the way back she told the cabbie to stick to the West Side Highway. To avoid Tante's old building and profitless nostalgia. Also the fare would be cheaper that way. Most of the ride she spent emptying out her handbag onto her lap in order to get together what bills and coins had scattered from the wallet-purse. Then she tried to fix the purse clasp. No good; her fingers hurt from pressing the hard metal. On Madison Avenue, already quite near the Waldorf, the car stopped for a red light. *Summer Sale,* it said on the window of a leather shop.

"Driver, I'll get out right here." she said.

Sure enough, she found a bargain in that shop. A purse combined with an ample billfold (for odd-sized European banknotes) made of some clever leathery composition. Only $7.95. But the salesgirl suddenly looked up while figuring the city tax.

"Trudy Spieger? . . . Right? Oh! Could I have an autograph?"

Customers swiveled heads. Faces seemed to mushroom against the glass door. Trudy scribbled, paid, probably blushed furiously.

All that éclat and she couldn't afford a real leather purse. Getting out of that store was like escaping a lynch mob.

While half-running she put on her dark glasses. This very act brought home to her the murderous dichotomy of her life. Overblown hotel suites and money-grubbing for bargains. New York made everything worse. Maybe only Bachberg could save her. A smaller, more cohesive life. The thing was to get her business done in the city and get out. She headed directly for the Waldorf Towers.

"There's some furniture Mr. Letarpo wanted to show me in the storage room."

Old Butler Nail Eyes bowed. He shepherded her along the gallery. She had a glimpse of Letarpo by the terrace, five business-suit backs around him, then Nail Eyes bowed her down a service corridor into a room that really looked like storage space.

Musty typewriters on shelves, electric fans on the floor, an air conditioner with its bowels open, an Exercycle. No furniture whatsoever.

It hit her like a cold punch between the breasts. This on top of such a day. She was the victim of some charade. Nothing made sense. She felt the weight of all the vain rushing, straining, trying since Nick's death; trying, reaching, stooping to pick up little bits of purpose in her world. All no good. All the fragments splintered further around the naked light bulb above that Exercycle.

She was tapped, almost harshly, from behind.

"Forgive this!"

Letarpo, with a steel tubing under his arm.

"Nobody told me! They sent all furniture to Pilcic."

"Oh," she said.

"To my island. And nobody told me! Terrible! We go there tomorrow. I canceled everything. Please!"

She'd never seen this tense shirtsleeved Letarpo before. His shirt was lean and white. He rubbed his hands across it. His ribbed metal watchband chirped against the silver buckle of his belt.

"It's all right," she said.

"We fly to Pilcic."

"That's ridiculous," she said.

215

"I got you here for nothing. All the way to New York. I make up for it. I canceled everything."

"Forget it," she said.

"No. We fly tonight."

He seemed to have lost all joviality and humor. For some reason that made enormous relief flood through her, a reaction so irrational she almost had to laugh at herself. Her mouth had to be restrained from smiling.

"It's not *that* important," she said.

"Very important!"

If this man gave her such great relief, why did she feel a perverse great need to test him?

"What about my son?" she said.

"Okay. We all fly to my island for the furniture."

"My son has a cold."

"It's warm on the island. Or he stays here and rests. We will only be a couple days. Please!"

"I must ask my son," she said.

But Letarpo was already on the phone, asking for her suite. Everything went so fast. She hadn't expected even this utility room to have an extension.

"Ask," Letarpo said. He thrust the receiver at her. There was too much speed in the room.

"Ronnie?" she said. "Did we wake you?"

"I was just on the phone," Ronnie's voice said, surprisingly alert. "Yussuf called."

"At least I didn't wake you."

"Yussuf traced me through Paris. He'll be flying over. A friend of yours is here. Miss Berg."

"Jennifer!" Trudy said. "Great! I'll be there in a minute. Listen, Ronnie, I've been invited to go to Mr. Letarpo's island because that's where the furniture is now. Would you like to come along tonight?"

"Well, Yussuf's coming tomorrow. I said I'd be here, just two minutes ago."

"You don't mind if I'm gone for a couple of days?"

"No," Ronnie said. "You know, there's room in this suite for Yussuf."

"I'll be over in a few minutes to discuss it," she said.

216

"That's okay. Yussuf's coming."

"We'll discuss it in a few minutes," she said, and hung up.

"We leave tonight," Letarpo said, the tubing under his arm.

"Why so fast?" she said. Though she sensed that whatever this was, it was reasonable only if it was head-over-heels.

"I canceled everything," he said. "I got nothing to do if we don't fly."

"Let me catch my breath," she said.

"I go crazy doing nothing. It's not nice, my going crazy."

"You'll have to let me discuss it further with my son."

"We get him the best governess while you're in Pilcic. A-one."

"I'm not sure I'm going."

"You unpacked already?"

"No," she said. "But I should discuss it further with my son."

She didn't discuss it further with her son. Back in the suite she found Ronnie asleep once more on the sofa, and Jennifer, her old friend Jenn, sitting with very strictly crossed legs on a gilt chair.

"Jenn!" she said.

They half-hugged. Jennifer's face was as dry as her hair now and her dress so aggressively plain brown and anti-stylish; and this suite was so big and the circumstances so peculiar. They had to whisper.

"So glad to see you, Jenn!" she whispered. "How was Israel? Let's go into the next room where we can talk."

They tiptoed past Ronnie who was breathing deeply, the color returned to his faintly freckled cheeks. His forehead felt cool to her touch.

"I came back to the States last month," Jennifer said in the next room. "Elihu is still there."

"What are you up to now?"

"Waiting to get my job back in the library," Jennifer said. "I won't ask you. I'd sound like a reporter."

"Oh shut up," Trudy said. "How come your goddamn complexion is better than mine?"

They laughed. It broke the ice a little.

"Jenn!" Trudy said. "Would you do me a terrific favor? How'd you get along with Ronnie?"

"He's very sweet," Jennifer said. "And sleepy."

"This is such a crazy moment," Trudy said. "I'll be going off for a couple of days. There'll be a governess coming in for that time. Could you stay till she comes tonight? Sort of look her over? I mean, how she gets on with Ronnie? And maybe drop by for a couple of minutes tomorrow?"

"All right," Jennifer said.

"Ronnie will have his best friend visiting him too — but I'd be so grateful. And for any time you lose on my account —"

"Now *you* shut up," Jennifer said.

They laughed again. Now Trudy could kiss her and run over to the embossed escritoire.

"*Dear Ronnie,*" she wrote on Waldorf stationery. "*My big tall darling. By Thursday latest I'll be back. A lady will come to keep you company and see to things. My friend Jennifer Berg might also butt in now and then. Letarpo says you can reach me any time through his office here. Drink lots of liquids. Have a good time with Yussuf. Call me any time. If you want to, I'll be back right away. I sent something to you at Bachberg. It'll be great there! I love you terribly much. Mother.*"

It was the first time she had not signed *Mummy*.

4

What struck her about Pilcic when they got there was that everything on the island had such sunny leafy-rich ease. It was almost blinding. She could hardly take it in during the first hour. Perhaps she didn't even want to. The wealth coming in through the window — the rainbow of scents — eucalyptus? tangerine? mimosa? manure? oleander? — she could deal with the blended opulence of that only after she'd dealt with her own wrinkledness. Naturally everything was crushed by the time she reached Pilcic. Her clothes hadn't been unpacked for days. The tan slacks, the only ones right for the heat of the island, consisted of nothing but wrinkles. A wizened maid, smiling and mute, helped her hang up her clothes in that odd timbered guest house.

"Possible to iron?" Trudy asked.

The maid just smiled. Naturally Trudy's hair was all kinks. None of the scarves with which she tried to cover it were exactly smooth. She'd folded the scarves on top of her Hot Weather suitcase, but somebody must have upended her luggage. She was a walking anthology of crinkles. She felt sleepless and crumpled.

Letarpo stared at her. During the trip he'd mostly stayed in the business part of the plane up front, working with the three assistants who wore turtleneck shirts and who looked like triplets. Trudy had dozed off, out of some sense of self-defense. Now, as she walked out of the guest house, she found him waiting, staring, introducing her to a babushka that turned out to be his mother. Mother stared too. They didn't explain the sights, those two. Just walked alongside her, silent. One of the turtlenecked triplets followed behind and at one point came up to say, in a thick accent, and with odd formality, that they were in the Gulf of Trieste, this was the Italian shoreline over there, except over there, this hill, where Yugoslavia commenced, thank you. Silence. The turtlenecked triplet fell behind again. Letarpo and Mother stared at her.

The silence somehow made it harder to accept the reality of the island. It was lovely, with a small harbor full of white loggias, terraces, lyric sails, vineyards and, higher up, olive trees twinkling the silvery underside of leaves in the pretty breeze. There were even three women mending fishnets on a stone bench. After Manhattan yesterday, this was a sudden lantern slide showing impossible and gorgeous innocence.

She was sleepless, dazed. Since the whole thing was impossible, the incongruities within impossibility didn't bother her: the long airstrip between the orange trees; three gray speedboats cruising at the end of the harbor jetties — three destroyer-colored praetorian prows that kept other craft at a distance. Telex clatter talked to bird song as they passed a whitewashed house. And Mother Letarpo. Her babushka covered seamed bronze, a strong-nosed ancient face. She wore a long flowered skirt like the other women on the island. But her apron was sky-blue, not black like the others', and into its strings was tucked a fancy revolver: a collapsible umbrella with a sculptured ivory handle. Trudy remembered it from the Gucci window on Fifth Avenue.

219

And the villa with its arcades, its espaliered fruit trees like Antone's place in Bahama. Only it was too tall.

"Mr. Antone built that?" she asked.

The turtlenecked assistant looked at Letarpo. Letarpo and Mother just kept staring at her.

"The old Antone house, yes," the turtleneck said. "But Mr. Letarpo, he built a floor on top. Please."

He held open the heavy-paneled door. Letarpo & Mother stared. Trudy walked in. She was enchanted.

In the hall stood two chests she wanted instantly for Bachberg. They were renaissance, possibly Venetian, inlaid with simple blues and grays that had aged marvelously into paleness. The two rooms beyond were full of strong rustic colors, brown and blue; tables and chairs on legs that could have supported Michelangelo cherubs. But it was the beds upstairs that really got her. (She was surprised by her own greed — tried not to let it show, for he was still staring at her.) They stood in the master bedroom, and the soft headboards made of quilted silver-green country linen were perfect for leaning into, deep into the night; for reading and reading in a home of her own. She also loved the quilted bedspreads that seemed to be made of sherbet. From the half-open casements came the scent of eucalyptus; leisurely footsteps on gravel; bird cries. The back of her neck warmed to a thought: to possess some of the calm, solidity, cosiness possible in the world after all.

"Lovely," she said.

No answer. Letarpo & Mother kept watching her. Four black, alert eyes.

"Upstairs, please," said one of the triplet-looking assistants.

Upstairs on the top floor was a sauna, a bedroom (more or less an inappropriate copy of the one in the Towers apartment) and then an enormous peasanty living room — all like the Letarpo jet, part luxury, part folk. Letarpo himself suddenly came to life at a window.

"*Chey! Triplett! Stani! Stoj!*"

She looked out. In the distance hazed the curve of the Italian shore. But right below an assistant was pulling a donkey from what must be a stable.

"We go down," Letarpo said, and down they went.

"Did I hear you right?" she said. "You called him 'Triplet'?"

"Yes," Letarpo said.

"But that's my word for your assistants. They look alike and I don't know their names."

"They got terribly mixed-up Croat names," he said. "I like 'Tripletts.' I heard you say that yesterday."

"I better watch myself," she said.

"Too late. Now on they are 'Tripletts.' "

Mother Letarpo stared and Trudy became aware of something. "What happened to Bic?"

"Bic, sometimes he irritates you." He held the door open and she stepped outside quickly.

"Whoever told you that?" she said.

"We keep him away for a little while."

"Don't be silly," she said.

"He's busy for me in Rome. Now this is my extraspecial old donkey."

They were on the lawn before the house. Somewhere on the way out they had lost Mother Gucci. The Tripletts were gone. Everybody else had left. Letarpo wore a black polo shirt and the glasses hanging from the powerful chain. He wrapped his arm around the animal's neck so that it staggered.

"This boy made me rich," he said. "This one smuggled for me all over the war. Two hundred I had like that, but he's the only one alive now, this one."

What do you say about an old embraced donkey? Especially if you're really aching for some lovely furniture with which to start a new life? She stroked the donkey's ears because they looked the least furry. Inside the left ear she noticed a number in half-faded ink. *A——136–1380.*

"What is that?"

"Bravo!" he said. "You saw! People don't see usually. And I don't tell. It's my Jew Donkey, this one."

"He is?" she said.

"I smuggled many things in the war. Thousands. Also seventeen Jews, Greece to Turkey. Jews sat on this one. Clop, clop, clop, over the Byka Pass, away from the Nazis. Sometimes I smuggled Je s

for money, sometimes free. This one, maybe he saved twelve. I put
my money-number in his ear."

"You'll have to be a little clearer," she said.

He looked at her, stroked the donkey.

"All right. You I tell," he said. "That number. My first Swiss
bank account."

"You wrote it in his ear?"

He nodded.

"The Jews I smuggled free, I ask: 'You get to Turkey, you write
me a letter. To Whom It May Concern. Alexander Letarpo smuggled a Jew, me, free. God is my witness, and signature. Send it to
my account A——136–1380, Schweizerische Bankgesellschaft,
Zurich, that's the payment.' It's a little crazy of me."

"No — just unusual," she said.

"Seven really sent the letter," he said, stroking the donkey.
"Seven out of . . . maybe nine. Maybe nine I smuggled free. The
others for money."

"Seven out of nine is good," she said.

"Finally they caught me with this Jew. Crazy tailor with one
eye. But it was okay. No money on me, no letters, just this donkey-
boy here and nobody looks in his ear. They put me in this little
jail where I met Simon."

"Simon never told me about the letters," she said.

"I never told him. I never tell anybody. Sometimes in Zurich I
take out the letters. I show them to . . ." He shrugged a powerful,
big-shouldered, wry Mediterranean peasant shrug that seemed to
come from a much taller man. He shrugged and lifted flat palms
against the sky. Dozens of swallows swarmed up from an olive
grove and dove their shadows at the house. "You and Mama. The
only ones I tell," he said.

They stood side by side. That and the jet-lag and the Adriatic
idyll. She felt skin puckering between her shoulder blades.

"I tell you a lot," he said. He wrapped his arm round the
donkey. The donkey tottered.

"I wanted to tell *you,*" she said. "It's — it's so damn petty by
comparison, but I'd love to have some furniture, if the offer still
holds."

"You say which," he said. He looked at her, full and fierce.

"I doubt that it's the extra furniture you meant —"

"You say!"

"Some chests. And a bed. It would be right for Bachberg."

"Beds," he said. "Not bed."

"One is enough."

"Beds."

"I just need one," she said.

He was still looking at her in that head-on burning way. It made her turn to the house.

"I don't know why Antone had two," she said. "That time he wasn't married."

"You will be married," he said.

The swallows, a whole wind of them, blew up from behind the house and dove back into the olives.

"You and me," he said.

She felt the heat in her armpits: so he's not going to dump me like Nick. A terrific triumph together with shame at the triumphantness — and caution, a need to stay sober. This was a peasant emperor of cunning wooing her from behind a donkey.

"I've been ripened for this," she said out loud.

He put his hand on her elbow. Her legs took a step back.

"It doesn't make sense," she said. "On my part too. That isn't even the furniture you meant, the things in storage. I think we —"

"You are what I mean," he said.

"Mr. Letarpo," she said. "What have we got to do with each other?"

His arms dropped off the donkey. He took the chained spectacles off his neck as if he could look at her better without the chain.

"I'm trying to find a life now," she said. "I'm trying to put my life together. You understand? I don't want to make any more mistakes!"

She was trying not to make her voice too shrill with the things working inside her.

"You see, I've got Ronnie," she said. "And I'm trying to get back to my work. I want to finish my dissertation. I haven't even done *that* yet."

He'd stuffed the glasses with the chain into his pocket and he kept looking at her.

"I'm very tired from all the flying," she said. "I do appreciate your canceling all the important meetings and showing me this island, but —"

"I only show it to my wife," he said.

She heard her shoes creak on the gravel.

"Why *me?*" she said.

He shrugged and stared at her.

"That enormous suite was so unnecessary at the Waldorf," she said, stupidly.

"You are the first here since Michelle," he said.

"For God's sakes, make sense!" she said. "You could never live at Bachberg! But I will! I made up my mind. It'll be my home with Ronnie. Could you live there? Even fairly regularly? A man like you?"

"I will live there," he said.

"Do you know what you are saying?"

"I will live there. I told you yesterday. I want to change my places. I want to change everything with you."

"You'll make a home at Bachberg?"

"I will put my lizard there," he said. "And I will not make a golf out of the marsh, the marsh you like."

"I like it very much," she said, "but it's not important."

"It's important, you mentioned it."

His hands were thrust so deeply into his pockets, he stared at her out of a stoop. If it was possible for Alexander Letarpo to look humble, this was probably it.

You're probably such a bastard, she thought. And you're such a temptation. It's a complication you're likable.

"I can't think too well right now," she said. "I'll have to have more time."

"Trood," he said.

"I guess all I can say right now is Thank you."

"In my mind I have been saying 'Trood,' a lot. My secret name for you."

"Thank you," she said.

She found herself stroking the donkey ear. It was good for the strain. He stroked the other ear.

"We keep Mama waiting," he said.

A Triplett came out of nowhere and took the donkey, and they went back in.

Then the chapel next morning. The chapel behind the villa stood in an olive grove of its own. It was a maze of silver niches, bas-relief saints with askew necks and saviors swarthy on the cross. Mother Letarpo kneeled, unkneeled very swiftly, crossed herself, looked at Trudy who had remained standing. There was another old woman, much like Mother L., but her apron was black and she had no Gucci umbrella tucked into its strings. This woman handed Mother L. a small deep tin basin and Mother L. handed it on to Trudy. It was half-filled with incensed holy water. Mother L. crossed herself again very efficiently, fast, walked out. Before the chapel now stood the Volkswagen, the Rolls-motored two-seater of certain memory. A Triplett waited behind the wheel.

Mother L. got in, motioned for Trudy to follow. Both seats were taken: no room for Trudy. Mother L. pointed to her lap. White doves meandered round the white chapel tower. Trudy hadn't slept too well and her emotions moved in somnambulist angles. She sat down on Mother L.'s apron.

At this touch, the motor hummed, swelled, they moved up the steepness of a curve. Mother L.'s fingers hooked into Trudy's elbows. Trudy held onto the tin basin, trying not to make it spill. She smelled the incense and Mother L.'s clean linen. Up the car swerved between twigs. Trudy tried not to think about being giddy. She thought instead how difficult it must be to tame this island, to work the soil or make a runway. It was so willfully hilly. Yet there was the airport (with a green-brown knoll of its own — the jet under canvas). Everything was cultivated, nothing was simply meadow or wild garden. They skimmed boughs with little green apples. Branches beaded with pears and oranges whooshed past the window. Then a solid stand of olives through which there was just enough path for the car.

"You've got a lot of agriculture here," Trudy said.

Instantly the Triplett whispered Slavic at Mother L., who whispered right back.

"Yes," the Triplett said aloud. "I keep it in order, for my son when he comes back."

"He comes back a good deal, doesn't he?" Trudy said.

Slavic whisper.

"When my son comes back here for good," the Triplett said, "to be a farmer with you. Permanent."

There was a bluntness about the exchange and about the way the car tackled the next steep brow of the hill. On her somnambulist perch on a Croat apron, Trudy found this bluntness piquant.

"You think he'll be content to be a farmer?"

Slavic whisper.

"When the *conde* gives up, my son will be content," the Triplett said.

"The *conde?*"

"Mr. Nicholas Antone Senior," the Triplett said, this time not waiting for the whisper. He smiled. When he acted as mouthpiece for Mother L. he was a neuter translation-machine.

"*Conde,*" Trudy said. It came to her. That's what Nick used to call old Antone. "What do you mean 'when the *conde* gives up'?" she said.

Slavic whisper.

"When my son is so successful all over the world, the *conde* will see he can never destroy him," said the Triplett, once more the translation-machine.

The car had stopped. Trudy felt a tap on her arm. The kind which signals a child to get out of the car. Trudy got out. It wasn't easy with the basin. She stood on top of a hill and way down there in a workshed by the stable she saw three half-naked men stirring something blue in a huge vat. Letarpo had told her the dye came from a local berry and must be smeared on olive trees against beetles. She thought the smallest of the three men must be her future husband, but she couldn't be sure. Certainly she couldn't yell down and ask him to enlighten his mad mother with some yells back. Trudy wasn't even sure she wanted Mother L. enlightened. An enlightened Mother L. might be unmitigated murder.

"*Dobro jutro.*" This meant "good morning." One of the two Croat phrases Trudy had learned by then. It came in a chorus from the women working on top of the hill, tying vine shoots together.

"Please," the Triplett said. He took the basin from Trudy. The women stopped working, straightened up from their stoops to attention. Mother L. pulled the Gucci umbrella out of her apron strings. She uncollapsed it, raising it high, opened it into an art nouveau silk rainbow, closed it again. Immediately a bell, sweet and tinny, began to ring from the chapel tower; rang up the hill and down the harbor; rang across the pastel flutings of the Adriatic to the Istrian shore; rang robin wings into the air.

"We bless this new vine terrace," the Triplett said to Trudy. Mother L. put her hand in the basin the Triplett held out. With vigor she sprinkled holy water across vines and women workers. Whereupon the Triplett held out the basin to Trudy. Trudy was irritated; she was Jewish. She was also touched. So she sprinkled holy water too, but very briefly.

Mother Letarpo nodded. Something happened Trudy couldn't quite believe. Right in front of everybody Mother L. pointed at Trudy's breasts and said something Slavic.

"You are much better there than my first daughter-in-law," Triplett said perfectly blandly.

"Probably you weren't so bad yourself," Trudy said, pointing right back.

Slavic whisper. The bronze seams under the babushka fell into a novel pattern. Mother Letarpo was smiling. More Slavic whisper.

"Would you like to walk down the hill arm in arm with me?" Triplett said.

"I like walking," Trudy said.

Slavic whisper. The vineyard women bowed and Trudy bowed back. Triplett got into the car with the basin. Mother Letarpo opened her umbrella against the sun. Birds sang. Arm in arm Trudy and Mother Letarpo walked down the hill together.

She wanted to mention it to Letarpo. He had finished with the blue dye. He and his two fellow workers were washing their hands in a soapy barrel. Then they rinsed off their arms in a stone well that squeaked as a Triplett worked the lovely cast-iron handle. She smelled mimosa and wet earth. Tiny green birds chased each other with tiny screams. Smells and sights crowded round her that she wanted to take to Ronnie and to Bachberg, where she was dying to do root work of her own. She might not even mind settling on the island later, after Ronnie had finished school. After too many years of footloose ambitions, she was at a place that promised basics; even this earthy bitch of a Mother L. did.

"Alexander," she said.

The word felt funny on her tongue and so she stepped closer because she didn't want to repeat it too loudly. It was the first time she had seen him bare to the navel. His body was as tanned and firm as those of the young men he'd been working with. He dried himself on the towel they had used.

"Your mother says some peculiar things," she said.

He laughed. He slapped the towel at a fly. "You know how old Mama is?"

"It's something that ought to be cleared up," she said.

"Eighty-eight years old, Trood. She tests you. She wants my wife to be strong. Okay?"

"Okay," she said. "But one thing. I don't want to be married in the chapel here."

He put the towel round his neck. "Call me something," he said. "I call you 'Trood.' Don't call me 'Alexander.' "

She looked around. The other men had vanished.

"I'm not original. I'll say 'Tarp' like the others."

"Good!"

"Please, Tarp. No wedding in the chapel."

"Michelle got married in the chapel before we got married in the plane."

"No," she said. "No plane. Nothing fancy."

"I tell you," he said. "We get married here, and then we get married Jewish."

"No," she said. "I'm Jewish and that's important to me. But I got married Jewish before and it didn't work. We'll do something plain, but not in the chapel."

"Trood, you are strong," he said. He put the towel round her neck too.

"I better be," she said.

"Strong one, you win," he said. "Where is the wedding?"

"I thought about it. It'd be nice to have it in Miami, where my aunt lives."

"Miami! I got leases there."

"She is my only relative."

228

"We marry in Miami. First I ask for Trood's hand, huh?"

"No," she said, laughing. "But I better try to reach my son."

Because of the difference in hours, Ronnie didn't even know about the whole thing yet. But when she got back to the guest house it was past noon and he must be having breakfast in New York. The switchboard girl on the island, wherever she was, spoke a fine British English and got her through fast.

"Ronnie!" she said. "I'm coming back tonight!"

"You all right, Mother?"

"Yes, it's just that — there's some news."

"You all right? Tell me."

"I'll tell you in person."

"Something with Letarpo?"

"Don't be so impatient —"

"You'll marry him."

"You little fink," she said. "I wanted to tell you face to face!"

He didn't say anything for a couple of seconds.

"Is it okay with you?"

"Congratulations, Mother."

"Thank you! But is it okay with you? Because that's very crucial to me!"

"Sure. Am I supposed to be there?"

"The ceremony? Are you kidding? I'll kill you if you're not!"

"Can Mannritt come? And Yussuf?"

"If you wish, sure."

"Yussuf's right here."

"Wait a minute, it's not going to happen tomorrow morning, you know. Probably not till next month."

"I hope they can come."

"I wasn't thinking of something big, but if that's important to you, they'll be more than welcome. It's probably going to be at my aunt's."

"Congratulations," he said.

"My big tall darling," she said. "We'll live at Bachberg — even Letarpo. He'll surprise you! You should see this island! We'll be together! We'll have the means and the leisure to be ourselves — I can't wait to talk to you!"

"Fine."

"I love you!"

"I don't really need that governess. Yussuf and I are going to a lot of museums."

"Good! Can I call you again, your dinnertime? Will you be in?"

"Yes."

"By then I'll know when I'll be back."

"Fine."

"I love you," she said again.

The moment she hung up she said *Stupid!* to herself. She'd forgotten to ask about his cold.

Five weeks later, on a very hot August day, that convergence in Florida, secret and synchronized. Trudy arrived via Fort Lauderdale; the others by way of Freeport or Miami; all by regular flights and under cover names. By early evening, when the heat had gotten slightly better, Trudy sat with Tante in the garden of her little hotel in Miami Beach. In her hand Tante held an enormous red apple into which a Croat silver coin had been stuck. Apparently a traditional gift, delivered by a messenger an hour earlier. Tante had put on the long black skirt and the toque she'd worn at Trudy's wedding to Simon. Since Tante was an eccentric, nobody took much notice. Nobody took much notice of the small chartered yacht, no bigger than most on Indian Creek, which drew up to the pier. Trudy perspired in her pale green dress. Something inside her hammered as if it were still a seventeen-year-old heart.

"Excuse me!" said Tante's nervous young doctor, third in their party. Trudy had insisted that he attend. "I better check!" he said.

Over the gangplank he went, and into the ship, and very soon came out again.

"Impossible," he said. "The air conditioning! I can't let you go in now. I don't care what kind of V.I.P.'s. Not with your arthritis."

"It does not matter," Tante said.

"I don't care who they are," the doctor said. "I made them turn it off. Let them open the windows! It'll be all right in a few minutes."

"In that case we do *this* now," Tante said.

She put down the apple; unsnapped her handbag; uncrackled a legal form onto the garden table.

"You go in and call this Mr. Rapallo," she said to the doctor.

"Letarpo," Trudy said. She smiled. She loved Tante.

"You call him," Tante said.

"To come out here?" the nervous young doctor said.

"Right now, use the time," Tante said. "Read this."

Trudy read. The undersigned agreed that after their marriage they would arrange control of their assets according to the provisions and by-laws of the California Community Property Law regardless of the location where the ceremony was performed.

"I have consulted my lawyer on this," Tante said. "You have a son. You have responsibilities."

"Oh, Tante," she said. "You are something. We already had a session with one of his legal people, and later —"

"Not later. Now. And not just *his* lawyers. Ridiculous! This is not just another marriage."

She kissed the old cheek, thinking, He's got Mother Gucci but I've got my own.

"For a present I only give you my African violet," Tante said.

"Oh shut up," Trudy said and it was a good thing that Letarpo came out of the boat just then, behind the nervous doctor. Letarpo concealed under sunglasses and a yachting cap, with a newspaper held against his shirtfront to hide the formal black bow tie.

"This is my aunt," Trudy said. "You two once talked on the phone."

"Tante!" Letarpo said. "*Tetka!*" A Croatian hug.

"I thank you for the apple," Tante said, re-adjusting her toque. "Please sign this."

"Aha!" Letarpo said, bending over the form.

"All my idea," Tante said. "Trudy knew nothing."

"Trudy is very embarrassed," Trudy said.

"Chey, this is a fantastic Tante!" Letarpo said. "Next time I don't call the lawyers. I call you!"

He gave her another hug. The doctor looked away, nervous. Trudy's heart pounded.

"I think Dr. Banning has a pen," Tante said, righting her toque again. Letarpo took the pen, signed with a scrawl. Trudy signed it. Tante signed on one of the Witness lines with brittle large letters. The doctor squinched his name.

"You should make a classical music station here," Tante said to Letarpo. "This Florida is hopeless. Nothing but jungle on the dial."

"Hey — chokay!" Letarpo said and ran back into the ship.

Almost immediately the Gucci umbrella of Mother L. stuck out of a porthole, unfurled into an art nouveau, folded, retracted again. The signal. It was time.

They helped up Tante. With the apple in her hand, her handbag hanging from her elbow, her other arm leaning on Trudy, she marched heavily toward the gangplank and across it, across the deck into the cabin and through a gauntlet of non-airconditioned faces of Trudy's life: Bic in black tie like Letarpo, sweating. Ronnie sweating in a seersucker jacket next to the turbaned sweating Prince Yussuf of Macedonia. The princess sweating in what must be a very hot blue party dress. Mother Letarpo with a black silk scarf for a babushka and a long black skirt (matching Tante's) *without* an apron, sweating. Mannritt sweating hugely under a stole. Even, to Trudy's surprise, Jennifer, her old buddy Jennifer sweating the poignant sweat of the very thin. The Tripletts sweating, a yacht captain in stately dress-whites sweating, stewards sweating. . . . Past all these she marched with Tante up to a sweating justice of the Supreme Court of the sovereign state of Florida.

Trudy felt proud, stirred, especially because of the heat. The hardship of the turned-off air conditioning struck her as a tribute to Tante and therefore to herself. The sweating; these faces; her man, this catch-of-catches waiting for her by the justice with such tense warm eyes — it was such a fantastic blow against the universe-running-down, after Nick. It was a tremendous gathering-up and reforging of her life. It was tremendous. Drops ran down cheeks, waves tapped against the boat hull while Mr. Justice said, "With the authority vested in me . . . ," across a simple, single spray of jonquils, just as she had requested.

It was so simple, there was no meal afterward. Only champagne. Perspiration ran down Mother Letarpo's scored face, so Trudy didn't even mind the old witch pouring some incensed drops into her goblet, even if it made the champagne a bit acrid. Then it was time to kiss Ronnie and Tante and, yes, Mother Gucci. Trudy was pleased with herself because she didn't cry at this point either — fine thing if the famous strong Trudy had started bawling while the two old women controlled themselves!

She didn't cry. But when the speedboat took her and Letarpo away, she had to sit down. The dryness of her eyes had cost her a certain weakness in the knees. The strain began to liquefy her legs as they roared out into Biscayne Bay. By the time they got to the big ship, the Rough Diamonds cruiser, she suddenly missed old Antone, whose Key Bahama couldn't be too far away. Antone's absence sapped her. She asked her new husband for some coffee. Letarpo helped her into a cabin, with an incredibly tender smile on that strong face.

"I'm sorry," she said. "But I have to lie down."

They laid her down somewhere. For a few moments she was still lucid enough to be very embarrassed about swooning like that. Christ, like an excessively virginal bride. Then she dropped away, chuted into a dream that she was sitting somewhere in a high armchair, her head held up by someone behind her, and Letarpo sitting in an identical chair adjoining, and a black cassock in front, an ikon smelling of wine murmuring at them both, an object floating toward her face, a metal gleam cool against her lips, a cross, replaced by Mother L.'s wrinkles and the smell of incense just as at the vineyard blessing, and in a mist of anger and humor she pulled herself together and said, *You bastards, it's a Mickey Finn; I'm not dreaming this,* and then she really conked out.

VI

1

Of course, being Letarpo, he'd always used everything. He used a Mickey Finn to get in his Croat wedding. But who didn't use everything? Once she herself had used his using everything. A talmudic conceit. She'd even used that conceit to avoid having an orgasm with him.

Click! the door had gone in her Waldorf Towers bedroom. *Click!* (And mind, this must have been in the fifth year of their marriage by then.) *Click!* There he was, unexpected, absurd, looking like an attractively weathered Puerto Rican delivery boy gone mad. He carried a huge purple box and was naked to the waist. *Click!* At his Towers place you could lock every room, and only he and she had all the keys.

"You!" she said.

She was always dazed on her Waldorf Towers mornings. Trudy and the Renoir lady always stared out dazed together, down on six miles of Manhattan slanting away from the fortieth floor. The lady had the frame to hold her together. Trudy turned to her dissertation readings. Her dissertation, now that she'd come back to it, had changed. It now focused on the inability of the twentieth-century young to inherit the idea of redemption from their elders; on the trivialization of hope; on the consumer society trying grimly to upholster hopelessness.

She wasn't sure if the originality of the thesis would be acclaimed. But working on it staked out *her* sphere and persona against the imperial giddiness of the Towers. It gave spine to the rest of her day. She even liked to read Max Weber for breakfast, as a bravura gesture against the fortieth floor. Only she was interrupted.

Click!

"Chey, Trood," he said, half naked.

He kissed her. He smelled as usual of pinewoods (the shaving stuff he used), of distance and faintly, tangily, of sweat. Yesterday he'd called from Los Angeles and talking about taking the polar route to London, before joining her at Bachberg later.

"Aren't you supposed to be over the North Pole?"

"Over Trood."

Typical suddenness. He lip-tweaked a necklace of bitelets round her neck, and he still didn't let go of the box he carried in the other hand.

"When you're off to lunch, I'm off to London," he whispered deep into her ear, a voluptuous and decadent secret. Except that she knew what he really meant.

"Not that lunch," she said. "I told you yesterday."

"That lunch . . . ," growled his tongue in her ear.

"Stop," she said, laughing. "I told you, I'll phone in my excuses. Hey, I'll lunch with *you*."

"Trood, I go to London." He broke off a piece of breakfast roll, rubbed it softly against her breast, popped it into his mouth as if it were now scrumptiously marmaladed. "Chey, your lunch, it's going to be more fun than my London."

"Not for me," she said. "I haven't even got a hat. You forgot our whole phone conversation."

"You'll get a hat," he said, breast-marmalading another piece of roll. "What's the matter, don't want to help earthquake victims?"

"With a check, dumb Tarp," she said. "Not a hat. Who'd you lose your shirt to?"

He took a sip from her cup of tea and mugged a terrible face because it was so lemony.

"You scared of Mrs. Minsk?" he said. "That's why no lunch?"

"Mrs. Mynn, you hypocrite," she said. "You know better than me because you read the columns more than me. I just don't want to go to her lunch. What's in the box?"

"You can take Mrs. Minsk," he said.

Now he sat down on her lap in order to study her page of Max

Weber. He wrinkled his brow something awful and picked up her ballpoint and after much pondering made an enormously judicious comma between the second and third words of *The soteriological mythos of mystagogic salvation religions* and kissed her very abruptly and tonguely right in the middle of her laugh.

"Cut it out," she said, even though (always to her own surprise) she didn't really feel like cutting it out.

"Mysta-gogic," he said. "Mister Gogix." He stood up, bowed, dropped his pants, sat down on her lap, marmaladed more roll on her left breast, swallowed it and said with a soft snuggling passion, "You can take Mrs. Minsk at lunch."

"No," she said.

"You can take New York away from her."

"I haven't got the clothes to take New York away from anybody," she said. "Thank God. You haven't either right now."

His brief white undershorts looked like bathing trunks. The light gray socks played up the tan of his legs and the black hair. He was a real sex monkey.

"You got a lunch hat here."

His foot flipped open the box. His foot lifted out a black hat with a magnificent brim. His foot tossed up the hat, his hand caught it and plunked it on her head.

"Jesus," she said. "You flew here for *that?*"

"*Voilà*. Fits," he said.

"It can't fit," she said. "Hats never fit me."

"Fits you like the fur cap," he said, putting his head between her breasts to judge the hat better from that angle.

"All right, in my fur cap I'll go to lunch," she said. "Barefoot."

"Fits," he said. "You don't need the fur cap."

"I'll take it out of storage, barefoot," she said. She began to have a horrible feeling the hat really fit.

"Out of storage already," he said, kissing her. "Mr. John, he used the fur cap to figure out the size. . . . Fits beautiful."

"You stole my fur cap!" she said.

"A hat beauty," he said. She was amazed how he could talk with such a busy tongue. "You take . . . Mrs. Minsk . . . at lunch," he said, talking and tongueing.

"*You* take her, you maniac," she said.

"You take this," he said sweetly and tucked her hand round the erection that flourished through his shorts.

"All right," she said. "Let's have Mrs. Mynn eat that at lunch."

"Come over there," he said.

Intertwined, staggering, they passed the mirror on the way to bed, and the hat really fit even with her negligee.

"I'm keeping it on," she said, for he tried to remove it together with her negligee.

"You need it for lunch, Trood."

"I'm keeping it on."

She jammed it on again after the negligee had come off.

"I'm keeping it on!"

She kept it on. For the next half hour he could do everything to her in bed except get the hat off. She kept it on, stark naked as she was. She wedged it firmly between her head and the headboard, and he made swipes at it with bearlike grunts, though he never lost his beat inside her; in fact those swipes were humorous, insidious sophistications of his rhythm, and she had the same odd beef again, against this plutocrat goat. He could make her come much too fast. Sonofabitch Croat could bust in on her at breakfast time with an erection and a hatbox, with his jokes and social-climbing vanities absurd for an Alexander Letarpo, and within minutes he had her in bed panting for more and deeper, and the most annoying thing about it was that she was his inferior in the agon of the bed, though she should have been his superior because she was his superior in youth and looks.

Yes, in that forty-floor-high bed she longed for a touch of frigidity, for with Tarp frigidity was one of the last footholds of independence. To cool down the pulse in her hips (while the bed sighed faster and the morning traffic hummed like a romantic memory from far below) she tried to think frigid tough thoughts in her hat-brimmed head on the pillow. She thought: he isn't really fucking *me*. He is fucking the one live glamorous remnant of Nick Antone; he is fucking my newsprint self; he is fucking New York Society and American politics through my cunt and I'm not even in politics any longer and I hope I won't be sucked into Society, into any Mrs. Mynn lunches, fuck them. I don't want to be that kind of cunt. He is using me.

240

He grabbed for her hat in vain again; he wanted to get it off, preserve it unscathed for The Lunch. She kept it on. Fuck it. He grunted *grrr* and bit her amazingly slightly on a breast while switching to rotation below; and, still plumping for frigidity, she told herself that she was using him too. I am putting out for excellent good reasons, she thought. This fuck now, this legal lay, lets me build my life with Ronnie at Bachberg. Because of this grunter I'm fucking, my life isn't just a P.S. to Nick Antone. Yes, Mrs. Letarpo is fucking Mr. Letarpo at 9 A.M., fucking a jackpot, fucking Dow-Jones *lui-même,* fucking oodles of California Community Property and therefore I can say fuck you to all the panics all the cupcakes are suffering, even the most liberated ones, fuck you to the Getting-Fat? Getting-Wrinkled? panic, fuck the Invest-Your-Ass-But-Good-And-Fast panic. . . . Thanks to Grr-Grr, fuck off! to all that. Yes, thank you, a nice cold Thank You to you, my sweet-fucking Tarp, no matter how you piston down there, humming Croatian in my ear. Fuck you.

But he sure pistoned persuasively. And to cheat him somehow, she thought of the cocks in her life. Bic with his then-personable phallic swagger; poor Simon, esthetic, pathetic in his attempts; and Nick of the endless agility and irony, wielding one of the world's most adored groins, calling her a funny newly-coined bed-name each time . . . with none of them she had really come, but with the Croat gorilla here, this grabber for her hat, this beast of a people-user, this grunter and grrr-er and ear-spitter, this mogul-animal whom she hated to give the satisfaction of a scream, with whom she didn't want to, had tried for the last twenty minutes not to, with whom she downright hated to — with him she did. Goddamn it, she did. She came.

But the hat she kept on throughout. She kept it on after he left for his plane. It was still on her head when she went from bedroom to study. Even before their wedding Tarp had ordered his den in the Waldorf split in half. And by the time their Caribbean honeymoon was over, by the time she set foot in the city as Mrs. Letarpo, a lady-brain's idyll had awaited her on the fortieth floor. Rosewood desk, pink-veined marble desk set, pastel filing cabinets. An unknown decorator had worked with an unknown librarian. The book shelves were stocked with the *Britannica,* the

Encyclopedia of Social Sciences and nearly all the standard texts within the sociological ambit, from Durkheim to Lévi-Strauss. Altogether a super Bas Mitzvah present. Trudy felt it was good to garnish the perfection of it all with a ruin of a hat.

But apparently breakfast sex didn't go too well with Max Weber. She couldn't really get back into good old soteriology. A nutmeggy scent distracted her; a reminder of Tarp, who was already airborne on the way to London. The scent came from the cigarillo he liked to smoke afterward, naked, brown arms folded behind his head, cigarillo dangling from a smile. An amazingly lovable smile, not macho-smug, but warm, young, glad-to-be-alive. The smile of a young donkey driver into whose lap had fallen the Princess of the World. Touching, that she was that to him. And that he didn't even seem to mind about the hat. After all, the hat was what he'd flown to New York for, and now it was lust-mauled, a crumpled black piece of dusting cloth, still on her head. She'd had her way with the hat. So she decided she would go to The Lunch so precious to Tarp after all, and really dig into her work in the afternoon.

Hat on, she walked into what used to be the storage room of the apartment, now Jennifer's office, all comfortable walnut furniture, which Jennifer reduced to threadbareness by simply putting out her cigarette in the cold-coffee puddle of a plastic container.

"Believe it or not, I'm going to that lunch," Trudy said.

"I shouldn't call Mrs. Mynn to cancel?" said Jennifer.

"No. What have we got for me to wear in the Costume Shop? In the lunch rack?"

"Well," Jennifer said. "Let's go prospecting."

The Costume Shop was the clothes closet of the late Michelle Letarpo: Trudy had discovered that she and the first Mrs. L. were the same size 11, more or less. Not only that, but Michelle had stocked the closet with a huge assortment of Balenciagas, Diors, all the top-longevity designers. Michelle seemed to have had a classic eye for what would keep coming back into fashion. Some part of the Costume Shop was always *au courant* — either campily or for real. Whenever Trudy had to dress up for some tediousness in New York like the Macedonian Ambassador's dinner — that is, whenever such a tediousness forced her into a puppet role and into puppet clothes — she fought back via the Costume Shop. She refused to waste time, money, energy at Bendel's. She simply directed Giorgio to grab a likely armful out of the closet and from such a selection chose one. She'd gotten by each time so far. It was one way of remaining herself.

Certainly the lunch qualified as a tediousness. She and Jennifer smiled as Giorgio staggered in under the weight of half a dozen dresses. Butler Nail Eyes had been fired at Trudy's instigation. Giorgio had the same tough-chinned North Italian face as Nail Eyes (she suspected that Tarp liked to hire North Italians as servants since Antone was one); but Giorgio was new to the Letarpo Towers menage. Every three days he laid his household books on Trudy's desk because he assumed that Trudy spent all that time on all those papers studying tradesmen's accounts. He also seemed to think that Jennifer's chronic frown was directed specifically at him, and moved his arms a great deal when he walked to convey alacrity, and constantly smoothed down his white jacket. He was sort of a riot. Since she'd become Mrs. Letarpo, Trudy had learned to treat her relationship with domestics as a permanent comedy-game whose rules were agreed to by all concerned, but whose reality was not to be taken seriously.

Trudy looked at the five dresses laid before her.

"That one," she said. A nubby-tweed Chanel suit with lots of buttons — bound to look unpredictable under the shambles of a hat.

"Boy, will I be lunchy," she said.

Actually she'd been staving off the Hella Mynn lunch for years. It was the kind of lunch with which Mrs.-Letarpo-in-New-York must collide, sooner or later. It was one of the reasons why Trudy had evaded the city for a long time.

At first she'd lived mostly in Bachberg, in photocopy. That is, in the photocopy and reference room of what was to be the library of the transplanted École Mannritt. Meanwhile workers were hammering away on the Letarpos' residential floor on top of the building. Tarp wasn't around too much; nor could you blame him during the topsy-turviness of the unfinished school. Ronnie studied a lot and vanished into the intensity of his assistance to Mannritt

243

and Yussuf. Those two worked like fiends, remodeling chalets into dorms and classrooms, keeping the school going on a curtailed basis, and, incidentally, siphoning Ronnie's presence away from Trudy.

After too many months of that, their floor on top of the library was ready. Enter Letarpo, but not with carpet samples from Paris as planned. He had his hand flat against his mouth, swaying from side to side. The man could act shy in the most energetic way. Something was up.

"Trood," he said. "The stage from the drama department — we put it here in the library?"

Mannritt, Ronnie and the two Macedonians had come in too.

"Lots of room for the stage downstairs. You see, Trood? We just move books to this floor."

"*This* floor?" she said. "But we live here!"

"That's why I ask for the great permission. See, we transfer the stage here from Chalet C. Yussuf and Company, they need the whole Chalet C — very special plans, check?"

He grinned at Ronnie. Ronnie, not much less tall than his step-father now, stared at his sneakers, chewing gum. Prince Yussuf and his sister Dara were chewing gum — even Mannritt; eight cheeks moving to different chords of the same tune. Practically a fugue.

"It is the most exciting plan for Chalet C to be the religion department building," Mannritt said.

"Tarp, you kill me," Trudy said. "You're away most of the week but you know more about school plans than me."

"Also, *bing!bang! chimm!boom!* six in the morning, Jesus Christ," Letarpo said, with a fine combination of grin and sigh.

"Oh, the garbage collection," Trudy said. The trash bins happened to be right behind the library and the Tyroleans did empty them deafeningly at an unearthly hour. By then she knew about Tarp's sleeping problem.

"The garage is far off the *bing!bang! chimm!boom!*" Letarpo said.

"The garage? Your idea is we live in the *garage?*"

"Ex-garage. Books kick us out, we kick out cars. We make a villa out of the garage!" His hands whirled up into the shape of a great castle, fell into prayer. "You give your great permission?"

Of course she gave her great permission. Of course it delayed their settling down as a family. Shortly after the great permission the three of them flew to Pilcic. Ronnie lay alone in the vineyards all day, phoned Yussuf at night, soon had to return to school. Tarp was called to the States. And Trudy couldn't stand being alone with Mother Gucci. Where go? Not to the Bourbon tomb in Paris. Tarp cabled her to join him in New York. When she got there, it turned out that Tarp was at a refinery conference in Washington and that she had to join a yachting party he'd accepted for her because the hostess was a friend of Michelle, the first Mrs. Tarp.

Trudy felt that she was too good for, and yet not up to, that sort of thing. A terrific protest cold came down on her in the middle of a hot May. All she remembered of those days was reading Martin Buber in her mahogany bunk, driven bats by the preciosity of the style; and the three Rumanian princesses sticking scrawnily out of their bikinis up on deck, lying around in the oddest positions, for there was a bet on who'd get the most deeply tanned elbows. And the girlfriend of one of the amateur helmsmen (he was also a member of the Federal Reserve Board), a svelte blonde whom Trudy once caught on all fours before the toilet bowl in her flared pants and middy blouse; the poor creature didn't want to be seasick all over her satin. And when they docked at Southampton Mrs. Hella Mynn materialized, neck brace and all, generalissima of the East Coast, whom Tarp called Mrs. Minsk. "Why, Gertrude," she said after being piped aboard. "You've got to rap with the committee. Do lunch when you're in New York."

It was to avoid the lunch that she stayed so little in New York. Back she went to Bachberg to camp out with Ronnie.

Well, not exactly with him. Even photocopy was now a hive of carpenters. She slept in an attic above the administration office while Ronnie roomed with Prince Yussuf. And after a long, long time of this; after the oblong garage had been ordered into a more villalike shape; after the necessary fixtures had been installed; after the furniture had already been shipped from Pilcic and was waiting in Innsbruck storage; after all that, she finally walked to her dream house with a measuring tape, to start seriously on interior decor — and found a nightmare.

The place was a swamp. Workmen's ashtrays twitched on the

245

floor, moving to the flow of bilge. From the drain of a just-connected sink climbed a small black toad with a horn above its eyes, and hopped onto a faucet.

Mannritt came screaming, cursing, firing the Sicilian work crew. Ronnie, Yussuf and sister Dara arrived, all hiding under the same tense half-grin. The plumbing had backed up and broken; those additional bathrooms had put the entire pipe system of the school out of whack.

Trudy fired off a cable. Tarp alit almost instantly from Lisbon, with a wooden box. Out of it flicked Pilcic lizards that gulped down the toads with little girlish cries. Tarp also produced, within days, a whole work force of Macedonian plumbers.

Even so they took forever. The whole sewage and water system of the school had to be restored, amplified, reinforced. It had to be done in difficult Alpine terrain and rather piecemeal so as not to disrupt school too much. And when *that* was finally over, Tarp stepped from his Rolls-Volkswagen and held a blueprint before his face like a mask.

"Oh, oh," Trudy said.

Oh, oh was right. Pinned to the blueprint was an architect's sketch. It showed their ex-garage villa all right, but with such a delightfully mansarded, orieled, balconied second floor she didn't get as mad as she should.

"For Christ's sakes," she said. "When are we going to settle down?"

"Don't hit, don't hurt," he said. "Look, Trood: the new floor on top, it starts with our bedroom here; here, your study, the smart place; my study, here — little dumb place, no telex, not much work, I'll be a good boy. That's on top. Ground floor: Ronaldo's room — you see? More separation, more space for him, entertain, do terrible things, he'll be a young man soon. Over here, dining room, living room, kitchen. *Basta.* Okay?"

She looked at it, shaking her head.

"See?" he said. "No maid's room, no live-in help here. You teach Tarp the dishwasher. *Chachacha.*"

She didn't laugh with him. But she knew he was sort of right, the sonofabitch. Ronnie was growing up rapidly, still away from her rather than toward her. She'd worried about the day when

246

they'd all move into one tight floor together. It might help to have more space if they were going to start doing some real living together.

"Your great permission?" Tarp said. "We put a floor on top. We call it the Villa Make-Top?"

"You *momser*," she said. "When will enough be enough?"

"The top," he said. "The top is enough."

So another Macedonian work gang came to make the top. It was such a nuisance, waiting for the completion of their forever uncompletable home. But at least it drove her into completing something else. At last she really did get serious about finishing her dissertation.

During the delays she'd done a lot of reading on the sociology of the redemption concept. Now she thought the theme warranted a real book she could dedicate to Ronnie. This meant more resort to New York for longer periods, for the reference resources.

But God damn it, New York in turn meant The Lunch. The Lunch still waited for her in Manhattan. It swooped down inevitably on Mrs. Letarpo in the Waldorf Towers. So did the hat that came with The Lunch. And so did the hush, the awful hush with which The Lunch began.

The first thing that hit her was this hush. Perhaps the state of her clothes helped provoke it. She hadn't really planned to enter Elaine's that wet. She had only resolved to arrive non-chauffeur-driven, and the only way to escape the driver laying for her at the Towers entrance was to smile him away and walk quickly round the corner. She'd intended to catch a taxi on Lexington, but it started to come down all of a sudden and all the taxis were taken. So she just kept walking. The rain wasn't too bad. She could window-shop at her ease, stroll from boutique to boutique. This was such rare fun these days, she walked all the way up to 88th Street and the crosstown blocks east, and the hell with getting sopping wet. It went with her outfit. When she got to Elaine's, the chauffeurs grinned at her drippyness from the insides of their dry limousines.

"Sorry, private party," said the guard. He got a half-dissolved invitation for his trouble.

247

So naturally there was a hush inside. The hush of some sixty people suspended by her footfalls into silence. An enormously alert, fast-appraising, hardworking silence.

In her masquerade as Mrs. Letarpo, Trudy had become attuned to such silences and the work hidden inside them. Amazing how people on that level, especially the women, worked and scroll-worked their fun to the point of drudgery. Every social cigarette, every shared little laugh, every new pair of gloves, every convivial coffee cup, golf round or tennis doubles — God, every bit of gregariousness was a tactic. It was a reflection of one's position in the arena; was either thrust or parry or flaunt or feint or ambush. It was all work, all endless painstaking virtuosity that would be reviewed instantly by one's peer virtuosos, reported, deftly interpreted or skilfully ignored by the society columnists. It was amazing. In her bolshie teens Trudy had thought of the fatcats as frivolous oppressors of the world below. Now she knew that the poor things oppressed themselves too. They were like the medieval Chasidim, these people. All that was spontaneous in life had to be reduced to the strategic by those virtuosos of devoutness. At least with the Chasidim their obsession aimed for God's all-seeing approval; with the people in this room, for enhancement of one's ranking. (It came to Trudy, the parallel ought to be amplified into a chapter somewhere.) With both the Chasidim and the Beautiful Ones each routine act had a symbolic understructure that must be defined and refined, positively or negatively *ad infinitum* by fellow initiates. As in the Talmud, life was consumed in commentary. Therefore: what did it mean that Trudy Letarpo appeared among them at this moment, late, sopping wet, under a *Schande* of a hat? How align the phenomenon into the coordinates of the *Vogue* cabala?

"Trudy Letarpo!"

Hella Mynn had opened her arms (but not too wide). She stood in a cluster which moved slightly (not too slightly) to form a half circle around her not-too-widely-opened arms. This uncoiling of the central group had the effect of presenting to Trudy the entire mosaic of power in the room, from Warhol impassively seated in one corner, to tall Obolensky with a goblet in the other, to BAH, *B*erenice *A*stor *H*uxley, the giant bluestocking duchess of the

248

twenties, with her black satin galluses holding up the Marlene Dietrich slacks over her white blouse. Great BAH was an heirloom in Mrs. Mynn's possession, superprestigious. Of course BAH wore her enormous ocher shaggy mushroom — her trademark of a hat. To this hat of hats Hella Mynn paid homage campily with all-hat lunches. "Hats," it said on the invitation. What luncher dared disobey?

None.

Trudy noticed it on her walk toward Hella Mynn. It must have been damn hard to match all these instances of blue denim haute couture, the Trigère overalls and gypsy suedes with headgear. But they had all managed it somehow. Trudy walked past painters' caps made of leopard skin and hard-hat simulations over which, Jesus, a whole Hampton gay bar's worth of designer talent must have brooded through many a weekend. In this world, energized by chic paranoia, was it paranoid of Trudy to think they were all in league against her? Here she was, the fairly new Mrs. Letarpo (still silvered over by the *Nick Now!* Express), bursting in poodle-wet on their great dry carefulness, with a travesty of a hat. How would they interpret that?

"What a treat for us," Hella Mynn said.

She kept her arms half open. A tray dropped in the kitchen. Bing! At the same time a waiter emerged, bearing smoked salmon canapés under the mustaches of a herald. Of course Trudy had met Hella Mynn and some of the others before. But their convergence here had a ritual power — watch out! — an intricately coded, hierarchical status significance. A hundred eyes flickered in the room. A hundred expectancies. It made Trudy think of the seraphim Max Weber had mentioned, the burning angels who flew so high, so near to God, that they burned with love for Him. *You,* they seemed to say to her in this room, since you're flying so high on this altitude of ours, where's *your* flame? Sear yourself a little to deserve us! Give a big party! A vulnerable interview! None of these evasions like your quiche recipe in *Harper's Bazaar,* or your flower arrangements in the *Sunday News,* or your Towers Brainy Cell in *House and Garden.* Expend some light and substance! Burn! Work like us!

Or was that all only imaginary? Was Trudy ducking into intellectualization at such moments, that is, into her own turf — because she was scared to meet these people on their own? But the fact was that Hella Mynn burned awfully well. It became clearer and clearer as Trudy walked toward the woman. Hella Mynn glowed with dramaturgic energy. Her neck brace was the most cunning color, expressing attenuation and esthetics to the highest degree. It was no less precisely nuanced to her saffron pants suit than to her aviator glasses. Face and figure were one single slim mask between her half-open arms. The mask turned every aspect of the lunch into theater; from the choice of Elaine's Restaurant (probably both a concession and a challenge to Trudy's "cultural" reputation) to Hella's adjutant, a petite woman, wife of an Exxon senior vice president whose name Trudy couldn't remember. This high corporate lady carried a clipboard and a cigarette holder. At a smile of Hella's she rapped the holder against a glass.

Hella Mynn bent forward to mime a kiss. Trudy countermimed. She breathed in a potent subtle cloud of perfume. "I'm sorry, I'm wet," she said.

"Wet or dry, my dear," Hella Mynn said with her deep voice.

She left one arm on Trudy's moist shoulder in a mildly emphatic way.

"*My friends,*" she said.

All noise stopped.

"Friends, I don't have to tell you about Gertrude. I don't have to tell you what it means to have her with us and the kind of help she can give to the committee. But we are greedy, aren't we? We want more. It'd be beautiful if she could give us a few words of encouragement."

A speech? Nothing like that had been mentioned when Hella had asked her to come.

"Let's encourage her to encourage us," Hella Mynn said, applauding. Everybody joined her instantly. The smoked-salmon bearer froze into a statue and didn't come to life until the applause stopped. A car misfired in the street. Trudy stepped forward.

"I'm sorry I'm late and wet," Trudy said.

Hella Mynn laughed. It wasn't the laugh of a woman in a neck brace. It was a free gallop of a laugh and came from a face bent backward with enjoyment and had a certain magic — the quality of charming leadership. The whole room laughed. Hella hugged Trudy for a moment without much touching somehow. Then she stepped back.

"Lay it on us, Trudy," she said softly.

Trudy really had to make a speech.

"Well, I won't make a speech," she said. "I'll just say what our letter said, that Letarpo and I will be glad to take care of the Waldorf Grand Ball Room rental, plus the Macedonian king, make sure he'll show up. And I'm sure you all will do the very important rest. And I'm still sorry I'm late and wet."

They laughed. They applauded. Again Hella Mynn put her hand on Trudy's shoulder with that superb mild emphasis.

"Isn't that beautiful?" Hella Mynn said. "That'll be perfect next time around!"

More applause. She turned to her clipboard assistant. "You have that down, Heidi? We'll get to work on that in September. This time we'll prepare way ahead." She smiled: the Mephistopheles-faced photographer from the *Post* (apparently the only one allowed) flashed his bulb for the fiftieth time at Hella and at Trudy's wetness.

"And now I'll spread her among you," Hella Mynn said. She ushered Trudy toward the crowd. Trudy didn't move.

"*Next* time?" Trudy said.

"This year we'll have the thing at Jamaica," Mrs. Mynn said. "Heidi nailed the president of Turkey for sponsor poobah. Listen, Andy the Warhol wants to know your least favorite color and you've *got* to meet BAH."

Trudy didn't move.

"I don't follow," Trudy said.

Though she followed all right. A lot of eyes were on her through the buzz, eyes that wanted to watch her burning.

Hella no longer tried to usher her forward. "There's long been a feeling that we ought to have our winter affair someplace warm," Hella Mynn said.

"I just don't follow," Trudy said. "Our proposal was all set. You said all the members were informed and they all agreed."

"They did, angel. We just set it back a year. It'll be groovy next year, when there's enough time —"

251

"You sort of lost me," Trudy said. "Isn't there a vote?"

"Of course. At these things, Gertrude, if you don't do business right away, nobody pays any mind."

"You mean you already voted?"

"First thing, angel, while the mind is sober. We're not all great brains like you. Now Andy was just over there — "

"Hold it," Trudy said. "You'll never sell a third of the tickets. Not with some Turkish president, when you could have a reigning king."

"You think so?" Hella said, charmingly interested.

"Even I know that and I'm new to the game," Trudy said.

"Well then, we'll do it up doubly brown when we have your nice king next year."

"For God's sakes, it's *this* year," Trudy said, "this year right after the earthquake, that's when they need the money the most, the victims for whom we're all making that touching effort!"

"Oh my dear Gertrude," Hella said. "I've been making the effort for ten years. Maybe I learned something about it. But I'm always willing to learn more. Like —" She turned and took the clipboard away from her adjutant with a reasonant briskness. "Like for next year, a list of new names we could contact through you or your husband? Good people for whom we'd be grateful?"

Hella Mynn maintained the sweetness of her smile, her neck-braced head most amiably inclined. All around eyes stared through the buzz, to watch Trudy burn.

"I think I'll try to get a little less wet," Trudy said.

She took off her hat. She wrung it out, more or less at random over the clipboard. An odd expression traveled from under Hella Mynn's glasses. The upper lip curled as though she'd smelled something painful. She took a small dance step sideways. The next thing she did was unknown because Trudy had walked off after putting on her hat again. Trudy had decided not to walk out, for that would make an already juvenile situation altogether childish. She walked past flashbulb flashes, canapés, stares, toward BAH.

"Hello," she said to Berenice Astor Huxley. "I'm Trudy Letarpo. I've looked forward to meeting you."

"Aha," BAH said. *The New York Times* lay folded in her lap and she seemed to have dozed off. "Trudy? . . . Trudy, didn't you teach Hebrew to Clare Luce? What was the use of that?"

"As a matter of fact I never did," Trudy said.

"I bet she was!" BAH said. "Bully for you! You ought to tell Hella. Hella! . . . Damn, where is Hella"

But Hella, neck brace and all, had vanished into the ladies room, and pots banged from the kitchen like a far-off gong.

2

A few days later she flew to the Alps. After the Hella Mynn brutishness, Bachberg should have been refreshing. There she could be with Ronnie. She breathed in the tart cleansing air of the high valley in October. There was snow spanking-white on peaks, the oaks crimson and yellow against the green of the pines, smell of fresh-sawn wood, keenness of fresh paint, spice whiffs from the cigarettes the Macedonian workers smoked down to stubs they stuck under their dusty berets. . . . She had a great time antiquing in Innsbruck's Altstadt in her pidgin German. She needed cupboards and highboys in country Biedermeier. How integrate the silver-green quilted headboards and the provincial Venetian of the Antone furniture with the Tyrolean pieces needed to complete the rooms? . . . Great fun to assemble alternatives and make the final decision with Tarp when he came the following week.

So why was she depressed as the months went on? She was working well on her dissertation. And she blocked out the syllabus of the humanities and religion department Mannritt was to start next year (after all, Trudy was a consultant) and she looked over résumés of faculty applicants. But she loved drooling over decor plans for Villa Make-Top, where she'd finally settle into a life base — with a highboy in the bedroom? Or a baroque credenza not too fancy? And what about Ronnie's room?

Ronnie didn't show much interest. He had the Central Park West chair and a cot.

"I don't need more now," he said. "I'm so busy."

It was Ronnie she was depressed about. There was no real getting close to him, though they now lived in adjoining rooms in the staff building. Of course he actually *was* busy. Mornings he attended classes. Lunch he spent with Mannritt, Prince Yussuf and his sister as part of the liaison team between Mannritt and the Macedonian construction workers. They were finally finishing the religion building. Ronnie measured with yardsticks, compared paint samples; Mannritt queried; the prince translated and the princess jotted things down on the pad. Mannritt had explained to Trudy that all the building work had to be finished by the end of spring so that they could finally resume full complement next year — she needed all the help she could get. No quarreling with that, especially since it was good for Ronnie to feel useful. So she watched Mannritt and her helpers poking around amidst woodshavings and lathes, eating their sandwiches on the go. They looked like a patrol: Ronnie and Prince Yussuf both wore the same kind of epauletted white shirt. La Mannritt and the princess moved in culottes, and though the older woman was so ample and the younger so thin, they produced the same sort of flow under the garment. Among these four there was a self-contained momentum which Trudy watched from her balcony, eating a sandwich all by herself. She knew she should grab her Ronnie away. But she didn't know how.

Afternoons Ronnie shut himself up in his homework. He worked in his Central Park West chair, for which he'd become too big. So he doubled up, propped his copybook on his knees. The childlikeness of that in a tall freckled youth made her body ache for her son.

"How about joining your old lady for dinner?" she said. "We could drive to Innsbruck to make it worth your while."

"Oh," he said. "Oh, I'm supposed to have a bite with Madame Mannritt and the others."

"Again?"

A child-man, a gallant, a solemn cut-up, probably a secret heller, with a math book balanced on the knee of his curled-up leg. Sweet and sealed-off.

Gone the Ronnie that wanted to win and impress her. This youth here seemed to try to keep her at arm's length in the nicest way.

"Tomorrow I'm going to Vienna," she said.

"Have a good time, Mother."

"Just for one day. I'll be right back."

"That's nice," he said, and went off into the evening.

She listened to the swiftness with which his footsteps died. On the floor lay a pack of cigarettes with Arabic lettering. One of the Macedonian workers must have dropped it. She lit what was probably the first and last cigarette of her life. It stung her throat. She threw it down, stamped on it, walked out among dim raw silhouettes of half-reconstructed chalets, through a darkness tingling with pine scent and cicadas. She walked to the building that was to house the religion department. No electricity there as yet. The windows wavered golden-russet. Candlelight. Inside a woman's voice sang, bittersweetly, "Ave Maria." No doubt a tape recorder, but Trudy couldn't see it when she opened the door. In the candlelight she saw only Mannritt, Ronnie and Prince Yussuf crouched closely together while the princess moved wooden blocks on the floor. Mannritt got up fast and flowed in her culottes to Trudy.

"Those are the pews," Mannritt said. "Those blocks, Mrs. Letarpo. What we will create here, it will be a church-synagogue-mosque interchangeable, most exciting. We are also testing acoustics."

Mannritt spoke fast. All four lived in a candlelit velocity beyond the speed of normal life. Trudy felt she was slowing them down. Apparently Ronnie hadn't even noticed her.

"I don't want to interrupt," she said.

"Not at all, at all," La Mannritt said. "When we have progressed more, we will show you, for your advice." She reached toward her groin. "If I could ask a favor . . ." It was a pocket she'd reached into; out came a small warm package she pressed into Trudy's hand. "Would you be so kind? These Band-Aids. My students are used to a little attention at night. But nowadays, this terrible deadline to finish the building . . ."

"Yes," Trudy said.

"Thank you!" Mannritt said. "Oh Mrs. Letarpo that you yourself — I have such glamorous help! Thank you!"

So Trudy did a Madame Mannritt in the student lounge. The

kids were as exhausted as ever. Trudy passed among them gluing Band-Aids over an astounding variety of scrapes; she patted headaches and discussed with the nurse the color of the drinking water. Most of the students slumped over German illustrateds. Some stared at Trudy from the corners of their eyes. None of them was Ronnie.

Curfew was at eleven P.M. But on her way back Trudy saw the windows of the religion building still swimming in candlelight, this time to an oriental singsong. . . . The Koran sung by Yussuf?

In her bed later, she felt sleep coming, but Ronnie was still out. At least she didn't hear the door. She heard something calling in the marsh by the pinewoods. A bird. Too-witt . . . . . too-witt . . . too-witt . . .

Thank God, Vienna the next day was a perfect antidote. After the loneliness of being Ronnie's mother at Bachberg she could use a brief tumult of being Mrs. Letarpo in public. With some pangs she'd agreed to the date some weeks ago, but it turned out to be awfully painless. The flight to Vienna took only an hour. And the dining room of the occasion, a small sumptuous vault above the Sacher Hotel restaurant, she couldn't help find delightful.

Bic and Jennifer were waiting there. The only thing they'd done wrong was the centerpiece — overshowy, two dozen crimson roses in a Ming vase much too big for the table. She had it replaced by three single roses in three bud vases. She liked that much better. In the small gothic mirror she even liked herself — not unimportant if you're a couple of days away from forty-two. After Bachberg a little bit of vanity-indulging was therapeutic. She wore the one chic item in her Bachberg wardrobe, a silk shirtwaist. She pulled at it to do justice to the geometric pattern when a zither player started behind the Spanish screen and somebody came up from behind to clamp a hat on her head.

"Trood!" he said through his kiss. "You forgot that in the States!"

"I didn't forget, I left it," she said.

"*That* you left? With that you took away New York from Mrs. Minsk!"

"New York is still in the same place," she said, smiling.

"No sirree, Madame! That's a Trudy-Town now! You didn't see the paper? Chey, here they come."

Here they came indeed, up the exclusive little staircase. No time for the comb. Trudy decided the hat on looked slightly less grotesque than the hat off but with the hat-messed hair showing.

"Hokay," Tarp introduced. "This is my wife Trudy, and these people here, they're all His Honors and Highnesses with whom I make trouble. *This* Highness is von Mellen. I bought Bachberg from him — what is it? — fifteen years ago, and you know all the trouble we're making with the school there. . . . *This* Honor is Madrid mayor, he's got a lot of trouble with me; I'm taking a couple thousands workers away from him, for the pipeline factory in Paris. . . . Oh-oh, *this* Honor is speak of the devil. That's his Mayor-of-Paris Honor who's going to find out what trouble — *ah, mais oui, Monsieur!* — he'll find out what trouble after he won't give us cooperation. . . . Now *this* Highness here, I'm in real trouble. He's the president of — what's the exact name?"

"The Austrian-Spanish Chamber of Commerce," said the handsome man, kissing Trudy's hand.

"Him I'm in trouble with, I took away the mayors from his Chamber conference. The whole idea of this lunch is, all our guests get in terrible trouble with each other. So they won't get so mad at me. Anybody apéritifs?"

Everybody apéritifs. Nobody got mad at anybody. It was a small beautifully run lunch. Trudy seemed to get the credit for running it, though all she'd done was phone Jennifer about the menu. Tarp had put a spotlight on Trudy by making her the only woman present. That day he turned up his rough good humor an extra point, so that she could (on his lee side, as it were) lean back, smile, radiate reticence by contrast.

It was fun, particularly since all the men happened to be rather young and good-looking, considering their position. She sat between an Honor and a Highness. Both played jealous. Highness put a fretted gold watch on the table: Trudy had to promise not to talk longer than two minutes to one neighbor before turning to the other. The rule was violated with frequency and hilarity. And when, after coffee, His Spanish Honor rose to present His French Honor with the Medal of the Lion of Madrid, Trudy had to hang it round Monsieur, who kissed her on both cheeks before kissing — despite all the protests from the table — her lips.

Was it being almost forty-two — was that why she enjoyed all this so much? It was all such old-fashioned, effortless, playfully naïve flirtatiousness that seemed to be unknown in the States and by which she wasn't a bit jaded. That's how the lunch went. Much of the ambience was really due to Tarp. He managed an air of being both court jester and *éminence grise* at court of each of these potentates. When it was over, he bear-hugged them all goodby and then practically carried Trudy down the little staircase with tenderness. Quite as though they'd finished a tryst in a *chambre séparée*.

That afternoon he went on to Scandinavia somewhere in his plane, and she flew back to Bachberg, puzzling over him. He was at utterly successful, earthy ease with the politicians and aristocrats of Europe. Why bother to conquer the Hella Mynns of New York through his wife?

Back in Bachberg, though, America and Vienna dwindled away. Next day she ate her usual Ronnieless sandwich on the usual balcony in a sunny nippy wind, and watched her son walk munching past with Mannritt and the two Macedonians. All around the peaks, white, gray, gold, sealed her into scenic solitude. She got up, walked to the phone, yelled at the school's poor phone operator and kept yelling till she got results from an Innsbruck butcher. She made an attractive enough eating companion to some fairly spoiled people. She'd be bloody goddamned if she couldn't get her own son to share a meal with her.

Around three P.M. Ronnie arrived, to plummet straight into his homework. She bided her time; looked at tile samples for the kitchen of the future Villa Make-Top. When she heard him get up to leave, she struck.

"Hold it!"

She led him to what made do as dining nook.

"Don't tell me you don't remember that." She took the bell off the steak tartare platter. "Even as a little kid you used to eat it by the pound."

"Oh," he said. "That's nice of you."

"So don't go snacking elsewhere. Sit down and eat with me."

He took a small breath. Then he smiled and sat down with her. He mixed in the egg with deftness. The smile was more of a cavalier's smile than a teenage son's. His legs were crossed and the muscles of his short-sleeved arm moved slimly. She still suspected he was humoring her, but perhaps he was humoring her with affection. There was some wild deep engrossment here, on the surface of which he was a boy acting nicely to Mom.

"Let's talk, Ronnie."

"Okay."

"We haven't had much chance to get together. A lot has happened."

"How was Vienna?" he said.

"Pleasant," she said. "Maybe next time you'll come along."

"I saw your picture in the International *Herald Trib*."

Trudy found herself unprepared for that.

"When?" she said. Though she knew.

"Couple of days ago. One of the kids showed it to me. The big wrinkled New York hat fashion you started, or something."

"Oh that's such rot!"

"When is Gospodin coming?"

"Come on, don't call him that," she said.

"His servants do."

"You're not his servant. Call him Tarp, same as I do."

"When is Tarp coming?" he said evenly.

"Friday."

"I can move out, back into the dorm, the night before."

"Are you kidding?"

"It's not a big place here."

"Who cares about big?" she said. "The hell with bigness! All the *big* talk, just because I married Tarp!"

He looked away.

"That hat thing in the paper," she said. "Shall I tell you what happened in New York? There was a charity I was asked to join, but the woman boss there thought I was too big, I'd take it away from her! And because of that the charity is going to suffer! A lot of needy people! *That* should have been in the paper — not the stupid hat thing!"

She saw what he was looking at. A huge lovely suede-brown moth, settled on the lamplit wall. She wanted to put her fingers on its trembly wings. "Ronnie," she said. "There're too many things going on around me now. That's why it's so great to build a sort of shelter here — hole up with you in the Alps! I'm trying to focus on what's important. Use whatever leverage I have for important things. Like you, and the work I'm trying to do, and helping people. And Tarp, I'll try to make Tarp's leverage meaningful too. You follow me? I want to build a place where we can live together!"

He nodded. He was looking at the moth.

"You see, that's a strength in Tarp, the way he's close to his family and where he comes from. We ought to learn from that."

Ronnie nodded.

"And this bigness thing, just because I married him — I don't want it to run my life. I don't want to spend all my time defending it or fighting it — hell, this must be boring to you."

"No, no," he said.

"Tell me what you're doing. I mean with Mrs. Mannritt and the others."

"Oh, you know, the inside of the religion building."

"Is it fun?"

"Yes. We're experimenting with ideas." He looked at his watch. "The trouble is, I promised —"

"Go on! Get out of here!" She gave him a kiss and a push.

"Thank you," he said softly.

"Anyway, don't you dare move out!"

"Okay."

"And come back a little earlier tonight," she said, smiling.

When *did* he come back? It must have been past midnight when the door woke her. The door to her own room which had been opened.

It was Ronnie.

"Mother," he said. "It's about the synagogue."

She had to blink violently because she had dropped off with the light on. After her eyes adjusted, she saw that her first thought had been wrong. He wasn't drunk. But there was a disarray about him. He kept smoothing back an eyebrow, a very adult-male gesture out of sync with his sneakers and the crushed shirt.

"We're now on the synagogue side of the religion building," he said. "I don't want a modern synagogue. Do you happen to know the layout of the old kind?"

"The old kind," she said. She tried to clear her mind, but her eye got stuck on something like a new dark freckle on his neck. It might have been a toothmark too, but she couldn't be sure. He'd been pushed into her room by some urgency she couldn't grasp in her confusion. "The old synagogues," she said.

"I thought I'd ask for your advice," he said.

"An old Orthodox synagogue," she said. "It shouldn't be hard to research. Let me think about it tomorrow."

"Tomorrow," he said. "Yes, thanks."

"Ronnie!" she called after him.

"Thank you. Sorry to wake you up," he said. "Good night." And was gone.

She waited till next afternoon, when she knew Jennifer must be back in New York. She called and asked her to dig up pictures of medieval synagogues. To her surprise Jennifer wasn't prompt about calling back. Wednesday a call did come from the States — *Mademoiselle* magazine asking for a crushed-hat photo session against alpine background. The operator refused on standing orders, though Trudy got a ghoulish kick out of listening in. Friday the phone rang again.

"Trood? You postpone the birthday for one day?"

He hadn't forgotten. It was the day she became forty-two. She didn't mind spending it quietly, incredulously (each year her age became more of an artifact externally imposed on the same floundering wild-hearted adolescent) . . . no, she didn't mind spending No. 42 in Bachberg's green air, with her manuscript and Villa Make-Top blueprints and a birthday card from Tante. But she was glad he hadn't forgotten.

"Reason I don't come till tomorrow is that we got mayor problems in Paris," Tarp said.

"Don't apologize."

"Sonofabastard mayor! He knows why I got him the medal in

Vienna! He's supposed to make bike lanes on the highway! Sonofabastard kissed you on the mouth!"

She had to laugh.

"My Spanish workers got nothing but bikes! No bikelanes, no going to work! No pipeline! *O Bože,* the wires I had to pull for his medal, you know, that whole story!"

"Sure," she said. Now and then Tarp threw in some little business tidbit prefaced by "You know, that whole story." As if she were briefed on all Letarpo operations each day before breakfast and everything was familiar stuff.

"Next time buy all your factories complete with bike lanes, dummy," she said.

"*Ja dolazim sutra!*" Tarp said. "Tomorrow I come!"

Tomorrow he came. It took her a while to realize in what state, for he seemed the same as in Vienna. Two Tripletts jumped out of the station wagon with Bic, who opened the back door. Here was her husband staggering out behind a box.

"Happy birthday, Trood!"

The strong hug, the humorously erotic lip-kiss, the double cheek-kiss Balkan style, he swept the lid off the box.

It was the Altneu synagogue of ancient Prague, a model made of laminated wood, lovingly plainted.

"How'd you get *that?*"

"Little doing, Sotheby's. Not bad, huh?"

"Wait a minute!" she said. "That's for Ronnie!"

"Sure it's for Ronnie."

"But only Jennifer knows about it in New York."

"So she told me about it in New York."

"You're one lying Croat!" she said. "You were in Paris yesterday with all your mayor trouble!"

"What's the matter? I can't be in New York when I got Paris mayor trouble? Chey, Bic, don't we have Paris mayor trouble?"

"Sure we got Paris mayor trouble," Bic said. "Lots of Paris mayor trouble."

"Because of Paris mayor trouble I can't be in New York? You got a Jewish law against it?"

"There's a Jewish law against everything," she said, looking at the synagogue model. "But it's a very sweet surprise."

"Not for you — 's'not a birthday present. The birthday we do in little bits. Okay, first little bit."

He held out his hand. A Triplett reached into a pocket. Few of Tarp's presents ever came in wrappings, but naked and sudden out of a Triplett pocket.

"Happy birthday, Trood."

A brooch. Wrought of some green precious metal she couldn't even identify. She stepped back. This time the surprise was cold.

"Oh, Tarp," she said. "We talked about that sort of thing."

Such tycoonish gifts she hated with a passion that was no doubt puritan and a reverse vanity. But she couldn't help it. "Thank you," she said. "No Sugar Daddy jewelry."

"What jewelry! Jesus God!" He hefted it violently. "Weigh! *Wood!* From the olive tree at the Towers!" Violently he hit himself on the chest. "I carve it! I even paint it on the plane, I had no time before. It was wet an hour ago. Chey, Bic, it wasn't wet an hour ago?"

"Sure it was wet an hour ago," Bic said.

She took it. She'd forgotten. It was a Croat custom, the gift carved by the giver.

"Forgive me," she said. "That's darling."

It was really wood, a caterpillar whittled with considerable skill, yet with an endearingly primitive clasp. She kissed him.

"Then the other little birthday from Mama."

Now the Triplett came up with a manila folder; Tarp handed it on to Trudy. A huge pressed flower was inside.

"Madonna rose," Tarp said. "Very rare. Turn it this way. You see the face in the petals? Like a madonna."

She saw. The folder smelled of incense.

"Well, from Mama. Very Catholic." Tarp gave a grin and did a shoulder-shrugging quick jig and dabbed his chin with his tie. She knew him well by then. In Letarpo semaphore this meant embarrassment.

"It's lovely," she said. "I mean it. It's touching."

"And we throw a big birthday party at the Eiffel Tower. We invite the Big Boy from Macedonia, people like that, maybe even sonofabastard mayor if he makes bike lanes — we show Mrs. Minsk, huh?"

"Now hold it," Trudy said.

263

"Hey, Ronaldo! *Ciao,* Ronaldo! We got something for you!"

"Ronaldo" was what Ronnie had become as Letarpo's stepson. Ronnie had come up with the inevitable group: Mannritt and the Macedonians; that is, Yussuf and the princess. Tarp grabbed the synagogue model back from a Triplett, thrust it at Ronnie, slung his arms round the Macedonians to watch the boy's reaction.

Ronnie stood there, holding the *Altneuschul.*

"Something wrong, huh?" Tarp said. "Mama's got the birthday. *You* got the present."

"It's your birthday?" Ronnie said.

"Never mind," Trudy said. "But that's for your work on the religion building. It's a famous old Prague synagogue."

"Yes." Ronnie looked at her. "It was you I asked about old synagogues."

"Well, Tarp heard about your interest through me," Trudy said. "Isn't it beautiful?"

"Thank you," Ronnie said.

"Don't worry, Mama's going to get a nice big present too," Tarp said. "Big party on the Eiffel Tower, high enough the pigeons can't eat the caviar. Everybody invited. We do it weekend — weekends you got no school, right?"

Ronnie nodded, holding the synagogue.

"There's going to be no such party," Trudy said.

"Of course a party. King's already said okay for Sunday."

"Happy birthday, Mother," Ronnie said. He held the synagogue carefully, stiffly, while the crickets began in the marsh.

"The party's out," she said to Tarp. "For Christ's sakes, Tarp, mobilize all those fancy people for a good cause for a change, workers' bike lanes or something! Not because some poor woman is forty-two years old."

Tarp clapped his hands together so violently, some workers in the next chalet stopped.

"*Slažem se! No birthday party. Birthday demonstration!*"

When Tarp laughed out loud, every pore in that compact body jumped, from the black slippers to the brown sports jacket to the long black hair. He guffawed and shook like a powerful child, and everybody got little convulsed pats and strokes that were invitations to join the merriment. When he laughed like that he was a whole surging troop of laughers. It was commandingly infectious. Mannritt simpered, the prince showed teeth, his sister put her hand against her face to brake a giggle. Even Ronnie's mouth seemed to soften.

"Chey, we give Trood a demonstration! We treat her to a Class A demonstration!"

He sure knew how to back down uproariously.

"Okay, next year," Trudy said smiling. "This year we got work to do on our house. Come on."

He came on all right, at a speed high even for him, but she still didn't catch on. He inspected construction progress on various school buildings. He got his shoes sopping wet in the marsh, nailing a bird house for finches on a willow. He said "Oh boy, yeah!" to the nebulously complex plan Ronnie's group had for the inside of the religion building. He climbed halfway up a fir tree to see the alpine sunset better. And when they buckled down to the real work at the Villa Make-Top and put their heads together over decor sketches, he let her win a point: agreed to forget about the blue Picasso he'd wanted shipped from the Paris house to the future living room downstairs. Whew.

They settled on what chests would go with the Venetian pieces from Pilcic, and he himself phoned the Innsbruck carpenters in his laborious German. Tireless, he crawled into all corners of the bare Villa Make-Top, wielding the tapemeasure and managing to chew his dinner sausage while holding a pencil between his teeth. He insisted on drawing the new, maybe final, layout plan with his own hand and never mind that he constantly confused his centimeters with Trudy's inches. By eleven she was exhausted but also warmed. Their home would really be birthed by them both.

When she fell into bed in their temporary rooms, he hit himself on the forehead.

"*Zaburavio sam!* Forgot to call off your party." And ran for the phone downstairs.

It must have been a long call. Next morning the bed next to hers was untouched. She rushed down in her robe.

"Good morning," a Triplett said brightly.

The Triplett finger pointed. At a truck parked by the Villa Make-Top. Morning gusts tugged at her robe as she ran. Inside the house there was Tarp, still in yesterday's sports jacket and marsh-wet shoes, straining a credenza against the wall.

"You're crazy! We haven't even painted yet!"

"Just to try it out, Trood."

"The wiring isn't even done!"

"Just so we get an idea." He was breathing heavily, happily. "On paper it means nothing."

"But that's insane."

Some of the bedroom furniture already stood on casters in the hall.

"We look at it, we move it out again. Like a rehearsal. The credenza is okay against the wall?"

"You did all this overnight?" she said.

He didn't answer because he was pushing too hard. But the Triplett helping him nodded and ballooned dusty cheeks.

"I had to phone night calls anyhow. Persia and so on. After breakfast we do the upstairs."

It was then that she caught on at last.

"You've got your insomnia," she said.

"Sure. When it gets too boring, too many Paris mayor bastards and like that. I think the credenza works against the wall."

"Yes, it does," she said.

His insomnia spells were more like energy jags. Breakfast consisted of a donkey and long distance. The phone kept crying incongruously against the mountain morning, and another truck rumbled up. A Triplett led a very dark donkey down the gangplank.

"Look at this boy," Tarp said. "Maybe I can go to sleep on that boy!"

"Nairobi." Bic held up the receiver. "It's always Nairobi for breakfast."

"You make the extension longer?" Tarp said.

"I had them put in half a mile while you were working the furniture," Bic said.

"I'll take Nairobi on the boy. I want to get used to the boy."

He took Nairobi on the boy. He sat saddleless on the donkey, coffee mug in one hand, receiver clamped between ear and shoulder so that one hand was free to stroke the boy. He was instantly pals with the animal and rode it twenty yards off into inaudibility, extension trailing like a centaur's umbilical cord. He rode back, tossed the phone down to Bic, jumped off with the coffee mug half-drunk and unspilled and bussed the boy goodby.

"Okay. We do the upstairs now?"

They did the upstairs of the Villa Make-Top. For the next few hours they tried out all her various ideas for book shelves. He played the part of the stainless steel brackets that would hold up the transparent Lucite shelves in a floating-books effect against the dark wood walls. He insisted on holding up one shelf after another with the actual books on it — sundry Talcott Parsons volumes, Toynbees, Kierkegaards, dictionaries, etc. — while she stepped back to evaluate. She felt indulged, a little foolish, but she had such fun. They hit on an asymmetric shelf pattern that worked beautifully. After lunch it was the bedroom's turn, Tarp pushing furniture around endlessly, humming. They ended up with her original idea: the beds alongside the balcony view, not facing it. Then she had a hard time talking him out of a super-sauna which would have delayed their moving in for additional months.

"You win, Trood. You the champ. Now! I take a shower and I take a nap on the boy."

"All right," she said. "Meantime I'll go through the wallpaper swatches for the bathrooms."

Jennifer had sent a million of those. Innsbruck had sent a number. By mid-afternoon, when she'd made a preliminary selection, there was no Tarp. She found the bathroom damp, but his bed still untouched.

"He rides off on the boy," the one visible Triplett said.

Where?

A Triplett-shrug. All students had vanished into homework at that time of the day. The Macedonian construction gang was eating in their barracks. But voices came from the edge of the marsh. She found not only Tarp but Ronnie with Mannritt, Prince Yussuf and the princess. Tarp had his right arm around the donkey, the left round her son. It stung. For days she'd mooned around the fringes of Ronnie's bunch. With one leap Tarp had made himself at home with them.

"Hey, Trood!"

"Good evening," the prince said. "Mr. Letarpo made a smashing offer!"

"What smashing?" Tarp said. "Logical. What's so smashing about logical?"

"But Mr. Letarpo proposed an Agrarian Institute!" the prince said. "For my people! Right here in the Alps. To learn small-farm methods in the Tyrol, similar to their mountain lands! Then my people needn't stay my father's serfs! Or — or be work gangs in foreign countries. And we have good soil, rather like here! It would save my country!"

"We do it in the next valley," Tarp said. "Trood wants her quiet here. But in the next valley —"

"Wait a minute," Trudy said. Ronnie stood immobile under Tarp's arm.

"I'll ride the boy over to the next valley," Tarp said.

"Slow down," Trudy said. She had to keep things under control. "You'll gobble up the Alps if I don't stop you."

"But in this valley you don't want any more building."

"Maybe you don't need any," Trudy said. "Let the Macedonians be apprenticed to the farmers here, work and live with them, that's the best way to learn —"

"Right!" the prince said.

"You could administer the program here at Bachberg," Trudy said. "That would take only a few extra rooms in any of the houses."

"Marvelous!" the prince said. "Thank you!"

"We could coordinate it with the school," Mannritt said, pompadour tumescing with excitement.

"Einstein idea!" Tarp said. "And she doesn't even want a birthday party — girl like that!"

They all smiled. That is, Ronnie looked down, so she couldn't be sure he smiled too. From the woods came a smell of resin, and cicadas bore in on them from the marsh.

"Tonight I sleep," her husband said.

268

He didn't sleep. He did lie down with her. But when she woke up, her watch said 2:10 A.M. and his bed was empty, again. She discovered him downstairs, in his pajamas, coiled on the floor around the phone, earpiece against his ears, singing softly, "*Oh, mein Papa.*" . . . She'd heard him musicalize before during his nocturnal long distance fits, when the connection took long to get through and there was no secretary to hold the wire. But now, lying on the raw boards under the harshness of a light bulb and the marsh noise of the night — now he and the telephone seemed locked together into an inviolable rite. She groped her way upstairs again.

At breakfast time there was no sign of him. But the phone downstairs was still occupied, this time by a very curly-haired young man she recognized from the Paris office. He bowed to her as he talked. His French was rapid but apparently he was talking to the matron-in-charge of the Paris house, arguing that you couldn't possibly put Nureyev into a room with an untuned piano.

"Oh Mrs. Letarpo," he said after he hung up. "Everything's full for the weekend! The Crillon, the Meurice, all stuffed to the gills! We have to put some of them in the house."

"When did you come in?" she said.

"This morning. Same plane that took Mr. Bic to Paris to do the real tough organizing. I'm just a little provider of beds. Some we'll have to put in the house. Now Prince Yussuf —"

"Some *who?*" she said.

"Oh, but the guests at the affair tomorrow. Mr. Letarpo said it was your idea. It should be so exciting!"

"Thanks for the news," she said and went off to find Alexander Letarpo.

No Bic, of course. No Triplett either, visible or audible. But she knew she'd find her man in the marsh, and she did. He was riding the donkey in rubber boots. He leaned forward in the saddle with the thrust of someone intensely occupied.

"What are we doing *now?*" she said.

"Chey, Trood. Good morning. You like these bushes for Pilcic?"

He was pulling up long green things by the roots and putting them into a pouch strapped to the donkey's side. Swiftly, forcefully, he yanked out one shoot after another.

"Come on, slow down," she said. "Make sense."

Fat chance. He and the donkey moved with inevitable, cheerful expedition.

"Going to have these flown to Pilcic," he said. "Plant them right away again today. Okay with you?"

"There are other things I wish you'd check out with me," she said.

"It's a sedgeberry bush. Mama makes berry preserves. I'm going to tell Yussuf for the Agrarian Institute. See the little berries coming out?"

"Yes," she said.

"We got a little marsh on the island. Behind the airstrip. You notice?"

"Tarp," she said. "We agreed there'd be no birthday party."

"No, no. No party," he said, pulling shoots. "A demonstration in Paris. Get some big people out for a good cause, the way you said."

"Oh, come on," she said.

"Your idea, Trood! Make the mayor make bike lanes for the workers! Big Shot biking gala. Lots of fun."

His cheeks up on the donkey were not swollen exactly, but filled out youthfully, as if exhilarated by so much sustained awakeness. But the eyes gleamed lividly veined, hot and black, deep inside his skull. This was not the time to argue.

"Don't you think somebody should help you with all that work?"

"No, no. Puts me in condition. Good for biking."

All she could do was shake her head.

"Go back, Trood. Don't catch cold. Later I take a nap."

Apparently his insomnia had accelerated the whole valley. On her way back she ran into Yussuf, who looked like a turbaned Christmas tree on sprinter's legs. He was hung with sneakers and he almost ran over her.

"Forgive me! I didn't see! Oh, you know Ronnie's going to lose a bet?"

"He is?"

"He bet me Mr. Letarpo wouldn't give up the oil lease in my country when it runs out? Well, Mr. Letarpo just offered this: We develop oil entrepreneurs from the people of my country, the way we develop agrarians in the Agrarian Institute! Next year we set up an Oil Institute!"

The sneakers, all hanging by their laces round his neck, swayed with his high breath.

"Good!" she said.

"You know I shall bike with my father? At the gala! Father will let me choose candidates in Macedonia for the Agrarian Institute here — Mr. Letarpo arranged it last night."

"Good," she said. "What are all those sneakers?"

"Oh, a selection just in from Innsbruck. Madame Mannritt has no cycling gear."

"She's going to that thing too?"

"Everybody is! Smashing! Do excuse me!"

He ran on.

"*Dobro!*" she heard Tarp's voice from the marsh, talking to the donkey. "*Dobro. Da navastimo sa time!*"

There was no stopping him or the mad birthday bike happening. She knew he had to get it out of his system, dream it out into the world before he could sleep.

"Tomorrow you're the world Number One biking lady," he said, when he finally came back from the marsh in the evening. "Tomorrow you wear something biky — sailor pants or something with the big hat — knock'em out, Trood!"

"I'm more concerned about your knocking yourself out," she said.

He'd taken another shower, but he was sweating again. He didn't eat at all. He put a sweater over his wet face and a parka over that, and jumped into the Rolls Volkswagen waiting for him. He kissed her hand from inside the car.

"A little exercise," he said, and his Triplett stepped on the gas.

She knew where he was going. He was off to ski the night away on the glacier.

3

She saw him next the following evening at Orly. He met her there so they could copter to the gala together.

"For you," he said, kissing her and giving her a letter. He wore huge dark glasses now to hide his eyes, but seemed as ebullient as ever, pointing out the lights of l'Étoile below. Only now and then he'd suddenly inhale deeply through clenched teeth. The repressed, caged yawn of exhaustion. About his night on skis he said nothing. He must have installed the floodlit night-*piste* on the glacier for just such sleepless spells. But because of Nick's death he never mentioned the glacier to her. Even in his state he continued to exercise such tact. He just talked about the gala and asked her to open the letter.

Later she'd realized that his timing with that letter was also an act of deftness. She took the engraved card out of the envelope. Hella Mynn requested the pleasure of Mr. and Mrs. Alexander Letarpo at the Metropolitan Arts Forum Benefit Ball, this year in Jamaica.

It was as if the copter had been jolted.

"For the Metropolitan Arts Forum!" she said. "It's supposed to be for earthquake victims. This bitch! She's still punishing me!"

It wasn't just the new injustice to disaster victims. It was Trudy's own vulnerability. She kept assuming that her ego would be beyond the range of such vileness and she kept discovering that it wasn't. She wanted to sink her nails into Hella's neck.

"Don't worry, we show Mrs. Minsk," Tarp said.

Yes, handing her that invitation just then was terrific timing. Tarp had handed her an angry energy with which to enjoy his spectacle. That invitation swept any qualms away.

The helicopter sank toward a torchlit stretch of highway leading to a big chimneyed hulk which must be the pipeline factory. "We show Mrs. Minsk," Tarp said. "We show the mayor too. No bike lanes? Look who's biking."

She looked down at the ground, which had risen toward them like a flare-bright magic carpet. She looked at an enormous, festive flexing of Letarpo social power, pleasant to behold when somebody else's power had just slapped her in the face. They had descended into a roped-off red-carpeted area filled with people standing by their bikes. Highnesses and Honors she knew from Vienna. The king of Macedonia, Robert Redford, a dusting of Rothschilds and Gulbenkians, and more of the elevated ilk. The king wore a blazer. BAH — BAH was there! — sported her famous galluses over the handlebars; the others were mostly gym-suit-sporty-campy, and the moment before Trudy stepped out, she put on her big wrinkled hat after all. Hella Mynn's little missive mandated The Hat.

A crescendo of flashbulbs. Much illuminated kissing. A positioning of TV cameras and a mounting of bikes, and then the entire V.I.P. caravan pedaled toward the factory. Trudy had to smile. Madame Mannritt rode between His Macedonian Majesty and Baron de Hirsch, wearing under a long dark-blue skirt white sneakers for an athletic touch.

They arrived. Apparently the factory's truck garage had been cleared for the purpose. The illuminati dismounted in a vast ballroom cast in concrete. It was an echoing, clanking phantasmagoria, draped red, white and blue, studded with champagne bars and buffet tables, goblets, waiters, more photographers behind red ropes. Behind a festooned tier of gas tanks an orchestra played "Happy Birthday to You" the moment Trudy let go of the handlebars; and a lot of eminent palms applauded her into confusion.

"First we go here," Tarp said, and fortunately led her off to a little office where two thin men in business suits jumped from behind a littered desk. They looked like a pair of clerks left over from the gray of the factory's daytime life, grayly immune to the high mania of the party.

"That's Maître Dellas, greatest lawyer," Tarp introduced. "And Maître Armand, second greatest lawyer. They want you to look at something."

The second greatest lawyer buttoned the top button of his jacket and gave Trudy a sheaf of typing bound with baby-blue ribbons. The first page said *Proposed Articles, Letarpo Foundation.*

"What now?" she said.

"Another little birthday piece. I told you, we do it in bits."

"That's a birthday present?"

"You look at it, Trood."

She looked at it. It was legalese. The band played *"La Vie en Rose."* She put the documents down.

"Tarp," she said. "I wish you'd slow down."

"Slow? It took us couple of months to put it together, hey Maître? That's sixty million there. You can't go fast with sixty. You'll be president of sixty, okay? Happy foundation, Trood! Happy birthday!"

He took his dark glasses off and gave her a warm Balkan kiss, moist and hearty.

"Tarp long wanted to start a foundation," Bic said. "But he'll only do it if you'll be president."

"*Quand il me prend dans ses bras . . .*," the band singer was singing outside.

"I guess this tops just about everything else," Trudy said.

"Trood, your foundation, you do with it what you want," Tarp said. "But maybe the first thing you could do is the Agrarian Institute, for example. That's — how much, Bic?"

"Two million five."

"Two million five. But first you have a real happy birthday. And we show Mrs. Minsk."

"You're out of your mind," she said. "I mean — thank you! But I can't run a foundation. I'm not an executive."

"Oh, we'll have a complete staff. You just set policy," Bic said.

"You want to be just a big hat to the world?" Tarp said. "Gifted girl like you? No sir! You going to be a writer-brain and a founda-tion-brain! Oh yeah, and a helping brain! You know what sonofa-bastard mayor is going to do? Okay the bike lane! He already told the press. You did it with your demonstration idea! You do other things with the foundation!"

"My God," she said. "Almost thou persuadest me. But you know what's *involved?*"

"No, no. No *buts* to a tired man, Trood."

"With you I never have time to think," she said.

She went to the dusty curtains that screened the glass door of the little office. "I've got you under my skin . . . ," played the orchestra. She parted the curtain and saw the princess dancing with her father, the king's hand stroking her hair as they turned. She looked for Ronnie and finally found him by a champagne table, talking close with Madame Mannritt and the prince, and she was astounded. All that expensive, exclusive, enviable high cheer being staged for her. That enormous foundation was for her.

Yet she couldn't savor this glory except by imagining how it would explode off the *Daily News* social column into the face of goddamn Hella Mynn. She watched the hurried slight limp of a passing waiter and the marcelled hair of the orchestra leader, who appeared to have his eye peeled on the very door behind which she was standing. She was astounded by her lack of joy.

"Tarp," she said. "Remember a long time ago, the day I met you at the college library — you went to a party."

He put his arm around her. She could smell his sleeplessness.

"Simon Spieger was supposed to meet you there — some cocktail party at some club? Simon asked me to phone you there when he was at Tante's house — you know what I'm talking about?"

"After I get some rest I'll remember," he said. "First you enjoy your birthday here."

"That was about twenty years ago," she said. "I was scared to talk to you directly. So I just left a message for you at that party. It sounded so glamorous."

"You going to boss the foundation?" He squeezed her powerfully.

"It's too big a thing," she said.

"You say No, I don't sleep."

"All right," she said smiling. "If you'll sleep. And if we do a foundation gala for the earthquake victims."

"You say the word!"

"And if we give it in honor of Hella Mynn."

"Mrs. Minsk?"

"Yes, absolute condition."

"You're the boss." He was leaning against her.

"I want to use this to go against my own worst instincts," she said. "You follow? You unsleeping monster? I don't want this to spoil me rotten!"

"You say Yes to the foundation and I go to Pilcic to sleep."

"All right. Yes, if we go right now."

"Right now? Leave this?"

"It's lovely, Tarp, but it's not my style. I mean I'm glad about the bike lanes, but I think the others are getting a bigger kick out of it than me."

"Hey, Trood, you haven't danced!"

"All right, we dance our way out. How about that?"

"Chokay," he said.

"Nice and slow."

Bic did some signaling. A Triplett opened the door. The orchestra surged up. She blew a kiss across the shouts and the glitter to Ronnie as they danced through the huge floor toward the street.

And still he didn't sleep, not even when they got to his island. By that time his insomnia was a fact that covered the horizon. When they left the plane on Pilcic the rain rained as a boundless endless little stampede of his restlessness. Houses, boats, trees wavered wetly without repose. Mother Letarpo embraced her son, tapped Trudy on the cheek, and all throughout her mottled forefinger drummed on the Gucci umbrella, and that steady drumming was a tentacle of his sleeplessness.

They walked into the villa. All the furniture that had been moved to Bachberg was still there. For a few moments she thought she was inside the hallucination of someone who's been awake for many days. This was surreal simultaneity. There were the Venetian chests, the brown-and-blue Italian provincial and, yes, upstairs the beds with quilted headboards.

"Look at that! That's our furniture!" she said.

A Slavic exchange and a laugh which didn't sound like a laugh because his voice had become so gravelly and because it came from under his dark glasses. "Mama had copies made," he said.

Mother Letarpo made them sit down to a mutton dish. He didn't eat.

"Triplett!" he called.

He took *The Economist* and the *Financial Times* and spread the sheets on the floor to cut a Triplett's hair. On the plane he had cut Bic's hair with the *International Herald Tribune* on the floor. Now he stood by the dining table and skillfully cut little snips off an impassive Triplett while Mother Letarpo drummed and Trudy ate.

"Please stop it and have something," Trudy said.

He stopped, went to the window crawling with rain.

"The olive tree! Needs a doctor."

276

A moment later he had an oil slicker and was gone with pruning shears. Mother Letarpo said something Slavic to the Triplett, who gathered up *The Economist* from the floor.

"Oh yes," Triplett said to Trudy. "You would please only use the downstairs toilets."

"The upstairs ones don't work?"

"It's for Mr. Letarpo. His leavings will not be flushed away because a blessing will be said over them for sleep."

She would have gone with that. She would even have gone with the little yellow slips she saw Mother L. stick into the mattress on his side of the duplicate twin beds. She would have gone with the Croat sleep magic if it had helped. But Tarp didn't even come into the bedroom. After midnight she found herself an oil slicker in the closet, went down through the dark house into the garden.

There was nobody by the olive tree or anywhere else in the wet night. But she did see a light in the stable window.

Inside, he stood by the old donkey, currying the fur with a comb and talking to the animal in such soft husky Slavic, she felt she interrupted.

"Trood. You go to bed."

"Go yourself," she said. "Please. At least stretch out and try."

He walked to the other side of the donkey.

"What's wrong?" she said. "Can I help in any way?"

"No, no," he said. "But what you mentioned. That party. When I didn't really know you yet, a long time ago. Where was Simon supposed to meet us? I can't remember."

"Don't try until you're rested," she said.

"Something in New York," he said. "Something with Nick. But I can't remember."

"It's not important."

"Sure it's important. Trood remembers it, it's important."

"After a good night's sleep it will come back to you," she said.

"That Nick was great at parties," he said. "At his bike party you would have stayed."

"No," she said.

Suddenly he slumped against the donkey, both his arms flung across the animal's back, so that she was alarmed. The next moment he danced. He did a fast stamping jig, turned and stamped,

stamped and turned, oil slicker whirling, heels thumping, the donkey comb held aloft.

"Hey, that's not resting!" Trudy said.

"Nick could do that one." He stopped, not even much out of breath. "Nick's the only non-Croat could do the Dalmatian polka. You ever see Nick do it?"

"No," she said.

"He blew it after a while. One day in Paris he says, 'Let's do the Dalmatian.' He tried, but he'd lost it."

"Maybe I made him lose it," she said.

"No. That was before you. You think he would have added up?"

"How do you mean?"

Trudy had noticed only just now that a Triplett was stationed immobile at the corner of the stable.

"You think he would have added up in the White House?"

"I — I hope so," she said.

"Nobody ever adds up," he said, combing the donkey again.

"After a good night you might think different," she said.

"No, later on Nick got his father's feet. Kicking feet, not dancing feet. That old man got kicking feet."

She didn't know what to say.

"But I told him, 'With Trudy around you might add up. I'll support you for President.' "

"I never knew that," she said.

"You'll add up, Trood. You'll add up with the Foundation."

"I'll add up with a rested you," she said.

"Come on, I'll teach you the Dalmatian."

"Tomorrow."

"Right now. But not here. Not a stone floor." He stamped. "You need wood, double planking. We go to our house on the coast."

The Triplett had already moved to the door, seemed to know exactly what to do. He didn't have a slicker, but moved briskly ahead of them, down the lamplit dripping path to the harbor, straight into a motor boat, and during that furious five-minute splash Trudy felt again the pulse of hallucination all around, as if she'd been swept into Tarp's private and bedless dream. Water surged above no less than below, Triplett twisted the spoked wheel, Tarp steadied her against the seat, humming, "*Oh mein Papa. . . .*"

The boat screeched aground on the mainland beach. There was the garish blue neon she'd noticed from the island but hadn't been able to decipher till now: *Grand Hotel Conchiglia*. With humming little pokes Tarp pushed into the lobby, also garish blue. The floor tiles made a pop-art conch mosaic, but cigarette butts had been ground into the glaze. In the corner, bus-tour cockneys screamed a drunken late-night argument about soccer. Behind the desk, the concierge slouched bald and coughed down a swallow from his paper cup of coffee. He had a chipped conch in his buttonhole.

"Oh, Mr. Letarpo."

He coughed with an Italian-colored cockney accent.

"That was our place here," Tarp said to Trudy. "On this spot, before we moved to the island. Here was the stable for my boys, right this spot."

He folded back the concierge's desk. With little pushes he guided her through a back room smelling of vinegar and then they were by the hotel swimming pool, made of conch-shaped cracked marble. Spotlights lit up the turbidity of the water from underneath. The rain got worse.

"Come on," Tarp said. "Mama still owns the ground. In here."

They were in a shed filled with stacks of deck chairs.

"Look." His finger paused across a spot in the wall. "My knife mark from when I was a boy. You see?"

"Oh yes," she said.

But she couldn't really see. The light he had switched on was too feeble and the wall too shredded. It was a very old shed.

"That was your house?"

"Our house," Tarp said. "Now they put deck chairs in here, how do you like that? Our house. What's the matter, Triplett? Can't get them out?"

The Triplett had been trying to undo the chain that fastened the deck chairs to the ground.

"I'll fix it," the Triplett said, and ran out.

"You can't dance with all those chairs," Tarp said. "But you see, that's the right floor here." He stamped. "Double planking. Makes the right stamping noise. Wait till you see. You'll make a better dancer than Nick."

"I'll need a nice rested dancing teacher."

"Don't worry, you'll add up."

"I'm sorry, Mr. Letarpo," the concierge said, coming in.

"Get those chairs out of here!"

"I'm sorry, I haven't got the key to the chain, Mr. Letarpo. Only the pool man has the key."

"Get them out! I can't dance with all those chairs!"

"We got them chained since last month, because of all the theft," the concierge said.

"When is the pool man coming?"

"Eight A.M., Mr. Letarpo. I'm sorry."

"I'll wait for the fucking pool man," Tarp said, and lay down on a stack of deck chairs.

"Sir —" The concierge never finished the sentence. The Triplett, finger against mouth, had pushed him out.

"Wait for the pool man," Tarp said. He lay on the deck chair stack in the shroud of his oil slicker and dark glasses. Rain rumbled against the old wood of the house. Trudy lay down on a pile of chairs next to Tarp's. She smelled the smell of rain and rotting wood, of brine and fetid sweet harbor pollution. The Triplett, soaked through his turtleneck, had become a sentinel-silhouette by the door.

" . . . wait for the pool man . . . ," her husband said slowly against the rain. Side by side they lay on heaps of deck chairs and waited for his sleep.

4

Which could be the point: Tarp was anchored firmly to the very contradictions and crazinesses in his life, even when he lay on a heap of dirty deck chairs.

But Trudy? She tried to get herself firmly moored to Bachberg. But not too long after returning there from her odd Paris-Pilcic birthday, she had to leave again. Why did settling down always take forever? Of course she left only for a brief trip to New York.

And actually it was frustrating to live in the valley without being able to move into the family chalet. After all this time some final work at the Villa Make-Top was *still* going on. "Darling, it's just a quick hop," she said to Ronnie, kissing him goodby.

Not only quick but full of pleasant prospects. The détente lunch with Hella Mynn was on the agenda; shopping for slip-covers and rugs for Bachberg; and last not least, breaking another lance on behalf of the earthquake disaster area (would it be Trudy if it weren't do-goody?). Just that trip had to go out of control.

In New York she first put on her famous big hat for the *Women's Wear Daily* photographer and told the *Women's Wear Daily* reporter how to couture a library. This was strictly to give herself more clout to be humble on top of, during the détente lunch with Hella Mynn.

Then she took off her famous big crushed hat. She combed bangs down her forehead right into her dark glasses. Off she taxied to 42nd Street, to the New York Public Library. Jennifer waited for her at the big reading room with the material she'd taken out of the reference stacks for Trudy, mostly monographs on Parrington and Beard. For three hours Trudy gorged herself, reading, jotting, photostatting. A lot of booty in her shoulder bag, she walked out and crosstown. At a Florsheim on Madison Avenue she bought herself brogues. For old times' sake — hadn't she always bought her walking shoes at Florsheim's? Trudy still resisted the idea of having shoes made for her; it was like surrendering to a life-style cliché. She kept on the brogues, jammed her other shoes into the shoulder bag, kept walking toward the Waldorf Towers. New York had gotten dirtier. Occasionally heads rotated in her direction. All right, so Trudy Letarpo had become a hunk of media fodder. But she could handle that and still enjoy the streets and shop windows. She didn't have to take the town — she'd taken from the town what she wanted.

It didn't bother her that next day Bic phoned to say that her husband couldn't make New York after all; he was still detained in Iran. Fine. The détente lunch might have been jeopardized by Tarp. Who knows how Hella might take it if he called her Mrs. Minsk? And anyway, to make up for Tarp's no-show, some unexpected company arrived.

Mannritt materialized at the Towers door. She'd used the Easter recess plus a free ride on Mr. Letarpo's jet! To take advantage of the spring sales in New York! To buy fixtures for the school! Mannritt glowed with Big Apple fever. But Mannritt wasn't the point. There was an enormous surprise. Ronnie — *Ronnie* — walked in behind her with the princess. Trudy rushed to embrace him and received his courteous-gallant Hello-Mother kiss. They were here for the prince, Ronnie said. Yussuf had finished his interviewing of candidates in Macedonia for the Bachberg Agrarian Institute; he was due in New York to register the Institute with the U.N. Eco-Conference. He was overdue, in fact, and thanks to that he'd get here just in time to meet them on their Easter recess.

"Great," Trudy said. "The whole bunch of you are going to be my lodgers."

And that was great fun — easy, too, with Tarp not there. It was also a way for her of staying in control, of not just being a creature of the Waldorf Towers' fortieth floor. It was playing Young Dorm against all that luxury. She had cots for Mannritt and Princess Dara put in the living room, right under the Braque. The prince and Ronnie she put up in the den. Ronnie, who seemed to be in the same good mood as his mother, asked for a big sheet of paper, and crayoned on it first the Macedonian flag and then graffiti'd into its yellow-orange colors the female sex symbol alternating with the hammer-and-sickle. He spread the sheet as cover over Yussuf's cot. Giorgio the butler, who had to supervise the installation, looked at the whole thing, inhaled, and never exhaled again. Ronnie kept his even, pensive face. Mannritt suddenly suffered from postnasal drip, which probably meant a choked-back giggle. Whereupon her lodgers ran out to accompany Madame Headmistress on her shopping.

It was fun. That afternoon Trudy spent organizing the material she'd gotten out of the Public Library. She worked quite well despite interruptions. Hella Mynn's lispy social secretary rang to athk a thousand pardonths but (after postponing the lunch for three months) would Mrs. Letarpo mind very much, Thursday inthstead of Wednethday for lunch? No, Mrs. Letarpo didn't mind. Mrs. Letarpo didn't even much mind when Ronnie called and said they'd run into another Mannritt student, also on an Easter recess

lark here, and they'd all been invited by this student to stay overnight in Long Island.

"Well, enjoy yourself," she said.

"We'll be back early tomorrow. Has Yussuf arrived?"

"No."

"That's funny."

"Don't worry, his interviewing just took a little longer."

"Somebody's worrying about him," Ronnie said. "Those scholar-
ships he's interviewing for, they're supposed to stop all the share-
cropping and serf stuff in his country. At Bachberg they're supposed
to teach independent farm technique, so somebody's worrying."

"First we'll have to get the Institute *going*," she said. "You're just
sorry Yussuf can't tomcat with you, you heller."

"He's overdue. We sent him a cable."

"Probably he'll arrive tonight. If he does, he and I will have a
party. So there."

"Hope you'll have a party."

"Have a good time, darling," she said.

Of course she was disappointed Ronnie wouldn't sleep in the
bed she'd put in specially for him. On the other hand, his talking
to her on the phone at greater length like that, letting his hair
down a little on Yussuf — was that a way of soothing her? Making
up for leaving old mother home alone, for God knows what Long
Island capers?

At any rate Yussuf didn't come. She didn't have a party. She had
a good night's sleep. Next morning she woke into a realization: for
her détente lunch with Hella the following day, she had no détente
clothes. Michelle's passé party dresses in the Costume Shop were
out of the question, especially after the *Women's Wear* interview.
Trudy's own wardrobe, what there was of it, was probably too
jazzy/sporty not to arouse martial instincts in a Hella Mynn. She
needed something chic, yet distinctly subdued. It was off to Bergdorf's — just as Ronnie arrived with Mannritt and the princess.

"Hello, Mother — going out?"

The three were eating pretzels out of his brown paper bag.

"Suddenly so interested in me?" she said, smiling. "After your
gay night out?"

"I mean, you're leaving right now?"

"I have to do some shopping."

"Oh. You couldn't possibly do it later?"

"It's clothes for a lunch tomorrow."

She recognized how decadent that might sound to Ronnie.

"Actually," she said, "I want to get something plain for a very boring lunch. But it involves a charity that helps a lot of people."

"I mean, they couldn't bring the clothes here? Don't they do that for special customers?"

"Hey, Ronnie, it's just a small purchase comparatively! And I don't want to be that special. What's up?"

"You see, we're expecting a phone call about Yussuf," he said, eating his pretzel fast. "He didn't answer our cable."

"I guess he'll come today."

"Now he's a week overdue. The Macedonian Embassy says they don't know anything. So this morning we tried through Letarpo's office. I mean, Letarpo arranged that whole agrarian thing that made Yussuf go there."

"You should have let me know, you idiot."

"Actually, we inquired in your name. Because Letarpo's such a good friend of the king's. So you might get a phone call."

"Okay, you stay here while I'm gone —"

"No, they're acting funny about it. Maybe they'll give the facts only to you."

"Oh, I doubt that," she said.

But they all kept chewing pretzels at her intensely, even Mannritt.

"I have an idea," she said. "You come with me to Bergdorf and I'll have Jennifer watch the phone here and call me instantly at the store if something breaks, okay?"

Okay. The three of them accompanied her, down the rich greedy clangor of Madison Avenue. Her bangs and glasses sheltered Trudy. Rather pale, very energetic, Ronnie kept buying chestnuts, peanuts, more pretzels from vendors and doled them out to his bunch. Apparently they didn't feed their overnight guests too well at Long Island. If there'd been a Sands Point invitation in the first place.

But even if Sands Point was a fib and a front to hide hanky-panky, say, between Ronnie and Mannritt — all right; here was something long suspected and, ultimately, not even so unreasonable. Trudy had told herself a long time ago that she must come to terms with Ronnie's moral unpredictabilities. Ronnie had been denied a regular family situation. He had been denied the legitimacy of his father, and a unique father too. Perhaps by way of redress Ronnie now inflicted an illegitimacy of his own, namely Mannritt. In a way that eased Trudy's guilt. In another way it also touched her pride. Her sixteen-year-old making it between his school principal's cathedral thighs! Being deep buddies with a progressive and idealistic prince. . . . Deep down in the corny, overachieving part of Trudy's psyche something smiled. No, nothing was out of control.

And she liked having those three come into Bergdorf Goodman with her. The Bergdorfers were much less apt to sniff out Mrs. Letarpo if she slipped in as part of a group. And if she *was* recognized it was good to be armed with what others might consider a retinue.

That, too, was being in control, controlling New York's yeastiness, especially rampant that spring day. Even in spring Fifth Avenue managed to be sultry. Maybe Bachberg had spoiled Trudy. It seemed as though there were no walkers left in the city, only prowlers, skulkers, racers, hustlers. In Bendel's windows, bikinis thrust pelvises at the tropic spotlights. Bergdorf, too, had developed an elegant raunchiness. One Easter window burst out with mannequins who had lamb faces with hooker bodies under the evening sheaths. On the third floor, where Trudy led her group, they found a huge papier-mâché sheep which had a face vaguely resembling Marilyn Monroe. Ronnie began to do a flirt-dance around it with his peculiar, unsmiling grotesquerie. Mannritt and Dara tittered. The salesgirl, a little red in the face, laid out tan, gray, beige sweater-and-skirt combinations. The idea was to pick out something modishly nondescript for tomorrow. At that point Bic appeared.

"How did you know where to find me?" Trudy said.

"Jennifer. Actually it's a message from the Macedonians."

Ronnie stepped forward. "Is Yussuf coming?"

"I guess not yet."

"Where is he?" Ronnie said.

"Looks like he'll be at the capital tomorrow. He wants his sister to join him there."

Ronnie stood very straight and the princess walked closer to him and Mannritt.

"He wants her to join him in Macedonia!" Ronnie said. "Why didn't Yussuf call us himself?"

"He's still out there in the sticks, interviewing," Bic said. "But he should be back at the capital tomorrow. I think they'll have some ceremony about his agrarian program and he wants his sister to be in on that. I'll be glad to supply transport —"

"No, thank you," Ronnie said.

"We happen to have a plane —"

"*Thank you!*"

Trudy almost marveled at her son. Accompanied by a razor-sharp headshake, this *Thank you!* was absolute dismissal. "Yessir," Bic said, and went off with a mock salute.

"Are you really worried?" she asked Ronnie.

"It's all right," Ronnie walked up to the selection of clothes. "I like that one."

She didn't pursue it further, actually out of respect for him: he wanted to show that the prince was strictly part of *his* emotional cosmos; that he was old enough not only to send a Bic packing but to be in command of his own rich tensions. Furthermore, Trudy saw that he was pointing at a solid muddy-blue sweater with a glen-plaid gray skirt. An ensemble admirably boring, perfect for a détente lunch with a dressy bitch.

"Ronnie, you're quite a boy," she said.

Everything was still under control.

The next day Ronnie flew back to Bachberg and Trudy stayed to lunch with Hella Mynn. Hella had chosen to be fuschia-luminous, from pumps to silk pants suit to neck brace to sombrero. Trudy's Bergdorf dullness looked doubly dull by comparison. Furthermore, Trudy wore a mousy, gelded version of Her Hat. Anything for détente. Trudy hadn't objected to Dauphin, though that restaurant was down the block from the Museum of Modern Art and therefore in the very heart of Hella's turf. Did Trudy make a fuss that Hella had delayed this meeting over the whole winter? Of course not. And she'd muted her hair into a bun.

Maitre d' in front, Hella behind, Trudy was being marched to certainly the uppermost, innermost, mostmost table of them all. Trudy tried to look as a captured Phoenician monarch must have looked when a Roman consul marched his prisoner in triumph through the city. Muted or not, she was a splendid piece of booty. All those painterly, post-avant-garde geniuses looked up from their oysters to elevate eyebrows at the procession and to blow Hella kisses, Hella parading her Phoenician monarch.

"Hella, that was terrific!"

"Hella, you made Irving Trust look pretty!"

"Hella for mayor!"

"Oh, that was something we called *Dali at the Dime*," Hella said at the table. "We had every bank branch in the city stay open after hours and make like a gallery, you know? In every branch we put in a Dali or a de Kooning or like that, along with neighborhood artists. It really brought out the natives."

"Lovely idea," Trudy said.

"Well, a little consciousness-raising. But to get all those bank jokers to cooperate! And the galleries! The walls you've got to beat your head against."

"I guess your head would be the only one to do it," Trudy said. After all, Hella's husband was both museum president and bank board member.

"A tough number," Hella said. "That's why it took me so long to get myself together for our lunch. What will you have, Gertrude?"

What would she have? Here was another chance to display proper and subtle humility. (Trudy was beginning to have downright fun with this.) Hella selected avocado stuffed with crab, chicken Kiev and creamed potatoes Suisson. This was high-calorie bravado stressing the inviolability of Hella's slim-line (never mind that it was really tough, stringy, neurotic haggardness). Trudy confined herself to consommé double followed by shrimp salad; as if she were a diet-wracked flab-guilty *shlub* instead of a fairly effortless size eleven. Trudy also submitted to Hella's choice of Pouilly-Fuissé. But after her hostess had tasted and approved of the wine, had leaned back with a waiter-lit cigarette, with a warm, public, fuchsia-emblazoned smile, Trudy thought: Okay, enough. Enough preliminaries and propitiations.

287

"One of the things I wanted to ask you," Trudy said, "was about taking away the Jamaica benefit from the Earthquake Fund."

Service was prompt at Dauphin, at least for Hella. The consommé steamed, the stuffed avocado gleamed buttery.

"You know, about that earthquake thing," Hella said. "I came to agree with you. You said — was it at Elaine's? — you said Jamaica wouldn't work for the Earthquake Fund. And it's true. No way."

"I said a Waldorf affair would draw better than Jamaica," Trudy said. "But now the Fund even lost Jamaica."

"But Gertrude. You know what would draw best of all. Europe! That's where your earthquake sufferers are. And Europe is your baby anyway. I still get such great vibes from your Paris party."

"I didn't make myself understood," Trudy said. "I said that Jamaica isn't as good, but it's much better than nothing at all this spring."

"Gertrude, scout's honor," Hella said. "We cased the situation before we shifted Jamaica from the Fund. Jamaica won't pull any disaster money. That's strictly a culture crowd. Is the shrimp all right?"

"Relief is needed now," Trudy said. "People are suffering."

They confronted each other past waiters' arms, pouring wine, placing salads. Trudy realized this was no good.

"Actually we're doing just what you suggested," Trudy said. "Something in Europe. At the opening of the Agrarian Institute in Bachberg we'll have an Earthquake Fund benefit. It's still pretty far off, next year in October, but I hope you'll agree to be our guest of honor. That's one reason why I came here."

"Aren't you groovy," Hella said. "So sweet. The problem is the Metropolitan Arts Forum. It's on my neck every October."

"Well, it's a long way off. We can do it any weekend convenient for you."

"Angel, that bloody forum goes on every bloody weekend every bloody October."

"Then let's make it in September or November."

"Oh, God," Hella said. "The whole fall is always murder. Things don't get halfway sane till January. And that's Asiatic flu time."

"Yes," Trudy said. She disliked the too cunningly sauced shrimp salad.

"You don't need me, Gertrude. Much as I'd love to come into your European orbit sometime."

"I doubt I have a European orbit," Trudy said.

"Well, whatever I should have called it — BAH adored it! She loved your Paris factory thing!"

"It was really my husband's thing." Trudy wanted to try once more. "I know a call went out to invite you —"

"I was in Hawaii. Gertrude, don't ever agree to unveil a mural in Hawaii. You pay for it with your pancreas. But BAH's still crazy about your Paris factory."

"Of course we'll ask her to Bachberg once I've settled on a date with you."

"Oh," Hella said, savoring the Pouilly-Fuissé. "I believe she's already been asked."

"She must have mixed that up," Trudy said. "We haven't even fixed a date for the benefit."

"She's been asked to be a sponsor."

"By whom?"

"Your foundation sent her a letter. Some of my gallery pals got one too."

"Are you sure?"

"Angel, they called me about it. I told them, Sponsor away! Jump to it! It's bound to be the Wow!-of-the-year next year."

Trudy didn't know at whom to be more furious. Tarp, who must be behind all this, who was still Taking New York behind her back. Or this cool feral Hella, spearing the last of her chicken Kiev.

"There's been some confusion," Trudy said. "I've been so busy building us a place in Bachberg. I've let things go."

"Don't worry," Hella said. "Won't you try the mousse?"

"All that will change," Trudy said. "I promise you this: The Agrarian benefit will happen at your convenience, fall or winter, because you're the guest of honor. And about friends of yours being contacted by the foundation — that's the last time. Such contacts will be made only with your advice and approval and through the channels of your orbit. All right?"

"Oh Gertrude," Hella Mynn said. "Don't hassle yourself."

"Madame won't try the mousse?" the waiter said.

"Yes, I'll try the mousse," Trudy said. "I'm not hassling myself. It's my foundation and I'm responsible for all arrangements and problems."

"With you, Gertrude, I can't imagine there are ever any problems."

"I could easily say something as positive about you," Trudy said.

"No, with me it's much more cut and dried. Your career has been a wonder."

Hella leaned back, tasting the mousse, shaking her head. But she shook it a shade awkwardly, on the bias, perhaps because of the neck brace. It was a head-shake less controlled and graceful than her other motions. And for the first time since they'd entered Dauphin, Trudy felt that something had happened which wasn't a maneuver. Hella really meant that about No Problem. Hella — and God knows who else? — all the Hella Mynns really thought that Trudy's life had been a clever, smooth, no-problem frolic, up from Grub Street academe to Simon Spieger to Nick Antone to Letarpo. Tra-la-la. A daredevil game plan, brilliantly brought off. A wonder of a caper. A problemless wonder while Hella Mynn must drudge day and night at the burdens and privileges of royalty.

"My career," Trudy said. "Christ, that consists of being an imperfect mother and a dissertation I can't seem to finish. And I do sincerely beg you to give the Jamaica benefit back to the Earthquake Fund."

"But Gertrude," Hella Mynn was no longer awkward. She had lit a cigarette and released smoke with fluent dolor. "It's a bloody pity. The Jamaica contract's already signed with our fund-raiser."

"Can't you change it?"

"No, it's one of those double contracts. The same outfit will do the Farmers' Culturemobile Ball for us. We're locked in."

"Farmers' Culturemobile?"

"You know, grow a few brains on those poor people before the tractors drive them bonkers in Minnesota. The Grange is in on that with us next fall —"

"Next fall!" Trudy said. "I had Jennifer — that's my associate — she specially checked the social calendar! She said our Bachberg thing would be the only agrarian —"

"Now isn't that a drag?" Hella Mynn said. "That calendar has become totally useless." Between puffs she spooned up the very last dollop of mousse.

"You yourself are taking on the Culturemobile?" Trudy said.

"Angel, that's my curse. Everything seems to think it has to come down on me."

A busboy all in white, a swarthy cherub, slipped as he passed and almost dropped a tray of glasses. A waiter saved him, and he whispered "*Gracias!*" with such ardent innocent gratitude, it tightened Trudy's eyes with the corruption and mendacity at her table.

"But there's always another year, Gertrude. Ask me to your second alpine gala."

"Probably you'll have your second Culturemobile festival," Trudy said.

"I'll play hookey," Hella said, laughing the spontaneous hard silver of her laugh. It was a totally civilized declaration of total war: *You've met your match, you bloody wonder.*

"And thank you for being so patient about this lunch," Hella said.

"Check, please," Trudy said.

"Are you serious?" Hella said. "I'll sign, Guillaume."

"I pay my share," Trudy said. It was a Stouffer's-ladies argument, very offensive here and therefore satisfying to Trudy. She put down twenty bucks.

"Angel, that's much too big a tip," Hella said, rising with a sovereign smile. And Trudy was marched out again between Mrs. Mynn and the maitre d', through an espalier of little "Hella!" exclamations. Instead of détente, this was Armageddon out of control and she cursed herself for not having unleashed her full-size hat.

⤖ 5 ⤖

Out of control. How did it happen? To fall so fast into just the velvet nastiness to which she'd thought herself superior! The goddamn ease with which a Hella Mynn could turn Trudy into just another haute-bitch like Hella herself! Each trying to bite the other with her husband's importance. For Hella such dogfights were a way of life, a grand manner, a *raffiné* style. To Trudy it was being out of control. Something had to be done to regain control.

As a start the foundation people must be more tightly reined. She cabled Paris to set up a meeting about that, in Bachberg. From the fortieth Towers floor, New York looked glamorous, young, a Cole Porter mirage, traffic dancing down the canyons' shine, nothing but finely syncopated grace notes, but she knew that even the dogwood blossoms (flaming up from Central Park with the bottle splinters all around) were out of control. She ached for Bachberg. Ronnie had already returned there. After Hella Mynn she needed repose in her mountain nook, in her family-crevice and Ronnie's nearness.

She arrived after ten at night. Instantly she noticed the flower boxes. The wind rustled leaves and petals at all the windows. The flower boxes were already up at the Villa Make-Top. She ran upstairs.

Sure enough, all the furniture was already there, already in place, for keeps now. Everything just as Tarp and she had planned. And the bookshelves worked out beautifully, Lucite against dark wood wall; except that the books themselves stood higgledy-piggledy in no order whatsoever, despite the instructions left to the school librarian.

Which turned out to be just dandy: Trudy didn't even take off her coat. For the next hour or two she had the greatest therapeutic time arranging some of the shelves, the two history shelves and the fiction shelf. And she felt much more in control again.

Then the door banged. Ronnie! She rushed down. It was only the wind. Her watch said near midnight. Typical Ronnie: She'd cabled him her arrival, but he would stay out all night, as usual, with his peculiar gang. She took the book Jennifer had found for him in New York: *A Pictorial History of Jewish Worship*. A bit too coffee-table-gorgeous, but the curse taken off it by the fact that it was secondhand, with a wine-stained dust jacket. Book under her arm, she set off to find him outside, in the lamplit piney breeze-thrusts. Of course the religion building was finished. It was still lit at this late hour, just as she had figured. Yellow wavered through the curtains. Still no electricity here? She knocked. No answer. So she used her master key.

What first surprised her was her own composure. Ordering the bookshelves had really put things under control again. And the three bodies stretched on oriental bolsters had at first less relation to each other than to the lantern which hung from the ceiling and moved to the draft, swinging slowly, producing, erasing, producing again the dim huge heaving nakedness of Mannritt's breasts (and the frown of Mannritt's closed eyes as if something wonderful had slipped her mind), and Ronnie next to her, clothed, lying on his stomach, one arm round the telephone, the other round the princess, who slept smiling, a smile Trudy had never seen before, just as she'd never before seen the princess's blouse unbuttoned down to a nipple as small and dark as a truffle.

The three sleepers dropped away into darkness, surfaced with the lantern's swing, vanished, reappeared, a slide projection that flashed on, off, on; and Trudy, to comprehend this better, bent forward and lost hold of the book in her hand. The heavy *Pictorial History of Jewish Worship* dropped.

Thud.

Instinctively she picked up the book, coiled back from the door into the chill moon-shade of some poplars. Poplar branches rustled and twitched, but inside her eyes these three remained immobile, lapidary, perennial, sleeping like bronze statuary together, flashing on and off together like a fixed star through a secret and grotesque eternity.

She had to grasp that, and started forward again. Footfalls stopped her. Footfalls kicked things completely out of control again. Two faces floated toward her in the dark. Ronnie's and the princess's, so close they looked unkempt with each other's hair, brunette tousle and black strands, blown through one another by the wind. They were chewing gum. Two punk ghosts, grim and gamey.

"Mannritt went to her house," Ronnie said.

No greeting. Just "Mannritt went to her house."

Ronnie knew she'd seen the carnal three of them; that she'd seen

Mannritt. "Mannritt went to her house." Nothing more. The two were chewing gum together in this defiant heartbreaking hard unison, and Ronnie had his arm round the girl's waist.

"Ronnie, what's the matter?"

Now he looked at her. Dark child-eyes in that wind-battered youth-face. Trudy had to look away.

"You didn't go to Macedonia," Trudy said to the princess. No answer. To avoid Ronnie's eyes, Trudy had to keep talking to the princess. "I thought your brother asked you to join him in Macedonia," Trudy said to the princess.

"He didn't ask me. They just *say* he asked me."

The princess's voice was new. She'd never sounded or looked like that before. In Ronnie's arm she looked taller, more rounded. Her voice was marble. The wind had blown hardness into her cheeks.

"My brother Yussuf warned me," the princess said. "I should be careful if he is overdue and we don't hear from him directly. He said, 'Don't go, if they suddenly say, Go.' "

"When did he warn you?" Trudy said.

"Before he left. When my father invited him to interview agrarians in our country."

"He won't come back," Ronnie said. "He'll be lucky if he gets a funeral."

"But — *why?*" Trudy said.

"Oh, subversion," Ronnie said. "They'll think up something. Letarpo will explain it to you. He arranged it all. The whole Agrarian Institute was his idea. He is such nice pals with the king."

"But what makes you talk about funerals!"

"What makes my father the king like that?" The princess was talking with her hard new voice. "What makes three million starve in our country?"

"We tried to reach the king by phone," Ronnie said.

"Why didn't you let me do something?" Trudy said. "I know Yussuf is your best friend —"

"You're always very *busy*, Mother."

"Not always, Ronnie!"

"Always with very important beautiful things."

"But this is important!"

"Letarpo always has more important ideas, Mother. You lead a very important life with him."

"But this is as important as anything!"

"Maybe now it is," the princess said. With a small iron laugh which nobody would have thought was in her. Ronnie's hand came round her waist and rested on her belly. A very rounded, perhaps newly rounded belly. Pregnant? Before Trudy could see what that really was in the dark, they had turned around and walked back to the religion building.

"Ronnie!" she called. "We'll get this straightened out. I'll talk to Tarp. . . . Ronnie! You're wrong!"

They kept walking.

"It'll come out all right!" she called. In her hand she discovered the gift book, still ungiven, and the wind blew.

She went to work, dialing. Most of the night she spent on the phone, finger stuck into her other ear against the wind's racket outside. Tarp was not in Paris. Nor at Pilcic. Nor in New York. Nobody in his various offices knew how he could be reached. Nor was Bic anywhere reachable. She gave up. It occurred to her that she ought to phone or cable Paris to cancel the meeting with the foundation people. But she didn't give a damn about the foundation people. In the window, the gusts had turned from black to gray. Dawn smelled not of spring, but of ice and dead leaves. An exhausting and exhausted riddle. The dial tone hovered in the room after she hung up and passed into a space behind her eyes.

"Trood?"

"Oh — hello," she said into the receiver.

"Big doings, huh? I wake you up?"

"I've been trying to reach you!"

She was dizzy. She'd sat up abruptly from an ocher dream.

"Where are you?" she said.

"Malta. I tell you, a lousy place to phone the king."

"There's a problem, Tarp!"

"Sure there's a problem. King says Yussuf wasn't interviewing! Yussuf was making trouble —"

"Then you know about the prince!"

"He was organizing Reds! King says he was even making troubles with the construction gang, the Macedonian boys in Bachberg —"

"I don't care about that —"

"King cares about it! He was choking on the phone!"

"Tarp," she said. "The problem is my son is very close to Yussuf —"

"I told Yussuf a hundred times, careful. Wait. Nobody lives forever —"

"You better do something! Your good friend, the king —"

"I give him a pipeline."

"Listen! This is very serious!"

"So's the pipeline serious to the king! Our big negotiating hoo-hoo! Who pays the pipeline? Okay, I'm the hoo-hoo. I pay. Special pipeline to his oil fields, double their value."

"I'm talking about Ronnie!"

"That's what I'm talking! King gets pipeline free. For that the king gives back Yussuf to Ronaldo. That's the deal."

"Oh," she said. She dug her thumbnail sharply into her palm, to sting herself into alertness. "Will that work?"

"Sure. Why you think Ronaldo's in my plane with her? Off to the best clinic in Sweden. Fix that up quiet."

"But I talked to Ronnie here last night —"

"Last night. Now it's the next day, and we get that uncompli-cated in Sweden. I talked with Ronnie after you. I sent him my ship. So now I'm sitting here, drinking ants."

"Tarp, I just woke up," she said. "I don't get —"

"Why do you think Tarp sits here? Waiting to charter something for Rio? Because I gave my ship to Ronaldo, fly the princess to a clinic. You know how they make coffee in Malta? Grind up ants, pour hot water over them."

"God, I hope it works with Ronnie," she said.

"We uncomplicate everything. We do everything, even drink ant coffee. You go have lunch. Here comes my charter man."

"Where can I reach you?" she asked.

"I call you in a couple of hours. Have lunch and go back to sleep, Trood."

Lunch? Her watch said twenty after twelve.

"Watch out for the kiss."

An explosion in the earpiece. Click. Dial tone.

"Lunch?" she said to herself.

She had never gotten up so late before. The lateness was the only thing she felt. Or let herself feel. The rest of reality was shaped by that malformation in time: the cold water coming out of the hot water faucet in the bathroom. And the maid, wrapped in a lambs-wool jacket, saying in her Sicilian English, two gennamen down-stairs, Signora Letarpo wants to have coffee 'ith them?

Downstairs the two gentlemen turned out to be the foundation lawyers. The lateness of the hour had encumbered them with over-coats and gloves they took off to shake hands, and goosepimply chins, with which they nodded when Trudy said, "Excuse me. I'll be right back!"

She had seen from the open door that Ronnie wasn't in his room downstairs. Tarp was right. She couldn't find Ronnie outside either. The lateness of the hour had emptied the shrub-lined lanes of Bachberg; had stopped the wind, brightened and thinned the sun, tightened Trudy's pores, sharpened the green of the young oak leaves. It had drained the whole place of faces. The religion building looked laconic-empty after last night, just another chalet. Building, slopes, mountains — no people.

But from the gym she heard a pulse. Mannritt was doing jumps, *un-deux-trois* with a dozen students, all zipped up in gym suits.

"Ronnie is really gone?" Trudy said.

Un-deux-trois the students kept jumping, though Mannritt had stopped. Flushing an extraordinary purple, Mannritt stared down at Trudy's shower sandals as if they represented the lateness of the hour.

"Yes," Mannritt said. "It is lucky most students went away for the weekend. The ones here I keep warm with exercises."

Un-deux-trois, the students jumped.

"We have no heat," Mannritt said to Trudy's sandals. "Our boiler man, he is also a Macedonian. He also had to go into the truck."

"What truck?"

"Where all the Macedonian workers had to go. I didn't want to have you waked, Madame. It was legal. The gendarmes showed me the paper."

"What paper?" Trudy said.

297

"An extradition paper to Macedonia. It said the workers did wrong political things —"

"They took Ronnie too?"

"No, no." Mannritt took a step back, still fixing on Trudy's late-hour sandals. "Ronaud went afterwards with the princess."

"Voluntarily?"

"Oh yes. A limousine."

"Even after the extradition?"

"Oh yes."

Un-deux-trois the students jumped. Mannritt's flush subsided but her eyes grew larger at Trudy's sandals.

"You will catch cold, Madame."

Trudy had begun to realize it. A very cold spring day. Her toes were being nipped. Through the chill bright emptiness she went back to the chill Villa Make-Top where the coffeepot still steamed on the hot table. The lawyers, the two *maîtres,* still waited in their overcoats.

"You know about the Macedonian workers they took away?"

Both lawyers had gray, nicely barbered mustaches. Their double smiles were sallow, bland, impervious.

"The Macedonians, Madame?"

"My husband mentioned nothing to you?"

"No, Madame."

"They took away all the construction workers from here! They sent them to Macedonia!"

"Indeed. Unfortunately, Madame Letarpo, we are limited to the foundation."

"They'll be arrested in Macedonia. Probably like the prince."

"Unfortunately we have no information. We have only just arrived."

They spoke alternately, with the same adenoidal voice.

"If we may proceed, Point A of Madame's memorandum. We apologize about the matter of invitations."

"What?"

"Invitations to Mrs. Hella Mynn's friends to participate in plans for the foundation gala."

"Oh yes," she said. "I have other things on my mind now."

"Anytime Madame wishes she will supervise invitations. We were only concerned to broaden the social base. Point B in Madame's memorandum, a very worthwhile point, one million dollars direct gift to the earthquake area. Only it is beyond the foundation's ability this year."

The older *maître* had a silver chronometer on his wrist, without hands or face, just a slot that said in sans-serif lettering *twelve forty-five*.

"The foundation has many millions," she said sharply, to make up for the fact that Point B had also slipped her mind.

"Yes, Madame. But we are spending two million five on the Agrarian Institute, plus nine million on buying pipeline equipment for one Limited plus a loan of five million six to another Limited, low interest, plus —"

"You lost me," she said.

The skin of her entire back contracted. Just as she was recovering from her grogginess and lateness, the cold was getting her.

"What Limiteds?" she said, though she didn't really want to know.

"The first is Letarpo Mineral Limited. Its option rights are in the foundation articles Madame has —"

"The foundation is not in the pipeline business!" she said. "And at the moment I have other urgent problems!"

"Madame is right — not in the pipeline business. We will lease back the pipeline to the first Limited."

"You are not explaining or helping!" she said.

"Madame." The chronometer flicked to *twelve forty-six*. "We must give the Limiteds a good fiscal position. Or the foundation is not possible at all, and all the benefactions." Two bland impervious smiles. "Thank you, no sugar."

The maid in the lambswool jacket carried the tray from *maître* to *maître*. The maid seemed to understand these guests much better than Trudy and was better protected against the cold. And the *maîtres* were drinking their coffee on their feet, in their overcoats, as if that were the only way to drink it: in upturned velvet collars, with thin, ribbed suede gloves holding the cups. They were professionals at such sipping, at making such lukewarm steely statements in the midst of other people's shivers.

"It is regular foundation practice, Madame. Next year we hope to budget more for direct gifts."

Trudy discovered Mannritt. Mannritt had appeared outside the window, against the yew framing Villa Make-Top. It was amazing. In the cold sunshine out there, Mannritt's whole stately body contorted into gesture. She was trying to translate the lawyers' sentences into more accessible and admissible pantomime. Mannritt's arm strained up, her neck arched back in a ballet of exegesis.

"It is traditional," the *maître* was saying. "The first foundation year one spends on staff and donor fiscals. The second, one begins larger allocations."

Mannritt had come nearer still. Her arms embroidered the air. The pompadour had collapsed into a half-mane, blonde down the blue gym suit, which made her look absurdly innocent, like an agitated, distended child. Mannritt was hanging by her arm, hopping around it in the cold brass of the sunshine, she was warmly beserk, perhaps from Ronnie's arms, she was beckoning Trudy and Trudy wanted to be by her.

"Next year," the *maître* was saying, "we will compile a list of major possible beneficiaries for Monsieur and Madame Letarpo to choose."

"*Pardon me*," Trudy said.

She ran outside, still in her shower sandals.

"Telephone!" Mannritt said. "Just for you, very secret, about Ronald! From Liechtenstein."

"I thought there was something!"

"Liechtenstein police — they said not to connect to you if you're with somebody else."

"About Ronnie?"

"Yes, Ronnie! Come on, in my house."

Trudy flung her arm about Mannritt. For one moment, child to child. Then they ran together like children. Out of control.

VII

When she stopped rubbing her eyes in Liechtenstein, two things began to define themselves. One was Jennifer, who'd tapped her awake. Jennifer smoking a cigarette. The other was her, Trudy's, hat, hanging on the wall, with little bloody feet sticking out from under it. The hat hung big and wrinkled on a crucifix. She'd hung it there because she wanted to sleep a little and could take only one agony at a time.

She scooped the hat off the crucifix. She put it on, deeply, into her face. With the hat deep into her face it was easier to ask Jennifer to ask a kepi'd cop where the bathroom was.

In the bathroom, after she'd gotten the pressure out of her bladder and some good cold tap water onto her face and some minimal order into her hair — in that little bathroom with the roller towel squawking hoarse Delphic phrases at her every time she pulled at it — in that bathroom she became awake enough at last. She burst out of the door.

She passed two rooms and sure enough, here was the Liechtenstein police captain's office, but no captain, no radio equipment, no Letarpo. Just Jennifer.

"Where are they?" Trudy said.

"At the hotel."

"But that's why I slept here at the station! So that I could be right next to the radio gear! So that when we make contact with Ronnie in the plane, I'm right here."

"They moved the radio and everything to the hotel," Jennifer said.

"While I slept!"

"Letarpo asked me to bring you over."

By that time they were in the Volkswagen, scooting through the dewy little morning town, dew shining on shingles, on picket fences, on garden roses, dew even on the bikes of bikers they passed and on the church spire where the cast-iron rooster gleamed above seven o'clock.

"Why the hell did they move to the hotel?" Trudy said.

"Bic told me they needed room for their preparations."

Jennifer coughed smoke and looked very pale.

"You didn't sleep, did you?" Trudy said. "I shouldn't have either."

"You need your strength more than I," Jennifer said.

"You didn't sleep and you're not even Ronnie's mother."

"I slept before."

"What preparations?" Trudy said. "What are they doing?"

"I don't know," Jennifer said. "They wanted old Antone out of the way. I took him to breakfast at the inn across the street."

Gravel from the hotel driveway scoured the fenders. The car stopped. They got out. The town smelled of wet cobbles and fresh rolls.

"Oh Jenn!" Trudy said.

Then she had to knock on the tall door of the hotel.

A Triplett opened.

Inside, in those huge wooden bowels, in that high-ceilinged antlered hollow, it had become very different. It stirred so busily with faces, for an instant she hoped Ronnie would be there too. Perhaps everything was over and all right.

Another Triplett pointed down: she shouldn't stumble over mummy-limbs wrapped in canvas. Bic's golf clubs that must have been brought to the hotel. Then Bic himself (in the empty bar she'd never particularly noticed before) with his back to her, practicing a putt. She rushed past. The dining hall had almost become a ballroom now, very bright with all the wagon-wheel chandeliers burning and the cloth covers pulled off tables and chairs, naked, so that the beech wood gleamed. Captain Doss of the Liechtenstein police sat in a corner (jacket tossed capelike over his shoulders) surrounded by his shortwave Erector set and two kepi'd officers. Two assistant maitre d's assisting the boss at the opening of a great surrealist restaurant.

Captain Doss rose to kiss her hand, but didn't quite because he was wired to the Erector set. His smile flicked between earphones. Letarpo bent with Turk over a long cake. A cake of all things. And, in the midst of such a delirium of familiars, a weird stranger half hidden behind the Captain, smallish, blond, comely, a little too old to be still so handsome, with enormous spectacles and a shirtsleeved intensity, standing stooped down to a microphone and a machine, as if he were scooping the event for NBC. No Ronnie.

Plaster bits looped down from the ceiling, the same everlasting indoor snow of the Grand Hotel. And the dog, the big dog whose name she didn't know, sat by a naked table and beat his tail against the parquet floor. Everyone but Ronnie.

"Ronnie," she heard someone whisper, probably herself. Yussuf answered.

"*Ladies and gentlemen,*" Prince Yussuf said, invisible but loud. His high Oxonian voice, his somewhat guttural tremolos made the ceiling-snow jitter in midair. "*It affords me great pleasure to open the Macedonian Culture Institute in London on a day which in the history of our country —*"

Snap.

The blond man had snapped off Yussuf on the machine. This man raised his shoulders now, took off his glasses and said with the exact same Yussuf voice, even with the same loudness, "*Hello, Ronnie! It's Yussuf. I'm all right, they let us go. The workers too. You had better come down.*"

He stopped. Letarpo's hand had gone up, stopping him. Tarp had seen her.

"Trood!"

He ran over, hugged her. She stepped away.

"Where's Ronnie now?" she said.

"Over Zurich someplace. We get him down nice. Look." With a little push he made her face the blond man, the pseudo-Yussuf. "Old Vic. We flew him in special."

"When're you going to talk to Ronnie?" she said.

"Anytime between now and eight, Madame," said Captain Doss.

"An actor!" Trudy said. "You expect to fool Ronnie like that?"

"Fool him," Tarp said. "Fool him is save him. Come, I show you something."

She didn't move.

"Where is Yussuf?"

"Ah, Yussuf," Tarp said, shaking his head.

"You said you'd fix it with the pipeline."

"When did I say? Two days ago. But after Ronaldo acts up like that? My plane? *The princess?*" He whistled, sucking in his breath. He gave Trudy a tap. "All right, we fix it different."

"What happened to Yussuf and the workers?"

"I got the best actor from Old Vic here —"

"They'll never be seen again. Is that what happened?"

"Hey, Trood! Ronaldo's up there! And the princess! What hap-. pens with *them,* huh? That's first!"

"You're going to fix it with an actor?"

"He's the best actor —"

"Ronnie won't believe you," she said. "He never did. He's much smarter than I."

"*You* he'll believe," Letarpo said.

"Me?"

"He smells it's an actor, you tell him I got a gun on you."

A pistol of a Letarpo-forefinger was pointing at her. At the same time his teeth swelled white and sharp out of the bronzed face. He was repressing an insomnia yawn, but he was also smiling at that crazy very long cake. She almost admired his *élan* riding even across this misery. She hated herself for the admiration: Was that the trouble? Had she been a Big-Man addict all her life? Simon? Nick? Letarpo? Trudy, woman-on-her-own intellectual, a Big Man addict like a tootsie combing the singles bars for at least an assistant movie director? . . . Desperately she tried to focus, as if figuring how the mess started would end it.

"Old Vic doesn't work, you tell Ronaldo my gun's on you. You tell him, Trood: he doesn't land the plane — my gun goes boom! Mr. Police Captain?"

"Yes, Mr. Letarpo," the Captain said between earphones. "If necessary we shall confirm, Madame is Mr. Letarpo's counter-hostage."

"Heet-heet! . . ." a giggle-wail came from behind. Everybody turned. It wasn't a giggle. It was Jennifer, her secretary, crying and running out.

"But who needs the gun thing?" Letarpo said, turning back. "We fix it with our friend Old Vic."

"He sounds precisely right," the police captain said.

"A couple hours, and Ronaldo's down safe. I order something to celebrate. You imagine? You can get champagne in this little town?"

"Yes, marvelous. . . . I've been to the liquor store here," Trudy said. The big dog had recognized her. Simultaneously she felt its tongue rough against her knee, and her pulse like an icepick down her neck, and plaster snowflakes brushing her temple. It seemed to snow faster in the dining room.

"Here. I show you," Letarpo said. A little push guided her to Turk, who was putting almonds on the cake. It was a long chocolate log. "This I had baked in Paris, extra-pronto. This cake got a meaning."

"Ronnie's going to crash," she said.

"It means the pipeline! We show it to Ronaldo. Number One, get him down safe. Number Two, keep him down happy. This pipeline cake is for Number Two. You see those candles? Know what they mean?"

"*Ladies and gentlemen,*" Yussuf's voice said again. "*It affords me great pleasure . . .*"

"Now five candles — you like the color? They go on the cake. Five candles for five million people Ronaldo helped with the airplane heist. That'll make him happy."

"He could have been such a young man," Trudy said.

"Listen!" Letarpo said. "Each candle is a million. Two million poor people in the Turkey earthquake area, three million poor in Macedonia, the pipeline goes through the whole area — you listening, Trood? Because Letarpo says to both governments: You want my pipeline benefits? My cheap transportation to your oil? Okay, first you stop epidemics in that area, you get the point? Stop starvation, stop all kinds trouble, really take care of the people, otherwise it's not safe, spending all that money to build the pipe. See?"

"*. . . the Macedonian Culture Institute in London,*" Yussuf's voice

307

said, *"on a day which in the history of our country marks the liberation . . ."*

"How did we two get involved?" Trudy said.

"Big bad Tarp, huh?" Letarpo said. "Okay, that's the point! Tell Ronaldo he helped five million people, heisting that plane. Without the heist big bad Tarp wouldn't do the pipeline. The heist helped five million people! That'll make Ronaldo happy! Even after he's down. Five million people helped for ten years. I'll ask a ten-year program, guaranteed. . . ."

"I thought you'd be letting your oil lease go pretty soon now," she said.

"Not now. Got to hang on, to help long-range —"

She scooped a salt shaker off the sideboard and threw it into the cake, and something squeaked. Old Antone had walked in, on Jennifer's arm. Blind, erect, careful, he strode along in his trench-coat. His face was the color of the plaster flakes that floated from the ceiling.

"I brought him for help," Jennifer said with a wracked, hiccupy voice. The squeak came from behind her. A delivery boy in blue jeans. He wheeled a case of champagne bottles on a trundle whose casters squeaked.

The Captain jumped up. Bic rushed in with a golf club.

"This delivery fellow came in with Antone!" Bic said. "We couldn't stop him —"

"It's all right," the Captain said. "He'll just have to stay until this is over." *Squeak!* went the casters and the dog, the big dog whose name Trudy didn't know, gave a bellow at the squeak. The delivery boy jumped. He stopped the truck; looked about; twitched a comb out of his pocket and gave his red curls a stroke. He had a pencil stuck behind one ear, this delivery boy, and a cigarette stuck behind the other. Water heaved into Trudy's eyes. She'd never seen him before, but she knew this boy combed himself whenever he was astonished.

"Hello, Ronnie," the actor said. *"It's Yussuf, I'm all right. I'm all right. The workers too. They let us go. You had better come down."*

"They brought in an actor!" Trudy said to old Antone.

"I thought it was the prince. Very good," Antone said.

"But if it doesn't work they want me to go through a whole charade!"

"A charade might be good. That's all right," Antone said.

"They want me to deceive Ronnie!"

"He'll be undeceived when he comes down," Antone said. "That's healthy. My son Nick never was undeceived enough."

"You're supposed to help!" Trudy said.

He stood erect in his trenchcoat and Letarpo, whom he was supposed to help against, had begun to chocolate-ice the cake with Turk.

"Survive and be undeceived, my dear," Antone said. "The best help he can get. Then he can live with me at Bahama."

With a flat knife Letarpo smoothed icing over the salt shaker she'd thrown at the cake. Now it looked like a decorative spike, an inventive detail. Turk put a cherry on top of it. It looked like a cute representation of an oil derrick.

"*Ladies and gentlemen, it affords me great pleasure,*" said Yussuf's voice.

"Ah!" the Captain said at a noise in his earphones.

Letarpo stopped, then went on smoothing icing. Old Antone stood erect. The way they ignored each other was insane and superb. Bic gripped his golf club with both hands, like a bell bar. The two *képis* stared at the delivery boy, and this boy, with wide blue eyes, reached for the cigarette behind his ears. Turk had put more almonds on the cake and blew away some flakes of ceiling snow.

Trudy had no idea how she'd gotten to stand on this parquet scarred by ski boots. Had there ever been a way out? Out of the maze leading into this infernal dining room? She looked around, eyes burning, for a door that would open on Tante's plants or at least Ronnie's baby cries. She had no way to get away from the desperations that ruled the earth, from a tall man rigid in a trenchcoat and a smaller man icing a cake. For the first time in her life she really wanted to pray. But she knew no prayers that made any sense. There was no shelter. Except a cough.

The delivery boy coughed. He coughed, holding on to the edge of the champagne case. He coughed smoke from the cigarette he had lit, his narrow white forehead wrinkled, frowning at the irritation he couldn't get out of his throat, and the young naïveté of that was the only undoomed thing in the room. She ran to him.

"I'm sorry," she said to the delivery boy. "I'm sorry you got trapped here."

His eyes, two astounded blue irises, were on her. He unpinned the bill that had been pinned to the champagne case.

"You won't be detained long," she said.

"Gangsters — in hotel?" the delivery boy said, with a solemn deep voice.

"No," she said. "Not gangsters. You speak English?"

"In winter I ski-instruct."

Boo-oot . . . , went the short-wave Erector set.

"I'd like to hold your hand," Trudy said.

"Please. Signature on receipt," the delivery boy said. The hand that was still clamped around the comb reached up to his ear and opened two fingers to take down the pencil.

"Give me your hand," Trudy said.

The delivery boy stuck the pencil back behind the ear; he dropped the comb into his pocket. He gave her his hand. It was cool and narrow, with young hair on the back. Her eyes were dry, though she heard Jennifer sniffle. Snow fell from the ceiling, and the dog, the big dog whose name she didn't know, beat its tail against the floor.